The Alien Years

Robert Silverberg was born in New York in 1935. He sold his first novel while still a student at Columbia University, and has been a full-time writer since graduation. He has published more than fifty novels as well as serious works of history and archaeology, and has been nominated for more awards for his fiction than any other science fiction writer, alive or dead. He and his wife now live in San Francisco.

Voyager

ROBERT SILVERBERG

The Alien Years

HarperCollins*Publishers*

This novel is entirely a work of fiction.
The names, characters and incidents portrayed in it
are the work of the author's imagination.
Any resemblance to actual persons, living or dead,
events or locations are entirely coincidental.

Voyager
An imprint of HarperCollins*Publishers*
77–85 Fulham Palace Road,
Hammersmith, London w6 8jb
www.voyager-books.com

This paperback edition 1999
3 5 7 9 8 6 4

First published by HarperCollins*Publishers* 1998

Copyright © Agberg Ltd 1998

The author asserts the moral right
to be identified as the author of the work

A catalogue record for this book
is available from the British Library

ISBN 0 586 21110 1

Printed in Great Britain by
Omnia Books Limited, Glasgow

For H.G. Wells
The father of us all

When the sun no longer shines, when the stars drop from the sky and the mountains are blown away, when camels great with young are left untended and the wild beasts come together, when the seas are set on fire and men's souls are reunited, when . . . the record of men's deeds are laid open, and heaven is stripped bare, when Hell burns fiercely and Paradise approaches; then each soul shall understand what it has done.

The Koran
81st Surah

I

Seven Years
from Now

Carmichael might have been the only person west of the Rocky Mountains that morning who didn't know what was going on. What was going on was the end of the world, more or less, but Carmichael – his name was Myron, though everybody called him Mike – had been away for a while, reveling in a week of lovely solitude and inner retuning in the bleak beautiful wasteland that was northwestern New Mexico, not paying close attention to current events.

On this crisp, clear autumn morning he had taken off long before dawn from a bumpy rural airstrip, heading westward, homeward, in his little Cessna 104-FG. The flight was rough and wild all the way, a fierce wind out of the heart of the continent pushing his plane around, giving it a scary clobbering practically from the moment he was aloft.

That wasn't so good, the wind. An east wind as strong as this one, Carmichael knew, could mean trouble for coastal California – particularly at this time of year. It was late October, the height of Southern California's brushfire season. The last time there had been rain along the coast was the fifth of April, so the whole region was one big tinderbox, and this hard hot dry wind blowing out of the desert was capable of fanning any little spark it might encounter into a devastating conflagration of blowtorch ferocity. It happened just about every year. So he wasn't surprised to see a thin, blurry line of brown smoke far ahead of him on the horizon by the time he was in the vicinity of San Bernardino.

The line thickened and darkened as he came up over the crest of the San Gabriels into Los Angeles proper, and there seemed to be lesser zones of brown sky-stain off to the north and south now, as well as that long east-west line somewhere out near the ocean. Evidently there were several fires at once. Perhaps a little bigger than usual, too. That was scary. This time of year in Los Angeles, everything was always at risk. With a wind as strong as this blowing, the whole crazy town could go in one big firestorm.

The air traffic controller's voice sounded hoarse and ragged as he guided Carmichael toward his landing at Burbank Airport, which might have been an indication that something special was happening. Those guys always sounded hoarse and ragged, though. Carmichael took a little comfort from that thought.

He felt the smoke stabbing at his nostrils the moment he stepped out of the plane: the familiar old acrid stink, the sour prickly reek of a bad October. Another instant and his eyes were stinging. You could almost draw pictures in the dirty air with the tip of your finger. This one must indeed be a lulu, Carmichael realized.

A long, skinny fellow in mechanic's overalls went trotting past him on the field. 'Hey, guy,' Carmichael called. 'Where's it burning?'

The man stopped, gaped, gave him a strange look, a disbelieving blink, as though Carmichael had just come down from six months in a space satellite. 'You don't know?'

'If I knew, I wouldn't have asked.'

'Hell, it's everywhere. All over the goddamn L.A. basin.'

'Everywhere?'

The mechanic nodded. He looked half crazed. Again the sagging jaw, again that dopey bozo blink. 'Wow, you actually mean to say you haven't heard about –'

'No. I haven't heard.' Carmichael wanted to shake him. He ran into this kind of cloddish stupidity all the time, and he hated it. He gestured impatiently toward the smoke-fouled sky. 'Is it as bad as it looks?'

'Oh, it's bad, man, real bad! The worst ever, for damn sure. Like I say, burning all over the place. They've called out every general aviation plane there is for firefighting duty. You better get with your warden right away.'

'Yeah,' Carmichael said, already in motion. 'I guess I'd better.'

He sprinted into the main airport building. People got out of his way as he ran through. Carmichael was a sturdily built man, not particularly tall but wide through the shoulders and deep through the chest, and like all the Carmichaels he had fierce blue eyes that seemed to cast a searchlight beam before him. When he moved fast, as he was doing now, people got out of his way.

You could smell the bitter aroma of the smoke even inside the terminal. The place was a madhouse of panicky commuters running back and forth and yelling at each other, waving briefcases around. Somehow Carmichael jostled his way to an open data terminal. It was the old-fashioned kind, no newfangled biochip-implant stuff. He put a call through to the district warden on the emergency net, and the district warden said, as soon as he heard who was talking, 'Get your ass out here on the line double fast, Mike.'

'Where do you want me?'

'The nastiest one's a little way northwest of Chatsworth. We've got planes loaded and ready to go out of Van Nuys Airport.'

'I need time to pee and phone my wife, okay?' Carmichael said. 'I'll be in Van Nuys in fifteen.'

He was so tired that he could feel it in his teeth. It was nine in the morning and he'd been flying since half past four, and battling that bastardly east wind, the same wind that was threatening now to fan the flames in L.A., had been miserable work every single mile. He was fifty-six years old, no kid any more, the old juices flowing more sluggishly every year. At this moment all he wanted was home and shower and Cindy and bed. But Carmichael didn't regard firefighting work as optional. Not with the possibility of a firestorm always hanging over the city.

There were times when he almost wished that it would happen, one great purging fire to wipe the whole damned place out.

That wasn't a catastrophe he really wanted to see, not even remotely; but Carmichael hated this giant smoggy tawdry Babylon of a city, its endless tangle of clotted freeways, the peculiar-looking houses, the filthy polluted air, the thick choking glossy exotic foliage everywhere, the drugs, the booze, the divorces, the laziness, the sleaziness, the street bums, the street crime, the shyster lawyers and their loathsome clients, the whips and chains, the porno shops and the naked encounter parlors and the massage joints, the virtual-reality chopshops, the weird people speaking their weird trendy lingo and wearing their weird clothes and driving their weird cars and cutting their hair in weird ways and sticking bones through their noses like the savages they really were. There was a cheapness, a trashiness, about everything here, Carmichael thought. Even the grand mansions and the fancy restaurants were that way: hollow, like slick movie sets.

He sometimes felt that he was bothered more by the petty trashiness of almost everything than by the out-and-out evil that lurked in the truly dark corners. If you watched where you were going you could stay out of reach of the evil most or even all of the time, but the trashiness slipped up sneakily around you no matter how well you kept sight of your own values, and there was no doing battle with it: it infiltrated your soul without your even knowing it. He hoped that his sojourn in Los Angeles was not doing that to him.

There had been Carmichaels living in Southern California ever since General Fremont's time, but never any in Los Angeles itself, not one. He was the first of his tribe that had managed somehow to wind up there. The family came from the Valley, and what Carmichaels meant when they spoke of 'the Valley' was the great flat agricultural San Joaquin, out behind Bakersfield and stretching off far to the north, and not the miserable congested string of hideous suburbs just over the hills from Beverly Hills and Santa Monica that Angelenos understood the term to connote. As for Los Angeles itself, they ignored it: it was the cinder in the eye, the unspeakable blotch on the Southern California landscape.

But L.A. was Cindy's city and Cindy loved L.A. and Mike Carmichael loved Cindy, everything about her, the contrast of her slim pixy daintiness against his big blunt burly potato-nosed self, her warmth, her intensity, her playful quirky sense of fun, her dark lively eyes and glossy curling jet-black bangs, even the strange goofy philosophies that were the air of life to her. She was everything he had never been and had never even wanted to be, and he had fallen for her as he had never fallen before; and for Cindy's sake he had become the family Angeleno, much as he detested the place, because she could not and would not live anywhere else.

So Mike Carmichael had been living there the past seven years, in a little wooden house up in Laurel Canyon amidst the lush green shrubbery, and for seven Octobers in a row he had dutifully gone out to dump chemical retardants on the annual brush-fires, to save the locals from their own idiotic carelessness. One thing that just about every Carmichael grew up believing was that you had to accept your responsibilities, no complaining, no questions asked. Even Mike, who was as near to being a rebel as the family had ever produced, understood that.

There would be fires. That was a given. Qualified pilots were needed to go up there and drop retardants on them and put them out. Mike Carmichael was a qualified pilot. He was needed, and he would go. It was as simple as that.

The phone rang seven times at the home number before Carmichael hung up. Cindy had never liked answering machines or call forwarding or screen-mail or anything like that. Things like that were dehumanizing, mechanistic, she said. Which made them practically the last people in the world without such gadgets; but so be it, Carmichael figured. That was the way Cindy wanted it to be.

Next he tried the little studio just off Colfax where she made her jewelry, but she didn't answer there either. Probably she was on her way to the gallery, which was out in Santa Monica, but she wouldn't be there yet – the freeways would be worse even than on a normal day, what with all these fires going – and so there was no sense even trying her there.

That bothered him, not being able to say hello to her right away after his six-day absence, and no likely chance for it now for another eight or ten hours. But there was nothing he could do about that.

He took off from Burbank on emergency clearance, firefighting authorization. As soon as he was aloft again he could see the fire not far to the northwest. It was denser now, a greasy black column against the pale sky. And when he stepped from his plane a few minutes later at Van Nuys Airport he felt an immediate blast of sudden unthinkable warmth. The temperature had been in the low eighties at Burbank, damned well hot enough for nine in the morning, but here it was over a hundred. The air itself was sweating. He could see the congealed heat, like droplets of fat. It seemed to him that he heard the distant roar of flames, the popping and crackling of burning underbrush, the troublesome whistling sound of dry grass catching fire. It was just as though the fire was two miles away. Maybe it was, he thought.

The airport looked like a combat center. Planes were coming and going with lunatic frenzy, and they were lunatic planes, too. The fire was so serious, apparently, that the regular fleet of conventional airborne tankers had been supplemented with antiques of every sort, planes forty and fifty years old and even older, converted B-17 Flying Fortresses and DC-3s and a Douglas Invader and, to Carmichael's astonishment, a Ford Trimotor from the 1930s that had been hauled, maybe, out of some movie studio's collection. Some were equipped with tanks that held fire-retardant chemicals, some were water-pumpers, some were mappers with infrared and electronic scanning equipment glistening on their snouts. Harried-looking men and women were in frantic motion everywhere, making wild gestures to each other across great distances or shouting into CB handsets as they tried to keep the loading process orderly. It didn't seem very orderly.

Carmichael found his way to Operations HQ, which was full of haggard people peering into computer screens. He knew most of them from other fire seasons. They knew him.

He waited for a break in the frenzy and tapped one of the dispatchers on the shoulder. She looked up, nodded in a goggly-eyed way, then grinned in recognition and said, 'Mike. Good. We've got a DC-3 waiting for you.' She traced a line with her finger across the screen in front of her. 'You'll dump retardants along this arc, from Ybarra Canyon eastward to Horse Flats. The fire's in the Santa Susana foothills and so far the wind is from the east, but if it shifts to northerly it's going to take out everything from Chatsworth to Granada Hills, right on down to Ventura Boulevard. And that's only *this* fire.'

'Holy shit! How many are there?'

The dispatcher gave her mouse a couple of clicks. The map of the San Fernando Valley that had been showing on the screen went swirling into oblivion and was replaced by one of the entire

Los Angeles basin. Carmichael stared, aghast. Three great scarlet streaks indicated fire zones: this one out at the western end of things along the Santa Susanas, another nearly as big way off to the east in the grasslands north of the 210 Freeway around Glendora or San Dimas, and a third down in eastern Orange County, back of Anaheim Hills. 'Ours is the big one so far,' the dispatcher said. 'But these other two are only about forty miles apart, and if they should join up somehow –'

'Yeah,' Carmichael said. A single wall of fire running along the whole eastern rim of the basin, maybe – with ferocious Santa Ana winds blowing, carrying airborne rivers of sparks westward across Pasadena, across downtown L.A., across Hollywood, across Beverly Hills, all the way to the coast, to Venice, Santa Monica, Malibu. He shivered. Laurel Canyon would go. The house, the studio. Hell, *everything* would go. Worse than Sodom and Gomorrah, worse than the fall of Nineveh. Nothing but ashes for hundreds of miles. 'Jesus,' he said. 'Everybody scared silly of terrorist nukes, and three carloads of dumb kids tossing cigarettes can do the job just as easily.'

'But this time it wasn't cigarettes, Mike,' the dispatcher said.

'No? What then, arson?'

Again that strange stare and blink, much like the one the field mechanic had given him. 'You serious? You haven't heard?'

'I've been in New Mexico the last six days. Way off in the outback.'

'You're the only one in the world who hasn't heard, then. Hey, don't you ever tune in the radio news when you drive?'

'I flew there and back. The Cessna. Listening to the radio is one of the things that I go to New Mexico to get away from having to do. – For Christ's sake, heard *what*?'

'About the E-Ts,' said the dispatcher wearily. 'They started the fires. Three spaceships landing at five this morning in three different corners of the L.A. basin. The heat of their engines ignited the dry grass.'

Carmichael did not smile. 'E-Ts, yeah. You've got one weird sense of humor, kiddo.'

The dispatcher said, 'You think it's a joke?'

'Spaceships? From another world?'

'With critters fifteen feet high on board,' the dispatcher at the next computer said. 'Linda's not kidding. They're out walking around on the freeways right this minute. Big purple squids fifteen feet high, Mike.'

'Men from Mars?'

'Nobody knows where the hell they're from.'

'Jesus,' Carmichael said. 'Jesus Christ God.'

Half past nine in the morning, and Mike Carmichael's older brother, Colonel Anson Carmichael III, whom everyone usually spoke of simply as 'the Colonel', was standing in front of his television set, gaping in disbelief. His daughter Rosalie had phoned fifteen minutes before from Newport Beach to tell him to turn it on. That would not have occurred to him, otherwise. The television was here for the grandchildren, not for him. But there he was, now, a lean, long-legged, resolutely straight-backed and stiff-necked retired army officer in his early sixties with piercing blue eyes and a full head of white hair, gaping like a kindergarten kid at his television set in the middle of the morning.

On the huge state-of-the-art screen, set flush into the pink ashlar facing of the Colonel's recreation-room wall, the same two stupefying scenes had been alternating on every channel, over and over and over again, for the entire fifteen minutes that he had been watching.

One was the aerial shot of the big fire on the northwestern flank of the Los Angeles basin: black billowing clouds, vivid red tongues of flame, an occasional glimpse of a house on fire, or a whole row of houses. The other was the grotesque, unbelievable, even absurd sight of half a dozen titanic alien beings moving solemnly around in the half-empty parking lot of a huge shopping mall in a place called Porter Ranch, with the sleek slender shaft of what he supposed was an alien ground vehicle of some sort rearing up like a shining needle behind them out of a tumbled cluster of charred cars, nose tilted upward at a 45-degree angle.

The camera angles varied from time to time, but the scenes were always the same. A shot of the fire, and then cut to the aliens at the shopping mall. The fire again, looking worse than before; and then cut again to the aliens in the mall. Over and over and over.

And, over and over and over, the same string of words kept running through the Colonel's mind:

This is an invasion. We are at war. This is an invasion. We are at war.

His mind could handle the fire part of it readily enough. He had seen houses burning before. Huge catastrophic fires were an ugly part of California life, but they were inevitable in a place where thirty-odd million people had decided to settle in a region that had, as an absolutely normal feature of the climate, a dry season lasting from April to November every year. October was the fire month, when the grassy hills were bone-dry and the diabolical Santa Ana winds came roaring up out of the desert to the east. There was never a year without its batch of fires, and every five or ten years there was a really monstrous one – the Hollywood Hills fire of 1961, when he had been in his late teens, and that one right down below here in Santa Barbara in 1990, and the huge Bay Area blaze that wiped out so much of Oakland a year or two after that, and that Pasadena fire on Thanksgiving Day, and on and on.

But this other thing – alien spaceships landing in Los Angeles, and, so they seemed to be saying on the tube now, touching down also in at least a dozen other places around the world – bizarre visitors, very likely hostile and belligerent, coming without warning – intruding, for God only knew what reason, on the generally peaceful and prosperous place that was the planet Earth in the early years of the twenty-first century –

That was movie stuff. That was science fiction. It hammered at your sense of the orderly structure of the world, of the predictable flow of the events of life.

The Colonel had read only one science fiction book in his life, *The War of the Worlds*, H.G. Wells, long ago. He hadn't been the Colonel, then, but just a tall, skinny high-school kid diligently making himself ready for the life that he already knew he was going to lead. It was an intelligent, entertaining novel, but ultimately the book had annoyed him, because it asked an interesting question – *What do you do when you find yourself up against an utterly unbeatable enemy?* – and then had supplied no useful answer. The Martian conquest of Earth had been thwarted not by any kind of clever military strategy but only by the merest of fortuitous flukes, a convenient biological accident.

He didn't mind tough questions, but he believed in trying to find good answers for them, and he had been expecting Wells to supply something more satisfying than having the invincible Martian conquerors succumb to unfamiliar Earthly disease bacteria even as the armies of Earth lay flattened and helpless before their advance. That was ingenious of Wells, but it wasn't the right kind of ingenuity, because it left no scope for human mental ability or courage; it was simply a case of one external event cancelling out another, like a tremendous downpour suddenly showing up to extinguish a raging forest fire while all the firefighters stood around sucking their thumbs.

Well, here, strange to say, was Wells's book come to life. The Martians actually had landed, real ones, though surely not from Mars. Descending out of nowhere – what had happened to our orbital early warning systems, he wondered, the space-based telescopes that were supposed to be scanning for incoming asteroids and other little cosmic surprises? – and, if what he was seeing on the teevee was any fair sample, they were already strutting around very much like conquerors. Willy-nilly, the world seemed to be at war, and with creatures of a superior technology, evidently, since they had managed to get here from some other star and that was something we could not have achieved.

It remained to be seen, of course, what these invaders wanted. Maybe this wasn't even an invasion, but just an embassy that had arrived in a singularly clumsy way. But if it was war, the Colonel thought, and these creatures had weapons and abilities beyond our fathoming, then we were about to get our chance to deal squarely with the problem that H.G. Wells a hundred years ago had preferred to finesse with an expedient nick-of-time gimmick.

Already the Colonel's mind was beginning to tick through a litany of options, wondering about which people he needed to call in Washington, wondering whether any of them would call him. If indeed there was going to be war against these aliens, and he *was* intuitively certain that there would be, he intended to play a part in it.

The Colonel had no love for war and very little eagerness to become involved in it, and not just because he had been retired from the armed services for close to a dozen years. He had never glamorized war. War was a nasty, stupid, ugly business, usually signifying nothing more than the failure of rational policy. His father, Anson II, the Old Colonel, had fought – and fought plenty, and had the scars to show for it – in the Second World War, and nevertheless had raised his three sons to be soldiers. The Old Colonel had liked to say, 'People like us go into the military in order to see to it that nobody will ever have to fight again.' His eldest son Anson had never ceased to believe that.

Sometimes, though, you simply had war thrust upon you without any choice, and then it was necessary to fight or be obliterated, and this looked like one of those times. In that case, retired though he was, he might have something to offer. The psychology of alien cultures, after all, had been his big specialty from his Vietnam days onward, although he had never imagined having to deal with a culture as alien as *this*. But still, there were certain general principles that probably would apply, even in this case –

Abruptly the idiot repetitiousness of the stuff they were showing on the screen began to irritate and anger him. He went back outside.

Wild updrafts from the blaze buffeted Carmichael's plane as he took it aloft. That gave him a few bad moments. But he moved easily and automatically to gain control, pulling the moves out of the underground territories of his nervous system. It was essential, he believed, to have the moves in your fingers, your shoulders, your thighs, rather than in the conscious realms of your brain. Consciousness could get you a long way, but ultimately you had to work out of the underground territories or you were dead.

This was nothing, after all, compared with the stuff he had had to deal with in Vietnam. At least today nobody would be shooting at him from below. Vietnam was where he had learned all he knew about flying through thermal updrafts, too.

The dry season in the swampy south of that unhappy land was the time of year when the farmers burned the stubble from their fields, and things were all smoke and heat down on the ground, with visibility maybe a thousand yards, tops. That was in daytime. More than half of his combat missions had been at night. A lot of the time he flew during the monsoon season, notable for thick sideways gusts of rain, a time that was nearly as bad for flying in as the field-burning season was. The Viet Cong folks and their buddies of the North Vietnamese Army battalions generally preferred carrying out troop movements mostly during bad weather, when nobody in their right minds would be flying. So that was when Carmichael had been up there above them, of course.

The war was thirty-plus years behind him, and it was still as fresh and vivid in his life as though it had been Saigon and not New Mexico where he had just spent the past six days. Because he was too much the family bad boy to have gone docilely into the Army as he had been expected to do, and nevertheless was enough of a Carmichael so that he would never have dreamed of shirking his obligation to help his country defend its security perimeter, he had been a Navy pilot during the war, flying twin-engine turbo-prop OV-10s as a member of Light Attack Squadron 4, operating out of Bin Thuy.

His tour of duty had been twelve months, July 1971 through June 1972. That had been enough. The OV-10s were supposed to be observation planes, but in Vietnam they flew close support for an air-cavalry pack and went out equipped with rockets, Gatling guns, 20-millimeter cannons, strapped-on clusters of cluster bombs, and all sorts of other stuff. Carrying a full load, they could barely make it up higher than 3500 feet. Most of the time they flew below the clouds, sometimes down around treetop level, no more than a hundred feet up, seven days a week, mostly at night. Carmichael figured he had fulfilled his military obligation to his nation, and then some.

But the obligation to go out and fight these fires – you never finished fulfilling that.

He felt the plane responding now, and managed a grin. DC-3s were tough old birds. He loved flying them, though the newest of them had been manufactured before he was born. He loved flying anything. Flying wasn't what Carmichael did for a living – he didn't actually do anything for a living, not any more – but flying was what he did. There were months when he spent more time in the air than on the ground, or so it seemed to him, because the hours he spent on the ground often slid by unnoticed, while time in the air was heightened, intensified, magnified.

He swung south over Encino and Tarzana before heading up across Chatsworth and Canoga Park into the fire zone. A fine haze of ash masked the sun. Looking down, he could see the tiny houses, the tiny blue swimming pools, the tiny people scurrying about with berserk fervor, trying to hose down their roofs before the flames arrived. So many houses, so many people, great human swarms filling every inch of space between the sea and the desert, and now it was all in jeopardy.

The southbound lanes of Topanga Canyon Boulevard were as jammed with cars, here in mid-morning, as the Hollywood Freeway at rush hour. No, it was worse than that. They were even driving on the shoulders of the road, and here and there were gnarly tangles where there had been accidents, cars overturned, cars slewed around sideways. The others just kept on going, fighting their way right around them.

Where were they all going? Anywhere. Anywhere that was away from the fire, at least. With big pieces of furniture strapped to the tops of their cars, baby cribs, footlockers, dressers, chairs, tables, even beds. He could imagine what was within those cars, too – mounds of family photographs, computer disks, television sets, toys, clothing, whatever they prized the most, or however much of it they had been able to stash before the panicky urge to flee overtook them.

They were heading toward the beaches, it seemed. Maybe some television preacher had told them there was an ark sitting out there in the Pacific, waiting to carry them to safety while God rained brimstone down on Los Angeles. And maybe there really was one out there, too. In Los Angeles anything was possible. Invaders from space walking around on the freeways, even. Jesus.

Jesus. Carmichael hardly knew how to begin thinking about that.

He wondered where Cindy was, what *she* was thinking about it. Most likely she found it very funny. Cindy had a wonderful ability to be amused by things. There was a line of poetry she liked to quote, from that old Roman, Virgil: a storm is rising, the ship has sprung a leak, there's a whirlpool to one side and sea-monsters on the other, and the captain turns to his men and says, 'One day perhaps we'll look back and laugh even at all this.'

That was Cindy's way, Carmichael thought. The Santa Anas are blowing and three horrendous brush fires are burning all around the town and invaders from space have arrived at the same time, and one day perhaps we'll look back and laugh even at all this.

His heart overflowed with love for her, and longing.

Carmichael had never known anything about poetry before he had met her. He closed his eyes a moment and brought her onto the screen of his mind. Thick cascades of jet-black hair, quick dazzling smile, little slender tanned body all aglitter with those amazing rings and bead necklaces and pendants she designed and fashioned. And her eyes. No one else he knew had eyes like hers, bright with strange mischief, with that altogether original way of vision that was the thing he most loved about her. *Damn* this fire, getting between them now, just when he'd been away almost a whole week! Damn the stupid men from Mars! Damn them! Damn them!

As the Colonel emerged onto the patio he felt the wind coming hard out of the east, a hot one, and stronger than it had been earlier that morning, with a real edge on it. He could hear the ominous whooshing sound of fallen leaves, dry and brittle, whipping along the hillside trails that began just below the main house. East winds always meant trouble. And this one was bringing it for sure: already there was a faint taste of smoke in the air.

The ranch was situated on gently sloping land well up on the south side of the Santa Ynez Mountains back of Santa Barbara, a majestic site sprawling over many acres, looking down on the city and the ocean beyond. It was too high up for growing avocado or citrus, but very nice for such crops as walnuts and almonds. The air here was almost always clear and pure, the big dome of the sky extended a million miles in every direction, the sight-lines were spectacular. The land had been in the Colonel's wife's family for a hundred years; but she was gone now, leaving him to look after it by himself, and so, by an odd succession of events, one of the military Carmichaels found himself transformed into a farming Carmichael also, here in the seventh decade of his life. He had lived here alone in this big, imposing country house for the past five years, though he had a resident staff of five to help him with the work.

There was some irony in that, that the Colonel should be finishing his days as a farmer. It was the other branch of the Carmichael family, the senior branch, that had always been the farmers. The junior branch – the Colonel's branch, Mike Carmichael's branch – had customarily gone in for professional soldiering.

The Colonel's father's cousin Clyde, dead almost thirty years now, had been the last of the farming Carmichaels. The family farm now was a 300-home subdivision, slick and shiny. Most of Clyde's sons and daughters and their families still lived scattered up and down the Valley cities from Fresno and Visalia to Bakersfield, selling insurance or tractors or mutual funds. The Colonel hadn't had contact with any of them in years.

As for the other branch, the military branch, it had long ago drifted away from its Valley roots. The Colonel's late father Anson II, the Old Colonel, had settled in a San Diego suburb after his retirement from the Service. One of his three sons, Mike, who had wanted to be a Navy pilot, Lord love him, had wound up in L.A., right there in the belly of the beast. Another son, Lee, the baby of the family – he was dead now, killed ten years back while testing an experimental fighter plane – had lived out in Mojave, near Edwards Air Force Base. And here he was, the oldest of the three boys, Anson III, stern and straight and righteous, once called the Young Colonel to distinguish him from his father but now no longer young, dwelling in more or less placid retirement on a pretty ranch high up on a mountain back of Santa Barbara. Strange, very strange, all of it.

From the wraparound porch of the main house Colonel Carmichael had unimpeded views for vast distances. The front aspect allowed him to look straight out over the series of hills that descended toward the south, down to the red-tile roofs of the city of Santa Barbara and the dark ocean beyond, and on a clear day like this he could see all the way to the Channel Islands. From the side patio he had a tremendous angle eastward over the irregular summits of the low mountains of the coastal range at least to Ventura and Oxnard, and sometimes he even caught a hint of the grayish-white edge of the smog wall that came boiling up into the sky out of Los Angeles itself, ninety miles away.

The air off in that direction wasn't grayish-white today. A great brownish-black column was climbing toward the stratosphere out of the fire zone – rising from Moorpark, he guessed, or Simi Valley or Calabasas, one of those mushrooming suburban towns strung out along Highway 101 on the way into Los Angeles. As it hit some obstruction of the upper air it turned blunt and spread laterally, forming a dismal horizontal dirty smear across the middle of the sky. At this distance the Colonel was unable to see the fire itself, not even with the field glasses. He imagined that he could – persuaded himself that he could make out six or eight vermilion spires of flame ascending vertically in the center of that awful filthy pall – but he knew it was only a trick of his mind, that there was no way he could see a blaze that was more than sixty miles down the coast. The smoke, yes. Not the fire.

But the smoke was enough to get his pulse racing. A plume that big – whole towns must be going up in flames! He wondered about his brother Mike, living right there in the middle of the city: whether he was okay, whether the fire was threatening his neighborhood at all. The Colonel reached tentatively for the phone at his hip. But Mike had gone to New Mexico last week, hadn't he? Hiking around by himself in some desolate back corner of the Navajo reservation, getting his head clear, as he seemed to need to do two or three times a year. And in any case Mike was usually was part of the volunteer airborne fire-fighting crew that went up to dump chemicals on fires like this. If he was back from New Mexico, he was in all likelihood up there right now fluttering around in some rickety little plane.

I really should call him anyway, the Colonel thought. But I'd probably just get Cindy on the phone.

The Colonel didn't enjoy talking to his brother Mike's wife Cindy. She was too aggressively perky, too emotional, too god-damned *strange*. She spoke and acted and dressed and thought like some hippie living thirty years out of her proper era. The Colonel didn't like the whole idea of having someone like Cindy being part of the family, and he had never concealed his dislike of her from Mike. It was a problem between them.

In all probability Cindy wouldn't be there either, he decided. No doubt a panicky evacuation was in progress, hundreds of thousands of people heading for the freeways, racing off in all directions. A lot of them would come this way, the Colonel supposed, up the Pacific Coast Highway or the Ventura Freeway. Unless they were cut off from Santa Barbara County by a stray arm of the fire and were forced to go the other way, into the chaotic maelstrom of Los Angeles proper. God pity them if that was so. He could imagine what it must be like in the central city now, what with so much craziness going on at the edges of the basin.

He found himself tapping the keys for Mike's number, all the same. He simply had to call, whether or not nobody was home. Or even if it was Cindy who answered. He *had* to.

Where the neat rows and circles of suburban streets ended there was a great open stretch of grassy land, parched by the long dry summer to the color of a lion's hide, and beyond that were the mountains, and between the grassland and the mountains lay the fire, an enormous lateral red crest topped by a plume of foul black smoke. It seemed already to cover hundreds of acres, maybe thousands. A hundred acres of burning brush, Carmichael had heard once, creates as much heat energy as the original atomic bomb that they had dropped on Hiroshima. Through the crackle of radio static came the voice of the line boss, directing operations from a bubble-domed helicopter hovering at about four o'clock:

'DC-3, who are you?'

'Carmichael.'

'We're trying to contain it on three sides, Carmichael. You work on the east, Limekiln Canyon, down the flank of Porter Ranch Park. Got it?'

'Got it,' Carmichael said.

He flew low, less than a thousand feet. That gave him a good view of all the action: sawyers in hard hats and orange shirts cutting burning trees to make them fall toward the fire, bulldozer crews clearing brush ahead of the blaze, shovelers carving fire-breaks, helicopters pumping water into isolated outbursts of flame. He climbed five hundred feet to avoid a single-engine observer plane, then went up five hundred more to avoid the smoke and air turbulence of the fire itself. From that altitude he had a clear picture of it, running like a bloody gash from west to east, wider at its western end.

Just east of the fire's far tip he saw a circular zone of grassland perhaps a hundred acres in extent that had already burned out, and precisely at the center of that zone stood a massive gray something that looked vaguely like an aluminum silo, the size of a ten-story building, surrounded at a considerable distance by a cordon of military vehicles.

Carmichael felt a wave of dizziness go rocking through his mind.

That thing, he realized, had to be the E-T spaceship. It had come out of the west in the night, they said, floating over the ocean like a tremendous meteor over Oxnard and Camarillo, sliding toward the western end of the San Fernando Valley, kiss-ing the grass with its searing exhaust and leaving a trail of flame behind it. And then it had gently set itself down over there and extinguished its own brush-fire in a neat little circle about itself, not caring at all about the blaze it had kindled farther back, and God knows what kind of creatures had come forth from it to inspect Los Angeles.

It figured, didn't it, that when the UFOs finally did make a landing out in the open, it would be in L.A.? Probably they had chosen to land there because they had seen the place so often on television – didn't all the stories say that UFO people always monitored our TV transmissions? So they saw L.A. on every other show and they probably figured it was the capital of the world, the perfect place for the first landing. But why, Carmichael wondered, had the bastards needed to pick the height of the fire season to put their ships down here?

He thought of Cindy again, how fascinated she was by all this UFO and E-T stuff, those books she read, the ideas she had, the way she had looked toward the stars one night when they were camping in the high country of Kings Canyon and talked of the beings that must live up there. 'I'd love to see them,' she said. 'I'd love to get to know them and find out what their heads are like.'

She believed in them, all right.

She knew, *knew*, that they would be coming one day.

They would come, not from Mars – any kid could tell you that, there were no living beings on Mars – but from a planet called HESTEGHON. That was how she always wrote it, in capital letters, in the little poetic fragments he sometimes found around the house. Even when she spoke the name aloud that was how it seemed to come out, with extra-special emphasis. HESTEGHON was on a different vibratory plane from Earth, and the people of HESTEGHON were intellectually and morally superior beings, and one day they would materialize right out of the blue in our midst to set everything to rights on our poor sorry world.

Carmichael had never asked her whether HESTEGHON was her own invention, or something that she had heard about from a West Hollywood guru or read about in one of the cheaply printed books of spiritual teachings that she liked to buy. He preferred not to get into any kind of discussion with her about it.

And yet he had never thought she was insane. Los Angeles was full of nut cases who wanted to ride in flying saucers, or claimed they already had, but it didn't sound nutty to Carmichael when Cindy talked that way. She had the innate Angeleno love of the exotic and the bizarre, yes, but he felt certain that her soul had never been touched by the crazy corruption here, that she was untainted by the prevailing craving for the weird and irrational that made him loathe the place so much. If she turned her imagination toward the stars, it was out of wonder, not out of madness: it was simply part of her nature, that curiosity, that hunger for what lay outside her experience, to embrace the unknowable.

Carmichael had had no more belief in E-Ts than he did in the tooth fairy, but for her sake he had told her that he hoped she'd get her wish. And now the UFO people were really here. He could imagine her, eyes shining, standing at the edge of that cordon staring lovingly at the spaceship.

He almost hoped she was. It was a pity he couldn't be with her now, feeling all that excitement surging through her, the joy, the wonder, the magic.

But he had work to do. Swinging the DC-3 back around toward the west, he swooped down as close as he dared to the edge of the fire and hit the release button on his dump lines. Behind him, a great crimson cloud spread out: a slurry of ammonium sulphate and water, thick as paint, with a red dye mixed into it so they could tell which areas had been sprayed. The retardant clung in globs to anything, and would keep it damp for hours.

Emptying his four 500-gallon tanks quickly, he headed back to Van Nuys to reload. His eyes were throbbing with fatigue and the bitter stink of the wet charred earth below was filtering through every plate of the old plane. It was not quite noon. He had been up all night.

The Colonel stood holding the phone while it rang and rang and rang, but there was no answer at his brother's house, and no way to leave a message, either. A backup number came up on the phone's little screen: Cindy's jewelry studio. What the hell, the Colonel thought. He was committed to this thing now; he would keep on going. He hit the key for the studio. But no one answered there either. A second backup number appeared. This one was the gallery in Santa Monica where she had her retail shop. Unhesitatingly, now, the Colonel hit that one. A clerk answered, a boy who by the sound of his high scratchy voice was probably about sixteen, and the Colonel asked for Mrs Carmichael. Hasn't been in yet today, the clerk said. Should have been in by now, but somehow she wasn't. The kid didn't sound very concerned. He made it seem as if he was doing the Colonel a favor by answering the telephone at all. Nobody under twenty-five had any respect for telephones. They were all getting biochips implanted, the Colonel had heard. That was the hottest thing now, passing data around with your forearm pressed against an X-plate. Or so his nephew Paul had said. Paul was twenty-seven, or so: young enough to know about these things. Telephones, Paul had said, were for dinosaurs.

'I'm Mrs Carmichael's brother-in-law,' the Colonel said. It was a phrase he could not remember having used before. 'Ask her to call me when she comes in, will you, please?' he told the boy, and hung up.

Then he realized that a more detailed message might have been useful. He hit the redial key and when the boy came back on the line he said, 'It's Colonel Carmichael again, Mrs Carmichael's brother-in-law. I should have told you that I'm actually trying to find my brother, who's been out of town all week. I thought perhaps Mrs Carmichael might know when he's due back.'

'She said last night that he was supposed to be coming back today,' the boy said. 'But like I told you, I haven't spoken to her yet today. Is there some problem?'

'I don't know if there is or not. I'm up in Santa Barbara, and I was wondering whether – the fire, you know – their house –'

'Oh. Right. The fire. It's, like, out by Simi Valley somewhere, right?' The kid spoke as though that were in some other country. 'The Carmichaels live, like, in L.A., you know, the hills just above Sunset. I wouldn't worry about them if I were you. But I'll have her phone you if she checks in with me. Does she have your implant access code?'

'I just use the regular data web.' I'm a dinosaur, the Colonel thought. I come from a long line of them. 'She knows the number. Tell her to call right away. Please.'

As soon as he clipped the cellphone back in his waistband it made the little bleeping sound of an incoming call. He yanked it out again and flipped it open.

'Yes?' he said, a little too eagerly.

'It's Anse, dad.' His older son's deep baritone. The Colonel had three children, Rosalie and the two boys. Anse – Anson Carmichael IV – was the good son, decent family man, sober, steady, predictable. The other one, Ronald, hadn't worked out quite as expected. 'Have you heard what's going on?' Anse asked.

'The fire? The critters from Mars? Yes. Rosalie called me about it about half an hour ago. I've been watching the teevee. I can see the smoke from out here on the porch.'

'Dad, are you going to be all right?' There was an unmistakable undertone of tension in Anse's voice. 'The wind's blowing east to west, straight toward you. They say the Santa Susana fire's moving into Ventura County already.'

'That's a whole county away from me,' the Colonel said. 'It would have to get to Camarillo and Ventura and a lot of other places first. Somehow I don't think that's going to happen. – How are things down your way, Anse?'

'Here? We're getting Santa Anas, sure, but the nearest fire's up back of Anaheim. Not a chance it'll move down toward us. Ronnie and Paul and Helena are okay too.' Mike Carmichael had never gone in for parenthood at all, but the Colonel's baby brother Lee had managed to sire two kids in his short life. All of the Colonel's immediate kin – his two sons and his daughter, and his niece and nephew Paul and Helena, who were in their late twenties now and married – lived in nice respectable suburban places along the lower coast, places like Costa Mesa and Huntington Beach and Newport Beach and La Jolla. Even Anse's brother Ronald, who was not so nice and not so respectable, was down there. 'It's you I'm worried about, dad.'

'Don't. Fire comes anywhere within thirty miles of here, I'll get in the car and drive up to Monterey, San Francisco, Oregon, someplace like that. But it won't happen. We know how to cope with fires in this state. I'm more interested in these E-Ts. What the devil do you suppose they are? This isn't all just some kind of movie stunt, is it?'

'I don't think so, dad.'

'No. Neither do I, really. Nobody's that dumb, to set half of L.A. on fire for a publicity event. I hear that they're in New York and London and a lot of other places too.'

'Washington?' Anse asked.

'Haven't heard anything about Washington,' said the Colonel.

'Haven't heard anything *from* Washington, either. Odd that the President hasn't been on the air yet.'

'You don't think they've captured him, do you, dad?'

He didn't sound serious. The Colonel laughed. 'This is all so crazy, isn't it? Men from Mars marching through our cities. – No, I don't suppose they've captured him. I figure he must be stashed away somewhere very deep, having an extremely lively meeting with the National Security Council. Wouldn't you say so?'

'We don't have any kind of contingency plans for alien invasions, so far as I know,' Anse said. 'But I'm not up on that sort of stuff these days.' Anse had been an officer in the Army's materiel-procurement arm, but he had left the Service about two years back, tempted away by a goodly aerospace-industry paycheck. The Colonel hadn't been too pleased about that. After a moment Anse said, sounding a little uncomfortable, as he always did when he said something he didn't really believe for no other reason than that he suspected the Colonel wanted to hear it, 'Well, if it's war with Mars, or wherever it is they come from, so be it. I'm ready to go back in, if I'm needed.'

'So am I. I'm not too old. If I spoke Martian, I'd volunteer my services as an interpreter. But I don't, and nobody's been calling me for my advice so far, either.'

'They should,' Anse said.

'Yes,' the Colonel said, perhaps a little too vehemently. 'They really should.'

There was silence at the other end for a moment. They were treading on dangerous territory. The Colonel had been reluctant to leave the Service, even after putting in his thirty years, and had never ceased regretting his retirement; Anse had scarcely hesitated, the moment he was eligible to claim his own. Anse said, finally, 'You want to hear one more crazy thing, dad? I think I caught a glimpse of Cindy on the news this morning, in the crowd at the Porter Ranch mall.'

'Cindy?'

'Or her twin sister, if she has one. Looked just like her, that was for sure. There were five, six hundred people standing outside the entrance of the Wal-Mart watching the E-Ts go walking by, and for a second the camera zoomed down and I was sure I saw Cindy right in the front row. With her eyes as bright as a kid's on Christmas morning. I was certain it was her.'

'Porter Ranch, that's up beyond Northridge, isn't it? What would she have been doing out there early in the morning when she lives way to hell and gone east of there and south, the other side of Mulholland?'

'The hair was just like hers, dark, cut in bangs. And big earrings, the hoops she always wears. – Well, maybe not. But I wouldn't put it past her, going up to that mall to look at the E-Ts.'

'It would have been cordoned off right away, the moment the critters arrived,' the Colonel said, while the thought went through his mind that she should have been at her gallery in Santa Monica by this time of morning, and hadn't been there. 'Not likely that the police would have been letting rubberneckers in. You must have been mistaken. Someone else, similar appearance.'

'Maybe so. – Mike's out of town, right? The back end of New Mexico, again?'

'Yes,' said the Colonel. 'Supposed to be getting back today. I called his house but I got no answer. If he's back already, I suspect he's gone out on volunteer fire duty the way he does every year. Right in the thick of things, I imagine.'

'I imagine so. That's exactly what he would be doing.' Anse laughed. 'Old Mike would have a fit if it turned out that that really was Cindy out there at the mall with the E-Ts, wouldn't he, dad?'

'I suppose he would. But that wasn't Cindy out there. – Listen, Anse, I do appreciate your calling, okay? Stay in touch. Give my love to Carole.'

'You know I will, dad.'

The Colonel clapped the phone shut, and then, as it rang again, opened it almost immediately, thinking, Let it be Mike, let it be Mike.

But no, it was Paul calling – his nephew, Lee's boy, the one who taught computer sciences at the Oceanside branch of the University. Worried about the old man and checking in with him,

Paul was. The basic California catastrophe procedure, same drill good for earthquakes, fires, race riots, floods, and mudslides: call all your kinfolks within a hundred fifty miles of the event, call all your friends, too, make sure everybody's all right, tie up the phone lines good and proper, overload the entire Net with needless well-meant communication. He would have expected Paul, at least, to have known better. But of course the Colonel had done the same thing himself only about ten minutes ago, calling all around town trying to track down his brother's wife.

'Hell, I'm fine,' the Colonel said. 'Air's getting a little smoky from what's going on down there, that's all. I've got four Martians sitting in the livingroom with me right now and I'm teaching them how to play bridge.'

At the airport they had coffee ready, sandwiches, tacos, burritos. While Carmichael was waiting for the ground crew to fill his tanks he went inside to call Cindy again, and again there was no answer at home, none at the studio. He phoned the gallery, which was open by this time, and the shiftless kid who worked there said lazily that she hadn't been in touch all morning.

'If you happen to hear from her,' Carmichael said, 'tell her I'm flying fire control out of Van Nuys Airport, working the Chatsworth fire, and I'll be home as soon as things calm down a little. Tell her I miss her, too. And tell her that if I run into an E-T I'll give it a big hug for her. You got that? Tell her just that.'

'Will do. Oh, by the way, Mr Carmichael –'

'Yes?'

'Your brother called, twice. Colonel Carmichael, that is. He said he thought you were, like, still in New Mexico and he was trying to find Mrs Carmichael. I told him you were supposed to be coming back today, and that I didn't know where she was, but that the fire was, like, nowhere near your house.'

'Good. If he calls again, let him know what I'm doing.'

That was odd, Carmichael thought, Anson trying to phone Cindy. The Colonel had done a pretty good job over the past five or six years of pretending that Cindy didn't exist. Carmichael hadn't even known that his brother *had* the gallery number, nor could he understand why he would want to call there. Unless the Colonel was worried about him for some reason, so worried that he didn't mind having to put up with talking with Cindy.

Probably I should phone him right now, Carmichael thought, before I go back upstairs.

But there was no dial tone now. System overload, most likely. Everybody was calling everybody all around the area. It was a miracle that he'd been able to do as well as he had with the phone just now. He hung up, tried again, still got nothing. And there were other people lined up waiting for the phone.

'Go ahead,' he said to the first man in line, stepping back from the booth. 'You try. The line's dead.'

He went looking for a different phone. Across the way in the main hall he saw a crowd gathered around someone carrying a portable television set, one of those jobs with a postcard-sized screen. Carmichael shouldered his way in just as the announcer was saying, 'There has been no sign yet of the occupants of the San Gabriel or Orange County spaceships. But this was the horrifying sight that astounded residents of the Porter Ranch area beheld this morning between nine and ten o'clock.'

The tiny screen showed two upright tubular figures that looked like big squids walking on the tips of the tentacles that sprouted in clusters at their lower ends. Their skins were purplish and leathery-looking, with rows of luminescent orange spots glowing along the sides. They were moving cautiously through the parking lot of a shopping center, peering this way and that out of round yellow eyes as big as saucers. There was something almost dainty about their movements, but Carmichael saw that the aliens were taller than the lampposts – which would make them at least twelve feet high, maybe fifteen. At least a thousand onlookers were watching them at a wary distance, appearing both repelled and at the same time irresistibly drawn.

Now and then the creatures paused to touch their foreheads together in some sort of communion. The camera zoomed in for a close-up, then jiggled and swerved wildly just as an enormously long elastic tongue sprang from the chest of one of the alien beings and whipped out into the crowd.

For an instant the only thing visible on the screen was a view of the sky; then Carmichael saw a shot of a stunned-looking girl of about fourteen who had been caught around the waist by that long tongue, and was being hoisted into the air and popped like a collected specimen into a narrow green sack.

'Teams of the giant creatures roamed the mall for nearly an hour,' the announcer intoned. 'It has definitely been confirmed that between twenty and thirty human hostages were captured before they returned to their vehicle, which now has taken off and gone back to the mother ship eleven miles to the west. Meanwhile, fire-fighting activities desperately continue under Santa Ana conditions in the vicinity of all three landing sites, and –'

Carmichael shook his head.

Los Angeles, he thought, disgusted. Jesus! The kind of people that live here, they just walk right up and let the E-Ts gobble them like flies. Maybe they think it's just a movie, and everything will be okay by the last reel.

And then he remembered that Cindy was the kind of people who would walk right up to one of these E-Ts. Cindy was the kind of people who lived in Los Angeles, he told himself, except that Cindy was *different*. Somehow.

There was still a long line in front of every telephone booth. People were angrily banging the useless receivers against the walls. So there was no point even thinking about attempting to call Anson now. Carmichael went back outside. The DC-3 was loaded and ready.

In the forty-five minutes since he had left the fire line, the blaze seemed to have spread noticeably toward the south. This time the line boss had him lay down the retardant from the De Soto Avenue freeway interchange to the northeast corner of Porter Ranch. He emptied his tanks quickly and went back once more to the airport. Maybe they would have a working phone in Operations HQ that they would let him use to try to get quick calls through to his wife and his brother.

But as he was crossing the field a man in military uniform came out of the HQ building and beckoned to him. Carmichael walked over, frowning.

The man said, 'You Mike Carmichael? Live in Laurel Canyon?'

'That's right.'

'I've got a little troublesome news for you. Let's go inside.'

Carmichael was too tired even to feel alarm. 'Suppose you tell me here, okay?' The officer moistened his lips. He looked very uneasy. He had one of those blank featureless baby-faces, nothing interesting about it at all except the incongruously big eyebrows that crawled across his forehead like shaggy caterpillars. He was very young, a lot younger than Carmichael expected officers of his rank to be, and obviously he wasn't good at this stuff, whatever kind of stuff it was.

'It's about your wife,' he said. 'Cynthia Carmichael? That's your wife's name?'

'Come *on*,' Carmichael said. 'God damn it, get to the point!'

'She's one of the hostages, Mr Carmichael.'

'Hostages?'

'The space hostages. Haven't you heard? The people who were captured by the aliens?'

Carmichael shut his eyes for a moment. His breath went from him as though he had been kicked.

'Where did it happen?' he demanded. 'How did they get her?'

The young officer gave him a strange strained smile. 'It was the shopping-center lot, Porter Ranch. Maybe you saw some of it on the TV.'

Carmichael nodded, feeling more numb by the moment. That girl jerked off her feet by that immense elastic tongue, swept through the air, popped into that green pouch.

And Cindy – Cindy –?

'You saw the part where the creatures were moving around? And then suddenly they were grabbing people, and everyone was running from them?'

'No. I must have missed that part.'

'That was when they got her. She was right up front when they began grabbing, and maybe she would have had a chance to get away, but she waited just a little bit too long. She started to run, I understand, but then she stopped – she looked back at them – she may have called something out to them – and then – well, and then –'

'Then they scooped her up?'

'I have to tell you, sir, that they did.' The baby-face worked hard at looking tragic. 'I'm terribly sorry, Mr Carmichael.'

'I'm sure you are,' Carmichael said stonily. An abyss had begun to open within him. 'So am I.'

'One thing all the witnesses agreed, she didn't panic, she didn't scream. We can show it to you on tape inside. She was very brave when those monsters grabbed her. How in God's name you can be brave when something that size is holding you in mid-air is something I don't understand, but I have to assure you, sir, that those who saw it –'

'It makes sense to me,' Carmichael said.

He turned away. He shut his eyes again, for a moment, and took deep, heavy pulls of the hot smoky air.

It figures, he thought. It makes complete sense.

Of *course* she had gone right out to the landing site, as soon as the news of their arrival began to get around. Of course. If there was anyone in Los Angeles who would have wanted to get to those creatures and see them with her own eyes and perhaps try to talk to them and establish some sort of rapport with them, it was Cindy. She wouldn't have been afraid of them. She had never seemed to be afraid of anything. And these were the wise superior beings from HESTEGHON, anyway, weren't they? It wasn't hard for Carmichael to imagine her in that panicky mob in the parking lot, cool and radiant, staring at the giant aliens, smiling at them even in the moment when they seized her.

In a way Carmichael felt very proud of her. But it terrified him to think that she was in their grasp.

'She's on the ship?' he asked. 'The one that I saw sitting in that field just beyond the fire zone?'

'Yes.'

'Have there been any messages from the hostages yet? Or from the aliens, for that matter?'

'I'm sorry. I'm not in a position to divulge that information.'

'I've been risking my ass all afternoon trying to put that fire out and my wife is a prisoner on the spaceship and you're not in a position to divulge any information?'

The officer gave him a dead-fish sort of smile. Carmichael tried to tell himself that he was just a kid, the way the cops and the high-school teachers and the mayors and governors and everybody else mysteriously seemed to be just kids these days. A kid with a nasty job to do.

'I was instructed to tell you the news about your wife,' the kid said, after a moment. 'I'm not allowed to say anything about any other aspect of this event to anyone, not to anyone at all. Military security.'

'Yes,' Carmichael said, and for an instant he was back in the war again, trying to find out something, anything, about Cong movements in the area he was supposed to be patrolling the next day, and running into that same dead-fish smile, that same solemn meaningless invocation of military security. His head swam and names that he hadn't thought of in decades ran through his brain, Phu Loi, Bin Thuy, Tuy Hoa, Song Bo. Cam Ranh Bay. The U Minh Forest. Images from the past, swimming around. The greasy sidewalks of Tu Do Street in Saigon, skinny whores grinning out of every bar, ARVNs in red berets all over the place. White sand beaches lined with coconut palms, pretty as a picture; native kids with one leg each, hobbling on improvised crutches; Delta hooches going up in flames. And the briefing officers lying to you, lying, lying, always lying. His buried past, evoked by a single sickly smile.

'Can you at least tell me whether there *is* any information?'

'I'm sorry, sir, I'm not at liberty to –'

'I refuse to believe,' Carmichael said, 'that that ship is just sitting there, that nothing at all is being done to make contact with –'

'A command center has been established, Mr Carmichael, and certain efforts are under way. That much I can tell you. I can tell you that Washington is involved. But beyond that, at the present point in time –'

Another kid, a pink-faced one who looked like an Eagle Scout, came running up. 'Your plane's all loaded and ready to go, Mike!'

'Yeah,' Carmichael said. The fire, the fucking fire! He had almost managed to forget about it. *Almost*.

He hesitated a moment, torn between conflicting responsibilities. Then he said to the officer, 'Look, I've got to get back out on the fire line. I want to look at that tape of Cindy getting captured, but I can't do it now. Can you stay here a little while?'

Foundation
Isaac Asimov

The first volume in Isaac Asimov's world-famous saga, winner of the Hugo Award for Best All-Time Novel Series.

'One of the most staggering achievements in modern SF'
The Times

Long after Earth was forgotten, a peaceful and unified galaxy took shape, an Empire governed from the majestic city-planet of Trantor. The system worked, and grew, for countless generations. Everyone believed it would work forever. Everyone except Hari Seldon.

As the great scientific thinker of his age, Seldon could not be ignored. Reluctantly, the Commission of Public Safety agreed to finance the Seldon Plan. The coming disaster was predicted by Seldon's advances in psychohistory, the mathematics of very large human numbers, and it could not be averted. The Empire was doomed. Soon Trantor would lie in ruins. Chaos would overtake humanity. But the Seldon Plan was a long-term strategy to minimize the worst of what was to come.

Two Foundations were set up at opposite ends of the galaxy. Of the Second nothing can be told. It guards the secrets of psychohistory. *FOUNDATION* is the story of the First Foundation, on the remote planet of Terminus, from which those secrets were withheld.

SBN 0 586 01080 7

Arthur C. Clarke

The Songs of Distant Earth

The Voyagers Awoke in Paradise

When Earth's sun went nova, the *Magellan* barely escaped in time with its precious cargo of one million sleepers and gene banks of plants and animals.

Five hundred years into the voyage they stopped for repairs on the idyllic planet of Thalassa. But whilst the awakened Earth people envied them their stable, harmonious world, the hospitable Thalassans were drawn by the long quest of the interstellar voyagers. And when Lieutenant Commander Loren Lorenson met beautiful Thalassan Mirissa, their alien destinies became inextricably – and tragically – entwined.

The Songs of Distant Earth blends sound scientific speculation with a moving story of life and love on an alien and beautiful world.

ISBN 0 586 06623 3

'Well –'

'Maybe half an hour. I have to do a retardant dump. Then I want you to show me the tape. And then to take me over to that spaceship and get me through the cordon, so I can talk to those critters myself. If my wife's on that ship, I mean to get her off it.'

'I don't see how it would be possible for –'

'Well, try to see,' Carmichael said. 'I'll meet you right here in half an hour, okay?'

She had never seen anything so beautiful. She had never even imagined that such beauty could exist. If this was how their spaceship looked, Cindy thought, what could their home world possibly be like?

The place was palatial. The aliens had taken them up and up on a kind of escalator, rising through a seemingly endless series of spiral chambers. Every chamber was at least twenty feet high, as was to be expected, considering how big the aliens themselves were. The shining walls tapered upward in eerie zigzag angles, meeting far overhead in a kind of Gothic vault, but not rigid-looking the way Gothic was. Instead there was a sudden twist and leap up there, a quick baffling shift of direction, as though the ceilings were partly in one dimension and partly in another.

And the ship was one huge hall of mirrors. Every surface, *every single one*, had a reflective metallic sheen. Wherever your eye came to rest you saw a million ricocheting shimmering images, receding dizzyingly to infinity. There didn't seem to be any actual sources of illumination in here, just a luminous glow that came out of nowhere, as though being generated by the back-and-forth interaction of all those mirror-bright metal surfaces.

And the plants – the flowers –

Cindy loved plants, the stranger the better. The garden of their little Laurel Canyon house was dense with them, ferns and orchids and cacti and bromeliads and aloes and philodendrons and miniature palms and all manner of other things from the abundantly stocked nurseries of Los Angeles. Something was in bloom every day of the year. 'My science-fiction garden,' she called it. She had picked things for their tropical strangeness, their corkscrew stems and spiky leaves and unusual variegations. Every imaginable shape and texture and color was represented there.

But her garden looked like a dull prosaic bunch of petunias and marigolds compared with the fantasy-land plants that grew everywhere about the ship, drifting freely in mid-air, seemingly having no need of soil or water.

There were forking things with immense, fleshy turquoise leaves, big enough to serve as mattresses for elephants; there were plants that looked like clusters of spears, there was one that had a lightning-bolt shape, there were some that grew upside-down, standing on fanned-out sprays of delicate purple foliage. And the flowers! Green blossoms with bright inquisitive magenta eyes at their centers; furry black flowers, tipped with splashes of gold, that throbbed like moth-wings; flowers that seemed to be made out of silver wire; flowers that looked like tufts of flame; flowers that emitted low musical tones.

She loved them all. She yearned to know their names. Her mind went soaring into ecstasy at the thought of what a botanical garden on Planet Hesteghon must look like.

There were eight hostages in this chamber with her, three male, five female. The youngest was a girl of about eleven; the oldest, a man who looked to be in his eighties. They all seemed terrified. They were sitting together in a sorry little heap, sobbing, shivering, praying, muttering. Only Cindy was up and around, wandering through the immense room like Alice let loose in Wonderland, gazing delightedly at the marvelous flowers, looking in wonder at the miraculous cascades of interlacing mirror images.

It weirded her out to see how miserable the others all were in the presence of such fantastic beauty.

'No,' Cindy told them, coming over and standing in front of them. 'Stop crying! This is going to be the most wonderful moment of your lives. They don't intend to harm us.'

A couple of them glared at her. The ones who were sobbing sobbed harder.

'I mean it,' she said. I know. These people are from the planet Hesteghon, which you could have read about in the Testimony of Hermes. That's a book that was published about six years ago, translated from the ancient Greek. The Hesteghon people come to Earth every five thousand years. They were the original Sumerian gods, you know. Taught the Sumerians how to write on clay tablets. On an earlier visit they taught the Cro-Magnons to paint on cave walls.'

'She's a lunatic,' one of the women said. 'Will somebody please shut her up?'

'Hear me out,' Cindy said. 'I promise you, we're absolutely safe in their hands. On this visit their job is to teach us at long last how to live in peace, forever and ever. We'll be their communicants. They'll speak through us, and we'll carry their message to all the world.' She smiled. 'You think I'm a nut case, I know, but I'm actually the sanest one here. And I tell you –'

Someone screamed. Someone pointed, stabbing her finger wildly into the air. They all began to cower and cringe.

Cindy felt a glow of sudden warmth behind her, and looked about.

One of the aliens had entered the huge room. It stood about ten yards to her rear, swaying gently on the little tips of its walking-tentacles. There was an aura of great tranquility about it. Cindy felt a wonderful stream of love and peace emanating from it. Its two enormous golden eyes were benign wells of serene radiance.

They are like gods, she thought. *Gods.*

'My name is Cindy Carmichael,' she told the alien straight away. 'I want to welcome you to Earth. I want you to know how glad I am that you've come to fulfill your ancient promise.'

The giant creature continued to rock pleasantly back and forth. It did not appear to notice that she had spoken.

'Talk to me with your mind,' Cindy said to it. 'I'm not afraid of you. *They* are, but I'm not. Tell me about Hesteghon. I want to know everything there is to know about it.'

One of the airborne flowers, a velvety black one with pale green spots on its two fleshy petals, drifted nearer to her. There was a crevice at its center that looked remarkably like a vagina. From that long dark slit emerged a little tendril that quivered once and gave off a little low-pitched blurt of sound, and abruptly Cindy found herself unable to speak. She had lost the power of shaping words entirely. But there was nothing upsetting about that; she understood without any doubt that the alien simply did not want her to speak just now, and when it was ready to restore her ability to speak it would certainly do so.

A second quick sound came from the slit at the heart of the black flower, a higher-pitched one than before. And Cindy felt the alien entering her mind.

It was almost a sexual thing. It went inside her smoothly and easily and completely, and it filled her just as thoroughly as a hand fills a glove. She was still there inside herself, but there was something else in there too, something immense and omnipotent, causing her no injury, displacing nothing, but making itself at home in her as though there had always been a space within her large enough for the mind of a gigantic alien being to occupy.

She felt it massaging her brain.

That was the only word for it: *massaging.* A gentle soothing kneading sensation, as of fingertips lovingly caressing the folds and convolutions of her brain. What the alien was doing, she realized, was methodically going through her entire accumulation of knowledge and memory, examining every single experience of her life from the moment of birth until this second, absorbing it all. In the course of – what? Two seconds? – it was done with the job, and now, she knew, it would be able to write her complete biography, if it wanted to. It knew whatever she knew, the street she had lived on when she was a little girl and the name of her first lover and the exact design of the star sapphire ring she had finished making last Tuesday. And it also had learned from her the multiplication table and how to say 'Where is the bathroom, please?' in Spanish and the way to get from the westbound Ventura Freeway to the southbound San Diego Freeway, and all the rest of the things in her mind, including a good many things, very probably, that she had long ago forgotten herself.

Then it withdrew from her and she could speak again and she said as soon as she could, 'You know now, don't you, that I'm not frightened of you. That I love you and want to do everything I can to help you fulfill your mission.'

And, since she suspected it preferred to communicate telepathically instead of by voice, she said to it also, silently, with all the mental force that she could muster:

Tell me everything about Hesteghon.

But the alien did not seem to be ready to tell her anything. For a moment it contemplated her gravely and, Cindy thought, tenderly, but she felt no sense of contact with its mind. And then it went away.

When Carmichael was aloft again he noticed at once that the fire was spreading. The wind was even rougher and wilder than before, and now it was blowing hard from the northwest, pushing the flames down toward the edge of Chatsworth. Already some glowing cinders had blown across the city limits and Carmichael saw houses afire to his left, maybe half a dozen of them.

There would be more houses going up, he knew, many more, strings of them exploding into flame one after another as the heat coming from next door became irresistible. He had no doubt of it. In firefighting you come to develop an odd sixth sense of the way the struggle is going, whether you're gaining on the blaze or the blaze is gaining on you. And that sixth sense told him now that the vast effort that was under way was failing, that the fire was still on the upcurve, that whole neighborhoods were going to be ashes by nightfall.

He held on tight as the DC-3 entered the fire zone. The fire was sucking air like crazy, now, and the turbulence was astounding: it felt as if a giant's hand had grabbed the ship by the nose. The line boss's helicopter was tossing around like a balloon on a string.

Carmichael called in for orders and was sent over to the southwest side of the zone, close by the outermost street of houses. Firefighters with shovels were beating on wisps of flame rising out of people's gardens down there. The heavy skirts of dry dead leaves that dangled down the trunks of a row of towering palm trees running along the edge of the curb for the entire length of the block were starting to blaze into flame, going up in a neat consecutive sequence, pop pop pop pop. The neighborhood dogs had formed a crazed pack, running bewilderedly back and forth. Dogs were weirdly loyal during fires: they stuck around. The

neighborhood cats, he figured, were halfway to San Francisco by
now.

Swooping down to treetop height, Carmichael let go with a
red gush of chemicals, swathing everything that looked combust-
ible with the stuff. The shovelers looked up and waved at him
and grinned, and he dipped his wings to them and headed off
to the north, around the western edge of the blaze – it was edging
farther to the west too, he saw, leaping up into the high canyons
out by the Ventura County line – and then he flew eastward
along the Santa Susana foothills until he spotted the alien spaceship once more, standing isolated in its circle of blackened earth
like a high-rise building of strange futuristic design that some
real-estate developer had absentmindedly built out here in the
middle of nowhere. The cordon of military vehicles seemed now
to be even larger, what looked like a whole armored division
deployed in concentric rings beginning half a mile or so from
the ship.

Carmichael stared intently at the alien vessel as though he
might be able to see right through its shining walls to Cindy
within.

He imagined her sitting at a table, or whatever the aliens might
use instead of tables – sitting at a table with seven or eight of
the huge beings, calmly explaining Earth to them and then asking
them to explain their world to her.

He was altogether certain that she was safe, that no harm
would come to her, that they were not torturing her or dissecting
her or sending electric currents through her just for the sake of
seeing how she reacted. Things like that would never happen to
Cindy, he knew. The only thing he feared was that they would
depart for their home star without releasing her. That notion
was truly frightening. The terror that that thought generated
in him was as powerful as any kind of fear he had ever felt,
rising up through his chest like a lump of molten lead, spreading out to fill his throat and send red shafts of pain into his
skull.

As Carmichael continued to approach the aliens' landing site
he saw the guns of some of the tanks below swiveling around
to point at him, and he picked up a radio voice telling him

brusquely, 'You're off limits, DC-3. Get back to the fire zone. This is prohibited air space.'

'Sorry,' Carmichael replied. 'My mistake. No entry intended.'

But as he began to make his turn he dropped down even lower, so that he could have one last good look at the huge spaceship. If it had portholes, and Cindy was looking out one of those portholes, he wanted her to know that he was nearby. That he was watching, that he was waiting for her to come back. But the ship's vast hull was blind-faced, entirely blank.

– Cindy? Cindy?

It was like something happening in a dream, that she should be inside that spaceship. And yet it was so very much like her that she should have made it happen.

She was always questing after the strange, the mysterious, the unfamiliar. The people she brought to the house: a Navajo once, a bewildered Turkish tourist, a kid from New York. The music she played, the way she chanted along with it. The incense, the lights, the meditation. 'I'm searching,' she liked to say. Trying always to find a route that would take her into something that was wholly outside herself. Trying to become something more than she was. That was how they had fallen in love in the first place, an unlikely couple, she with her beads and sandals, he with his steady no-nonsense view of the world: she had come up to him that day long ago when he was in the record shop in Studio City, and God only knew what he was doing in that part of the world in the first place, and she had asked him something and they had started to talk, and they had talked and talked, talked all night, she wanting to know everything there was to know about him, and when dawn came up they were still together and they had rarely been parted since. He never had really been able to understand what it was that she had wanted him for – the Central Valley redneck, the aging flyboy – although he felt certain that she wanted him for something real, that he filled some need for her, as she did for him, which could for lack of a more specific term be called love. She had always been searching for that, too. Who wasn't? And he knew that she loved him truly and well, though he couldn't quite see why. 'Love is understanding,' she liked to say. 'Understanding is loving.' Was

she trying to tell the spaceship people about love right this
minute? *Cindy, Cindy, Cindy* –

The Colonel's phone bleeped again. He grabbed for it, eager and
ready for his brother's voice.

Wrong again. Not Mike. This was a hearty booming unfamiliar
voice, one that said, 'Anson? Anson Carmichael? Lloyd Buckley
here!'

'I'm sorry,' the Colonel said, a little too quickly. 'I'm afraid I
don't know –'

Then he placed the name, and his heart began to pound, and
a prickle of excitement began running up and down his back.

'Calling from Washington.'

I'll be damned, the Colonel thought. So they haven't forgotten
about me after all!

'Lloyd, how the hell are you? You know, I was just sitting
here fifteen minutes ago hoping you'd call! *Expecting* you to
call.'

It was only partly a lie. Certainly he had hoped Washington
would call, though he hadn't actually expected anything. And
the name of Lloyd Buckley hadn't been one of those that had
gone through his mind, although the Colonel realized now that
it really should have been.

Buckley, yes. Big meaty red-faced man, loud, cheery, smart,
though perhaps not altogether as smart as he thought himself to
be. Career State Department man; during the latter years of the
Clinton administration an assistant secretary of state for third-
world cultural liaison who had done diplomatic shuttle service in
Somalia, Bosnia, Afghanistan, Turkey, the Seychelles, and other
post-Cold-War hot-spots, working closely with the military side
of things. Probably still working in that line these days. A student
of military history, he liked to call himself, brandishing the names
of Clausewitz, Churchill, Fuller, Creasy. Fancied himself something of an anthropologist, too. Had audited one semester of the
course that the Colonel had taught at the Academy, the one in
the psychology of non-western cultures. Had had lunch with him
a few times, too, seven or eight years back.

'You've been keeping up with the situation, naturally,' Buckley said. 'Pretty sensational, isn't it? You're not having any problem with those fires, are you?'

'Not here. They're a couple of counties away. Some smoke riding on the wind, but I think we'll be okay around here.'

'Good. Good. Splendid. – Seen the Entities on the tube yet? The shopping-mall thing, and all?'

'Of course. The Entities, is that what we're calling them, then?'

'The Entities, yes. The aliens. The extraterrestrials. The space invaders. "Entities" seems like the best handle, at least for now. It's a nice neutral term. "E-T" sounds too Hollywood and "Aliens" makes it sound too much like a problem for the Immigration & Naturalization Service.'

'And we don't know that they're invaders yet, do we?' the Colonel said. 'Do we? Lloyd, will you tell me what the hell this is all about?'

Buckley chuckled. 'As a matter of fact, Anson, we were hoping you might be able to tell us. I know that you're theoretically retired, but do you think you could get your aging bones off to Washington first thing tomorrow? The White House has called a meeting of high honchos and overlords to discuss our likely response to the – ah – event, and we're bringing in a little cadre of special consultants who might just be of some help.'

'That's pretty short notice,' the Colonel heard himself saying, to his own horror. The last thing he wanted was to sound reluctant. Quickly he said: 'But yes, yes, absolutely yes. I'd be delighted.'

'The whole thing came on pretty short notice for all of us, my friend. If we have an Air Force helicopter on your front lawn at half past five tomorrow morning to pick you up, do you think you could manage to clamber aboard?'

'You know I could, Lloyd.'

'Good. I was sure you'd come through. Be outside and waiting for us, yes?'

'Right. Absolutely.'

'*Hasta la mañana*,' Buckley said, and he was gone.

The Colonel stared in wonder at the phone in his hand. Then he slowly folded it up and put it away.

Washington? Him? Tomorrow?

A great goulash of emotions surged through him as the realization that they had actually called him sank in: relief, satisfaction, surprise, pride, vindication, curiosity, and five or six other things, including a certain sneaky and unsettling measure of apprehensiveness about whether he was really up to the job. Fundamentally, he was thrilled. On the simplest human level it was good, at his age, just to be wanted, considering how unimportant he had felt when he had finally packed in his career and headed for the ranch. On the loftier level of Carmichael tradition, it was fine to have a chance to serve his country once more, to be able to make oneself useful again in a time of crisis.

All of that felt very, very good.

Provided that he *could* be of some use, of course, in the current – ah – event.

Provided.

The only way that Mike Carmichael could keep himself from keeling over from fatigue, as he guided his DC-3 back to Van Nuys to load up for his next flight over the fire zone, was to imagine himself back in New Mexico where he had been only twenty-four hours before, alone out there under a bare hard sky flecked by occasional purple clouds. Dark sandstone monoliths all around him, mesas stippled with sparse clumps of sage and mesquite, and, straight ahead, the jagged brown upthrusting pinnacle that was holy Ship Rock – *Tse Bit'a'i*, the Navajo called it, the Rock with Wings – that spear of congealed magma standing high above the flat arid silver-gray flatness of the desert floor like a mountain that had wandered down from the moon.

He loved that place. He had been entirely at peace there.

And to have come back from there smack into this – frantic hordes jamming every freeway in panicky escape from they knew not what, columns of filthy smoke staining the sky, houses erupting into flame, nightmare creatures parading around in a shopping-mall parking lot, Cindy a captive aboard *a spaceship from another star, a spaceship from another star, a spaceship from another star* –

No. No. No. No.

Think of New Mexico. Think of the emptiness, the solitude,

the quiet. The mountains, the mesas, the perfection of the unblem-
ished sky. Clear your mind of everything else.

Everything.

Everything.

He landed the plane at Van Nuys a few minutes later like a man
who was flying in his sleep, and went on into Operations HQ.

Everybody there seemed to know by this time that his wife
was one of the hostages. The officer that Carmichael had asked
to wait for him was gone. He wasn't very surprised by that. He
thought for a moment of trying to go over to the ship by himself,
to get through the cordon and do something about getting Cindy
free, but he realized that that was a dumb idea: the military was
in charge and they wouldn't let him or anybody else get within
a mile of that ship, and he'd only get snarled up in stuff with
the television interviewers looking for poignant crap about the
families of those who had been captured.

Then the head dispatcher came over to him, a tanned smooth-
featured man named Hal Andersen who had the look of a movie
star going to seed. Andersen seemed almost about ready to burst
with compassion, and in throbbing funereal tones told Carmichael that it would be all right with him if he called it quits
for the day and went home to await whatever might happen.
But Carmichael shook him off. 'Listen, Hal, I won't get her back
by sitting in the livingroom. And this fire isn't going to go out
by itself, either. I'll do one more go-round up there.'

It took twenty minutes for the ground crew to pump the retardant slurry into the DC-3's tanks. Carmichael stood to one side,
drinking Cokes and watching the planes come and go. People
stared at him, and those who knew him waved from a distance,
and three or four pilots came over and silently squeezed his arm
or rested a hand consolingly on his shoulder. It was all very
touching and dramatic. Everybody saw himself as starring in a
movie, in this town. Well, this one was a horror movie. The
northern sky was black with soot, shading to gray to the east
and west. The air was sauna-hot and frighteningly dry: you could
set fire to it, Carmichael thought, with a snap of your fingers.

Somebody running by said that a new fire had broken out in

Pasadena, near the Jet Propulsion Lab, and there was another in Griffith Park. The wind was starting to carry firebrands westward toward the center of Los Angeles from the two inland fires, then. Dodgers Stadium was burning, someone said. So is Santa Anita Racetrack, said someone else. The whole damned place is going to go, Carmichael thought. And meanwhile my wife is sitting inside a spaceship from another planet having tea with the boys from HESTEGHON.

When his plane was ready he took it up and laid down a new line of retardant, flying just above the trees, practically in the faces of the firefighters working on the outskirts of Chatsworth. This time they were too busy to wave. In order to get back to the airport he had to make a big loop behind the fire, over the Santa Susanas and down the flank of the Golden State Freeway, and for the first time he saw the fires burning to the east, two huge conflagrations marking the places where the exhaust streams of the other two spaceships had grazed the dry grass, and a bunch of smaller blazes strung out on a south-veering line that ran from Burbank or Glendale deep into Orange County. His hands were shaking as he touched down at Van Nuys. He had gone without rest now for something like thirty-two hours, and he could feel himself beginning to pass into that blank white exhaustion that lies somewhere beyond ordinary fatigue.

The head dispatcher was waiting for him again as he left his plane. This time there was an odd sappy smile on his implausibly handsome face, and Carmichael thought he understood what it meant. 'All right, Hal,' he said at once. 'I give in. I'll knock off for five or six hours and grab some shut-eye, and then you can call me back to –'

'No. That isn't it.'

'That isn't what?'

'What I came out here to tell you, Mike. They've released some of the hostages.'

'Cindy?'

'I think so. There's an Air Force car here to take you to Sylmar. That's where they've got the command center set up. They said to find you as soon as you came off your last dump mission and send you over there so you can talk with your wife.'

'So she's free,' Carmichael cried. 'Oh, Jesus, she's free!'

'You go on along, Mike. We can work on the fire without you for a while, if that's okay with you.'

The Air Force car looked like a general's limousine, long and low and sleek, with a square-jawed driver in front and a couple of very tough-looking young officers to sit with him in back. They said hardly anything, and they looked as weary as Carmichael felt. 'How's my wife?' he asked, as the car pulled away, and one of them said, 'We understand that she hasn't been harmed.' The way he said it, deep and somber, was stiff and strange and melodramatic. Carmichael shrugged. Another one who thinks he's an actor, he told himself. This one's seen too many old Air Force movies.

The whole city seemed to be on fire now. Within the air-conditioned limo there was only the faintest whiff of smoke, but the sky to the east was terrifying, with apocalyptic streaks of red shooting up like meteors traveling in reverse through the blackness. Carmichael asked the Air Force men about that, but all he got was a clipped, 'It looks pretty bad, we understand.'

Somewhere along the San Diego Freeway between Mission Hills and Sylmar Carmichael fell asleep, and the next thing he knew they were waking him gently and leading him into a vast bleak hangar-like building near the reservoir.

The place was a maze of cables and screens, with military personnel operating assorted mysterious biochip gizmos and what looked like a thousand conventional computers and ten thousand telephones. He let himself be shuffled along, moving mechanically and barely able to focus his eyes, to an inner office where a lieutenant colonel with blond hair perhaps just beginning to shade into gray greeted him in his best this-is-the-tense-part-of-the-movie style and said, 'This may be the most difficult job you've ever had to handle, Mr Carmichael.'

Carmichael scowled. Everybody was Hollywood to the core in this damned city, he thought. And even the colonels were too young nowadays.

'They told me that the hostages were being freed,' he said. 'Where's my wife?'

The lieutenant colonel pointed to a television screen. 'We're going to let you talk to her right now.'

'Are you saying I don't get to see her?'

'Not immediately.'

'Why not? Is she all right?'

'As far as we know, yes.'

'You mean she hasn't been released? They told me the hostages were being freed.'

'All but three have been let go,' said the lieutenant colonel. 'Two people, according to the aliens, were slightly injured as they were captured, and are undergoing medical treatment aboard the ship. They'll be released shortly. The third is your wife, Mr Carmichael.' Just the merest bit of a pause, now, for that terrific dramatic effect that seemed to be so important to these people. 'She is unwilling to leave the ship.'

The effect was dramatic, all right. For Carmichael it was like hitting an air-pocket.

'*Unwilling –?*'

'She claims to have volunteered to make the journey to the home world of the aliens. She says she's going to serve as our ambassador, our special emissary. – Mr Carmichael, does your wife have any history of mental imbalance?'

Glaring, Carmichael said, 'Cindy is very sane. Believe me.'

'You are aware that she showed no display of fear when the aliens seized her in the shopping-center incident this morning?'

'I know that, yes. That doesn't mean she's crazy. She's unusual. She has unusual ideas. But she's not crazy. Neither am I, incidentally.' He put his hands to his face for a moment and pressed his fingertips lightly against his eyes. 'All right,' he said. 'Let me talk to her.'

'Do you think you can persuade her to leave that ship?'

'I'm sure as hell going to try.'

'You are not yourself sympathetic to what she's doing, are you?' the blond-haired lieutenant colonel asked.

Carmichael looked up. 'Yes, I am sympathetic. She's an intelligent woman doing something that she thinks is important, and doing it of her own free will. Why the hell shouldn't I be sympathetic? But I'm going to try to talk her out of it, you bet. I love her. I want her back. Somebody else can be the goddamned ambassador to Betelgeuse. Let me talk to her, will you?'

The lieutenant colonel gestured with a little wand the size of a pencil, and the big television screen came to life. For a moment mysterious colored patterns flashed across it in a disturbing random way; then Carmichael caught glimpses of shadowy catwalks, intricate gleaming metal strutworks crossing and recrossing at peculiar angles; and then for an instant one of the aliens appeared on the screen. Yellow saucer-sized eyes – gigantic eyes – looked complacently back at him. Carmichael felt altogether wide awake now.

The alien's face vanished and Cindy came into view.

The moment he saw her, Carmichael knew that he had lost her.

Her face was glowing. There was a calm joy in her eyes verging on ecstasy. He had seen her look something like that on many occasions, but this was different: this was beyond anything she had attained before. It was nirvana. She had seen the beatific vision, this time.

'Cindy?'

'Hello, Mike.'

'Can you tell me what's been happening in there, Cindy?'

'It's incredible. The contact, the communication.'

Sure, he thought. If anyone could make contact with the space people from dear old HESTEGHON, land of enchantment, it would be Cindy. She had a certain kind of magic about her: the gift of being able to open any door.

She said, 'They speak mind to mind, you know, no barriers at all. No words. You just *know* what they mean. They've come in peace, to get to know us, to join in harmony with us, to welcome us into the confederation of worlds.'

He moistened his lips. 'What have they done to you, Cindy? Have they brainwashed you or something?'

'No, Mike, no! It isn't anything like that! They haven't done a thing to me, I swear. We've just talked.'

'Talked!'

'They've showed me how to touch my mind to theirs. That

isn't brainwashing. I'm still me. I, me, Cindy. I'm okay. Do I look as though I'm being harmed? They aren't dangerous. Believe me.'

'They've set fire to half the city with their exhaust trails, do you know that?'

'That grieves them terribly. It was an accident. They didn't understand how dry the hills were. If they had some way of extinguishing the flames, they would, but the fires are too big even for them. They ask us to forgive them. They want everyone to know how sorry they are.' She paused a moment. Then she said, very gently, 'Mike, will you come on board? I want you to experience them as I'm experiencing them.'

'I can't do that, Cindy.'

'Of course you can! Anyone can! You just open your mind, and they touch you, and –'

'I know. I don't want to. Come out of there and come home, Cindy. Please. Please. It's been six days – seven, now. It feels like a month. I want to hug you, I want to hold you –'

'You can hold me as tight as you like. They'll let you on board. We can go to their world together. You know that I'm going to go with them to their world, don't you?'

'You aren't. Not really.'

She nodded gravely. She seemed to be terribly serious about it.

'They'll be leaving in a few weeks, as soon as they've had a chance to exchange gifts with Earth. This was intended just as a quick diplomatic visit. I've seen images of their planet – like movies, only they do it with their minds – Mike, you can't imagine how beautiful everything is, the buildings, the lakes and hills, the plants! And they want so much to have me come, to have me experience it first hand!'

Sweat rolled out of his hair into his eyes, making him blink, but he did not dare wipe it away, for fear she would think he was crying.

'I don't want to go to their planet, Cindy. And I don't want you to go either.' She was silent for a time.

Then she smiled delicately and said, 'I know you don't, Mike.'

He clenched his fists and let go and clenched them again. 'I *can't* go there.'

'No. You can't. I understand that. Los Angeles is alien enough for you, I think. You need to be in your own places, in your own real world, not running off to some far star. I won't try to coax you.'

'But you're going to go anyway?' he asked, and it was not really a question.

'You already know what I'm going to do.'

'Yes.'

'I'm sorry. But not really.'

'Do you love me?' Carmichael said, and regretted saying it the moment it had passed his lips.

She smiled sadly. 'You know I do. And you know I don't want to leave you. But once they touched my mind with theirs, once I saw what kind of beings they are – do you understand what I'm saying? I don't have to explain, do I? You always know what I'm saying.'

'Cindy –'

'Oh, Mike, I do love you so much.'

'And I love you, babe. And I wish you'd come down out of that goddamned ship.'

Her gaze was unwavering. 'You won't ask that. Because you love me, right? Just as I won't ask you again to come on board with me, because I really love you. Do you understand what I'm saying, Mike?'

He wanted to reach into the screen and grab her. 'I understand, yes,' he made himself say.

'I love you, Mike.'

'I love you, Cindy.'

'They tell me the trip takes forty-eight of our years, even by hyperspace, but it will only seem like a few weeks to me. Oh, Mike! Goodbye, Mike! God bless, Mike!' She blew kisses to him. He could see her favorite rings on her fingers, the three little strange star sapphire ones that she had made when she first began to design jewelry. They were his favorite rings too. She loved star sapphires, and so did he, because she did.

Carmichael searched his mind for some new way to reason with her, some line of argument that would work. But he couldn't find any. He felt that vast emptiness beginning to expand within him again, that abyss, as though he were being made hollow by some whirling blade.

Her face was shining. She seemed like a complete stranger to him, all of a sudden.

She seemed now entirely like a Los Angeles person, one of *those*, lost in kooky fantasies and dreams, and it was as though he had never known her, or as though he had pretended she was something other than she was. No. No, that isn't right, he told himself. She's not one of *those*, she's Cindy. Following her own star, as always.

Suddenly he was unable to look at the screen any longer, and he turned away, biting his lip, making a shoving gesture with his left hand. The Air Force men in the room wore the awkward expressions of people who had inadvertently eavesdropped on someone's most intimate moments and were trying to pretend that they hadn't heard a thing. 'She isn't crazy, Colonel,' Carmichael said vehemently. 'I don't want anyone believing she's some kind of nut.'

'Of course not, Mr Carmichael.'

'But she isn't going to leave that spaceship. You heard her. She's staying aboard, going back with them to wherever the hell they came from. I can't do anything about that. You see that, don't you? Nothing I could do, short of going aboard that ship and dragging her off physically, would get her out of there. And I wouldn't ever do that.'

'Naturally not. In any case, you understand that it would be impossible for us to permit you to go on board, even for the sake of attempting to remove her?'

'That's all right,' Carmichael said. 'I wouldn't dream of it. To remove her or even just to join her for the trip. I don't have the right to force her to leave and I certainly don't want to go to that place myself. Let her go: that's what she was meant to do in this world. Not me. Not me, Colonel. That's simply not my thing.' He took a deep breath. He thought he might be trembling. He was starting to feel sick. 'Colonel, would you mind very much if I got the hell out of here? Maybe I would feel better if I went back out there and dumped some more gunk on that fire. I think that might help. That's what I think, Colonel. All right? Would you send me back to Van Nuys, Colonel?'

So he went up one last time in the DC-3. He had lost track of the number of missions he had flown that day. They wanted him to dump the retardants along the western face of the fire, but instead he went to the east, where the spaceship was, and flew in a wide circle around it. A radio voice warned him to move out of the area, and he said that he would.

As he circled, a hatch opened in the spaceship's side and one of the aliens appeared, looking colossal even from Carmichael's altitude. The huge purplish thing stepped from the ship, extended its tentacles, seemed to be sniffing the smoky air. It appeared very calm, standing there like that.

Carmichael thought vaguely of flying down low and dropping his whole load of retardants on the creature, drowning it in gunk, getting even with the aliens for having taken Cindy from him. He shook his head. That's crazy, he told himself. Cindy would be appalled if she knew he had ever considered any such thing.

But that's what I'm like, he thought. Just an ordinary ugly vengeful Earthman. And that's why I'm not going to go to that other planet, and that's why she is.

He swung around past the spaceship and headed straight across Granada Hills and Northridge into Van Nuys Airport. When he was on the ground he sat at the controls of his plane a long while, not moving at all. Finally one of the dispatchers came out and called up to him, 'Mike, are you okay?'

'Yeah. I'm fine.'

'How come you came back without dropping your load?'

Carmichael peered at his gauges. 'Did I do that? I guess I did do that, didn't I?'

'You're *not* okay, are you?'

'I forgot to dump, I guess. No, I didn't forget. I just didn't bother. I didn't feel like doing it.'

'Mike, come on out of that plane. You've flown enough for one day.'

'I didn't feel like dumping,' Carmichael said again. 'Why the hell bother? This crazy city – there's nothing left in it that I would want to save, anyway.' His control deserted him at last, and rage swept through him like fire racing up the slopes of a dry canyon. He understood what Cindy was doing, and he respected it, but he didn't have to like it. He didn't like it at all. He had lost his one and only wife, and he felt somehow that he had lost his war with Los Angeles as well. 'Fuck it,' he said. 'Let it burn. This crazy city. I always hated it. It deserves what it gets. The only reason I stayed here was for her. She was all that mattered. But she's going away, now. Let the fucking place burn.'

The dispatcher gaped at him in amazement. 'Hey, Mike –'

Carmichael moved his head slowly from side to side as though trying to shake off an intolerable headache. Then he frowned. 'No, that's wrong,' he said, and all the anger was gone from his voice. 'You've got to do the job anyway, right? No matter how you feel. You have to put the fires out. You have to save what you can. Listen, Tim, I'm going to fly one last load today, you hear? And then I'll go home and get some sleep. Okay? Okay?'

He had the plane in motion as he spoke, going down the short runway. Dimly he realized that he had not requested clearance. The tinny squawks of somebody in the control tower came over his phones, but he ignored them. A little Cessna spotter plane moved hastily out of his way, and then he was aloft.

The sky was black and red. The fire was completely uncontained now, and maybe uncontainable. But you had to keep trying, he thought. You had to save what you could. He gunned and went forward, flying calmly into the inferno in the foothills, dumping his chemicals as he went. He felt the plane fighting him as wild thermals caught his wings from below, and, glassy-eyed, more than half asleep, he fought back, doing whatever he could to regain control, but it was no use, no use at all, and after a little while he stopped fighting it and sat back, at peace at last, as the air currents lifted him and tossed him like a toy skimming over the top, and sent him hurtling toward the waiting hills to the north.

The invasion happened differently, less apocalyptically, in New York City. Great devastating grass fires, with accompanying panicky evacuations, had never been a feature of life in New

York. New York's specialty, then as always, was inconvenience rather than apocalypse, and that was how the invasion began, as simply one more goddamned New York inconvenience.

It was one of those glorious gold-and-blue dance-and-sing days that New York City provides in October, right after the season of hot-and-sticky has taken itself off stage and the season of cold-and-nasty is not quite ready to come on.

There were seventeen witnesses to the onset of the invasion. The point of initial disembarkation was the meadow near the southern end of Central Park. There were many more than seventeen people on the meadow when the aliens arrived, of course, but most of them didn't seem to have been paying attention.

It had begun, so said the seventeen, with a strange pale blue shimmering about thirty feet off the ground. The shimmering rapidly became a churning, like water going down a drain. Then a light breeze started to blow and very quickly turned into a brisk gale. It lifted people's hats and whirled them in a startling corkscrew spiral around the churning shimmering blue place. At the same time you had a sense of rising tension, a something's-got-to-give feeling. All this lasted perhaps forty-five seconds.

Then came a pop and a whoosh and a ping and a thunk – everybody agreed on the sequence of the sound effects – and the instantly famous not-quite-egg-shaped spaceship of the invaders was there, hovering about in mid-air twenty yards above the surface of the grass, and gliding gently toward the ground. An absolutely unforgettable sight: the gleaming silvery skin of it, the disturbing angle of the slope from its wide top to its narrow bottom, the odd hieroglyphics on its flanks that tended to slide out of your field of vision if you stared at them for more than a moment.

A hatch opened and a dozen of the invaders stepped out. Or *floated* out, rather.

They looked strange. They looked exceedingly strange. Where humans have feet they had a single oval pedestal, maybe five inches thick and a yard in diameter. From this fleshy base their wraithlike bodies sprouted like tethered balloons. They had no arms, no legs, not even discernible heads: just a broad dome-shaped summit, dwindling away to a rope-like termination that was attached to the pedestal. Their lavender skins were glossy, with a metallic sheen. Dark eye-like spots sometimes formed on them but didn't last long. There was no sign of mouths. As they moved about they seemed to exercise great care never to touch one another.

The first thing they did was to seize half a dozen squirrels, three stray dogs, a softball, and a baby carriage, unoccupied. No one will never know what the second thing was that they did, because no one stayed around to watch. The park emptied with impressive rapidity.

All of this created, naturally, no small degree of excitement in midtown Manhattan. Police sirens began to sound. Car horns were honking, too: not the ordinary routine everyday exasperated when-do-things-start-to-move random honkings that many cities experience, but the special rhythmic New York City oh-for-Christ's-sake-what-now kind of honk that arouses terror in the hearts of visitors to the city. People with berserk expressions ran fleeing from the vicinity of the park as though King Kong had just emerged from the monkey house at the Central Park Zoo and was personally coming after them, and other people were running just as hard in the opposite direction, *toward* the park, as though they absolutely had to see what was happening. New Yorkers were like that.

But the police moved swiftly in to seal off the park, and for the next three hours the aliens had the meadow to themselves. Later in the day the video networks sent up spy-eyes that recorded the scene for the evening news. The aliens tolerated them for perhaps an hour, and then shot them down, casually, as if they were swatting flies, with spurts of pink light that emerged from the tip of their vehicle.

Until then it was possible for the viewers to see ghostly gleaming aliens wandering around within a radius of perhaps five hundred yards of their ship, collecting newspapers, soft-drink dispensers, discarded items of clothing, and something that was generally agreed to be a set of dentures. Whatever they picked up they wrapped in a sort of pillow made of a glowing fabric with the same shining texture as their own bodies, which immediately began floating off with its contents toward the hatch of the ship.

After the spy-eyes were shot down, New Yorkers were forced to rely for their information on government spy satellites monitoring the Earth from space, and on whatever observers equipped with binoculars could glimpse from the taller apartment houses and hotels bordering the park. Neither of these arrangements was entirely satisfactory. But it soon became apparent that a second spaceship had arrived just as the first one had, pop whoosh ping thunk, out of some pocket of hyperspace. More aliens emerged from this one.

But these were of a different sort: monsters, behemoths. They looked like double-humped medium-sized bluish-gray mountains with legs. Their prodigious bodies were rounded, with a sort of valley a couple of feet deep running crosswise along their backs, and they were covered all over with a dense stiff growth midway in texture between fur and feathers. There were three yellow eyes the size of platters at one end and three rigid purple rod-like projections that stuck out seven or eight feet at the other.

The legs were their most elephantine feature – thick and rough-skinned, like tree trunks – and worked on some sort of telescoping principle, capable of being collapsed swiftly back up into the bodies of their owners. Eight was the normal number of legs, but as they moved about they always kept at least one pair withdrawn. From time to time they would let that pair descend and pull up another one, in what seemed to be a completely random way. Now and then they might withdraw two pairs at once, which would cause them to sink down to ground level at one end like a camel kneeling. The purpose of that, it seemed, was to feed. Their mouths were in their bellies; when they wanted to eat something, they simply collapsed all eight of their legs at the same time and sat down on it. It was a mouth big enough to swallow a very large animal at a single gulp – an animal as big as a bison, say. A little later on, when the smaller aliens had opened the cages in the park zoo, the big ones did just that.

Then, well along into the night, a third kind of alien made its appearance. These were wholly different from the other two: towering, tubular, purplish squid-like things that had rows of gleaming orange spots running up and down their sides. There were not many of this sort, and they seemed distinctly to be in charge: the two other kinds, at any rate, appeared to be taking orders from them. By now news was coming in about the alien landing that had occurred a little earlier that same day just west of Los Angeles. Only the squid type had been observed out there.

There had been landings in other places, too. Plenty of them, mostly major cities, though not exclusively. One ship came down in Serengeti National Park in Tanzania, on a broad grassy plain occupied only by a huge herd of wildebeests and a few hundred zebras, who paid little attention. One landing occurred in the midst of a raging sandstorm that was taking place in the Taklimakan Desert of Central Asia, and the storm abruptly ceased, according to the mystified but essentially grateful drivers of a convoy of Chinese trucks who were the sole wayfarers in the vicinity at the time. A landing in Sicily, among the dry forlorn hills west of Catania, aroused interest only among some donkeys and sheep and the eighty-year-old owner of a scraggly grove of olive trees, who fell on his knees and crossed himself again and again and again, keeping his eyes shut all the while.

But the main action was in cities. Rio de Janeiro. Johannesburg. Moscow. Istanbul. Frankfurt. London. Oslo. Bombay. Melbourne. Et cetera, et cetera, et cetera. There were aliens all over the place, in fact, except for a few strikingly obvious places where they had somehow not bothered to land, like Washington D.C., and Tokyo, and Beijing.

The ships they arrived in were of various kinds, driven by varying means of propulsion that ranged from noisy thrust-driven chemical rockets, as in Los Angeles, up to the mysterious and unfathomably silent. Some of the alien vessels came in on mighty trails of fire, like the big one that had landed near Los Angeles. Some just popped into view out of nowhere, as the one in New York City had done. Some landed right in the middle of big cities, like the one in Istanbul that set itself down on the grand plaza between Haghia Sophia and the Blue Mosque and the one in Rome that parked itself in front of St Peter's, but others chose suburban landing sites. In Johannesburg it was only the glistening spooky aliens that emerged, in Frankfurt only the behemoths, in Rio just the squids; elsewhere there were mixtures of the three kinds.

They made no announcements. They made no demands. They decreed no decrees. They offered no explanations. They didn't say a thing.

They were simply *here*.

The meeting, the Colonel discovered, was taking place at the Pentagon, not at the White House. That seemed unusual. But why should anything be usual today, with hordes of alien beings wandering the face of the Earth?

It was quite all right with the Colonel to be plodding around in the vast but familiar corridors of the Pentagon once again. He had no illusions about the activities that had gone on in this place over the years or some of the people who had taken part in them, but he was no more inclined to take umbrage at the building simply because stupid or even evil decisions had been made within it than a bishop recalled to Rome would take umbrage at the Vatican because some of its occupants over the centuries had been other than saintly. The Pentagon was just a building, after all. And it had been the center of his professional life for three decades.

Very little had changed in the twelve or thirteen years since he had last set foot within it. The air in the long corridors had the same stale synthetic smell, the lighting fixtures were no more beautiful than they had been and still cast that sickly light, the walls were as drab as ever. One difference he noticed was that the guards at the various checkpoints were much younger – he would easily have believed that they were high-school boys and girls, though he suspected they actually were a little older than that – and some of the security procedures were different, now, too.

These days they screened people to see whether they had biochip implants in their arms, for example. 'Sorry,' the Colonel said, grinning. 'I'm not that modern.' But they screened him for implants anyway, and very thoroughly. And moved him on through pretty quickly after that, though the other three who had flown with him from California, the ruddy-bearded UCLA professor and the Cal Tech astronomer with the British accent and that lovely but somewhat dazed young dark-haired woman who had actually been held for a short time as a hostage aboard the alien spaceship, were kept back for more elaborate interrogation, as civilians usually were.

As he approached the meeting room itself, the Colonel began to ratchet himself up a couple of gears, getting himself up to speed for whatever lay ahead.

Once upon a time, some thirty years ago, he had been part of the strategic planning team in Saigon, helping to run a war that could not possibly have been won, coping on a day-by-day basis with the task of tracking down the worms that kept wriggling up through the quicksand and trying to put them in their proper cans, while simultaneously searching for the light at the end of the tunnel. He had distinguished himself pretty considerably in that capacity, which was why he had started his Vietnam tour as a second lieutenant and finished it as a major, with further promotions ahead.

But he had given all that high-powered stuff up, long ago, first for a post-Vietnam doctorate in Asian Studies and a teaching appointment at the Academy, and then, after his wife's death, for the quiet life of a fuddy-duddy walnut farmer in the hills above Santa Barbara. He was, here and now in the charming first decade of the charming twenty-first century, too far out of things to know or care much about the contemporary world, having participated neither in the glorious Net that everybody was plugged into, nor the even newer and glitzier world of biochip implants, nor, in fact, anything else of importance that had happened since about 1995.

Today, though, he needed to reactivate his thinking cap and call upon the smarts that had been at his command in the good old days of the epic battle for the hearts and minds of those pleasant but complicated people out there in the rice-paddies of the Mekong Delta.

Even if he had been, after all, part of the losing team, that other time.

But through no fault of his own, that time.

*   *   *

The meeting, which was being held in a big, bleak, surprisingly unpretentious conference room on the third floor, had been going on for some hours by the time the Colonel was ushered into it, which was about two in the afternoon Eastern time on the day after the arrival of the Entities. Neckties had been loosened all over the room, coats had come off, the male faces were beginning to look stubbly, pyramids and ziggurats of empty white plastic coffee containers were stacked up everywhere. Lloyd Buckley, who came rumbling forward to seize the Colonel's hand the moment the Colonel entered, had the eroded look of a man who had gone without sleep the night before. Probably that was true of most of them. The Colonel hadn't had very much himself.

'Anson Carmichael!' Buckley bellowed. 'God damn, it's good to see you again after all this time! Man, you haven't aged half a minute!'

Buckley had. The Colonel remembered a lot of rumpled brown hair; it was mostly gray now, and there was much less of it. The State Department man had added fifty pounds or so, which surely had brought him up into the 270–280 range; his heavy features had thickened and coarsened, his shrewd gray-green eyes seemed lost now beneath heavy lids circled by puffy rings of fat.

To the room in general Buckley cried, 'Gentlemen, ladies, may I introduce Colonel Anson Carmichael III, U.S. Army, Retired – former professor of non-western psychology and Asian linguistics at West Point, and a distinguished military career before that, including, I suppose I should say, a creditable tour of duty during that unfortunate circus we staged long ago in Southeast Asia. A brilliant man and a devoted public servant, whose special insights, I know, are going to be invaluable to us today.'

The Colonel wondered what position Buckley held these days that entitled him to make a windy speech like that to people such as these.

Turning back to the Colonel now, Buckley said, 'I assume you recognize most if not all of these folks, Anson. But just to avoid any confusions, let me rattle off the cast of characters.'

The Colonel recognized the Vice President, naturally, and the Speaker of the House. The President did not seem to be in the

room, nor the Secretary of State. There was an assortment of
Navy people and Air Force people and Army people and Marines
people, plenty of braid. The Colonel knew most of the Army men
at least by sight, and a couple of the Air Force ones. The Chairman
of the Joint Chiefs of Staff, General Joseph F. Steele, gave the
Colonel a warm smile. They had served together in Saigon in '67
under General Matheson, when the Colonel of future times had
been a brand new second lieutenant assigned to the Field Advis-
ory Unit of the U.S. Military Assistance Command, dear old
gummed-up MAC-V, as an interpreter, and Joe Steele, four years
younger and a green kid just out of West Point, had started
out with some exceedingly humble flunky position for MAC-V's
Intelligence guys, though he had risen very quickly. And had
kept on rising ever since.

Buckley went around the room, making introductions. 'The
Secretary of Defense, Mr Gallagher –' A slight, almost incon-
sequential-looking man, lantern jaw, close-cropped gray hair
forming a kind of skullcap on his narrow head, formidable glint
of Jesuitical intelligence and dedication in his chilly dark-brown
eyes. 'The Secretary of Communications, Ms Crawford –' Elegant
woman, coppery glints in her dark hair, a Native American sharpness to her cheekbones and lips. 'The Senate Majority Leader, Mr
Bacon of your very own state –' Rangy, athletic-looking fellow,
probably a terrific tennis player. 'Dr Kaufman of Harvard's
Physics department –' Plump, sleepy-looking, badly dressed.
'The Presidential Science Advisor, Dr Elias –' Impressive woman,
stocky, self-contained, a mighty fortress unto herself. The heads
of the House Armed Services Committee and the Senate Armed
Services Committee. The Chief of Naval Operations. The Marine
Commandant. The top brass of the Army and Air Force as well.
The Secretaries of the Army and Navy. And so on and so on, a
goodly number in all, the high and the mighty of the land. The
Colonel noticed that Buckley had left two men in civilian clothes
completely unintroduced, and assumed he had some good reason
for that. CIA, he supposed, something like that.

'And your own title these days, Lloyd?' the Colonel asked
quietly, when Buckley seemed to have finished.

Buckley seemed nonplussed at that. It was the Vice President who said, while Buckley merely gaped, 'Mr Buckley is the National Security Advisor, Colonel Carmichael.'

Ah, so. A long way up from being an assistant secretary of state for cultural affairs. But of course Buckley had surely been angling for something like this all the time, turning his expertise in anthropology and history and the psychology of nationalistic fervor into credentials for a quasi-military post of Cabinet status in this era of resurgent cultural rivalries with roots going back beyond medieval times. The Colonel murmured something in an apologetic tone about not keeping up with the news as assiduously as he once did, now that he was retired to his hillside walnut groves and his almond trees.

There was action at the conference-room door, now. A flurry among the guards; new people arriving. The rest of the passengers from the Colonel's cross-country flight filed in at last: Joshua Leonards, the rotund UCLA anthropologist, who with his untrimmed red beard and ratty argyle sweater looked like some nineteenth-century Russian anarchist, and Peter Carlyle-Macavoy, the British astronomer from the Cal Tech extraterrestrial-intelligence search program, extremely elongated of body and fiercely bright of eye, and the shopping-mall abductee, Margaret Something-or-Other, a petite, rather attractive woman of thirty or so who was either still in shock from her experiences or else was under sedation, because she had said essentially nothing during the entire journey from California.

'Good,' Buckley said. 'We're all here, now. This would be a good moment to bring our newcomers up to date on the situation as it now stands.' He clapped a data wand to his wrist – that was interesting, the Colonel thought, a man of Buckley's age has had a biochip implant – and uttered a quick command into it, and a screen blossomed into vivid colors on the wall behind him.

'These,' said Buckley, 'are the sites of known Entity landings. As you see, their ships have touched down on every continent except Antarctica and in most of the capital cities of the world, not including this city and three or four other places where they would have been expected to land. As of the noon recap, we believe that at least thirty-four large-scale ships, containing hundreds or even thousands of aliens, have arrived. Landings are apparently continuing; and aliens of various kinds are coming forth from the big ships in smaller vehicles, also of various kinds. So far we have identified five different types of Entity vehicles and three distinct species of alien life, as so –'

He touched the wand to the implanted biochip node in his forearm and said the magic word, and pictures of strange life-forms appeared on the screen. The Colonel recognized the upright squid-like things that he had seen on television, stalking around that shopping mall in Porter Ranch, and Margaret Some-thing-or-Other recognized them too, uttering a little gasp of shock or distaste. But then the squids went away and some creatures that looked like faceless, limbless ghosts appeared, and, after those, some truly monstrous things as big as houses that were galumphing around in a park on clusters of immense legs, knock-ing over tall trees as they went.

'Up till now,' Buckley went on, 'the Entities have made no attempt at communicating with us, insofar as we are aware. We have sent messages to them by every means we could think of, in a variety of languages and artificial information-organizing systems, but we have no way of telling whether they've received them, or, if they have, whether they're capable of understanding them. At the present time –'

'What means have you actually used for sending these mes-sages?' asked Carlyle-Macavoy, the Cal Tech man, crisply.

'Radio, of course. Short wave, AM, FM, right on up the com-munications spectrum. Plus semaphore signals of various kinds, laser flashes and such, Morse code: you name it. Just about every-thing but smoke signals, as a matter of fact, and we hope Sec-retary of Communications Crawford will have someone working on that route pretty soon.'

Thin laughter went through the room. Secretary of Communi-cations Crawford was not among those who seemed amused.

Carlyle-Macavoy said, 'How about coded emissions at 1420 megahertz? The universal hydrogen emission frequency, I mean.'

'First thing they tried,' said Kaufman of Harvard. '*Nada*. Zilch.'

'So,' Buckley said, 'the aliens are here, we somehow didn't see them coming in any way, and they're prowling around unhindered in thirty or forty cities. We don't know what they want, we don't know what they plan to do. Of course, if they have any kind of hostile intent, we intend to be on guard against it. I should tell you, though, that we have discussed already today, and already ruled out, the thought of an immediate pre-emptive attack against them.'

The Colonel raised an eyebrow at that. But Joshua Leonards, the burly, shaggy UCLA anthropology professor, went ballistic. 'You mean,' he said, 'that at one point you were seriously considering tossing a few nuclear bombs at them as they sat there in midtown Manhattan and the middle of London and a shopping mall in the San Fernando Valley?'

Buckley's florid cheeks turned very red. 'We've explored all sorts of options today, Dr Leonards. Including some that obviously needed to be rejected instantly.'

'A nuclear attack was never for a moment under consideration,' said General Steele of the Joint Chiefs of Staff, in the tone of voice he might have used to a bright but obstreperous eleven-year-old boy. 'Never. But going nuclear isn't our only offensive choice. We have plenty of ways of making war by means of conventional methods. For the time being, though, we have decided that any sort of offensive move would be –'

'*The time being?*' Leonards cried. He waved his arms around wildly and flung his head back, unkempt russet beard jabbing upward, which made him look more than ever like some primordial Marxist getting ready to toss a grenade at the Czar. 'Mr Buckley, is it too soon after my arrival at this meeting for me to be butting in? Because I think I need to do some butting in right away.'

'Go ahead, Dr Leonards.'

'I know you say you've already ruled out a pre-emptive strike. Which I assume that you mean that *we*, the United States of America, aren't planning any such thing. And I assume that there's nobody on Earth crazy enough to be in favor of nuking ships that happen to be occupying sites right in the middle of big cities. But, as you say, that doesn't rule out other kinds of military action. I don't see anyone in this room representing Russia or England or France, to name just three of the countries where spaceships have landed that can be considered major military powers. Are we making any attempt to coordinate our response with such countries as those?'

Buckley looked toward the Vice President.

She said, 'We are, Dr Leonards, and we will be continuing to do so on a round-the-clock basis. Let me assure you of that.'

'Good. Because Mr Buckley has said that every imaginable means has been used in trying to communicate with the aliens, but he also said that we had been at least *considering* making them targets for our weaponry. May I point out that suddenly firing a cannon at somebody is a form of communication too? Which I think would indeed result in the opening of a dialog with the aliens, but it probably wouldn't be a conversation we'd enjoy having. And the Russians and the French and everybody else ought to be told that, if they haven't figured it out already themselves.'

'You're suggesting that if we attacked, we'd be met with unanswerable force?' asked Secretary of Defense Gallagher, sounding displeased by the thought. 'You're saying that we're fundamentally helpless before them?'

Leonards said, 'We don't know that. Very possibly we are. But it's not a hypothesis that we really need to test right this minute by doing something stupid.'

At least seven people spoke at once. But Peter Carlyle-Macavoy said, in the kind of quiet, chipped-around-the-edges voice that cuts through any sort of hubbub, 'I think we can safely assume that we'd be completely out of our depth in any kind of military encounter with them. Attacking those ships would be the most suicidal thing we could possibly do.'

The Colonel, a silent witness to all this, nodded.

But the Joint Chiefs and more than a few others in the room began once again to stir and thrash about in their seats and show other signs of agitation before the astronomer was halfway through his statement.

The Secretary of the Army was the first to voice his objections. 'You're taking the same pessimistic position as Dr Leonards, aren't you?' he demanded. 'You're essentially telling us that we're beaten already, without our firing a shot, right?' He was quickly followed by half a dozen others saying approximately the same thing.

'Essentially, yes, that's the situation,' replied Carlyle-Macavoy. 'If we try to fight, I have no doubt we'll be met with a display of insuperable power.' Which set off a second and louder uproar that was interrupted only by the impressive clapping of Buckley's hands.

'Please, gentlemen. *Please!*'

The room actually grew quiet.

Buckley said, 'Colonel Carmichael, I saw you nodding a moment ago. As our expert on interactions with alien cultures, what do you think of the situation?'

'That we are absolutely in the dark at the present moment and we should damned well not do anything until we know what's what. We don't even know whether we've been invaded. This may simply be a friendly visit. It may be a bunch of harmless tourists making a summer cruise of the galaxy. On the other hand, if it *is* an invasion, it's being undertaken by a vastly superior civilization and there's every chance that we are just as helpless before it as Dr Carlyle-Macavoy says we are.'

Defense, Navy, Army, and three or four others were standing by that time, waving their arms for attention. The Colonel wasn't through speaking, though.

'We know nothing about these beings,' he said, with great firmness. '*Nothing.* We don't even know how to go about *learning* anything about them. Do they understand any of our languages? Who knows? We sure don't understand any of theirs. Among the many things we don't know about this collection of Entities,' he went on, 'is, for example, which of them is the dominant species. We suspect that the big squid-like ones are, but how can we be sure? For all we know, the various kinds we've seen up till now are just drones, and the real masters are still up in space aboard a mother ship that they've made invisible and indetectable to us, waiting for the lesser breeds to get done with the initial phases of the conquest.'

That was quite a wild idea to have come from the lips of an

elderly, retired, walnut-farming colonel. Lloyd Buckley looked startled. So did the scientists, Carlyle-Macavoy and Kaufman and Elias. The Colonel was pretty startled by it himself.

'I have another thought,' the Colonel went on, 'about their failure so far to attempt any kind of communication with us, and how it reflects on their sense of their relative superiority to us. Speaking now in my academic capacity as a professor of non-western psychology, rather than as a former military man, I want to put forth the point that their refusal to speak with us might not be a function of their ignorance so much as it is a way of making that overwhelming superiority obvious. I mean, how could they not have learned our languages, if they had wanted to? Considering all the other capabilities they obviously have. Races that can travel between the stars shouldn't have any difficulty decoding simple stuff like Indo-European-based languages. But if they're looking for a way to show us that we are altogether insignificant to them, well, not bothering to say hello to us in our own language is a pretty good way of doing it. I could cite plenty of precedent for that kind of attitude right out of Japanese or Chinese history.'

Buckley said to Carlyle-Macavoy, 'Can we have some of your thoughts about all this, if you will?'

'What the Colonel has proposed is an interesting notion, though of course I have no way of telling whether there's any substance to it. But let me point out this: these aliens appeared in our skies without having given us a whisper of radio noise and not a smidgen of visual evidence that they were approaching us. Let's not even mention the various Starguard groups that keep watch for unexpected incoming asteroids. Let's just consider the radio evidence. Do you know about the SETI project that's been going on under that and several other names for the last forty or fifty years? Scanning the heavens for radio signals from intelligent beings elsewhere in the galaxy? I happen to be affiliated with one branch of that project. Don't you think we had instruments looking all up and down the electromagnetic spectrum for signs of alien life at the very moment the aliens arrived? And we didn't detect a thing until they began showing up on airport radar screens.'

'So you think there *can* be a hidden mother ship sitting out there in orbit,' Steele said.

'It's perfectly possible that there is. But the main point, as I know Colonel Carmichael will agree, is that the only thing we can say about these aliens for certain at this moment is that they're representatives of a race vastly more advanced than ourselves, and we had bloody well better be cautious about how we react to their arrival here.'

'You keep telling us that,' the Army Secretary grumbled, 'but you don't support it with any –'

'Look,' said Peter Carlyle-Macavoy, 'either they materialized right bang out of hyperspace somewhere inside the orbit of the moon, a concept which I think will make Dr Kaufman and some of the rest of you extremely uncomfortable on the level of theoretical physics, or else they used some method of shielding themselves from all of our detecting devices as they came sneaking up on us. But however they managed to conceal themselves from us as they made their final approach to Earth, it shows that we are dealing with beings who possess an exceedingly superior technology. It's reasonable to believe that they would easily be able to cope with any sort of firepower we might throw at them. Our most frightful nuclear weapons would be so much bows-and-arrows stuff to them. And they might, if sufficiently annoyed, retaliate even to a non-nuclear attack in a way intended to teach us to be less bothersome.'

'Agreed,' said Joshua Leonards. 'Completely.'

'They may be superior,' said a voice from the back, 'but we've got the superiority of numbers on our side. We're a whole planet full of human beings on our home turf and they're just forty shiploads of –'

'Perhaps we outnumber them, yes,' Colonel Carmichael said, 'but may I remind you that the Aztecs considerably outnumbered the Spaniards and were also on their home turf, and people speak Spanish in Mexico today?'

'So is it an invasion, do you think, Colonel?' General Steele asked.

'I told you: I can't say. Certainly it has the look of one. But the only real fact we have about these – ah – Entities – is that they're here. We can't make any assumptions at all about their behavior. If we learned anything at all out of our unhappy entanglement in Vietnam, it's that there are plenty of peoples on this planet whose minds don't necessarily operate the way ours do, who work off an entirely different set of basic assumptions from ours; and even so those are all human beings with the same inner mental wiring that we have. The Entities aren't even remotely human, and their way of thinking is entirely beyond my expertise right now. Until we know how to communicate with them – or, to put it another way, until they have deigned to communicate with us – we need to simply sit tight and –'

'Maybe they *have* communicated with us, if what I was told aboard the ship was true,' said the woman who had been taken hostage at the shopping mall, suddenly, in a tiny and dreamy but perfectly audible voice. 'With one of us, at least. And they told her lots of things about themselves. So it's already happened. If you can believe what she said, that is.'

More hubbub. Sounds of surprise, even shock, and a few low exasperated expostulations. Some of these high masters and over-lords plainly were not enjoying the experience of finding them-selves transformed into characters in a science-fiction movie.

Lloyd Buckley asked the dark-haired woman to stand and introduce herself. The Colonel yielded the floor to her with a little formal bow. She got a bit unsteadily to her feet and said, not looking at anyone in particular and speaking in a breathy monotone, 'My name is Margaret Gabrielson and I live on Wilbur Avenue in Northridge, California, and yesterday morning I was on my way to visit my sister who lives in Thousand Oaks when I stopped for gas at a Chevron station in a mall in Porter Ranch. And I was captured by an alien and taken aboard their spaceship, which is the truth and nothing but truth, so help me God.'

'This isn't a courtroom, Ms Gabrielson,' said Buckley gently. 'You aren't testifying now. Just tell us what happened to you when you were on board the alien ship.'

'Yes,' she said. 'What happened to me when I was on board the alien ship.'

And then she was silent for about ten thousand years.

Was she abashed at finding herself inside the actual and literal Pentagon, standing in front of a largely though not entirely male group of highly important governmental personages and asked to describe the wholly improbable, even absurd, events that had befallen her? Was she still befuddled and bewildered by her strange experiences among the Entities, or by the sedatives that had been given to her afterward? Or was she simply your basic inarticulate early-twenty-first-century American, who had not in any way been equipped during the thirty years of her life with the technical skill required in order to express herself in public in linear and connected sentences?

Some of each, no doubt, the Colonel thought.

Everyone was very patient with her. What choice was there?

And after that interminable-seeming silence she said, 'It was like, mirrors, everywhere. The ship. All metal and everything shining and it was gigantic inside, like some sort of stadium with walls around it.'

It was a start. The Colonel, sitting just beside her, gave her a warm encouraging smile. Lloyd Buckley beamed encouragement at her too. So did Ms Crawford, the Cherokee-faced Secretary of Communications. Carlyle-Macavoy, though, who obviously didn't suffer fools gladly, glared at her with barely veiled contempt.

'There were, you know, around twenty of us, maybe twenty-five,' she continued, after another immense terrified pause. 'They put us, like, in two groups in different rooms. Mine was a little girl and an old man and a bunch of women around my age and then three men. One of the men had been hurt when they caught him, like, I think, a broken leg, and the other two men were trying to make him, you know, comfortable. It was this giant-sized room, like maybe as big as a movie theater, with weird enormous flowers floating through the air everywhere, and we were all in one corner of it. And very scared, most of us. We figured they were, like, going to cut us up, you know, to see what was inside of us. Like, you know, what they do to laboratory animals. Somebody said that and after that we couldn't stop thinking about it.'

She dabbed away tears.

There was another interminable silence.

'The aliens,' Buckley prompted softly. 'Tell us about them.'

They were big, the woman said. Huge. Terrifying. But they came by only occasionally, perhaps every hour or two, never more than one at a time, just checking up, gazing at them for a little while and then going away again. It was, she said, like seeing your worst nightmares come to life, whenever one of those monsters entered the chamber where they were being kept. She had felt sick to her stomach every time she looked at one of them. She had wanted to curl up and cry. She looked as though she wanted to curl up and cry right this minute, here and now, in front of the Vice President and the chairman of the Joint Chiefs of Staff and all these Cabinet members.

'You said,' Buckley reminded her, 'that one woman in your group experienced some sort of communication with them?'

'Yes. Yes. There was this woman, who was, like, a little strange, I have to say – she was from Los Angeles, I guess about forty years old, with shiny black hair, and she had a lot of fantastic jewelry on, earrings like big hoops and three or four strings of beads and, like, a whole bunch of rings, and she was wearing this big wide bright-colored skirt like my grandmother used to wear in the Sixties, and sandals, and stuff. Cindy, her name was.'

The Colonel gasped.

The hair was just like hers, Anse had told him, *dark, cut in bangs. And big earrings, the hoops she always wears*. The Colonel hadn't believed it. The police would have had the site cordoned off, he had said. Not likely that they'd be letting rubberneckers near the alien ship, he had said. But no: Anse had been right. It was indeed Cindy that Anse had seen on the television news early yesterday morning in the crowd at that shopping mall; and later the aliens had grabbed her, and she had been taken aboard that ship. Did Mike know? Where *was* Mike, anyway?

Margaret Gabrielson was speaking again.

This woman Cindy, she said, was the only one in the group who had no fear of the aliens. When one of the aliens came into the chamber, she walked right up to it and greeted it like it was an old friend, and told it that it and all its people were welcome on Earth, that she was glad that they were here.

'And did the aliens reply to her in any way?' Buckley asked.

Not that Margaret Gabrielson had been able to notice. While Cindy was saying things to the alien it would just stand there looming high above her, looking down at her the way you might look at a dog or a cat, without showing any kind of reaction or understanding. But after the alien left the room, Cindy told everyone that the alien had spoken to her, like in a mental way, telepathy.

'And said what to her?' asked Buckley.

Silence. Hesitation.

'Like pulling teeth,' said Carlyle-Macavoy, through his own clenched ones.

But then it came out, all in a rush:

' – that the aliens wanted us to know that they weren't going to harm the world in any way, that they were, like, here on a diplomatic mission, that they were part of some huge United Nations of planets and they had come to invite us to join. And that they were just going to stay for a few weeks and then most of them were going back to their own world, although some of them were going to stay here as ambassadors, you know, to teach us a new and better way of life.'

'Uh-oh,' Joshua Leonards muttered. 'Scary stuff. The missionaries *always* have some new and better way of life that they want to teach. And you know what happens next.'

'They also said,' Margaret Gabrielson continued, 'that they were going to take a few Earth people back to their own world to show them what sort of place it was. Volunteers, only. And, like, this woman Cindy had volunteered. When they took us off the ship a few hours later, she was the only one who stayed behind.'

'And she seemed happy about that?' Buckley asked.

'She was, like, ecstatic.'

The Colonel winced. That sounded like Cindy, all right. *Oh, Mike!* How he loved her, Mike did. But in the twinkling of an eye she had abandoned him for monsters from some far star. Poor Mike. Poor, poor Mike.

Buckley said, 'You heard all of this, you say, only from this woman Cindy? None of the others of you had any kind of, ah, mental contact with the aliens?'

'None. It was only Cindy who had it, or said she did. All that stuff about ambassadors, coming in peace, that was all hers. But it couldn't have been true. She was really crazy, that woman. She was like, "The coming of the aliens was prophesied in this book that I read years and years ago, and everything is following the prophecy exactly." That's what she said, and you knew it was impossible. So the whole thing was just in her head. She was crazy, that woman. *Crazy*.'

Yes, the Colonel thought. *Crazy*. And Margaret Gabrielson, at that moment reaching her snapping point at last, burst into hysterical tears and began to collapse into herself and sink toward the floor. The Colonel rose in one smooth motion and caught her deftly as she fell, and steadied her and held her against his chest, murmuring soothing things to her while she wept. He felt very paternal. It reminded him of nothing so much as the time, some seven or eight years back, when Irene's diagnosis had come through and he had had to tell Rosalie that her mother had inoperable cancer, and then had had to hold her for what seemed like hours until she had cried it all out.

'It was awful, awful, awful,' Margaret Gabrielson was saying, voice muffled, head still pressed against the Colonel's ribs. 'Those hideous E-T monsters wandering around – and us not knowing what they were going to do to us – that crazy woman and all her looney-tunes nonsense – crazy, she was, crazy –'

'Well,' Lloyd Buckley said. 'So much for the first report of communications with the aliens, I guess.' He looked bemused, perhaps a little irritated by the messiness and uselessness of Margaret Gabrielson's account. No doubt he had been expecting something more. The Colonel, on the other hand, felt that he had had more than he wanted.

But there was still more to come.

A chime of some sort went off, just then. An aide jumped up, pressed his wrist-implant to a data node in the wall, gave a one-syllable command. Something lit up on a wall-mounted ribbon screen next to the node and a yellow printout came gliding from a slot below it. The aide brought it to Buckley, who glanced at it and coughed and tugged at his lower lip and made a sour face. And eventually said, 'Colonel Carmichael – Anson – do you happen to have a brother named Myron?'

'Everyone calls him Mike,' the Colonel said. 'But yes, yes, he's my younger brother.'

'Message just in from California about him that I'm supposed to pass along to you. It's bad news, I'm afraid, Anson.'

All things considered, it hadn't been much of a meeting, the Colonel thought, lost in gloom, leaden-hearted over his brother's heroic but shocking and altogether unacceptable death, as he headed for home sixteen hours later aboard the same plush Air Force VIP jet that had carried him to Washington the day before. He could not bear to think about Mike in his last moments in some rickety little plane, struggling frenetically and ultimately unsuccessfully against the violent air currents above the roiling horror of the Ventura County fire. But when he shifted his attention back to the Entities crisis and the meeting that had been called to discuss it, he felt even worse.

An embarrassment, that meeting. A ghastly waste of time. And a stunning revelation of the hollowness and futility of humanity's self-aggrandizing pretensions.

Buckley had offered to let him go back to his hotel after the news about Mike had come in: but no, no, what good would that have done? He was needed. He stayed. And sat there in mounting despair during all the dreary pointless remainder of it. All those important cabinet officers and lavishly decorated generals and admirals and the rest of them too, the whole grand crowd of lofty honchos arrayed in solemn conclave, interminably masticating the situation, and to what end? Ultimately the meeting had broken up without any significant information having been brought forth beyond the mere fact of the landings, no conclusions reached, no policy decisions taken. Aside from Wait and See, that is.

Wait; yes. And See.

The secure blue wall of the sky had been breached without warning; mysterious alien Entities had landed simultaneously all over Earth; yea, out of nowhere bizarre visitors had come, and they had seen, and after two and a half days they were already acting as though they had conquered. And in the face of all that, none of our best and brightest seemed to have the slightest idea of how we should respond.

Not that the Colonel himself had been of much help. That was perhaps the worst part of it: that he was as befuddled as the rest of them, that he had had nothing useful of his own to offer.

What was there to say, though?

We must fight and fight and fight until the last of these vile enemy invaders is eradicated from the sacred soil of Earth.

Yes. Yes. Of course. Went without saying. We shall fight on the beaches, we shall fight in the fields and in the streets, et cetera, et cetera. No flagging, no failing: fight with growing confidence, go on to the end. *We shall never surrender.*

But was this actually an invasion?

And if indeed it was, how did we go about fighting back, and what would happen to us if we tried?

Three seats ahead of him, Leonards and Carlyle-Macavoy were having the same discussion with each other that the Colonel was having with himself. And, so it appeared, coming to the same melancholy conclusions.

'Oh, Colonel, I feel so sad for you,' Margaret Gabrielson said, materializing like a wraith in front of him in the aisle. They were all flying back to California together, the valued special consultants, he and she and squat grubby Leonards and the long-legged Brit. 'Do you mind if I sit here next to you?'

With a vague indifferent gesture he beckoned her to the vacant seat.

She settled in beside him, pivoting around to give him a warm, earnest, compassionate smile. 'You and your brother were very close, weren't you, Colonel?' she said, pulling him abruptly back from one slough of despond to the other. 'I know how terribly upset you must be. The pain is written all over your face.'

He had comforted her at the meeting in Washington, and now she meant to comfort him. She means well, he thought. Be nice.

He said, 'I was the oldest of three boys. Now I'm the only one left. I think that's the biggest shock, that I'm still here and they're both gone.'

'How awful that must be, to outlive your younger brothers. Were they in the Army too?'

'The youngest one was Air Force. A test pilot, he was. Flew one experimental plane too many, about ten years ago. And the other one, Mike, the one that just – died, he decided to go in for the Navy, because no one in our family had ever been Navy, and Mike always had to do what nobody else in the family would even dream of doing. Like heading out for weeks at a time on camping trips all alone. Like buying his own little plane and flying it around the country by himself, not actually *going* any-where, just enjoying being up in the air with nobody else around him. And like marrying that weird woman Cindy and moving to Los Angeles with her.'

'Cindy?'

'The one who was a hostage while you were, the one who volunteered to stay with the aliens. That was Mike's wife. My sister-in-law.'

Margaret put her hand over her mouth. 'Oh, and I said such horrible things about her! I'm sorry! I'm so sorry!'

The Colonel smiled. She seemed to have shed, he noticed, all of those annoying little childish verbal tics, the 'likes' and 'you knows' with which she had spattered every sentence while she was speaking at the meeting. As though perhaps in her trembling nervousness in front of all those formidable high officials she had reverted to blathery little-girl locutions, but now, in one-to-one human communication, she was once again capable of speaking adult English. She was, the Colonel realized, probably not as stupid as she had sounded earlier.

'I never could stand her, myself,' he said. 'Simply not my kind of person. Too – *bohemian* for me, do you know what I mean? Too wild. I'm your standard-model straight-arrow guy, conservative, old-fashioned, boring.' Which was not entirely true, he hoped, but true enough. 'They train us to be that way in the Service. And it's a good bet that I was born that way, besides.'

'But Mike wasn't?'

'He was a little bit of a mutant, I suppose. We were a military family, and I guess we were raised to be military types, whatever that means. But Mike had a touch of something else in him, and we always knew it.' He closed his eyes a moment, letting his memories of Mike's strangeness flood upward in him – Mike's monumental untidiness, his sudden rages, his arbitrary dogmatic opinions, his willingness to let his life be dictated by the most bizarre whims. His mysterious feelings of inner emptiness and frosty dissatisfaction. And, especially, his fiery obsessive love for Cindy of the beads and sandals. 'He was nothing at all like either of us. I was my father's son all the way, the little soldier boy who was going to grow up to be a real one. And Lee – he was the baby – he was a good obedient kid like me, did what he was told, never wanted to know why. But Mike – Mike –'

'Went his own way, did he?'

'Always. I never understood him, not for a moment,' the Colonel said. 'Loved him, of course. But never understood him. – Let me tell you a story. We were six years apart in age, which is like a whole generation when you're kids. And one time when I was twelve and Mike was six I made some unkind comment about the sloppiness of his side of the room that we shared, and he decided then and there that he had to kill me.'

'*Kill* you?'

'With his fists. We had a horrendous fight. I was twice his age and twice as tall as he was, but he was always a chunky muscular kid, very strong, and I was always slender, and he came at me like a cannonball without the slightest warning and threw me down and sat on my chest and punched me black and blue before I knew what was happening. Hurt me plenty, too, the little lunatic. After about a minute I pushed him off me, and knocked him down and hurt *him* – that was how angry I was – but he got up still swinging, and kicking and biting and what-all else, and I held him at arm's length and told him that if he didn't calm down I was going to toss him in the pig-pond. We had a pig-pond then, where we lived out back of Bakersfield, and he didn't calm down, and I tossed him in. Then I went back to the house, and after a while so did he. I had a black eye and a split lip, and he was covered with muck and slop all over, and our mother never asked a single question.'

'And your father?'

'Wasn't around. This was 1955, a very scary time in the world, and the Army had just transferred him to what was called West Germany, then. We had military bases there. A few months later my mother and my brother Mike and I – Lee hadn't been born yet – went over there ourselves to be with him. We spent a couple of years there.' The Colonel chuckled. 'Mike was the only one of us ever learned much German. All the dirty words first, naturally. People used to gape at him in the street when he cut loose. Oh, a wild one, he was. But not, I think, all that different from the rest of us deep down underneath. When it was Vietnam time and the kids were growing their hair long and smoking dope and wearing funny-colored clothing, you'd have thought Mike would have been a hippie out there with them, but instead of that he became a Navy pilot and saw plenty of action. Hated the war, but did his duty as a man and a soldier and a Carmichael.'

'Were you in that war too?' Margaret asked.

'Yes. I sure was. And came to hate it too, for that matter. But I was there.'

She looked at him wide-eyed, as if he had admitted being at Gettysburg.

'Actually killed people? Got shot at?'

He smiled and shook his head. 'I was part of a strategic planning group, behind the lines. But not so far back that I didn't get to be familiar with the sound of machine-gun fire.' The Colonel let his eyes droop shut once again for a moment or two. 'Damn, that was an ugly war! There aren't any pretty ones, but that one was ugly. Still, you do whatever they ask you to do, and you don't complain and you don't ask any questions, because that's what's needed if there's going to be civilized life – somebody to do the uncivilized things, which nevertheless are necessary to be done. Usually, anyway.'

He was silent for a time.

Then he said, 'I got my fill of doing uncivilized things in Vietnam, I guess. A few years after the war I took a leave of absence and went back east, got me a degree in Asian Studies at Johns Hopkins, eventually wound up as a professor at West Point. In the course of ten years I saw Mike maybe three times at most.

He didn't say much any of those times. I could tell that something was missing from his life – like a life. Then when my wife got sick I came back to California, Santa Barbara – family land, her family – and there was Mike, living in L.A., of all places, and married to this peculiar modern-day hippie woman Cindy. He wanted me to like her. I tried, Margaret, I tried! I swear that I did. But we were people from two different worlds. The one single thing we had in common was that we both loved Mike Carmichael.'

'Peggy,' she said.

'What?'

'My name. Peggy. Nobody really calls me Margaret.'

'Ah-hah. I see. Right. *Peggy*.'

'Did she like you?'

'Cindy? I have no idea. She was polite enough to me. Her husband's old stuffed shirt of a brother. No doubt thought I was as much of a Martian as she seemed to me. We didn't see a whole lot of each other. Better that way, I figure. Basically we each pretended the other one didn't exist.'

'And yet yesterday at the meeting, right at the end, you asked that general if there was some way she could be rescued from the E-T spaceship.'

The Colonel felt his cheeks growing hot. He wished she hadn't brought up that silly little moment. 'That was dumb of me, wasn't it? But somehow I felt I owed it to her, to try to get her off of it. A member of my family, after all. In need of rescue. So I will ask. The proper thing to do, is it not?'

'But she volunteered to stay,' Peggy pointed out.

'Yes. Indeed she did. Besides which, Mike is dead and she's got nothing to come back to, anyway. And furthermore there's no way in hell that we could have removed her from that ship even if she was asking us to, which she wasn't. But you see the tradition-bound mind at work, do you, Peggy? The knee-jerk reflex of the virtuous man? My sister-in-law is in jeopardy, or so it seems to me, and therefore I turn to the powers that be and say, "Do you think there might be some way by which –"'

He stopped speaking abruptly. The lights had gone out aboard the plane.

Not just the overhead lights, but the little reading lights, and the auxiliary lights at floor level in the aisle, and everything else, so far as the Colonel could tell, that depended in any way on the movement of electromagnetic waves in the visible part of the spectrum. They were sitting in absolute black darkness within a sealed metal tube that was traveling at hundreds of miles an hour, 35,000 feet above the surface of the Earth. 'Power failure?' Peggy asked, very quietly.

'An extremely odd one, if it is,' said the Colonel.

A voice out of the blackness said, from the front of the cabin, 'Ah, we have a little problem here, folks.'

It was the second officer, and despite the attempted joviality of his words he sounded shaken, and the Colonel began to feel a little shaken too as he listened to the man's report. Every one of the ship's electrical systems, he said, had conked out simultaneously. All the instruments had failed, *all*, including the navigation devices and the ones responsible for feeding fuel to the engines. The big jet was without power of any sort now. It had effectively been transformed in the last couple of moments into a giant glider; it was coasting, right now, traveling on its accumulated momentum and nothing more.

They were somewhere over southern Nevada, the second officer said. There seemed to be some sort of little electrical problem down there, too, because the lights of the city of Las Vegas had been visible off to the left a moment ago and now they were not. The world outside the ship was as dark as the ship's interior. But there was no way of finding out what was actually going on out there, because the radio had gone dead, of course, as well as all other instrumentation linking them to the ground. Including air traffic control, of course.

And therefore we are dead also, the Colonel thought, a bit surprised at his own calmness; because how much longer could a plane of this size go on coasting without power through the upper reaches of the atmosphere before it went into free fall? And even if the pilot tried to jolly it down for a landing, how was he possibly going to control the plane with every one of its components kaput, no navigational capacity whatever, and where would he land it in the absolute dark that prevailed?

But then the lights came back on, showing the second officer standing just at the cockpit door, pale and trembling and with the glossy lines of tears showing on his cheeks; and the audio voice of the pilot now was heard, a good old solid deep pilot-voice with only the hint of a tremor in it, saying, 'Well, people, I don't have the foggiest idea of what just happened, but I'm going to be making an emergency landing at the Naval Weapons Center before it happens again. Fasten seat-belts, everybody, and hang on tight.'

He had the plane safely on the ground six and a half minutes before the lights went off a second time.

This time, they stayed off.

II

Nine Years
from Now

It was the greatest catastrophe in human history, beyond any question, because in one moment the world's entire technological capability had been pushed back three and a half centuries. Somehow the Entities had flipped a gigantic switch and turned everything off, *everything*, at some fundamental level.

In 1845 that would have been a serious matter but not, perhaps, catastrophic, and it would have been even less of a problem in 1635 or 1425, and it certainly wouldn't have mattered much in 1215. But in the first decade of the twenty-first century it was a stupendous calamity. When the electricity stopped, all of modern civilization stopped, and there were no backup systems – candles and windmills, could they really be considered backup systems? – to get things going again. This was more than a mere power failure; it was an immense paradigm shift. It wasn't just the huge generating stations that had failed; nothing at all electrical would work, right down to battery-operated flashlights. Nobody had ever drawn up a plan for what to do if electricity went away on a world-wide and apparently permanent basis.

No one could begin to figure out how the Entities had done it, and that was almost as frightening as the thing itself. Had they changed the behavior of electrons? Had they altered the lattice structure of terrestrial matter so that conductivity was no longer a reality? Or, perhaps, achieved some modification of the dielectric constant itself?

However they had managed it, it had happened. Electromagnetic waves no longer traveled anywhere controllable or useful, and electricity as a going concept was apparently extinct all over Earth. *Zap, zap, zap!* and the whole electrical revolution, incomprehensibly, was undone in a flash, the entire immense technological pyramid that had been built atop the little friction generator that old Otto von Guericke of Magdeburg had constructed in 1650 and the Leyden jar that Pieter van Musschenbroek concocted to store the energy the Guericke friction machine created, and Alessandro Volta's silver-and-zinc batteries, and Humphry Davy's arc lights and Michael Faraday's dynamos and the life's work of Thomas Alva Edison and all the rest.

Goodbye, then – for how long, nobody knew – to telephones and computers and radio and television, to alarm clocks and burglar alarms, to doorbells, garage-door openers, and radar, to oscilloscopes and electron microscopes, to cardiac pacemakers, to electric toothbrushes, to amplifiers of any and every sort, to vacuum tubes and microprocessors. Bicycles were still all right, and rowboats, and graphite pencils. So were hand-guns and rifles. But anything that required electrical energy in order to function was now inoperative. What became known as the Great Silence had fallen.

The electrons simply would not flow, that was the problem. The electrical functions of biological organisms were unaffected, but everything else was kaput.

Any sort of circuitry through which a voltage might pass now had become as nonconductive as mud. Voltages themselves, wattages, amperages, sine waves, bands and bandwidths, signal-to-noise ratios, and, for that matter, both signals and noise, et cetera ad infinitum, became non-concepts.

Drawbridges and canal locks remained frozen in whatever position they might have been in at the time when the current stopped. Planes unlucky enough to be aloft then, suddenly bereft of all navigational aid and the functioning of their most trivial internal mechanisms, crashed. So did some millions of automobiles that were in transit when the roads·went dark, the traffic-control computers went dead, and their own internal guidance systems failed. Cars not in transit at the moment of the death of electricity now were incapable of being started, except for the ancient crank-starting models, and there weren't very many of those still operating. The various computer nets were snuffed in an instant, of course. All commercial records that had not already been printed out became inaccessible. As did the world's currency reserves, safely sealed behind electronic security gates that now became very secure indeed. But currency reserves, those represented by such inert things as bars of gold as well as those represented by such lively though abstract things as digital entries coursing from mainframe to mainframe among the world's central banks, were pretty meaningless all of a sudden.

Most things were. The world as we had known it had ended.

The apparent precipitating factor of the blackout was that someone, somewhere, had in a moment of foolish exasperation lobbed a couple of bombs at one of the alien ships. No one knew who had done it – the French, the Iraqis, the Russians? – and nobody was claiming responsibility; and in the confusions of the moment there was no reliable way of finding out, though there were plenty of rumors, of course. Perhaps they had been nuclear bombs; perhaps they were only archaic firecrackers. There was no way for anyone to know that, either, because very shortly after the attack all the military detection systems that would have been capable of picking up a sudden release of radiation became just as non-functional as all the rest of the world's dismantled technology.

Whatever kind of attack had been made on the Entities, it was an altogether futile one. It did no damage, naturally. The Entity spaceships were, as everyone would swiftly discover, surrounded by force-fields that made it impossible for anyone to approach them without permission or to damage them in attacks from a distance.

What the attack did succeed in doing was to *annoy* the Entities. It was annoying in the way that a mosquito's humming can be annoying, and so they retaliated with what could have been the alien equivalent of a slap that one might aim at the mosquito's general vicinity on one's arm. Or, as the anthropologist Joshua Leonards had put it at the Pentagon, the attempted destruction of an Entity vessel had been the opening statement in a kind of conversation, to which the Entities had replied in a very much louder voice.

The first power shutdown, the two-minute one, may simply have represented a tune-up of the equipment. The second one that followed a few hours later was the real thing. The Great

Silence. The end of the world that had been, and the beginning of a nightmare time of murderous anarchy and terror and utter despair.

After a couple of hellish weeks in the cold and the dark, the power began returning. Sporadically. Selectively. Bewilderingly. Some things like automotive engines and deep-freeze units and water-purification plants began to work again; other things like television sets and tape recorders and radar screens didn't, though electric lights and gas-station pumps did.

The general effect was to bring mankind back from a medieval level of existence to something like that of about 1937, but with strange and seemingly random exceptions. Who could explain it? There was no rhyme, no reason. Why telephones, but not modems? Why compact-disc players, but not pocket calculators? And when modems eventually did come back, they didn't always work quite the way they had worked before.

But by then explanations didn't really matter. The basic point had been made, anyway: the world had been conquered, good and proper, just like that, by an unknown enemy for unknown reasons, no explanations given: not a word, in fact, said at all. The invaders had not bothered with a declaration of war, nor had any battles had been fought, and there had been no peace negotiations, and no articles of surrender had been signed; but nevertheless the thing had been accomplished, in a single night, quite definitively accomplished. Resistance would be punished; and serious resistance would be punished seriously.

Who, in any case, was going to resist? The government? The armed forces? How? With what? Overnight, all governments and armed forces had been rendered obsolescent, if not downright obsolete. Attempts to hold things together, to proceed with existing forms and procedures, were swept away in whirlwinds of chaos. Governmental structures began to corrode and sag like buildings that had gone without maintenance for centuries; but this was a corrosion that happened within days. Whole governmental sectors simply vanished. Others maintained a ghostly presence and pretended they still were functioning, but no one paid very much attention to them. The social contract that had sustained them had been repealed.

Many people simply accepted what had happened to the world, and tried to understand it as well as they could, which was not very well, and went about their business as well as they could, which also was not very well. Others – a great many – simply went berserk.

The police and the courts could not cope with the new anarchy; indeed, the whole law-enforcement structure fairly swiftly dissolved as though it had been dipped in acid, and vanished. Only by common consent, one could see now, had any of it been sustained in the first place. The mandate of the law had been withdrawn. Authority itself had been decapitated in a single stroke. Armies and police forces began to melt away. No formal orders for disbanding were given – quite the contrary – but, as their members went on unofficial leave by ones and twos and threes like water molecules boiling off, preferring to protect themselves and their own families rather than to serve the general good, such organizations simply ceased to exist.

And so the law was dead. Personal conscience was the only governor left. What had been neighborhoods turned into independent kingdoms, their borders guarded by quick-on-the-trigger vigilantes. Theft, looting, robbery, violent crime of all sorts: these things, never far below the surface in the turn-of-the-century world, now became epidemic.

In the first three weeks after the invasion – the Conquest – hundreds of thousands of people died by the hands of their fellow citizens in the United States alone. It was the war of everyone against everyone, days of frenzy and blood. In Western Europe, matters were not quite as bad; in Russia and many Third World countries, worse.

This was the time that became known as the Troubles. After the first few wild weeks, things became a little more calm, once electricity began to return, and then calmer still. But they never went back to the pre-Conquest norm.

And from time to time over the months that followed the Entities would turn the power off again, all over the world, sometimes for a couple of hours, sometimes for three or four days at a stretch. Just to remind people that they could do it. Just to warn them not to get too cozy, because another dose of chaos could hit at any time. Just to let them know who was boss here now, forever and a day, world without end.

People attempted to recreate some semblance of their former lives, nevertheless. But the old structures, having fallen apart so completely at the first shove, were maddeningly difficult to rebuild.

The global banking system had been shattered by the death of the computers. The stock exchanges, which had closed 'temporarily' at the time of the alien landing, did not reopen, and all the abstract store of wealth that was represented by ownership of shares and funds vanished into some incomprehensible limbo. That was devastating. Everybody became a pauper overnight, and only the shrewdest and toughest and meanest knew what to do about it. National currencies ceased to find acceptance, and were largely replaced by improvised regional ones, or corporate scrip, or units of precious metals, or barter. The whole economy, such as it now was, was built on improvisations of that sort. Credit-card use was unthinkable now. Personal checks were no more acceptable than they had been in the Neolithic.

A surprising number of businesses remained going concerns, but their modes of doing business had to be radically reinvented. Computer communication resumed, but it, too, was a pallid and eerily transmogrified version of its former self, full of gaps and unpredictabilities. A sort of postal service continued, but only a sort. Private security forces emerged to fill the void left by the evaporation of the public ones.

Some unofficial underground resistance movements sprang up, too, almost immediately, but they wisely stayed very far underground, and in the first two years did no actual resisting. There were other groups that simply wanted to *talk* with the Entities, but the Entities did not appear to be interested in talking, though they did, as it soon turned out, have ways of communicating in their own fashion with those with whom they chose to communicate.

A dreamlike new reality had settled upon the world. The texture of life now, for nearly everyone, was like the way life is the morning after some great local catastrophe, an earthquake, a flood, a huge fire, a hurricane. Everything has changed in a flash.

You look around for familiar landmarks – a bridge, a row of buildings, the front porch of your house – to see if they're still there. And usually they are; but some degree of solidity seems to have been subtracted from them in the night. Everything is now conditional. Everything is now impermanent. That was the way it was now, all over the world.

After a time, people began to shuffle through their newly dysfunctional lives as though things had always been this way, though they knew in their hearts that that was not so. The only really functional entities in the world now were the Entities. Civilization, as the term had been understood in the early twenty-first century, had just about fallen apart. Some new form would surely evolve, sooner or later. But when? And what?

Anse was the first of the Carmichael tribe to arrive at the Colonel's ranch for the Christmas-week family gathering, the third such gathering of the clan since the Conquest.

That was a pretty time of year, California Christmas. The hills all up and down the coast were green from recent rains. The air was soft and sweet, that lovely Southern California December warmth pervading everything, even though there was the usual incongruous fringe of snow right at the highest crest of the mountains back of town. The birds were caroling away, here in the late afternoon as Anse approached his father's place. There was bright festive bloom in every garden, masses of purple or red bougainvillea, the red flower-spikes of aloes, the joyous scarlet splash of woody-branched poinsettias taller than a tall man. A steady flow of traffic could be seen heading up from the beach as Anse swung inland off the main highway and went looking for the road that led upward toward the ranch. It must have been a good day for some merry pre-Christmas surfing.

Merry Christmas, yes, merry, merry, merry, merry! God bless us every one!

The cooler air of higher altitude came through the open car window as Anse made his way along the narrow mountain road, which took vehicles up and behind the ranch a little way before curving down again and delivering them to the entrance. He honked three times as he started down the final approach. Peggy, the woman who served as his father's secretary these days, came out to open the ranch gate for him.

She gave him a grin and a cheery hello. She was always cheery, Peggy was. Small fine-boned brunette, quite ornamental. The wild thought came to Anse that the old man must be sleeping with her. Anything could be true, here in these grim latter days. 'Oh, the Colonel will be so happy to see you!' she cried, peering in, flashing her ever-ready smile at Anse's wife Carole and at the three weary kids in the back of the car. 'He's been pacing around on the porch all day, restless as a cat, waiting for someone to show up.'

'My sister Rosalie's not here yet, then? What about my cousins?'

'None of them, not yet. Not your brother, either. – Your brother *will* be coming, won't he?'

'He said he would, yes,' Anse replied, no vast amount of conviction in his tone.

'Oh, terrific! Terrific! The Colonel's so eager to see him after all this time. – How was your drive?'

'Wonderful,' Anse said, a little more sourly than was really proper. But Peggy didn't seem to notice his tone.

Getting here was a grueling all-day business for him now. He had had to set out before sunrise from his home in Costa Mesa, well down the coast in Orange County, if he wanted to get to Santa Barbara before the early dark of this midwinter day. Once upon a time he had needed no more than about three hours, door to door. But the roads weren't what they had been back then. Very little was.

In the old days Anse would have taken the San Diego Freeway north to Highway 101 and zipped right on up to the ranch. But the San Diego was a mess from Long Beach to Carson because it had never been repaved after the Troubles, and you didn't want to go inland to take the Golden State Freeway, the other main northbound artery, because the Golden State ran straight through *bandido* territory and there were vigilante roadblocks everywhere, and so the only thing to do was to creep along surface streets from town to town, avoiding the more dangerous ones, and picking up a stretch of usable freeway wherever you could. You went zigzagging on and on through places like Garden Grove and Artesia and Compton and in the fullness of time you found yourself getting back to Highway 405 in Culver City, which was one of the safer parts of central Los Angeles.

From there it was a reasonably decent straight run north to the San Fernando Valley and you could, with only a couple of minor detours, get yourself on Highway 118 somewhere near Granada Hills, and that took you clear on out to the coast, eventually, via Saticoy and Ventura. Anse didn't like driving 118 because it brought him uncomfortably close to the burned-out area where his Uncle Mike had died on the day of the big fires. Mike had been practically like an older brother to him. But taking that route was the most efficient way to do things, now that the Entities had shut off Highway 101 between Agoura and Thousand Oaks. Simply shut it off, northbound and southbound, big concrete-block wall right across all eight lanes at each end of the requisitioned zone.

They were building some sort of facility for themselves in there, it seemed. Using human labor. Slave labor. The way it went, Anse had heard, was that the gang boss, who was human but who had had the Touch and the Push applied to him, which left him considerably altered, came to your house with half a dozen armed men and said, 'Come. Work.' And you went with them, and you worked. Or else they shot you. If you didn't like the work and were nimble on your feet, you ran away when you got the chance and went underground. Those were the only choices, so it seemed. But once you had the Touch, once you got the Push, you had no choices left at all.

The Touch. The Push.

Oh, brave new world! And a merry Christmas to all.

It had been a difficult drive for Anse, hands clenching on the wheel, eyes fixed rigidly on the trash-strewn road, hour after hour. You didn't want to hit anything that might hurt the tires; new tires were impossible to get and your old ones could take only so much fixing. You didn't want to damage the car in any way at any time, for the same reason. Anse's car was an '03 Honda Acura, in decent enough shape but beginning to get a little tired around the edges. He had been thinking of trading it in for something bigger, just when the Invasion happened. But that was before everything changed.

There weren't any more new cars, period. There was a big Honda factory somewhere in Ohio that had survived the wild period of lunacy that had followed the Conquest and supposedly was still turning out replacement parts that came up to specs, only they weren't shipping anything west, apparently because they didn't trust the West Coast currency that had begun to circulate in place of Federal money. The Honda facilities in California, those that hadn't been wrecked in the Troubles, were being run on a hit-or-miss basis by the people that had been managing them the day the Entities came, who had seized them a few days after contact was lost with the parent company in Japan. But they didn't seem to be a very competent bunch of managers, and you couldn't count on the quality of what their factories turned out, assuming you could get the part you needed in the first place, which wasn't often easy.

Repair, not replacement, was the order of the day; and if you had the bad luck to total your car somehow, you had essentially totalled your life, and you might as well just sign up with one of the Entity work gangs, for whom transportation, at least, was never any problem. They gave you the Touch; they gave you the Push; and then you went wherever they said, and did whatever they wanted you to do, and that was that.

Anse pulled the car into the gravel-topped lot just north of the big main building and staggered out, stiff, cross-eyed with fatigue. He had driven the whole way himself. Carole still was willing to drive within about a ten-mile radius from their home, but she was spooked nowadays about freeway driving, or driving in any sort of unfamiliar neighborhood, and he did all of that now. It was something that they never even discussed.

The Colonel was waiting for them on the back porch of the ranch house. 'Look, guys, there's Grandpa,' Anse said. 'Give him a big hello.' But the kids were already out of the car and running toward him. The Colonel scooped them up like puppies, first the twins in one big swoop, then Jill afterward.

'He looks good,' Carole said. 'Stands as straight as ever, still has that sparkle in his eyes –'

Anse shook his head. 'Very tired, is how he looks to me. And old. A lot older than he looked at Eastertime. His hair is thinning, finally. His face looks gray.'

'He's – what, sixty-eight, seventy?'

'Only sixty-four,' Anse said. But Carole was right: the Colonel was aging fast. His trim, erect look had always been deceptive. The true weight of his years had been thundering down upon him ever since the first day of the Troubles. That time when darkness had fallen across the world, panic had been widespread, the bonds of civil behavior had for a time been loosed as though they had never existed, had been the ultimate nightmare for the Colonel, Anse knew: the instantaneous collapse of all discipline and morality, the shedding of all civility. The world had come back a long way from the ghastly early days just after the Conquest, and so had the Colonel. But neither of them was anything like what they had been before, and probably never would be again. The changes showed on the Colonel's face, as they did everywhere else.

Anse went crunching across the gravel and let his father gather him into his arms. He was an inch taller than the Colonel, and thirty or forty pounds heavier, but it was the older man who was in charge of the embrace, the Colonel enfolding Anse first and Anse hugging back. That was the deal. The Colonel was in charge, always. Always.

'You look a little weary, dad,' Anse said. 'Everything all right?'

'Everything's all right, yes. As right as can be, considering.' Even his voice had lost a little of the old ring. 'I've been negotiating with the Entities, and that's tiring stuff.'

Anse lifted one eyebrow. 'Negotiating?'

'Trying to. Tell you later, Anse. – By God, it's good to see you, boy! But you look a little peaked yourself. It must have been a nasty drive.' He punched Anse in the arm, sharply, a hard shot, knuckle against meat. Anse punched back, just as sincerely. That was also something that they always did.

They had had some difficult times, Anse and the Colonel. There was a spread of just twenty-one years in their ages, which for a time, when the Colonel was in his vigorous forties and fifties and Anse was in his twenties and thirties, made the Colonel seem more like Anse's older brother than his father. They were just enough like each other to have done a goodly amount of butting of heads whenever they came to some area where neither was capable of backing off, and just different enough so that there was plenty of head-butting also when they reached an area of total disagreement.

Anse's leaving the Army so young had been one of those bad times. Anse's spell of heavy drinking, fifteen years back, had been another. As for Anse's occasional adventures with women other than Carole since his marriage, the Colonel surely knew nothing about those, or he would in all likelihood have killed him. But they loved each other anyway. There was no doubt about that on either side.

Together Anse and his father pulled the suitcases out of the Honda and the Colonel, stubbornly carrying the heaviest one, showed them to their rooms. The ranch house was a huge rambling affair, wings stretching off this way and that, and Anse and Carole always were put up in the best of the guest suites, which had a big bedroom for them and an adjoining smaller one that long-legged golden-haired Jill, who was nine, could share with her four-year-old twin brothers Mike and Charlie. There was also a nice sitting-room with a view of the sea. Anse was the first-born son, after all. This was a family that went by the rules.

The Colonel, taking his leave of them, clapped Anse on the shoulder. 'Welcome back, boy.'

'It's good to *be* back.'

And it was. The ranch was a big, warm, comforting place, nestling securely here on its lofty hillside between the steep mountain wall and the beautiful Pacific, far from the congestion and turmoil and outright daily deadly peril that was most of Southern California. The old stone walls, the slate floors, the sturdy unpretentious furniture, the funny frilly curtains, the innumerable high-ceilinged rooms: how could anyone ever believe, living up here in craggy solitude high above the pretty red rooftops of Santa Barbara, that invincible alien monsters stalked the world at this very moment, randomly choosing human beings to do their bidding as they gradually rearranged the landscape of the world to suit their own incomprehensible needs?

Jill put herself in charge of getting the boys scrubbed up for dinner. She loved playing mommy, and that lifted a big burden from Carole. As Anse unpacked, Carole turned to him and said, 'Do you mind if I shower first? I feel so creaky and edgy, after that long drive. And filthy, too.'

Anse felt none too fresh himself, and he had done all the work that day. But he told her to go ahead. The dark signs of strain were evident in her. Her lips were clamped tight, her arms were close against her body, her left hand was balled into a fist.

Carole was still a couple of years short of forty, but she didn't have much stamina these days. She needed to be coddled, and Anse coddled her. Carrying the twins had taken a lot out of her; and then, two years later, the Conquest, the Troubles – those uncertain terrifying weeks of living without gas or electricity, without television or telephone, boiling all your water and trying to keep clean with sponge baths and cooking your scrappy meals over a Sterno-powered stove and taking turns sitting up all night with the shotgun, in case one of the looting parties that were roaming Orange County just then had decided that it was about time for them to investigate your nice tidy suburban neighborhood – those few weeks had wrecked her altogether. Carole had never been designed for frontier life. Even now she was still only partly recovered from that terrible time.

He watched her out of the corner of his eye as she undressed. One of his little covert pleasures: after eleven years he still loved the mere sight of her body, still youthful, almost girlish – the smooth supple legs, the small high breasts, the cascade of shining golden hair and that tight, springy little triangle, golden also, at the base of her belly. The familiar body, no surprises there but still exciting, still beloved, and yet so often betrayed. What had impelled him to step out on her again and again with those other, lesser women was something that Anse had never been able to understand. Nor had he ever really stopped feeling the pull from time to time.

A defect in the family genes, he supposed. A breakdown of the iron Carmichael virtue. The blood running thin at last, after all those generations of rugged God-fearing super-patriotic righteous-living American folks.

Not that Anse thought for a moment that his father was any kind of saint, neither he nor any of that long line of upright Carmichaels preceding him into the misty past. But he could not imagine the Colonel ever cheating on his wife, or even wanting to. Or flanging up some plausible excuse to get himself out of a dangerous or unpleasant assignment. Or putting a joint to his lips and taking a deep drag to while away some dreary night in Saigon. Or in any other way deviating from the proper path as he understood it. Anse couldn't really even see the old man tiptoeing into the bedroom of that cute young Peggy of his to grab himself a little late-life fun.

Well, maybe the part about smoking a joint, yes. Considering that it had been the 1970s then, and Vietnam. But not any of the rest of it. The Colonel was a man of discipline, first and foremost. He must have been that way right from the cradle. Whereas Anse's own life had been a constant struggle between the things he *wanted* to do and the things he knew he *ought* to do, and though by and large he did not consider himself to be a disgrace to the family's staunch traditions, he knew that he had fallen from the true and righteous path many times more than he should, and most likely would again. In all probability his father knew it too, though not the full extent of his sins, oh, no, not nearly.

For Anse the mitigating factor in all this self-flagellation was that he was hardly the only member of the family who was something less than perfect. In the Colonel's generation there had been Mike, Anse's brooding, irascible uncle, dutifully putting in his time in the military for a little while, and just as dutifully doing the volunteer-firefighter thing that ultimately had killed him, but otherwise living such a strange reclusive irregular life, and eventually marrying that weird loopy jewelry-making Los Angeles woman whom the Colonel had loathed so much. And Anse's own siblings had the taint too: Rosalie, for instance, whose adolescence, Anse knew, had been one long secret circus of frantic promiscuity that would have sent the old man into apoplexy if he'd had the slightest inkling of it, though she had long since cleaned up her act. Or brother Ronnie –

Oh, God, yes, brother Ronnie –

'We're all invited to the ranch for the holidays,' Anse had said to brother Ronnie two weeks before, in the deepest Southland where all three of the Colonel's children had their homes. 'Rosalie and Doug, and Paul and Helena, and Carole and me and the kids,' Anse said. 'And you.'

Ronnie was the southernmost sibling of all, in La Jolla, just outside San Diego. Anse had driven all the way down there to deliver Ronnie's invitation in person. Once upon a time La Jolla had been about an hour's trip from Costa Mesa on the San Diego Freeway, but it wasn't an easy trip any more, nor a safe one. His brother lived a lively bachelor life in a nice oceanfront condominium there, pink walls, thick carpets, sauna and spa, big picture windows, a million-dollar place purchased with the profits from some shady pre-Conquest venture Anse had never wanted to know anything about. The less Anse knew about his younger brother's daily existence, the better: that had long been his policy.

Some houses on the landward side of Ronnie's street were heaps of blackened rubble, destroyed in the Troubles and never rebuilt, but Ronnie's own place looked fine. That was the way Ronnie's luck worked.

'Me?' Ronald Carmichael had cried, throwing up his hands in that smarmy mock-astonished way of his. The color deepened on his already ruddy face. He was a big-boned fair-haired man who looked as if he might easily run to fat before long, though in fact his body was muscular and solid. 'You've got to be joking. I haven't exchanged a word with him in five years!'

'You're invited, though. He's your father and he says come for Christmas, and this year he put a little extra spin on it. I don't know why, but he made it sound urgent. You can't say no.'

'Sure I can. He made it perfectly clear to me way back then that he didn't want anything whatever to do with me, and I've made my peace with that. We've been getting along very nicely without each other and I don't see any reason to change that now.'

'Well, I do. This year, apparently, something special is up. He said you were on the guest list this year, and this year, pal, you're going to be there. I'm simply not going to let you throw your own father's Christmas invitation back in his face.'

But there hadn't been any invitation, had there? Not directly from the Colonel to Ron, no. The old man had asked Anse to do the dirty work for him, and Ronnie took quick, easy advantage of that fact: 'Look, Anse, let him speak to me himself, if he wants me there so badly.'

'That's asking a lot of him, Ronnie. He can't unbend that far, not yet, not after all that's happened between you. But he wants you to come, that I know. It's his way of making peace. I think you ought to come. I *want* you to come.'

'What the hell does he want me there for? Why do you? Obviously he still despises me. You know that he thinks I'm nothing more than a con man.'

'Well? Aren't you?'

'Very funny, Anse.'

'This year he'll stay off your case. I promise you that.'

'I bet he will. Look, Anse, you know goddamned well that if I show up, there'll just be another fight. It'll spoil Christmas for everyone.'

'Ronnie –'

'No.'

'*Yes*,' Anse said sharply, looking straight into his brother's tricky, hooded, intensely blue Carmichael eyes and doing his patented imitation of the Colonel's crispest I-take-no-prisoners tone of voice. 'I'm notifying him of your acceptance. You be there, that's all.'

'Hey, now, Anse –'

'Done and done, kiddo, and that's that. One way or another, get your ass up to Santa Barbara by the afternoon of December 23.'

It sounded good as he said it, plenty of the old military zing in his tone. And Ron had shrugged and smiled in that charming, ingratiating way of his, and nodded and told him that he would give it real careful thought. Which was, of course, Ronnie's usual way of saying no. Anse had no more expectation that Ron was going to make an appearance at the ranch than he did that the Entities were going to pack up and go back home tomorrow as a Christmas present to the beleaguered peoples of Earth. He knew what his brother was like. An alien in their midst, was Ronnie. Nothing Carmichael about him except those goddamn blue eyes.

Well, the Colonel wanted him at the ranch for Christmas, God only knew why, and so Anse had obediently delivered the invitation. But privately he hoped Ronnie *would* stay home. Or get himself snatched up by a roving band of Entities, as occasionally happened to people, and spend the holiday aboard one of their ships, telling them sweet stories of the babe in the manger. There was no need for Ronnie to be there spoiling the holiday for the rest of them, was there, really? The black sheep, long strayed from the fold. The rotten apple. The bad seed.

Anse heard the sound of a car door slamming outside.

Carole heard it too. 'I think someone else just got here,' she called from the bathroom. She appeared in the doorway, all pink and gold, toweling herself dry. 'You don't think it's your brother, do you?'

Could it be? The troubled shadowy sibling, reunited with his family at last? But no: looking out into the gathering darkness toward the parking area, Anse saw a woman getting out of the car, followed by a big, ungainly man and a plump pre-adolescent boy.

'No,' he said. 'It's just Rosalie and Doug, with Steve.'

Then, no more than ten minutes later, he saw another set of headlights glowing on the mountain road below the ranch. His cousins Paul and Helena, probably, who were supposed to be driving up together from Newport Beach. Paul had lost his wife in the Troubles, Helena her husband. They had gravitated toward each other, brother and sister forming a solid little unit in this time of tragic loss for each. But no again: by the last fading gleam of daylight Anse was able to tell that this was a trim little sports car, not the great hulking ancient van that Paul would be driving. This was his brother's car. 'My God,' Anse gasped. 'I think it actually is Ron!'

*   *   *

In the beautiful city of Prague, which had been the capital of the Czech Republic until that day two years and two months ago when such things as capitals and republics had ceased to be of any real significance on Earth, and which now was the site of the central communications nexus for the Entities who occupied the mainland of Europe, the weather on this night, a few days before Christmas, was highly non-Californian, though it was pleasant enough for midwinter Prague. The temperature had been hovering just above the freezing mark all day and now, at nightfall, was beginning to slip below zero Celsius. It had snowed yesterday, though not really heavily, and much of the city was mantled now in a thin coating of white; but tonight the air was clear and still, just the slightest whisper of breeze rising off the river that ran through the heart of the old town but otherwise all was calm.

Karl-Heinrich Borgmann, sixteen years old, the son of a German electrical engineer who had been living in Prague since the mid-1990s, moved quickly through the gathering darkness, light on his feet like the predatory cat he conceived himself to be, stalking his prey. He was, in truth, something other than cat-like: short and thick-waisted, actually, flat face with jutting cheekbones, heavy wrists and ankles, dark hair and swarthy complexion, everything about him rather more Slavic than Teutonic in appearance. But in his mind he was a cat on the prowl, just now. His prey was the Swedish girl, Barbro Ekelund, the University professor's daughter, with whom he had been secretly, desperately, deliriously in love for the past four months, since the time they had met and briefly talked at the chopshop in Parizska Street, near the old Jewish quarter.

He trailed her now, staying twenty meters behind her and keeping his eyes fixed rigidly on her jeans-clad buttocks. This was the day he would at long last approach her again, speak to her, invite her to spend some time with him. His Christmas present to himself. A girl of his own, finally. The beginning of the new beginning of his life.

In his mind's eye he imagined her to be walking naked down the street. He could see with incandescent clarity those two smooth, fleshy white cheeks flaring startlingly out of her narrow waist. He could see everything. The slim pale back rising up and up above her rump, the thin dark line of her spine plainly visible. The delicate bones of her shoulder blades. The long thin arms. The wonderfully attenuated legs, so slender that they didn't meet and touch at the thighs the way the legs of Czech girls always did, but left a zone of open air from her knees all the way up to her loins.

He could spin her around to face him, too, if he wanted to, rotating her through a hundred-eighty-degree movement as easily as he could rotate an image on his computer screen with two quick keystrokes. He turned her now. Now he could see those ripe, round, pink-tipped breasts of hers, so incongruously full and heavy on her lean elongated form, and the long deep indentation of her navel framed to right and left by her jutting hip-bones, and the sliver of a birthmark beside it, and the dense, mysterious pubic jungle below, unexpectedly dark for all her Nordic fairness. He imagined her standing there stark naked on the snowy street, grinning at him, waving to him, excitedly calling his name.

Karl-Heinrich had never actually beheld the nakedness of Barbro Ekelund, nor that of any other girl. Not with his own eyes, at any rate. But he *had*, through much trial and error, managed to attach a tiny spy-eye to a thin catheter-like metal tube and slide it upward from the basement of her apartment building along the building's main data conduit into her very own bedroom. Karl-Heinrich was very good at managing such things. The spy-eye caught, now and then, delicious fugitive glimpses of Barbro Ekelund rising naked from her bed, moving about her room, doing her morning exercises, rummaging through her wardrobe for the clothes she meant to wear that day. It relayed those glimpses to the antenna atop the main post office that captured them for Karl-Heinrich's private data box, from which he could retrieve them with a single mouse-click.

Over the past two months Karl-Heinrich had assembled and enhanced and in various ways edited his collection of Barbro shots so that, by now, he possessed an elegant little video of her as seen from every angle, turning, reaching, stretching, unwittingly displaying herself to him with utter candor. He never tired of watching it.

But watching, of course, was nowhere near as good as touching. Caressing. *Experiencing.*

If only, if only, if only –

He walked faster, and then faster still. She was heading, Karl-Heinrich suspected, for that little coffee shop that she liked down toward the lower end of the square, just beyond the old Europa Hotel. He wanted to catch up with her before she entered it, so that she would enter it with *him*, instead of going immediately to some table filled with her friends.

'Barbro!' he called. His voice was husky with tension, little more than a hoarse ragged whisper. He had to force it out. It was always a formidable effort for him, making any sort of overture to a girl. Girls were more alien to him than the Entities themselves.

But she turned. Stared. Frowned, obviously puzzled.

'Karl-Heinrich,' he announced, coming up alongside her, compelling himself now to affect what he hoped was a jaunty, debonair ease. 'You remember. From the chopshop in the Stare Mesto. Borgmann, Karl-Heinrich Borgmann. I showed you how to jack the data wand to your implant.' He was speaking in English, as nearly everyone in Prague under twenty-five usually did.

'The chopshop –?' she said, sounding very doubtful. 'Stare Mesto?'

He grinned up at her hopefully. She was two centimeters taller than he was. He felt so stocky, so bestial, so coarse and thick-set, next to her willowy radiant long-legged beauty.

'It was in August. We had a long talk.' That was not strictly true. They had spoken for about three minutes. 'The psychology of the Entities as Kafka might have understood it, and everything. You had some fascinating things to say. I'm so glad to have run into you again. I've been looking all over for you.' The words were tumbling out of him, an unstoppable cascade. 'I wonder if I could buy you a coffee. I want to tell you about some wonderful new computer work that I've been doing.'

'I'm sorry,' she said, smiling almost shyly, plainly still mystified. 'I'm afraid I don't recall – look, I've got to go, I'm meeting some friends from the University here –'

Push onward, he ordered himself sternly.

He moistened his lips. 'What I've just accomplished, you see, is a way of jacking right into the main computers of the Entities. I can actually spy on their communications line!' He was astounded to hear himself say a thing like that, so fantastic, so untrue. But he waved his arm in a vague way in the direction of the river, and of the great looming medieval bulk of Hradcany Castle high on its hill beyond it, where the Entities had made their headquarters in the lofty halls of St. Vitus's Cathedral. 'Isn't that extraordinary? The first direct entry into their system. I'm dying to tell someone all about it, and it would make me very happy if you – if we – you and I – if we could –' He was babbling now, and knew it.

Her sea-green eyes were dishearteningly remote. 'I'm terribly sorry. My friends are waiting inside.'

Not only taller than he, but a year or two older. And as beautiful and unattainable as the rings of Saturn.

He wanted to say, Look, I know everything about your body, I know the shape of your breasts and the size of your nipples and I know that your hair down below is dark instead of blonde and that you've got a little brown birthmark on the left side of your belly, and I think you're absolutely beautiful and if you will only let me undress you and touch you a little I will worship you forever like a goddess.

But Karl-Heinrich said none of that, said nothing at all, just stood mute where he was, looking longingly at her as though she were a goddess in actual fact, Aphrodite, Astarte, Ishtar, and she gave him another sad little perplexed smile and turned from him and went into the coffee shop, leaving him alone and crimson-cheeked and gaping like a fish in the street.

He felt shock and anger, although no real surprise, at the rejection. He felt great sadness. But also, he realized, a touch of relief. She was too beautiful for him: a cold pale fire that would consume him if he came too near. He would only have behaved like a fool if she had gone inside with him, anyway. In his reckless hungry overeagerness, he knew, he would have ruined things almost immediately.

Beautiful girls were so frightening. But necessary. Necessary. Nothing ventured, nothing gained. Why, though, did it always end like this for him?

A swirling gust of snowy wind came roaring down the square at him and sent him shivering off toward the north, lost in a daze of bitter self-pity. Aimlessly, planlessly, he went wandering up along Melantrichova and into the maze of ancient little cobblestoned streets leading to the river. In ten minutes he was at the Charles Bridge, peering across at the somber mass of Hradcany Castle dominating the other bank.

They didn't floodlight the castle any more, now that the Entities were here. But you could still make it out, the great heavy blackness of it on the hill, blotting out the stars of the western sky.

The whole castle area was sealed off now, not just the cathedral but the museums, the courtyards, the old royal palace, the gardens, and all the rest that had made the place so attractive to tourists. Not that there were any tourists coming to Prague these days, of course. Karl-Heinrich's mind summoned the image of the gigantic aliens, the Entities, moving around within the cathedral as they went about their unfathomable tasks. He thought with some astonishment of the boast that had so unexpectedly sprung from his lips. *What I've just accomplished, you see, is a way of jacking right into the main computers of the Entities. I can actually spy on their communications line!* Of course there was no truth to it. But could it be done? he wondered. Could it? Could it?

I'll show her, he thought wildly. Yes.

Go up to the castle. Break in somehow. Connect with their computers. There has to be a way. It's only a sequence of electrical impulses; even they need to use something like that, ultimately, in any sort of computational device. It will be an interesting experiment: an intellectual challenge. I am a failure with women but I have a very fine mind that needs constantly to be kept in play so that its edge will remain keen. I must forever improve my own range of mental ability through constant striving toward excellence.

And so. Connect with them. And not just connect! Open a line of communication with them. Offer to teach them things about our computers that they can't possibly know and want to learn. Be useful to them. Somebody has to be. They are here to stay; they are our masters now.

Be useful to them, that's the thing to do.

Earn their respect and admiration. I can be very helpful, that I know. Get them to trust me, to like me, to become dependent on me, to offer me nice rewards for my further cooperation.

And then –

Make them give her to me as a slave.

Yes. Yes.

Yes.

Anse said, 'You won't fuck around with him, will you, Ronnie? Promise me that. You won't do a single goddamn thing to ruin the old man's Christmas.'

'Cross my heart,' Ron said. 'Last thing I would want, anything that would hurt him. It's all up to him. Let's just hope that he doesn't start in. If he goes easy on me, I won't have any quarrel with him. But remember, this was your idea, my coming up here.' Wearing only a bath towel around his waist, he moved briskly about the room, fastidiously unpacking, arranging his things just so, his shirts, his socks, his belts, his trousers. Ron was a very tidy man, Anse thought. Even a little prissy.

'*His* idea,' Anse said.

'Same thing. You be of one blood, you and he.'

'And so are you. Keep it in mind, is all I ask, all right?' They were four years apart in age, and they had never liked each other very much, though the animosity between them was nothing at all compared with that between Ronnie and his father. While they were growing up Anse had rarely been amused by Ronnie's habit of borrowing things from him without troubling to ask – sneakers, joints, girlfriends, cars, liquor, et cetera et cetera et cetera – but he hadn't regarded Ronnie's light-hearted unprincipled ways with the same sort of lofty condemnation that the Colonel had. 'You're his son and he loves you, whatever has gone on between you over the years, and this is Christmas and the whole family is together, and I don't want you to make trouble.'

Ronnie glanced back over his meaty shoulder. 'Enough already, Anse. I told you I'd be good. What do you say, bro? Can we let it go at that?' He selected a shirt from the dozen or more that he had brought with him, unfolded it and tweaked the fabric thoughtfully between two fingers, shook his head, selected another from the stack, unbuttoned it with maddening precision and began to put it on. – 'You have any idea why he wants us all here, Anse? Other than it being Christmas?'

'Isn't Christmas enough?'

'When you came down to see me in La Jolla you told me that you thought something special was up, that it was important for me to come. Urgent, even, you said.'

'Right. But I don't have a clue.'

'Could it be that he's sick? Something really serious?'

Anse shook his head. 'I don't think so. He looks pretty healthy to me. A little run down, that's all. Working too hard. He's supposed to be retired, but in fact he's become involved in some way in the government, you know. What passes for a government now. They pulled him out of retirement after the Conquest, or he pulled himself out. He keeps a lid on the details, but he told me he recently led a delegation to the Entities in an attempt to open negotiations with them.'

Ronnie's eyes widened. 'Are you kidding? Tell me more.'

'That's all I know.'

'Fascinating. Fascinating.' Ronnie tossed his towel aside, slipped on a pair of undershorts, set about the process of selecting the perfect slacks for the evening. He rejected one pair, two, three, and was studying a fourth quizzically, tugging at one tip and then the other of his drooping blond mustache, when Anse, beginning now to lose the very small quantity of patience that he had for his brother, said, 'Do you think you can move it along a little, Ron? It's practically seven. The before-dinner drinks are called for seven sharp and he's expecting us in the rec room right now. You remember how he is about punctuality, I hope.'

Ronnie laughed softly. 'I really bug you, don't I, Anse?'

'Anybody who needs to spend fifteen minutes picking out a shirt and a pair of pants for an informal family dinner would bug me.'

'It's been five years since he and I last saw each other. I want to look good for him.'

'Right. Right.'

'Tell me something else,' Ronnie said, choosing trousers at last and stepping into them. 'Who's the woman who showed me to my room? Peggy, she said her name was.'

There was something in his brother's eyes suddenly, a glint, that Anse didn't like.

'His secretary. Woman from Los Angeles, but he met her in Washington when he went back there for a meeting at the Pentagon right after the invasion. She was actually taken captive by the Entities the first day, in the shopping-mall thing, the way Cindy was, and she was in Washington to tell the chiefs of staff what she had seen. She ran into Cindy while she was aboard the alien ship, incidentally.'

'Small world.'

'Very small. Peggy says she thought Cindy was pretty nutty.'

'No argument there. And Peggy and the Colonel –?'

'Colonel needed someone to help him with the ranch, and he liked her and she didn't seem to have any entanglements in L.A., so he asked her to come up here. That's about all I know about her.'

'Quite an attractive woman, wouldn't you say?'

Anse let his eyes glide shut for a moment, and breathed slowly in and out.

'Don't mess with her, Ron.'

'For Christ's sake, Anse! I simply made an innocent comment!'

'The last innocent comment you made was "Goo goo goo", and you were seven months old.'

'Anse –'

'You know what I'm telling you. Leave her alone.'

An incredulous look came into Ronnie's eyes. 'Are you saying that she and the Colonel – that he – that they –'

'I don't know. I'd like to think so, but I doubt it very much.'

'If there's nothing between them, then, and I happen to be here by myself this weekend and she happens to be an unattached single woman – '

'She's important to the Colonel. She keeps this place running and I suspect that she keeps *him* running. I know what you do to women's heads, and I don't want you doing anything to hers.'

'Fuck you, Anse.' Very calmly, almost amiably.

'And you, bro. Will you be kind enough to put your shoes on, now, so that we can go up front and have drinks with our one and only father?'

For the past hour the locus of the tension had gone sliding downward in the Colonel's body from his head to his chest to his midsection, and now it was all gathered around his lower abdomen like a band of white-hot iron. In all his years in Vietnam he had never felt such profound uneasiness, verging on fear, as he did while waiting now for his reunion with his last-born child.

But in a war, he thought, you really only need to worry about whether your enemy will kill you or not, and with enough intelligence and enough luck you can manage to keep that from happening. Here, though, the enemy was himself, and the problem was self-control. He had to hold himself in check no matter what, refrain from lashing out at the son who had been such a grievous disappointment to him. This was the family Christmas. He dared not ruin it, and ruining it was what he feared. The Colonel had never particularly been afraid of dying, or of anything else, very much, but he was afraid now that at his first glimpse of Ronnie he would unload all the stored-up anger that was in his heart, and everything would be spoiled.

Nothing like that occurred. Anse came into the room with Ronnie half a step behind him; and the Colonel, who was standing at the sideboard with Rosalie on one side of him and Peggy on the other, felt his heart melting in an instant at the sight at long last, here in his own house, of his big, blocky, blond-haired, rosy-cheeked second son. The problem became not one of holding his anger in check but of holding back his tears.

It would be all right, the Colonel thought in giddy relief. Blood was still thicker than water, even now.

'Ronnie – Ronnie, boy – '

'Hey, dad, you're looking good! After all this time.'

'And you. Put on a little weight, haven't you? But you were always the chunky one of the family. Plus you're not a boy any more, after all.'

'Thirty-nine next month. One year away from miserable antiquity. Oh, dad – dad – it's been such a goddamn long time –' Suddenly they were in each other's arms, a big messy embrace, Ronnie slapping his hands lustily against the Colonel's back and the Colonel heartily squeezing Ronnie's ribs, and then they were apart again and the Colonel was fixing drinks, the stiff double Scotch that he knew Ronnie preferred and sherry for Anse, who never drank anything stronger nowadays; and Ronnie was going around the room hugging people, his sister Rosalie first, then Carole, then his moody cousin Helena and her even-tempered brother Paul, and then a big hello for Rosalie's clunky husband Doug Gannett and their overweight blotchy-faced kid Steve, and a whoop and a holler for Anse's kids, sweeping them up into the air all three together, the twins and Jill –

Oh, he was slick, Ronnie was, thought the Colonel. A real charmer. And cut the thought off before it ramified, because he knew it would lead him nowhere good.

Ronnie was introducing himself to Peggy Gabrielson, now. Peggy looked a little flustered, perhaps because of the way magnetic Ronnie was laying on the beguiling introductory charisma, or maybe because she knew that Ronnie was the family pariah, a shady unscrupulous character with whom the Colonel had had nothing to do for many years, but who now for some reason was being taken back into the tribe.

Loudly the Colonel said, when the highballs had been handed around, 'You may be wondering why I've called you all here tonight. And in fact I have a very full agenda for the next few days, which calls for a great quantity of eating and drinking, and also some discussion of Highly Serious Matters.' He made sure they heard the capital letters. 'The drinking is scheduled to occur –' He paused dramatically and shot back his cuff to reveal his wristwatch. '– at precisely 1900 hours. Which is in fact, right now. With dinner to follow, and the Highly Serious Discussion tomorrow or the day after.' He hoisted his glass. 'So: Merry

Christmas, all of you! Everyone that I love in the whole poor old battered world, standing right here in front of me. How wonderful that is. How absolutely wonderful. – I'm not getting too mushy in my old age, am I?'

They agreed that he was well within his rights to get too mushy tonight. But what they did not yet know and he did was that most of the mushiness – not all, but most – was little more than a tactical maneuver. As was the reconciliation with Ronnie. The Colonel had things up his sleeve.

He went around the room clockwise, giving a little time to each in turn, and Ronnie went around the other way, and eventually they were face to face again, father and son. The Colonel saw Anse watching protectively from a distance, as though considering the merits of joining them as a buffer; but the Colonel shook his head almost imperceptibly, and Anse backed off.

In a quiet voice the Colonel said to Ronnie, 'I'm tremendously glad you came here tonight, son. I mean that.'

'I'm glad too. I know we've had our problems, dad –'

'Put them away. I have. With the world in the mess it's in, we don't have the luxury of carrying on feuds with our own flesh and blood. You made certain choices about your life that weren't the choices I would have wanted you to make. All right. There are new choices to make, now. The Entities have changed everything, do you know what I mean? They've changed the future and they've damned well blotted out the past.'

'We'll find a way of getting them off our backs sooner or later, won't we, dad?'

'Will we? I wonder.'

'Is that a hint of defeatism that I hear in your voice?'

'Call it realism, maybe.'

'I can't believe I'm hearing Colonel Anson Carmichael III saying any such thing.'

'Strictly speaking,' said the Colonel, smiling obliquely, 'I'm a general now. In the California Army of Liberation, which hardly anybody knows about, and which I'm not going to discuss with you right now. But I still think of myself as a colonel, and you might as well too.'

'I hear that you went face-to-face with the Entities in their own lair. So to speak. They don't actually have faces, do they? But you went right in there, you looked them in the eye, you gave them what-for. Isn't that true, dad?'

Actually seems curious about it, the Colonel observed. Actually appears to be interested. That in itself is pretty unusual, for Ronnie.

'More or less true,' he said. 'Rather less than more.'

'Tell me about it?'

'I'd just as soon not, not right now. It wasn't pleasant. I want tonight, this whole week, to be nothing but pleasant. Oh, Ronnie, Ronnie, you scamp, you miserable rogue – oh, how happy I am to see you here –'

It had not been pleasant at all, the Colonel's meeting with the aliens. But it had been necessary, and, after a fashion, instructive.

The mystifying ease of the collapse of all human institutions almost immediately upon the arrival of the Entities was the thing that the Colonel had never been able to comprehend, let alone accept. All those governmental bodies, all those laws and consti- tutions, all those tightly structured military organizations with their elaborate codes of duty and performance: they had turned out, after thousands of years of civilization, to be just so many houses of cards. One quick gust of wind from outer space and they had all blown away overnight. And the little ad-hoc groups that had replaced them were nothing more than local aggrega- tions of thugs on the one hand and hot-headed vigilantes on the other. That wasn't government. That was anarchy's second cousin.

Why? Why? Goddamn it, *why*?

Some of it had to do with the dramatic breakdown of electronic communication, on which the world had become so dependent, and on the chaos that that had caused. What had taken three hundred years to happen to the Roman Empire was bound to happen a lot faster in a world that lived and died by data trans- mission. But that wasn't a sufficient explanation.

There hadn't been any overt onslaught, nor even any threat of it. The Entities, after all, had not gone riding out daily among mankind like the warriors of Sennacherib or the hordes of

Genghis Khan. For the most part they had remained, right from the beginning, immured within their own invulnerable starships, issuing no statements, making no demands. They went about their own inscrutable tasks in there and emerged only now and then, just a few at a time, to stroll casually around like so many mildly curious tourists.

Or, to put it more accurately, like haughty new landlords making their first inspection of properties that had recently come into their possession. Tourists would have been asking questions, buying souvenirs, flagging down taxi drivers. But the Entities asked no questions and hired no cabs and, though they did seem to have some interest in souvenirs, simply walked off with whatever they liked wherever they found it, no transaction having taken place, not even a semblance of by-your-leave being offered.

And the world stood helpless before them. Everything that was solid about human civilization had shattered by virtue of their mere presence here on Earth, as though the Entities radiated some high-pitched inaudible tone that had the capacity to shiver all human social structures into instant ruin like so much fragile glass.

What was the secret of their power? The Colonel yearned to know; for until you begin to understand your enemy, you have not a grasshopper's chance of defeating him, and it was the Colonel's hope above all else to see the world free again before the end of his days. That was something he could not help wanting, folly though the notion probably was. It was in his bones; it was in his genes.

And so when an opportunity presented itself for him to go right into the lair of the enemy and look him in the glittering yellow eye, he seized the chance unhesitatingly.

No one was quite able to say by what channels the invitation had come forth from them. The Entities did not speak to human beings in any of the languages of Earth; essentially, they did not speak at all. But somehow, *somehow*, their wishes were communicated. And they communicated a wish now to have two or three intelligent, perceptive Earthlings come aboard their Southern California flagship for a meeting of the minds.

The informal group that called itself the California Army of

Liberation, to which the Colonel belonged, had repeatedly pe-
titioned the Entities based in Los Angeles to allow just such a
delegation of human negotiators to come aboard their ship and
discuss the meaning and purpose of their visit to Earth. These
petitions met with total lack of response. The Entities paid no
attention at all. It was as if the ants were trying to negotiate with
the farmer who had turned his hose on their ant-hill. It was as
if the sheep were attempting to negotiate with the shearer, the
pigs and cattle with the slaughterer. The other side seemed not
to notice that any request whatever had been made.

But then, unexpectedly, they did seem to notice. It was all
very roundabout and indirect. It started with the exercise of the
telepathic means of compulsion that had become known as the
Push against the bearers of a similar petition that had been presented to the Entities of London; it had been a fairly complex
kind of Push, one that seemed to be *pulling*, after a fashion, as
well as repelling. In Resistance circles, an analysis was undertaken aimed at comprehending just what it was the Entities might
have been attempting to accomplish by Pushing the London
people in the way that they had; and a belief began to emerge
that the invaders had been letting it be known that they *would*
indeed entertain such a delegation, a maximum of three human
persons. In California, though, not in London.

That could all be a total misinterpretation of the facts, of course.
The whole theory was guesswork. Nothing explicit had been
said. It was a matter of actions and reactions, of powerful but
inarticulate forces operating in a certain way that could be construed as meaning such-and-such, and *had* been so construed.
But in years gone by astronomers had discovered entire hitherto-
unsuspected planets of the Solar System by studying cosmic
actions and reactions of that sort; the California people decided
that it was worth gambling on the hope that their interpretation
of the London maneuvers was correct, and going forward on that
basis with a delegation.

And so. The Liberation Army chose Joshua Leonards, for his
anthropological wisdom. Peter Carlyle-Macavoy, for general
savvy and scientific insight. Plus Colonel Anson Carmichael III
(US Army, Ret.) for any number of reasons. And there on a mild

autumn morning the Colonel stood with the other two in front
of the sleek gray bulk of the Entity vessel that had begun the
whole shebang by making that fiery landing in the San Fernando
Valley two years before – Leonards and Carlyle-Macavoy once
more, the only remaining residue in the Colonel's life, aside from
Peggy Gabrielson, of that grandiose, ambitious, utterly futile
What-Shall-We-Do-About-It meeting at the Pentagon the day
after the invasion.

'Is it a trap?' Joshua Leonards asked. 'I heard this morning that
they let five people on board a ship in Budapest last month. They
never came out again.'

'Are you saying you want to back out?' Peter Carlyle-Macavoy
asked, looking down almost distastefully at the stocky anthropologist from his great height.

'If they don't let us out, we can study them from within while
they study us,' said Leonards. 'That's fine with me.'

'And you, Colonel?'

The Colonel grinned. 'I'd surely hate to spend the rest of my
life aboard that ship. But I'd hate it worse to spend the rest of
my life knowing that I could have gone in there but I said no.'

There was always the curious possibility, he thought, that he
might wind up being shipped off to the Entities' home world the
way his former sister-in-law Cindy supposedly had been. That
would be strange, all right, finishing his days in a P.O.W. camp
on some weird alien world, undergoing perpetual telepathic
interrogation by fifteen-foot-tall squids. Well, he would take the
risk.

The big hatch in the side of the immense shining starship
opened and the covering slid some twenty feet downward along
an invisible track to become a platform on which all three of
them could stand. Leonards was the first to mount it, then Carlyle-Macavoy, then the Colonel. The moment the last of the three
men had come aboard, the platform silently ascended until it
reached the level of the dark opening in the ship's side. Dazzling
brightness came splashing out at them from within. 'Here we
go,' Leonards said. 'The three musketeers.'

The Colonel's mind in that initial moment of entry was full of
the questions he hoped to ask. All of them were variations on

Where have you come from and why are you here and what do you plan to do with us? but they were couched in an assortment of marginally more indirect conceptualizations. Such as: Were the Entities representatives of a galactic confederation of worlds? If so, would the entry of Earth into that confederation be possible, either now or at some time in the future? And was there any immediate intention of working toward more constructive human-Entity communication? And did they understand that their presence here, their interference with human institutions and the functioning of human economic life, had caused great distress to the inhabitants of a peaceful and by its own lights civilized world? And so on and so on, questions that once upon a time he would never in a million years have imagined himself ever asking, or ever needing to ask.

But the Colonel did not, of course, get to ask any of them, so far as he could tell.

Upon entering a kind of vestibule of the alien ship he was swallowed up in a world of bewildering light, out of which a pair of mountainous alien figures came swimming gracefully toward him amidst veils of even greater brightness. They moved in an air of glory. Long flickers of cold flame rose up about them.

When he could see them clearly, which they permitted him to do after some indeterminate period of time, he was startled to discover that they were *beautiful*. Awesome and immense, yes. Frightening, perhaps. But in the subtle opalescent shimmer of their glossy translucent integuments and the graceful eddying of their movements and the mellow liquid gaze of their great eyes there lay a potent and ineffable beauty – a delicacy of form, even – that surprised him with its benign impact.

You could disappear into the shining yellow seas of those eyes. You could vanish into the pulsing radiant luminosity of their powerful intelligences, which surrounded them like whirling capes of light, an aura that partook of something close to the divine. You were overwhelmed by that. You were amazed. You were humbled. You were suffused with a sensation that hovered bewilderingly midway between terror and love.

Kings of the universe, they were, lords of creation. And the new masters of Earth.

'Well,' the Colonel wanted to say, 'Here we are. We're very happy to have been given the opportunity to –'

But he did not say that, or anything else. Nor did Leonards and Carlyle-Macavoy say anything. Nor did either of the aliens, at least not as we understand the meaning of the verb *to say*.

The meeting that took place in that vestibule of the starship was defined, mostly, by what did not happen.

The three human delegates were not asked their names, nor given any chance to offer them. The two Entities who had come forth to interview them likewise proffered no introductions. There was no pleasant little speech of welcome by the hosts nor expression of gratitude for the invitation by the delegates. Cocktails and canapés were not served. Ceremonial gifts were not exchanged. The visitors were not taken on a tour of the ship.

No questions were asked, no answers given.

Not a word, in fact, was spoken by either side in any language either human or alien.

What *did* happen was that the Colonel and his two companions stood side by side in awe and wonder and utter stunned silence before the two extraterrestrial titans for a long moment, an infinitely prolonged moment, during which nothing in particular seemed to be happening. And then, gradually, each of the three humans found himself dwindling away within, experiencing in the most excruciating fashion an utter diminution and devaluation of the sense of self-worth that he had painstakingly constructed during the course of a lifetime of hard work, study, and outstanding accomplishment. The Colonel felt dwarfed, and not just in the physical sense, by these eerie giants. The Colonel felt deflated and impaired – shriveled, almost. Reduced in every way.

It was like becoming a small child again, confronted by stern, vast, incomprehensible, omnipotent, and distinctly unloving parents. The Colonel felt utterly and completely disempowered. He was nothing. He was nobody.

This was the experience that had already become known to its recipients as the Touch. It was caused by the silent and non-verbal penetration of a human mind in some telepathic way by the mind of an Entity.

Had the Entities, the Colonel wondered afterward, really

intended any such humiliation of their human guests? Perhaps that had been the whole purpose of the meeting: a reinforcement of the fact of their superiority. On the other hand, they had established that fact pretty damned thoroughly already. Why bother to make the point again in this fashion? When you've conquered a world overnight without lifting a tentacle in anger, you have no real need to rub it in. More likely the depressing effect of the meeting had merely been an inevitable thing: they are what they are, we are what we are, and when we stand before them we must unavoidably feel this way as an incidental byproduct of the disparity in general puissance and all-around effectuality between one species and the other. And so, he concluded, they probably hadn't meant them to come away from the meeting feeling quite as crappy as they did.

But understanding that did not make him feel much better, of course.

The Touch, the Colonel had already been informed, was usually followed by the Push. Which was the exertion of mental pressure by the infiltrating Entity against the infiltrated human mind, for the purpose of achieving something beneficial to the general welfare of the Entities.

That was what befell them next. The delegates from the California Army of Liberation now were subjected to the Push.

The Colonel felt something – he could not say what, but he felt it, felt himself somehow nudged, no, taken hold of and gently but firmly *shoved*, he knew not where – and then it was over. Over and gone and already becoming a non-event. But in the moment of that sensation the meeting, such as it had been, had reached its consummation. The Colonel saw that plainly. It was clear, from that point on, that they had already had whatever there was going to be, that the whole content of the meeting would be the Touch followed by the Push. A meeting of minds, indeed, in the most literal sense, but not a very satisfying one for the human delegates. No discussions of any sort. No exchange of statements, no discussion of aims and intents, most certainly no negotiations of any kind. The session was ended, though so far as the Colonel was concerned it had never really begun.

Another lengthy gray span of time without perceptible event

went by in an unquantifiable way, one more timeless kind of period in which nothing in particular took place, an absence of incident or even awareness; and then he and Leonards and Macavoy found themselves standing outside the ship again, reeling like drunkards but gradually getting themselves under control.

For some while none of them spoke. Did not want to; perhaps could not.

'Well!' Leonards said, finally, or perhaps it was Carlyle-Macavoy who said it first. The monosyllable came out sounding profound. 'And so now we know,' said Carlyle-Macavoy, and Leonards said the same thing half an instant later, just as profoundly. 'Now we know, all right,' said the Colonel.

He found himself oddly unable to make eye contact with them; and they too were looking anywhere but straight at him. But then they all came together in a rush like the fellow survivors that they were; they wrapped their arms around each other's shoulders, burly little Leonards in the middle and the two taller men close against him; and in a lurching, staggering way, not without laughter, they went blundering like some deranged six-legged creature across the barren brown field to the car that was waiting for them beyond the boundary of the Entities' compound.

And that was that. The Colonel was glad to have escaped with his sanity and independence of mind intact, if indeed he had. And it had been a valuable meeting, in its fashion. He saw now even more clearly than before that the Entities could do as they pleased with us; that they had powers so supreme that it was impossible even to describe them, let alone to comprehend them, and certainly not to do battle against them. That would be pure madness, the Colonel thought, doing battle against such creatures as these.

And yet it was not in him to accept that idea.

He still carried within himself, embedded in his awareness of the hopelessness of resistance, a congenital unwillingness to accede to the eternal slavery of mankind. Despite everything he had just experienced, he intended to fight on and on, in whatever fashion he could, against these invaders. Those were not compatible concepts, his awareness of the enemy's utter supremacy and his desire to defeat them anyway. The Colonel found himself skewered by that irresolvable incompatibility. And knew that he must remain so skewered until the end of his days, forever denying within himself that thing which he knew beyond all doubt could not be denied.

Ronnie and Peggy stood side by side by the edge of the flagstone patio, facing outward, looking into the wooded canyon that led down to the city of Santa Barbara. It was just before midnight, a bright moonlit night. Dinner was long over and the others had gone to sleep, and he and she, the last ones left, had simply walked outside together without the need for either of them to make the formal suggestion. She stood now very close to him, almost but not quite touching him. The top of her head was barely armpit-high against him.

The air was clear and eerily mild, even for a Southern California December, as though the silvery moonlight were bathing the landscape in mysterious warmth. The red rooftops of the little city far below were glowing purple-black in the darkness. A soft wind blew from the sea, perhaps portending rain in a day or two.

For a time neither of them spoke. It was very pleasant, he thought, just standing here next to this small, lithe, pretty woman in the peace and quiet of the gentle winter night.

If he said anything, he knew, he would find himself automatically dropping into the kind of games, seductive, manipulative, that he invariably played when he encountered an attractive new woman. He wanted not to do that with her, though he was not sure why. So he remained silent. So did she. She seemed to be expecting him to make some sort of move, but he did not, and that appeared to puzzle her. It puzzled him, too. But he let the silence continue.

Then she said, as though unable to allow it to last another moment, reaching for something and coming up with the most obvious gambit, 'What they tell me is that you're, like, the naughty boy of the family.'

Ronnie laughed. 'I have been, I suppose. At least by my father's standards. I never thought of myself as a particularly bad guy, just an opportunist, I guess. And some of the business deals I got myself involved with were, well, not altogether nice deals. The way the Colonel saw it, there was a certain element of chicanery about them. To me they were just deals. But the true issue, the basic thing for him, is that I never went into the military, which for the Colonel is an unpardonable sin for a member of our family. Though he seems to have pardoned me.'

'He loves you,' Peggy said. 'He can't understand where you went wrong.'

'Well, neither can I. But not for the same reason. By my lights I was just doing what made sense to me. Not every idea I had was a good one. But that doesn't make me a villain, does it? Of course Hitler could have said the same thing. – Hey, tell me about yourself, okay?'

'What's to tell?' But she told a little anyway: growing up on the outskirts of Los Angeles, family, high school, her first couple of jobs. Nothing unusual; nothing intimate. No mention of her sojourn aboard the Entities' starship.

She was perky, cheerful, straightforward, very likable, nothing tricky about her. Ronnie understood now why the Colonel had asked her to come to live with him and help him run the ranch. But ordinarily Ronnie's own tastes ran to women of a more baroque sort. He was surprised how attractive he found her. He began to see that he was getting snared more deeply than he had bargained for. Something was happening to him, here, something strange, even inexplicable. Well, so be it. A lot of inexplicable things were loose in the world these days.

'Ever been married?' he asked.

'No. Never occurred to me. What about you?'

'Only twice so far. Both youthful mistakes.'

'Everybody makes mistakes.'

'I think I've already had my full quota, though.'

'What does that mean?' she said. 'Like, no more marriages?'

'No more inappropriate ones.'

She didn't respond to that. After a while she said, 'It's a pretty night, isn't it?'

It certainly was. Big bright moon, glittering stars, soft balmy air. Crickets singing somewhere. The scent of gardenia blossoms aloft. The nearness of her, the sense of her trim little body within easy reach, of the powerful pull that it was exerting on him.

Where was the source of that pull, which seemed out of all proportion to her actual qualities? Did it lie in the fact that she was a planet in orbit around the sun that was his father, and by laying hold of her he would attach himself more firmly to the Colonel, which was something that apparently was important to him now? He didn't know. He refused even to seek an answer. That had been the root of Ronnie's success all through life, the refusal to look closely into that which he knew he was better off not understanding.

'We can't do white Christmases here in Southern California,' he said, after a short while, 'but we sure can do nice ones of the sort that we do.'

'I've never seen snow, do you know that? Except in the movies.'

'I have. I lived in Michigan for two years, my first marriage. Snow's a very pretty thing. You get tired of it when you live with it day after day, but it's nice to look at, especially when it's coming down. Everybody should see it once or twice in their lifetime. Maybe the Entities will arrange for it to start snowing in California as their next trick.'

'Do you seriously think so?' she asked.

'Actually, no. But you never can tell what they'll do, can you?'

And just at that moment a cold hard point of brilliant blue-white light blossomed suddenly in the sky, to the left of the moon. It was so intense that it seemed to be vibrating.

'Look,' Ronnie said quickly. 'The Star of Bethlehem, making a return appearance by popular demand.'

But Peggy wasn't amused. What she was was scared. She caught her breath with a little hissing intake and pressed herself up against his ribs, and without hesitating he slipped his arm around her and gathered her in.

The point now elongated, becoming a long streaking comet-like smear of brightness that went arcing across the sky from south to north, a blurry white blare, and was gone.

'An Entity ship,' he said. 'They're traveling around somewhere, delivering their Christmas presents a couple of days early.'

'Don't make jokes about them.'

'I can't help joking about things like the Entities. I'd go out of my mind if I had to take them as seriously as they deserve.'

'I know what you mean. I still can't believe it really happened, you know? That they dropped down out of the sky one day, these big hideous monstrous beings, and just took over the whole world. It doesn't seem possible. It's all like something you would read about in a comic book. Or a bad dream.'

Very cautiously Ronnie said, 'I understand that you were actually a captive on one of their ships.'

'For a little while, yes. That was *really* like a dream. The whole time I was there I was like, "This isn't really happening to me, this isn't really happening to me". But it was. It was the strangest thing I could ever have imagined. – I met a relative of yours while I was up there, did you know that?'

'Cindy, yes. My uncle's wife. A little on the eccentric side.'

'She sure was. What a weird woman! Went right up to the aliens, and she was like, "Hi, I'm Cindy, I want to welcome you to our planet". Just like they were long-lost friends.'

'To her they probably seemed that way.'

'I thought she was outrageous. A lunatic, too.'

'I never cared for her very much myself,' said Ronnie. 'Not that I knew her very well, or wanted to. And my father – he absolutely *loathed* her. So the invasion hasn't been such a bad thing for him, has it? In one stroke he gets rid of his sister-in-law Cindy and is reconciled with his rogue son Ronnie.'

Peggy seemed to think about that for a moment.

'Are you really such a rogue, then?' she asked.

He grinned. 'Through and through, top to bottom. But I can't help it. It's just the way I am, like some people have red hair and freckles.'

A second point of light appeared, elongated, streaked across the sky to the north.

She shivered against him.

'Where are they going? What are they doing?'

'Nobody knows. Nobody knows the first goddamned thing about them.'

'I hate it that they're here. I'd give everything to have them go back where they came from.'

'Me too,' he said. She was still shivering. He pivoted ninety degrees and bent from the hips until his face was opposite hers, and kissed her in a tentative way, and then, as she began to respond, uncertainly at first and then with enthusiasm, got less tentative about it, a good deal less tentative. Quite a good deal less.

And now it was Christmas eve, and they had had their festive dinner just as though everything was right in the world, plenty of turkey for all and the proper trimmings and any number of bottles from the Colonel's stock of quite decent Napa Valley wines. And then, when a glossy after-dinner glow had come over everybody, the Colonel stood up and announced, 'All right, now. It's time to get down to brass tacks, folks.'

Anse, who had been expecting this moment since his arrival but in the past thirty-six hours had not managed to garner a single clue about what was coming, sat up tensely, wholly sober even though he had allowed himself an extra glass or two of wine. The others appeared less attentive. Carole, sitting opposite Anse, had a glazed look of satiation. His brother-in-law Doug Gannett, untidy and uncouth as always, seemed actually to be asleep. Rosalie might have been dozing too. Anse's unhappy cousin Helena seemed several million miles away, as usual. Her brother Paul, ever vigilant for her, was watching her warily. Anse noticed disapprovingly that Ronnie, wide awake but looking even more than usually flushed from all the wine he had had, was nuzzling up against Peggy Gabrielson, who did not appear to mind.

The Colonel said, launching right into things in a crisp, overly fluent way that suggested that these were well-rehearsed words, 'I think you all know that I've moved quite some distance out of retirement since the beginning of the invasion crisis. I'm active in Southern California liberation-front circles and I'm in touch, as much as it's possible to be, with sectors of the former national government that still are operating in various eastern states. Contact is very iffy, you know. But news does reach me from time to time about what's going on back there. For example, to cite the most spectacular example: within the past five weeks New York City has been completely shut down and sealed off.'

'Shut – down – and – sealed – off?' Anse said. 'You mean, some kind of travel interdiction?'

'A very total one. The George Washington Bridge – that's the one across the Hudson River – has been severed at the Manhattan end. The bridges within the city have been blocked in one way and another also. The subway system is *kaput*. The various tunnels from New Jersey have been plugged. There are walls across the highways at the northern end of the city. Et cetera. The airports, of course, haven't been functioning for quite some time. The overall effect is to isolate the place completely from the rest of the country.'

'What about the people who live there?' Ronnie asked. 'New York City isn't a great farming area. What are they going to be eating from now on? Each other?'

'So far as I'm aware,' the Colonel said, 'pretty much the whole population of New York is now living in the surrounding states. They were given three days' notice to evacuate, and apparently most of them did.'

Anse whistled. 'Jesus! The mother of all traffic jams!'

'Exactly. A few hundred thousand people were either physically incapable of leaving or simply didn't believe the Entities were serious, and they're still in there, where I suppose they'll gradually starve. The rest, seven million suddenly homeless people, are living in refugee camps in New Jersey and Connecticut, or as squatters wherever they find vacant housing, or in tents, or however they can. You can imagine the scene back there.' The Colonel paused to let them imagine it; and then, just in case they weren't up to the job, added, 'Utter chaos, of course. More or less an instant reversion to barbarism and savagery.'

Doug Gannett, who, as it turned out, had not been asleep, said now, 'It's true. I got the story from a hacker in Cleveland. People are killing each other right and left to find food and shelter. Plus it's twenty degrees back there now and snowing every third day and thousands are freezing to death in the woods. But there's nothing we can do about any of this stuff, can we? It's not our problem. So frankly I don't understand why you're bringing it up right here and now, Colonel Carmichael, all this depressing stuff right after such a nice fine meal,' Doug finished, his voice turning puzzled and morose and a little truculent.

The Colonel's lip-corners crinkled ever so minutely, the gesture that Anse knew was the outward sign of scathing disapproval verging on disgust, within. The old man had never been good at disguising the disdain and even contempt he felt for his daughter's husband, a slovenly and shambling man who was said to be a crackerjack computer programmer, but who in no other way had demonstrated any kind of worthiness in the Colonel's eyes. In thirteen years Doug had not figured out anything better to call his father-in-law than 'Colonel Carmichael', either.

The Colonel said, 'What if they were to do the same thing to Los Angeles? Give everybody from Santa Monica east to Pasadena and from Mulholland Drive south to Palos Verdes and Long Beach a couple of days to clear out, let's say, and then interdict all the freeways and cut the place off totally from the surrounding counties.'

There were gasps of shock. There were cries of incredulity.

'Do you have any information that this is about to take place, dad?' Ronnie asked.

'As a matter of fact, no. Or I would have brought the whole thing up a long time ago. But there's no reason why it can't happen – next month, next week, tomorrow. They've already made a start on it, you know. I doubt that I need to remind you that Highway 101's been shut down near Thousand Oaks for the past six months, north and south, concrete walls right across it both ways. Suppose they decided to do that everywhere else. Just consider what it would be like: a tremendous chaotic migration of refugees, everybody looking out for himself and to hell with the consequences. A million people go west to Malibu and Topanga, and a million more cross into Van Nuys and Sherman Oaks, and all the rest of them head for Orange County. Into Costa Mesa, Anse and Carole. Into Newport Beach, Rosalie, Doug. Huntington Beach. Even all the way down to La Jolla, Ronnie. What will it be like? You haven't forgotten the Troubles, have you? This will be ten times worse.'

Anse said, 'What are you trying to tell us, dad?'

'That I see a New York-style catastrophe shaping up for Los

Angeles, and I want all of you to move up here to the ranch before it happens.'

Anse had never before seen them all look so nonplussed. There were slack jaws all over the room, wide eyes, bewildered faces, astonished murmurs.

The Colonel overrode it all. His voice was as firm and strong as Anse had ever heard it.

'Listen to me. We have plenty of space here, and there are outbuildings that can easily be converted to additional residential units. We have our own well. With a little sweat we can make ourselves self-sufficient so far as food goes: we can grow any crop except the really tropical ones, and there's no reason why all this good land has to be given over to almonds and nuts. Also our position up here on the side of the mountain is a good strategic one, easily fortified and defended. We –'

'Hold it, dad. Please.'

'Just a minute, Anse. I'm not done.'

'Please. Let me say something, first.' Anse didn't wait for permission. 'Are you seriously asking us to abandon our houses, our jobs, our *lives* –'

'What jobs? What lives?' There was a sudden whipcrack tone in the Colonel's voice. 'Since the Troubles you've all been improvising, every bit of the time. There isn't one of you, is there, who's still got the same job they had the day before the Entities came. Or goes about any other part of their daily life in remotely the same way. So it isn't as if you're clinging to well-loved established routines. And what about your houses? Those nice pretty suburban houses of yours, Anse, Rosalie, Paul, Helena? With the whole population of central Los Angeles flooding down your way to look for a place to sleep, and everybody angry because their neighborhood got sealed off and yours didn't, what's going to become of your cute little towns? No. No. What's just ahead for us is going to be infinitely worse than anything that occurred during the Troubles. It's going to be like a Richter Nine earthquake, I warn you. I want you here, where you'll be safe, when that happens.'

Helena, who had been widowed at twenty-two in the fury of

the Troubles, and who had not even begun in the intervening two years to come to terms with her loss, now started to sob. Rosalie and Doug were staring at each other in consternation. Their pudgy son Steve seemed stunned; he looked as though he wanted to crawl under the table. The only ones in the room who appeared completely calm were Peggy Gabrielson, who surely had known in advance that this was what the Colonel had in mind, and Ronnie, whose face was a bland, noncommittal poker-player's mask.

Anse looked toward his wife. Panic was visible in her eyes. Leaning across to him, Carole whispered, 'He's gone completely around the bend, hasn't he? You've got to do something, Anse. Get him to calm down.'

'I'm afraid he *is* calm,' Anse said. 'That's the problem.'

Paul Carmichael, with one comforting arm across his sister's shoulders, said, level-headed as always, 'I don't have any doubt, Uncle Anson, that we'll be better off up here if the same thing takes place in Los Angeles that you say was done in New York. But just how likely a possibility is that? The Entities could shut down New York just by cutting half a dozen transportation arteries. Closing off Los Angeles would be a lot more complicated.'

The Colonel nodded. He moistened his lips thoughtfully.

'It would be, yes. But they could do it if they wanted to. I don't know whether they do: nobody does. Let me tell you, though, one further thing that may affect your decision. Or at least I'll *partly* tell you.'

That was too cryptic. There were frowns all over the room.

The Colonel said, 'As I told you, I've been more active in the Resistance than I've let you know, and thus I happen to be privy to a great deal of information that circulates in Resistance circles. I don't intend to share any classified details with you, obviously. But what I can tell you is that certain factions within the Resistance are considering making a very serious attempt at a military strike against an Entity compound right after the new year. It's a rash and stupid and very dangerous idea and I hope to God that it never comes to pass. But if it does, it will certainly fail, and then the Entities will beyond any doubt retaliate severely, and may the Lord help us all, then. Chaos beyond belief will be the result and you, wherever you may be at the time, will wish that you had taken me up on my offer to move up here. That's all I'm going to say. The rest is up to you.'

He looked around the room, steely-eyed, fierce, almost defiant, every inch the commanding officer.

'Well?'

The Colonel was looking straight at Anse. The oldest, the favorite. But Anse did not know what to say. Were things really going to be as apocalyptic as this? He respected the old man's concern for them. But even now, after all that had taken place, he could not bring himself to believe that the roof was going to fall in on Los Angeles like that. And he felt a powerful inner opposition to the idea of giving up whatever was left of the life he had made for himself down there in Orange County, uprooting the whole family on the Colonel's mere say-so and holing up like hermits on this mountainside. Settling in here with his father and his slippery rascal of a brother and all the rest of them. Fort Carmichael, they could call it.

He sat silent, stymied, stuck.

Then came a cheerful voice from the corner:

'I'm with you, dad. This is the only place to be. I'll go home right after Christmas and pack up my stuff and get myself back here before the first of the year.'

Ronnie.

Uttering words that fell on the astounded Anse like thunderbolts. *This is the only place to be.*

Even the Colonel seemed momentarily dumfounded to realize that Ronnie, of all people, had been the first one to agree. He, of all people, scurrying back ahead of the others to the parental nest. But he made a quick recovery.

'Good. Good. That's wonderful, Ronnie. What about the rest of you, now? Doug, Paul, you guys are both computer experts. I don't know beans about computers, and I need to. We get a little on-line communication with other places here, but it isn't nearly enough. If you were living here, you could click right into the Resistance net and do some very necessary programming for us. Rosalie, you're with a money broker of some sort now, is that right? In the next stage of the breakdown of society you could probably help us figure out how to cope with the changes that will be coming. And you, Anse –'

Anse's head was swimming. He still could not bring himself to accede. Across the way with him, Carole, reading his mind without the slightest difficulty, was saying silently, lips exaggeratedly pursed, *No. No. No. No.*

'Anse?' the Colonel said again.

'I think I could use a little fresh air,' Anse said.

He went outside before his father had any chance to respond to that.

It was cooler tonight than last night, but still on the mild side. There was rain coming soon: he could feel it. Anse stood looking down at little Santa Barbara and imagined that it was the gigantic city of Los Angeles, and imagined that city in flames, its freeways impenetrably blocked, vast armies of refugees on the march, heading toward his very street. Swarms of gleeful Entities floating along behind them, herding them along.

He wondered also what was behind Ronnie's quick acquiescence. Buttering the old man up, gliding cunningly toward the foremost place in his heart after the long estrangement? Why? What for?

Maybe Peggy Gabrielson had had something to do with it. Anse was pretty sure that Ronnie and Peggy had spent last night together. Did the Colonel know that? The body language was obvious enough. Except, perhaps, to the Colonel. The Colonel would not have been pleased. The Colonel took a very Victorian view of such goings-on. And he was so protective of Peggy. He would surely intervene.

Well, Colonel or no, Ronnie almost certainly was up to something with Peggy, and was even willing to move to the ranch to keep it going. For one wild moment Anse found himself arguing that he would have to move here too, to protect his father against Ronnie's schemes, whatever they might be. Because Ronnie was totally amoral. Ronnie was capable of anything.

Anse had been troubled by his younger brother's amorality since he was old enough to understand Ronnie's nature. That was what he was, Anse thought – not immoral, as the Colonel took him to be, but *amoral*. Someone who does as he pleases without ever pausing a millisecond to consider issues of right and wrong, of guilt or shame. You had to be very cautious when you were dealing with somebody like that.

But also Anse was, and always had been, intimidated by Ronnie's volatile intelligence. Ronnie's mind moved faster and took him into stranger places than Anse could ever enter.

Anse knew that he himself was a fundamentally ordinary, decent man, flawed, weaker than he would like to be, occasionally guilty of acts of which he disapproved. Ronnie never disapproved of anything having to do with Ronnie. That was frightening. He was demonic; diabolical, even. Capable of almost anything. To prosaic diligent imperfect Anse, who loved his wife and yet was often unfaithful to her, who obeyed his iron-souled father in all things and yet had not troubled himself to have the expected distinguished military career, Ronnie – who had not bothered with *any* sort of military career, nor offered the slightest explanation for bypassing one – was terrifying to Anse, a superior being, forever outflanking him with maneuvers he could not comprehend.

Ronnie was always a step ahead, acting out of motives that Anse could not fathom. His two quick marriages and lightning-fast divorces, no visible reasons for either. His equally swift and puzzling shifts from one sort of lucrative borderline-legal business operation to another. Or, for that matter, the time once when they were both still little boys and Ronnie had justified some terrible act of hostile mischief by explaining that it made him angry that Anse, and not he, had been given the sacred privilege of carrying the family name, Anson Carmichael IV, and that he, Ronald Jeffrey Carmichael, was going to get even with Anse for that a million times over during all the days of their lives.

And now here was Ronnie improbably jumping at the Colonel's unexpected offer, instantly agreeing to move up here and dwell forever after at the right hand of their father while the rest of Southern California went to hell around them. What did

Ronnie know? What did he see in the days ahead that was invisible to Anse?

Anse thought of his children in the midst of civil strife. A replay of the Troubles, only really *bad* this time. Gunfire in the street, fires raging on the northern horizon, black smoke filling the sky, maddened hordes of people converging on Costa Mesa, his very district: hundreds of thousands of people from Torrance and Carson and Long Beach and Gardena and Inglewood and Culver City and Redondo Beach and all those million other little places that made up the giant amoebic thing that was Los Angeles, people who had been driven from their own homes by Entity edict and now proposed to take shelter in his. And there were Jill and Mike and Charlie peeking hesitantly out from behind him on the porch, mystified, frightened, their faces gone completely bloodless, asking plaintively, 'Daddy, daddy, why are there so many people on our street, what do they want, why do they look so unhappy?' While Carole, from within the house, called to him again and again, a strangled terrified moan, 'Anse – Anse – Anse – Anse –'

It would never happen. Never. Never never never. It was just the old man's wild apocalyptic fantasy. Probably he was having Vietnam flashbacks again.

Even so, Anse was surprised to find that he had somehow decided to move to the ranch after all, in the time it took him to walk back from the edge of the patio to the door of the house. And he discovered, too, once he was inside, that all the others had come to the same decision also.

Christmas morning, very early. The Colonel lay dreaming. More often than not, what he dreamed of was that happy time right after the war, reunited with his family at last, his children around him and his wife in his bed every night in that pretty little rented house in that cheery Maryland suburb. He was dreaming of that time now. Halcyon days, at least when seen in the warm pink glow of a dream. The Johns Hopkins days, getting his doctorate, working toward it in the library all day, then coming home to robust little Anse, who was always ten or eleven in the dreams, and Rosalie, a pretty little girl in smudged jeans, and Ron, no more than two and already with that rapscallion gleam in his eye. And best of all Irene, still healthy, young, just turned thirty and delicious to look at, strong sturdy thighs, high taut breasts, long dazzling spill of golden hair. She was coming toward him now, smiling, radiant, wearing nothing but a filmy little amethyst-colored negligee –

But, as ever, he remained on the edge of wakefulness even while asleep, the ancient inescapable discipline of his profession. The soft bleebling of the telephone by the bedside sounded, the private line, and by the second ring Irene and her negligee were gone and the phone was in his hand.

'Carmichael.'

'General Carmichael, it's Sam Bacon.' The former Senate Majority Leader, with the fine tennis-player legs. Now one of the ranking civilian officials of the California Army of Liberation. 'I'm sorry to be awakening you so early on Christmas Day, but –'

'There's probably a good reason, Senator.'

'I'm afraid there is. Word has just come through from Denver. They're going to do the laser thing after all.'

'The stupid fucking sons of bitches,' said the Colonel.

'Ah – yes. Yes, definitely,' said Bacon. He seemed a little taken aback at the sound of such colorful language, coming from the Colonel. That was not the Colonel's custom. 'They've seen Joshua Leonards's report, and Peter's comments too, and the response is that they're going to go ahead with it anyway. They've got an anthropologist of their own – no, a sociologist – who says that if only for symbolic reasons we need to begin some sort of counteroffensive against the Entities, in fact it's long overdue, and now that we have the actual capacity to do so –'

'Symbolic lunacy,' the Colonel said.

'We all second that, sir.'

'When will it happen?'

'They're being very cagy. But we've also intercepted and decoded a Net message from the Colorado center to their adjuncts in Montana that seems pretty clearly to indicate that the strike will occur on January 1 or 2. That is, approximately seven days from now.'

'Shit. Shit. Shit.'

'We've already notified the President, and he's sending a countermanding order through to Denver.'

'The President,' said the Colonel, making that sound like an obscenity also. 'Why don't they notify God, too? And the Pope. And Professor Einstein. Denver isn't going to pay any attention to countermanding orders that come out of Washington. Washington's ancient history. It shouldn't be necessary for me to say that to *you*, Senator. What we need to do is get somebody into Denver ourselves and disable that damned laser trigger ourselves before they can use it.'

'I concur. And so do Joshua and Peter. But we have some serious opposition right within our own group.'

'On the grounds that an act of sabotage aimed against our beloved liberation-front comrades in Denver is treason against humanity in general, is that it?'

'Not exactly, General Carmichael. The opposition comes on straight military grounds, I'm afraid. General Brackenridge. General Comstock. They believe that the Denver laser strike is a good and proper thing to attempt at this present time.'

'Jesus Christ Almighty,' the Colonel said. 'So I'm outvoted, Sam?'

'I'm sorry to say that you are, sir.'

The Colonel's heart sank. He had been afraid of this.

Brackenridge had been something fairly high up in the Marines before the Conquest. Comstock was a Navy man. Even a Navy man could be a general in the California Army of Liberation. They were both much younger than the Colonel; they had never had any military experience whatsoever, not even a minor police action in some third-world boondock. Desk men, both of them. But they had two votes to his one in the military arm of the executive committee.

The Colonel had suspected they would take the position that they now had taken. And had fought with them about it.

Let me remind you, he had said, *of a remarkably ugly bit of military history. The Second World War, Czechoslovakia: the Czech underground managed to murder the local Nazi commander, a particularly monstrous character named Reinhard Heydrich. Whereupon the Nazis rounded up every single inhabitant of the village where it had happened, a place called Lidice, executed all the men, sent the women and children to concentration camps, where they died too. Don't you think the same thing is likely to happen, only at least twenty thousand times worse, if we lay a finger on one of these precious E-Ts?*

They had heard him out; he had given it whatever eloquence he could muster; it had not mattered.

'When was this vote held?' he asked.

'Twenty minutes ago. I thought it was best to let you know right away.'

The Colonel yearned to slide back into his dream. Once more, 17 Brewster Drive; the young Irene in her amethyst-colored negligee; the hard pink tips of the beautiful breasts that ultimately would kill her showing distinctly against the filmy fabric of the garment. But none of that was available just now.

What *was* available, sitting up there high above the Earth in its predictable orbit, was a three-year-old laser-armed military satellite that the Entities had curiously failed to notice when they had neutralized the other human orbital weapons, or had not understood, or simply were not afraid of. It had the capacity to shoot a beam of very potent energy indeed at any point on Earth that happened to pass beneath it. It had been intended, in those long ago idyllic pre-Entity days of three years ago, as the United States' all-purpose global policeman, equipped with the high-tech equivalent of a very long billy-club: the ability to cut a nifty scorch-line warning across the territory of any petty country whose tin-horn despot of a ruler might suffer from a sudden attack of delusions of grandeur.

The problem was that the software that activated the satellite's deadly laser beam had been lost during the Troubles, and so the thing was simply sitting up there, idle, useless, pointlessly going around and around and around.

There was a new and even bigger problem now, which was that the Colorado counterpart of the California Army of Liberation had discovered a backup copy of the activator program and was proudly planning to launch a laser strike against the Denver headquarters of the Entities.

The Colonel knew what the consequences of that were going to be. And dreaded them.

To Former Senate Majority Leader Sam Bacon he said simply,
'So there's no way, diplomatic or otherwise, of preventing them
from launching the strike?'

'It doesn't seem so, General.'

Lidice, he thought. *Lidice all over again.*

'Oh, the damned fools,' said the Colonel quietly. 'The hot-
headed suicidal idiots!'

Across the world in England, Christmas Day had long since
arrived.

A child had been born at Bethlehem on this day some two
thousand years before, and two thousand years later children
continued to be born at Christmastime all around the world,
though the coincidence could be an awkward one for mother and
child, who must contend with the risks inherent in the general
overcrowding and understaffing of hospitals at that time of year.
But prevailing hospital conditions were not an issue for the
mother of the child of uncertain parentage and dim prospects
who was about to come into the world in unhappy and disagree-
able circumstances in an unheated upstairs storeroom of a modest
Pakistani restaurant grandly named Khan's Mogul Palace in
Salisbury, England, very early in the morning of this third Christmas since the advent of the Entities.

Salisbury is a pleasant little city that lies to the south and west
of London and is the principal town of the county of Wiltshire.
It is noted particularly for its relatively unspoiled medieval
charm, for its graceful and imposing thirteenth-century cathedral,
and for the presence, eight miles away, of the celebrated prehistoric megalithic monument known as Stonehenge. Stonehenge,
in the darkness before the dawn of that Christmas Day, was
undergoing one of the most remarkable events in its long history,
and, despite the earliness (or lateness) of the hour, a goodly
number of Salisbury's inhabitants had turned out to witness the
spectacular goings-on.

But not Haleem Khan, the owner of Khan's Mogul Palace, nor
his wife Aissha, both of them asleep in their beds, for neither of
them had any interest in the pagan monument that was Stonehenge, let alone the strange thing that was happening to it now.

And certainly not Haleem's daughter Yasmeena Khan, who was seventeen years old and cold and frightened, and who was lying half naked on the bare floor of the upstairs storeroom of her father's restaurant, hidden between a huge sack of raw lentils and an even larger sack of flour, writhing in terrible pain as shame and illicit motherhood came sweeping down on her like the avenging sword of angry Allah.

She had sinned. She knew that. Her father, her plump, reticent, overworked, mortally weary, and in fact already dying father, had several times in the past year warned her of sin and its consequences, speaking with as much force as she had ever seen him muster; and yet she had chosen to take the risk. Just three times, three different boys, only one time each, all three of them English and white.

Andy.

Eddie.

Richie.

Names that blazed like bonfires in the neural pathways of her soul.

Her mother – not really her mother; her true mother had died when Yasmeena was three; this was Aissha, her father's second wife, the robust and stolid woman who had raised her, had held the family and the restaurant together all these years – had given her warnings too, but they had been couched in entirely different terms. 'You are a woman now, and a woman must allow herself some pleasure in life,' Aissha had told her. 'But you must be careful.' Not a word about sin, just taking care not to get into trouble.

Well, Yasmeena had been careful, or thought she had, but evidently not careful enough. Therefore she had failed Aissha. And failed her sad quiet father too, because she had certainly sinned despite all his warnings to remain virtuous, and Allah now would punish her for that. Was punishing her already. Punishing her terribly.

She had been very late discovering she was pregnant. She had not expected to be. Yasmeena wanted to believe that she was still too young for bearing babies, because her breasts were so small and her hips were so narrow, almost like a boy's. And each of the three times she had done It with a boy – impulsively, furtively, half reluctantly, once in a musty cellar and once in a ruined omnibus and once right here in this very storeroom – she had taken precautions afterward, diligently swallowing the pills she had secretly bought from the smirking Hindu woman at the shop in Winchester, two tiny green pills in the morning and the big yellow one at night, five days in a row.

The pills were so nauseating that they *had* to work. But they hadn't. She should never have trusted pills provided by a Hindu, Yasmeena would tell herself a thousand times over; but by then it was too late.

The first sign had come only about three months before. Her breasts suddenly began to fill out. That had pleased her, at first. She had always been so scrawny; but now it seemed that her body was developing at last. Boys liked breasts. You could see their eyes quickly flicking down to check out your chest, though they seemed to think you didn't notice it when they did. All three of her lovers had put their hands into her blouse to feel hers, such as they were; and at least one – Eddie, the second – had actually been disappointed at what he found there. He had said so, just like that: 'Is that *all*?'

But now her breasts were growing fuller and heavier every week, and they started to ache a little, and the dark nipples began to stand out oddly from the smooth little circles in which they were set. So Yasmeena began to feel fear; and when her bleeding did not come on time, she feared even more. But her bleeding had *never* come on time. Once last year it had been a whole month late, and she an absolute pure virgin then.

Still, there were the breasts; and then her hips seemed to be getting wider. Yasmeena said nothing, went about her business, chatted pleasantly with the customers, who liked her because she was slender and pretty and polite, and pretended all was well. Again and again at night her hand would slide down her flat boyish belly, anxiously searching for hidden life lurking beneath the taut skin. She felt nothing.

But something was there, all right, and by early November it was making the faintest of bulges, only a tiny knot pushing upward below her navel, but a little bigger every day. She began wearing her blouses untucked, to hide the new fullness of her breasts and the burgeoning rondure of her belly. She opened the seams of her trousers and punched two new holes in her belt. It became harder for her to do her work, to carry the heavy trays all evening long and to put in the hours afterward washing the dishes, but she forced herself to be strong. There was no one else to do the job. Her father took the orders and Aissha did the cooking and Yasmeena served the food and cleaned up after the restaurant closed. Her brother Khalid was gone, killed defending Aissha from a mob of white men during the riots that broke out after the Entities came, and her sister Leila was too small, only five, no use in the restaurant.

No one at home commented on the new way she was dressing. Perhaps they thought it was the current fashion.

Her father scarcely glanced at anyone these days; preoccupied with his failing restaurant and his failing health, he went about bowed over, coughing all the time, praying endlessly under his breath. He was forty years old and looked sixty. Khan's Mogul Palace was nearly empty, night after night, even on the weekends. People did not travel any more, now that the Entities were here. No foreigners came from distant parts of the world to spend the night at Salisbury before going on to see Stonehenge, these days.

As for her stepmother, Yasmeena imagined that she saw her giving her sidewise looks now and again, and worried over that. But Aissha said nothing. So there was probably no suspicion. Aissha was not the sort to keep silent, if she suspected something.

The Christmas season drew near. Now Yasmeena's swollen legs were as heavy as dead logs and her breasts were hard as boulders and she felt sick all the time. It was not going to be long, now. She could no longer hide from the truth. But she had no plan. If Khalid were here, he would know what to do. Khalid was gone, though. She would simply have to let things happen and trust that Allah, when He was through punishing her, would forgive her and be merciful.

Christmas eve, there were four tables of customers. That was a surprise, to be so busy on a night when most English people had dinner at home. Midway through the evening Yasmeena thought she would fall down in the middle of the room and send

her tray, laden with chicken biriani and mutton vindaloo and
roti kebabs and schooners of lager, spewing across the floor. She
steadied herself then; but an hour later she did fall, or, rather,
sag to her knees, in the hallway between the kitchen and the
garbage bin where no one could see her. She crouched there,
dizzy, sweating, gasping, nauseated, feeling her bowels quaking
and strange spasms running down the front of her body and into
her thighs; and after a time she rose and continued on with her
tray toward the bin.

It will be this very night, she thought.

And for the thousandth time that week she ran through the
little calculation in her mind: *December 24 minus nine months is
March 24. Therefore it is Richie Burke, the father. At least he was the
one who gave me pleasure also.*

Andy, he had been the first. Yasmeena couldn't remember his
last name. Pale and freckled and very thin, with a beguiling smile,
and on a summer night just after her sixteenth birthday when
the restaurant was closed because her father was in hospital for
a few days with the beginning of his trouble, he invited her
dancing and treated her to a couple of pints of brown ale and
then, late in the evening, told her of a special party at a friend's
house that he was invited to, only there turned out to be no
party, just a stale-smelling cellar room and an old couch, and his
hands roaming the front of her blouse and then going between
her legs and her trousers coming off and then, quick, *quick!*, the
long hard narrow reddened thing emerging from him and sliding
into her, done and done and done in just a couple of moments,
a gasp from him and a shudder and his head buried against her
cheek and that was that. She had thought it was supposed to
hurt, the first time, but she had felt almost nothing at all, neither
pain nor anything that might have been delight. The next time
Yasmeena saw him in the street he grinned and turned crimson
and winked at her, but said nothing to her, and they had never
exchanged a word since.

Then Eddie Glossop, in the autumn, the one who had found
her breasts insufficient and told her so. Big broad-shouldered
Eddie, who worked for the meat merchant and who had an air
of great worldliness about him. He was old, almost twenty-five.

She went with him because she knew there was supposed to be pleasure in it and she had not had it from Andy. But there was none from Eddie either, just a lot of huffing and puffing as he lay sprawled on top of her in the aisle of that burned-out omnibus by the side of the road that went toward Shaftesbury. He was much bigger down there than Andy, and it hurt when he went in, and she was glad that this had not been her first time. But she wished she had not done it at all.

And then Richie Burke, in this very storeroom on an oddly warm night in March, with everyone asleep in the family apartments downstairs at the back of the restaurant. She tiptoeing up the stairs, and Richie clambering up the drainpipe and through the window, tall, lithe, graceful Richie who played the guitar so well and sang and told everyone that some day he was going to be a general in the war against the Entities and wipe them from the face of the Earth. A wonderful lover, Richie. She kept her blouse on because Eddie had made her uneasy about her breasts. Richie caressed her and stroked her for what seemed like hours, though she was terrified that they would be discovered and wanted him to get on with it; and when he entered her, it was like an oiled shaft of smooth metal gliding into her, moving so easily, easily, easily, one gentle thrust after another, on and on and on until marvelous palpitations began to happen inside her and then she erupted with pleasure, moaning so loud that Richie had to put his hand over her mouth to keep her from waking everyone up.

That was the time the baby had been made. There could be no doubt of that. All the next day she dreamed of marrying Richie and spending the rest of the nights of her life in his arms. But at the end of that week Richie disappeared from Salisbury – some said he had gone off to join a secret underground army that was going to launch guerrilla warfare against the Entities – and no one had heard from him again.

Andy. Eddie. Richie.

And here she was on the floor of the storeroom again, with her trousers off and the shiny swollen hump of her belly sending messages of agony and shame through her body. Her only cover-

ing was a threadbare blanket that reeked of spilled cooking oil.
Her water had burst about midnight. That was when she had
crept up the stairs to wait in terror for the great disaster of her
life to finish happening. The contractions were coming closer and
closer together, like little earthquakes within her. Now the time
had to be two, three, maybe four in the morning. How long
would it be? Another hour? Six? Twelve?

Relent and call Aissha to help her?

No. No. She didn't dare.

Earlier in the night voices had drifted up from the streets to
her. The sound of footsteps. That was strange, shouting and running in the street, this late. The Christmas revelry didn't usually
go on through the night like this. It was hard to understand what
they were saying; but then out of the confusion there came, with
sudden clarity:

'The aliens! Pulling down Stonehenge, taking it apart!'

'Get your wagon, Charlie, we'll go and see!'

Pulling down Stonehenge. Strange. Strange. Why would they
do that? Yasmeena wondered. But the pain was becoming too
great for her to be able to give much thought to Stonehenge
just now, or to the Entities who had somehow overthrown the
invincible white men in the twinkling of an eye and now ruled
the world, or to anything else except what was happening within
her, the flames dancing through her brain, the ripplings of her
belly, the implacable downward movement of – of –

Something.

'Praise be to Allah, Lord of the Universe, the Compassionate,
the Merciful,' she murmured timidly. 'There is no god but Allah,
and Mohammed is His prophet.'

And again: 'Praise be to Allah, Lord of the Universe.'

And again.

And again.

The pain was terrible. She was splitting wide open.

'Abraham, Isaac, Ishmael!' That *something* had begun to move
in a spiral through her now, like a corkscrew driving a hot track
in her flesh. 'Mohammed! Mohammed! Mohammed! There is no
god but Allah!' The words burst from her with no timidity at all,
now. Let Mohammed and Allah save her, if they really existed.

What good were they, if they would not save her, she so innocent and ignorant, her life barely begun? And then, as a spear of fire gutted her and her pelvic bones seemed to crack apart, she let loose a torrent of other names, Moses, Solomon, Jesus, Mary, and even the forbidden Hindu names, Shiva, Krishna, Shakti, Kali, anyone at all who would help her through this, anyone, anyone, anyone, anyone –

She screamed three times, short, sharp, piercing screams.

She felt a terrible inner wrenching and the baby came spurting out of her with astonishing swiftness, and a gushing Ganges of blood followed it, a red river that would not stop flowing. Yasmeena knew at once that she was going to die. Something wrong had happened. Everything would come out of her insides and she would die. Already, just moments after the birth, an eerie new calmness was enfolding her. She had no energy left now for further screaming, or even to look after the baby. It was somewhere down between her spread thighs, that was all she knew. She lay back, drowning in a rising pool of blood and sweat. She raised her arms toward the ceiling and brought them down again to clutch her throbbing breasts, stiff now with milk. She called now upon no more holy names. She hardly remembered her own.

She sobbed quietly. She trembled. She tried not to move, because that would surely make the bleeding even worse.

An hour went by, or a week, or a year.

Then an anguished voice high above her in the dark:

'What? Yasmeena? Oh, my god, my god, my god! Your father will perish!'

Aissha, it was. Bending to her, engulfing her. The strong arm raising her head, lifting it against the warm motherly bosom.

'Can you hear me, Yasmeena? Oh, Yasmeena! My god, my god!' And then an ululation of grief rising from her stepmother's throat like some hot volcanic geyser bursting from the ground. 'Yasmeena! Yasmeena!'

'The baby?' Yasmeena said, in the tiniest of voices.

'Yes! Here! Here! Can you see?'

Yasmeena saw nothing but a red haze.

'A boy?' she asked, very faintly.

'A boy, yes.'

In the blur of her dimming vision she thought she saw something small and pinkish-brown, smeared with scarlet, resting in her stepmother's hands. Thought she could hear him crying, even.

'Do you want to hold him?'

'No. No.' Yasmeena understood clearly that she was going. The last of her strength had left her.

'He is strong and beautiful,' said Aissha. 'A splendid boy.'

'Then I am very happy.' Yasmeena fought for one last fragment of energy. 'His name – is – Khalid. Khalid Haleem Burke.'

'Burke?'

'Yes. Khalid Haleem Burke.'

'Is that the father, Yasmeena? Burke?'

'Burke. Richie Burke.' With her final sliver of strength she spelled the name.

'Tell me where he lives, this Richie Burke. I will get him. This is shameful, giving birth by yourself, alone in the dark, in this awful room! Why did you never say anything? Why did you hide it from me? I would have helped. I would – '

But Yasmeena Khan was already dead. The first shaft of morning light now came through the grimy window of the upstairs storeroom. Christmas Day had begun.

Eight miles away, at Stonehenge, the Entities had finished their night's work. Three of the towering alien creatures had supervised while a human work crew, using hand-held pistol-like devices that emitted a bright violet glow, had uprooted every single one of the ancient stone slabs of the celebrated megalithic monument on windswept Salisbury Plain as though they were so many jackstraws. And had rearranged them so that what had been the outer circle of immense sandstone blocks now had become two parallel rows running from north to south; the lesser inner ring of blue slabs had been moved about to form an equilateral triangle; and the sixteen-foot-long block of sandstone at the center of the formation that people called the Altar Stone had been raised to an upright position at the center.

A crowd of perhaps two thousand people from the adjacent

towns had watched through the night from a judicious distance as this inexplicable project was being carried out. Some were infuriated; some were saddened; some were indifferent; some were fascinated. Many had theories about what was going on, and one theory was as good as another, no better, no worse.

As for Khalid Haleem Burke, born on Christmas Day amidst his mother's pain and shame and his family's grief, he was not going to be the new Savior of mankind, however neat a coincidence that might have been. But he would live, though his mother had not, and in the fullness of time he would do his little part, strike his little blow, against the awesome beings who had with such contemptuous ease taken possession of the world into which he had been born.

On the first day of the new year, at half past four in the morning Prague time, Karl-Heinrich Borgmann achieved his first successful contact with the communications network of the Entities.

He didn't expect it to be easy, and it wasn't. But he wasn't expecting to fail, and he didn't.

– *Hello, there,* he said.

A good deal of information about the aliens' data-processing systems had already been accumulated, bit by bit, by this hacker and that one, here and there around the world. And, despite the deficiencies in the old global Net that had been caused by the Entities' interference with the steady flow of electrical power on Planet Earth at the time of the Great Silence, most of this information had already been disseminated quite extensively by way of the reconstituted post-Conquest hacker network.

Karl-Heinrich was part of that network. Operating under the cognomen of Bad Texas Vampire Lords, he had built up associations with such European and even American centers of information as Interstellar Stalin, Pirates of the Starways, Killer Crackers from Hell, Mars Incorporated, Dead Inside, and Ninth Dimension Bandits. From them, and others like them, he had picked up whatever shards of data about the Entities' computational modes that he could find, everything incomplete, a scintilla here and a particle there, a morsel here and a scrap there.

A lot of it was wrong. Much of it was excessively hypothetical.

Some of it was entirely the invention of its disseminators. But – here and there, in the two years and two months since the Conquest – certain gifted hackers had managed to learn a few things, little nuggets of fact, that actually seemed to make sense.

They had done it by interviewing anyone who had had a chance to observe the doings of the Entities at close range and seen Entity computers in action. That meant dredging through the recollections of anyone who had been taken aboard the Entity starships, for one thing. Some of these abductees were hackers themselves, who had paid very close attention. There even were hackers who had managed to infiltrate human slave-labor gangs and take part in the incomprehensible reconstruction schemes of which the Entities were so fond. There was much that could be learned from that nasty experience.

And so they had garnered a few clues about the way the invaders sorted and processed and transmitted information; and they had put it all out there on the Net for their fellow hackers to see and ponder. And out of that assortment of crumbs, driblets, rags, tags, tatters, and wild guesses, methodically filtering out the parts that were incompatible with the rest, Karl-Heinrich had eventually put together his own internally consistent picture of how the Entity computers might operate and how they could be hacked.

– *Hello, there. I am Karl-Heinrich Borgmann of Prague, the Czech Republic.*

The Bad Texas Vampire Lords, or, rather, the solitary and peculiar boy that lurked behind that particular nom-de-Net, did not rush to share these insights with the other subversive organizations of the hacker world. It might have been useful to the cause of humanity if he had, because it would have advanced everybody's knowledge of the situation and, very likely, led to even greater understanding. But Karl-Heinrich had never been good at sharing things. There had never been much of a way for him to learn how to do it. He was the only child of remote, austere, forbidding parents. He had never had a close friend, except via the Net, and those were always long-distance friendships, anonymous, carefully controlled. His love life, thus far, had not progressed beyond electronic voyeurism. He was an island unto himself.

Besides, he wanted full credit for cracking the Entity code. He wanted to be world-famous, the best hacker ever. He wanted to be immensely famous. If he couldn't be loved, he could at least be admired and respected. And – who knew? – if he became famous enough, platoons of girls might stand in line outside his door for a chance to give themselves to him. Which was the thing he wanted above all else.

– *Hello, there. I am Karl-Heinrich Borgmann, of Prague, the Czech Republic. I have made myself able to interface with your computers.*

Already, beyond any question, it had become clear to everyone who had worked on the problem that the Entities used a digital system of computation. That was welcome news. After all, being aliens, they might have had some altogether alien way of processing data that would be beyond all human fathoming. But it had turned out that even on the far-off unknown star of the Entities the good old binary system was the most efficient way of counting things, even as on primitive little Earth. Yes or no; on or off; go or no-go; positive or negative; open or closed; present or absent; one or zero – there was nothing simpler. Even for *them*.

The Entity mainframe computers themselves were bio-organic devices with liquid software reservoirs, apparently. In essence, huge synthetic brains. They seemed to be, as human brains are, chemically programmable, responding to hormonal inputs. But that was only an operational fact. In the most fundamental sense they could be understood to be, almost certainly, electrically operated mechanisms: again, just as human brains are. Computations were achieved by the manipulation of charge. The chemical inputs changed electrical polarities; they turned ones into zeros, presences into absences, ons into offs.

The chemical inputs, perhaps, could be duplicated electrically, just as they were in the implanted biochips that had become all the rage among hackers like Karl-Heinrich a year or two before the invasion. Karl-Heinrich set out to try.

– *Hello, there. I am Karl-Heinrich Borgmann, of Prague, the Czech Republic. I have made myself able to interface with your computers. This has been the great dream of my life, and now I have achieved it.*

He spent a couple of dark wintry days up on the steep hill

behind Hradcany Castle, snooping around the deserted streets
outside the ancient wall. It wasn't possible to get into the castle
grounds any more, of course, but that didn't mean you couldn't
tap into electrical conduits that did. Unless the aliens could pull
electricity out of the air by alien magic, they needed distribution
lines for their power just like anyone else. And unless they had
installed their own generating systems within the castle, which
was an altogether plausible possibility, the lines had to come in
from outside.

Karl-Heinrich went looking for them, and in short order he
found them. He was very good at such things. When other little
boys had been reading about pirates or spacemen, he was reading
his father's textbooks of electrical wiring.

Now – first contact –

Karl-Heinrich carried his own tiny computer with him at all
times, an implant, right there in his forearm – a biochip no bigger
than a snowflake, and even more elegant of design. It collected
and deployed body warmth to amplify and transmit coded signals that opened data channels, making possible all sorts of trans-
actions. Karl-Heinrich had been one of the first to get implanted,
the day after his thirteenth birthday. Perhaps ten percent of the
population, most of them young, had had implants installed by
the time of the arrival of the Entities. The implant revolution,
though still only in its earliest stages, had been widely seen as
full of promise for the fantastic flowering future – a future which,
unfortunately, the alien invasion had apparently aborted. But the
implants were still in place.

Tapping into an electrical meter was child's play for Karl-
Heinrich. Any power-company meter-reader could have done it.
Karl-Heinrich was something more than a meter-reader. He spent
two days measuring inductances and impedances, and then, too
excited now even to remember to breathe, he sent a tendril of
electrical energy into the meter and through it, down a surging
river of electrons, until he felt himself make contact with –

Something.

A data source. Alien data.

It made him shiver to feel the alienness of it, its shape, its
internal structure, its linkage configurations. He felt as though

he were walking the mysterious glades of an unutterably strange forest on an unknown world.

The system through which it was flowing was nothing like any computer he had ever known, or even imagined. Why should it have been? Nevertheless he sensed familiarity amidst the strangeness. The data, however strange, was still only data, a series of binary numbers. The shape of that digital flow was weird and bizarre and yet he felt somehow confident that it was well within the reach of ultimate comprehension by him. The alien device into which he had tapped was, after all, a system for the manipulation and storage of data in binary form. What was that, if not a computer?

And he was inside it. That was the important thing. A hot tingle of sheer intellectual joy ran through him at the contemplation of his triumph. It was almost orgasmic in its intensity. He doubted that sex itself could provide such a thrill. But of course Karl-Heinrich had very little grounds for such a comparison.

It took him quite some while to understand the particular nature of what it was that he had touched. But gradually it dawned on him that the program within which he was wandering must be the master template for the whole electrical distribution grid; and suddenly there was a map of the Entities' electrical system superimposed on the map of the castle grounds that he had in his head.

He explored it. Very quickly he found himself trapped in a blind alley, went back, took another path. Another and another. Hit a roadblock, went around it, plunged forward.

His confidence grew from hour to hour. He was discovering things. He was learning. Things were adding up. He was piecing together correlations. He had found channels. He was getting deeper and deeper in.

The delight was intense. He had never known such pleasure.

He copied a swatch of data from an Entity computer, downloaded it into his own, and was pleased to see that he was capable of manipulating it by adding or subtracting electrical charge. He had no way of knowing what changes he was making, because the underlying data was incomprehensible to him. But it was a good start. He was able to access the information; he was even able to process it; all that was missing was some way of understanding it.

He realized that even at this primitive stage of his penetration of the system he should be able to send the Entities messages that they would be able to understand, if they had bothered to learn any of the languages of Earth. And he suspected that he could even eventually learn to reprogram *their* data through this line of access, if only he could figure out their computer language. But that was something to deal with later on.

He went onward, inward, wondering whether he might be sounding any alarms within the system as he went. He didn't think so. They would have stopped him by now, if they knew that he was boring inward like this. Unless, of course, they were amused by what he was doing, watching him, applauding his progress.

Before long his head was aching miserably, but his heart had begun to swell with a gathering sense of triumph.

Karl-Heinrich was certain now that the center of everything, the main computational node, was, as was already generally suspected, inside the cathedral. He had located something major down at the far end, in the Imperial Chapel, and something almost as big in the Chapel of St. Sigismund. But these, he suspected, were subsidiary trunks. There was a huge floor-to-ceiling screen full of pulsing lights in front of the Wenceslas Chapel that was a raging circus of energy, in and out, in and out. He realized, after probing it for four or five hours, that it had to be the master interface of the whole set-up, the traffic manager for everything else on the premises.

He jacked in, via the power line, and let oceans of incomprehensible data surge through him.

The alien information came at him in a gigantic flood, too voluminous even to try to copy and download. He did not dare to attempt to process it and certainly had no way of decoding it. All it was was a stream of ones and zeros, but he had no key to help him translate the binary digits into anything meaningful. He would need some gigantic mainframe, like the one that the University once had had, even to begin making an attempt at that. The world's mainframes were down for good, though. The

Entities had blown them all out in the moment of the Great Silence and they had stayed that way. The present-day version of the Net worked by virtue of a jerry-built string of patched-together servers that was barely capable of handling ordinary traffic, let alone of processing anything as intricate as what Karl-Heinrich had stumbled upon.

But he had made contact. That was the key thing. He was on the inside.

And now, now, now, the big decision stared him in the face. Simply continue to spy in secrecy on the Entity computer as a skulking loner, soaking up all this interesting gibberish, tinkering with it on the sly purely for fun, making a nice gratifying private hobby out of it? Or should he link up with Interstellar Stalin, Ninth Dimension Bandits, and the rest of the hackers who were working at the problem of entering the Entity network, and show them what he had managed to achieve, so that they could build on his achievement and carry the process on to the next level?

The first alternative would bring him nothing but the pleasures of solitary vice. Karl-Heinrich already knew how limited those were. The second would give him a momentary flicker of fame in the hacker underground; but then others would seize what he had done and run onward with it and he would be forgotten.

But there was a third choice, and it was the one he had favored all along.

All the hacker talk of mastering Entity computer code and using the knowledge somehow to overthrow them was mere childish stupidity. Nobody was going to overthrow the Entities. They were too powerful. The world was theirs, and that was that.

Accept that, then. Work with it. Offer them your services. They need an interface between themselves and humanity for the more efficient carrying out of their purposes. Very well. Here's an opportunity for you, Karl-Heinrich Borgmann. You have everything to gain and nothing but your misery to lose.

Their signals were incomprehensible to him, but his would not be to them, and contact had been made. Very well. *Do* something with it.

– Hello, there. I am Karl-Heinrich Borgmann, of Prague, the Czech Republic. I have made myself able to interface with your computers. This has been the great dream of my life, and now I have achieved it.

– I think I can be of great help to you. And I know that you can be of great help to me.

About seventeen hours later, on the other side of the world, someone in the Denver command headquarters of the Colorado Freedom Front keyed three handshake commands into a ten-year-old desktop computer, waited for a response from space, received it within thirty seconds, and keyed in four further commands. This time they were the signals that would activate the laser cannon in orbit 22,000 miles overhead.

These commands required acknowledgment, which came, and repetition, which was given.

From the military satellite overhead there now instantly descended a crackling bolt of energy in the form of an intensely focused beam of light, which homed in on the compound in which the Denver Entity forces had set up their operations, and for the next ninety seconds bathed its central building in flame. What effect this action had on the Entities within the building was not possible to determine, and, indeed, was destined never to be known.

But evidently it caused them some distress, for there were two immediate retaliatory consequences, both of them quite harsh.

The first was that electrical power began going off all over the Earth almost at once. In the initial few days the outages were spotty and irregular, but then a total planetwide interdiction took hold. The power stayed off for the next thirty-nine days, an outage more severe and disruptive than the so-called Great Silence of two years previously. With all electronic communication knocked out, it became impossible, among other things, for the members of the Colorado Freedom Front to carry out the additional laser strikes that had been planned to follow the opening salvo in the so-called War of Liberation.

The second consequence of the laser attack was that sealed canisters stored in eleven of the world's major cities sprang open within three hours of the Denver event, releasing microorganisms of an apparently synthetic nature that induced an infectious and highly contagious disease of a previously unknown kind across much of the planet. The symptoms were inordinately high fever followed by structural degradation of the larger veins and arteries followed by systemic breakdown and death. There was no known treatment. Quarantines seemed to have little value. Of those infected, about a third who evidently had some sort of natural immunity threw off the fever before reaching the stage of circulatory-system breakdown, and recovered completely. The rest died within three or four days of onset.

It was Doug Gannett who brought the news to the Colonel, in the early days when limited e-mail communication still was possible. 'Everybody's dying out there,' he said. 'I'm getting the same story from whoever's been able to stay on line. It's a huge epidemic and there doesn't seem to be any way to stop it.'

The Colonel, raging within, reacted outwardly only with a weary nod. 'Well, we can try to hide from it,' he said.

He called the ranch hands together and told the ones who lived on the premises that they would continue to be free to go down into Santa Barbara, as before, but that they would not be allowed to return if they did. As for the ones who lived in town, mainly in the Mexican neighborhood on the south side, he let them know that they could choose between remaining at the ranch or going back down to their homes and families, but that if they did leave the ranch there would be no coming back.

'The same, of course, goes for all of you,' he told the various assembled Carmichaels, giving each of them a long, slow look. 'You go out there, you don't get back in. No exceptions.'

'And how long does this rule stay in effect?' Ronnie asked.

'As long as it needs to,' said the Colonel.

The worldwide plague continued to rage until early July, bringing what had been left of the world's economy to a total standstill. Then it vanished as suddenly as it had come, as though the beings who had loosed it upon the world had now concluded that it had done its job to sufficiently good effect.

The effects had been considerable. On the lofty, isolated hillside where Rancho Carmichael was situated, there had been no impact at all, except for the loss of the ranch hands who had opted to return to their families, and who, it was presumed, had perished with them. Down below, things went quite differently. When the damage finally could be reckoned up, it turned out that close to fifty percent of the world's population had perished. The actual death rate varied, of course, from country to country, depending on local standards of sanitation and the availability of convalescent care; but none went unscathed, and some were virtually wiped out. Across the face of the world a new kind of Great Silence had fallen, the silence of depopulation. And though some three billion human beings had somehow managed to survive, very few of them had any further inclination to attempt or even consider hostile action against the alien conquerors of Earth.

III

Nineteen Years
from Now

The Colonel, waiting out on the ranch-house porch for the members of the Resistance Committee to assemble for the monthly meeting, believed himself to be awake. But in these latter days he moved all too easily between the world of sunlight and the realm of shadows, and as he sat there slowly rocking, lost in swirling daydreams, he found it difficult to be certain which side of the line he was really on.

It was a bright April day, clear and dry after one of the wettest rainy seasons on record. The air was warm and vibrant, and the hills were thick with a dense, lush growth of tall green grass that soon would be taking on its tawny summertime hue.

A bad business, all that thick grass. Great fuel for the autumn fire season, once it dried out.

The fires – the fires –

The Colonel's drowsy mind drifted backward across the years to show him Los Angeles burning, the day the Entities came. The scene on the television: the angry, reddened sky, the leaping tongues of flame, the gigantic, terrifying black column of smoke rising toward the stratosphere. Houses exploding like firecrackers, bim bam boom, block after block. And the plucky little firefighting planes soaring above the holocaust, trying to get down close enough to do some good with their cargoes of water and fire-retardant chemicals.

His brother Mike aboard one of those planes – Mike –

Up there over the fire, threading a difficult course through the treacherous upgusts of heat and wind –

Be careful, Mike – please, Mike –

'It's okay, grandpa. I'm right here.'

The Colonel blinked his eyes open. Took in the scene. No fires, no smoke, no little planes tossing about. Just the wide cloudless sky, the green hills all around, and a tall fair-haired adolescent boy with the long red scar on his cheek standing beside him. Anse's son, that one was. The nicer one. The Colonel observed that he was slouching in his chair, and pulled himself irritatedly upright.

'Did I say something, boy?'

'You called my name. "*Mike*", you said. "*Be careful, Mike!*" But I wasn't doing anything, just waiting for you to wake up. Were you having a dream?'

'I might have been, yes. A daydream, anyway. What time is it?'

'Half past one. My father sent me out to tell you that the Resistance meeting is about ready to get going.'

From the Colonel, a grunt of assent, awareness. But he remained seated where he was.

A moment later Anse himself appeared, coming slowly toward them across the broad flagstone patio. His limp seemed a little worse than usual today, the Colonel thought. He sometimes wondered whether it was all just a theatrical act, that limp of Anse's, an excuse for him to do a little extra drinking. But the Colonel had not yet forgotten the white shard of bone jutting through Anse's flesh after the horse had fallen on him three years back, down along the steep trail leading to the well. Nor the hellish sweaty hour when he and Ronnie had struggled to clean the wound and set the fracture, two amateur surgeons working without benefit of anesthesia.

'What's going on?' Anse asked the boy gruffly. 'Didn't I tell you to bring your grandfather inside for the meeting?'

'Well, grandpa was asleep, and I didn't feel good about waking him.'

'Not sleeping,' said the Colonel, 'just dozing.'

'Seemed mighty like sleep to me, grandpa. You were dreaming, and you called out my name.'

'Not his name,' the Colonel explained to Anse. 'Mike's. In fact I was thinking about the day of the fire. Remembering.'

Anse turned to his son and said, 'He means his brother. The one you were named for.'

The boy said, 'I know. The one who died in battle against the Entities.'

'He died battling a fire that the Entities happened to start, by accident, the day they first landed,' the Colonel said. 'That's not quite the same thing.' But he knew it was hopeless. The legends were already beginning to entrench themselves; in twenty or thirty years no one would know fact from fantasy. Well, in twenty years he wouldn't give a damn.

'Come on,' Anse said, offering the Colonel a hand. 'Let's go inside, dad.'

Rising from his chair with all the swiftness he could summon, the Colonel shook the hand away. 'I can manage,' he said testily, knowing exactly how testy he sounded, knowing too that he sounded that way too much of the time now. It wasn't anything that he could help. He was seventy-four, and usually felt considerably older than that these days. He hadn't expected that. He had always felt younger than his years. But there were no medicines any more that could turn back the clock for you when you began to get old, as there had been fifteen or twenty years ago, and doctoring was practiced now, mostly, by people without training who looked things up in whatever medical books they might have on hand and hoped for the best. So seventy-four was once again a ripe old age, beginning to approach the limit.

They walked slowly into the house, the stiff-jointed old man and the limping younger one. A cloudy aura of alcohol fumes surrounded Anse like a helmet.

'Leg bothering you a lot?' the Colonel asked.

'Comes and goes. Some days worse than others. This is one of the bad ones.'

'And a little booze helps, does it? But there isn't much of the old stock left, I'd imagine.'

'Enough for a few more years,' Anse said. He and Ronnie had, the Colonel knew, descended into deserted Santa Barbara one morning after the Great Plague had at last abated – a ghost town, was Santa Barbara now, inhabited only by a few spectral squatters – and had cleaned out most of the contents of an abandoned liquor warehouse they had found there. 'After that, if I live that long, I'll rig up a still, I guess. That's not a lost art yet.'

'You know, I wish you'd take it easier on the drinking, son.'

Anse hesitated for just a beat before replying, and the Colonel knew that he was fighting off anger. Anger rose all too quickly in Anse these days, but he seemed better at controlling it than he once had been.

'I wish a lot of things were different from what they are, but they aren't going to be,' Anse said tightly. 'We do what we can to get through the day. – Mind the door, dad. Here you go. Here.'

The members of the Resistance Committee – they had changed the name of it a few years back; Army of Liberation had begun to seem much too grandiose – had gathered in the dining room. They stood at once as the Colonel entered. A tribute to the valiant old chairman, yes. However pathetic the valiant old chairman had become, however superannuated. Anse did most of the work these days, Anse and Ronnie. But Anson Senior, the Colonel, was still chairman, at least in name. He chose to accept the accolade at face value, acknowledging it with a cool smile, stiff little nods to each of them.

'Gentlemen,' he said. 'Please – sit, if you will –'

He stood. He could still do that much. Square-shouldered, straight-backed as ever. Standing here before them, he felt much less the sleepy oldster nodding off on the porch, much more the keen-minded military strategist of decades past, the vigorous and incisive planner, the shrewd leader of men, the enemy of self-deception and failure of inner discipline and all the other kinds of insidious moral sloppiness.

Looking toward Anse, the Colonel said, 'Is everybody here?'

'All but Jackman, who sends word that he couldn't swing an exit permit from L.A. because of a sudden labor-requisition reassignment, and Quarles, whose sister seems to have started keeping company with a quisling and who therefore doesn't think it's a smart idea for him to come up here for the meeting today.'

'Is the sister aware of Quarles's Resistance activities?'

'Not clear,' Anse said. 'Maybe he needs to check that out before he feels it's safe to begin attending again.'

'At any rate, we have a quorum,' the Colonel said, taking the vacant seat beside Anse.

There were ten other committee members present, all of them men. Two were his sons Anse and Ronnie, one his son-in-law Doug Gannett, one his nephew Paul: with the Carmichael ranch standing high and safe above everything, all alone on its mountainside, untouched by the horrors of the plague year and largely unaffected by the transformations that had overtaken the world's shrunken population in the decade since, the local Resistance Committee had become virtually a Carmichael family enterprise.

Of course there were other Resistance Committees elsewhere, in California and beyond it, and Liberation Armies, and Undergrounds, and other such things.

But with communications even within what once had been the United States so chaotic and unpredictable, it was hard to keep in touch with these small, elusive groups in any consistent way, and easy to develop the illusion that you and these few men that were here with you were just about the only people on Earth who still maintained the fiction that the Entities would someday be driven from the world.

The meeting now began. Meetings of this group followed a rigid format, as much of a ritual as a solemn high mass.

An invocation of the Deity, first. Somehow that had crept into the order of events three or four years back, and no one seemed willing to question its presence. Jack Hastings was always the man who intoned the prayer: a former business associate of Ronnie's from San Diego, who had had some kind of religious conversion not long after the Conquest, and was, so it certainly seemed, passionately sincere about his beliefs.

Hastings rose now. Touched his fingertips together, solemnly inclined his head.

'Our Father, who looketh down from heaven upon our unhappy world, we beseech You to lend Your might to our cause, and to help us sweep from this Your world the creatures who have dispossessed us of it.'

The words were always the same, blandly acceptable to all, no particular sectarian tinge, though Ronnie had privately given the Colonel to understand that Hastings' own religion was some kind of very strange neo-apocalyptic Christian sect, speaking in tongues, handling of serpents, things like that.

'Amen,' said Ronnie loudly, and Sam Bacon half a second later, and then all the others, the Colonel included. The Colonel had never been much for any sort of organized religious activity, not even in Vietnam where the body-bags were brought in daily; but he was no atheist, either, far from it, and aside from all that he understood the value of formal observance in maintaining the structures of life in a time of stress.

After the prayer came the Progress Report, usually given by Dan Cantelli or Andy Jackman, and more appropriately termed the No Progress Report. This was an account of such success, or lack of it, that had been attained since the last meeting, especially in the way of penetrating Entity security codes and developing information that might be of value in some eventual attempt at launching an attack against the conquerors.

In Jackman's absence, Cantelli delivered the Progress Report today. He was a short, round, indestructible-looking man of about fifty, who had been an olive grower at the upper end of the Santa Ynez Valley before the Conquest, and still was. His entire family, parents and wife and five or six children, had perished in the Great Plague; but he had married again, a Mexican girl from Lompoc, and had four more children now.

This month's Progress was, as usual, mainly No Progress. 'There was, as you know, a project under way in Seattle last month aimed at finding some means of accessing high-security internal Entity messages and diverting them to Resistance computer centers. I'm sorry to say that that project has ended in complete failure, thanks to the activities of a couple of treacherous borgmanns who wrote counterintrusion software for the Entities. I understand that the Seattle hackers were detected and, I'm afraid, eradicated.'

'Borgmanns!' muttered Ronnie bitterly. 'What we need is a program that will detect and eradicate *them*!'

There were nods of approval all around the room.

The Colonel, puzzled by the strange word, leaned over to Anse and whispered, 'Borgmanns? What the devil are borgmanns?'

'Quislings,' Anse said. 'The worst kind of quislings, too, because they don't just work for the Entities, they actively aid and abet them.'

'Doing computer stuff, you mean?'

Anse nodded. 'They're computer experts who show the Entities better ways of spying on us, and teach them how to keep our hackers out of Entity computers. Ronnie tells me that the name came from someone in Europe who was the first to break through into the Entity computer net and offer them his services. He's the one who showed them how we can link our personal computers to their big ones so that they could order us around more efficiently.'

The Colonel shook his head sadly.

Borgmanns. *Traitors.* There had always been those, in every era of history. Some flaw in human nature, impossible to extirpate. He filed the word away in his memory.

A new vocabulary was springing up, he realized. Just as Vietnam had produced words like 'fragging' and 'hooch' and 'gook' and 'Victor Charlie' that no one remembered now but old men like him, so, too, did the Conquest seem to be producing its set of special words. *Entity. Borgmann. Quisling.* Although that last one, he reflected, was actually a retread from Second World War days, recently dusted off and put back into service.

Cantelli finished his report. Ronnie now stood up and delivered his, which had to do with the Colonel's own pet enterprise, the establishment of underground educational facilities whose purpose was to instill a passion for the ultimate rebirth of human civilization in the younger generation. It was what the Colonel called 'inner resistance,' a sort of holding action, aimed at the maintenance of the old patriotic traditions, a belief in the ultimate providence of God, a determined resolve to transmit to future Americans some sense of the old-line American values, so that when we finally did get the Entities off our backs we would still have some recollection of what we had been before they came.

The Colonel was only too thoroughly aware of the irony of placing Ronnie in charge of any project that was centered around such concepts as the ultimate providence of God and the maintenance of grand old patriotic American traditions. But the Colonel didn't have the energy to handle the work himself any more, nor did Anse seem capable of taking it on, and Ronnie had volunteered for the assignment with a hearty if somewhat suspicious show of enthusiasm. He spoke now with eloquence and zeal of what was being done by way of sending out instructional material to groups newly organized in Sacramento, San Francisco, San Luis Obispo, and San Diego. He made it sound, the Colonel thought, as though he believed there really was some point in it.

And there was. There *was*. Even in this strange new world of borgmanns and quislings, where people seemed to be falling all over themselves in their eagerness to collaborate with the Entities. You had to keep on working toward what you knew to be right, even so, the Colonel thought. Just as in that other era of hooches and fraggings and gooks and all the other fleeting terminology of that misbegotten war, there still had been sound fundamental reasons for taking action to contain the spread of imperialist Communism throughout the world, however cockeyed in actuality our involvement in Vietnam might have been.

The meeting was moving right along. The Colonel realized that Ronnie had sat down and Paul was speaking now, some item of new business. The Colonel, much of his mind still somewhere back there in 1971, glanced toward his nephew and frowned. He was noticing, as though for the first time, that Paul no longer looked like a young man. It was as if the Colonel had not seen him in many years, although Paul had lived right here at the ranch for the entire decade past. For a long while Paul had borne an astonishing resemblance to his late father Lee, but not any more: his heavy thatch of dark hair had gone gray and eroded far back from his forehead, his smooth oval face had grown longer and become creased with deep parallel lines, as Lee's had never been, and his eyes, once glitteringly bright with the hunger for knowledge, had lost their sheen.

How old the boy looked, how frayed and worn! *The boy!* What boy? Paul was at least forty now. Lee had died at thirty-nine, destined to remain forever young in the Colonel's memory.

Paul was saying something about the latest all-points Resistance bulletin: a roster, a worldwide census, of Entities, that had been compiled by some colleague of his from his University days, when he had been a brilliant young professor of computer sciences. The colleague, who was part of the San Diego Resistance cell and whose field was statistics – the Colonel had managed to miss his name, but that didn't matter – had over the course of the past eighteen months collected, sifted, collated, and analyzed a mass of fragmentary espionage reports from the far corners of the world and had come to the conclusion that the total number of Entities currently to be found on Earth was –

'Excuse me,' the Colonel said, finding himself lost as Paul went rattling onward with a flurry of correlatives and corollaries. '*What* was that number again, Paul?'

'Nine hundred, plus or minus some, as stated. You understand I'm speaking just of the big tubular kind, the purplish squid-like ones with the spots, which everyone agrees are the dominant form. We haven't tried to come up with figures for the other two types, the Spooks and the Behemoths. Those types seem somewhat more numerous, but –'

'Hold it,' said the Colonel. 'This sounds like craziness to me. How can anybody have come up with a reliable count of the Entities, when they hide in their compounds most of the time, and when there doesn't seem to be any way of telling one from another in the first place?'

There was some murmuring in the room at that.

Paul said, his voice oddly gentle, 'I've just pointed out, Uncle Anson, that the numbers are only approximate, the result mainly of stochastic analysis, but they're based on very careful observations of the known movements of the dominant Entities, the traffic flow in and around their various compounds. The figure we have isn't entirely hard and precise – I guess you missed what I was saying when I mentioned that there might well be another fifty or a hundred of them – but we're confident that it's close enough. Certainly there can't be many more than a thousand, all told.'

'It took just a thousand of them to conquer the entire Earth?'

'So it would seem. I agree that it seemed like more, when it was happening. But that was evidently an illusion. A deliberately induced exaggeration.'

'I don't trust these numbers,' said the Colonel stubbornly. 'How could anybody really know? How could they?'

Sam Bacon said, in a tone just as patient and gentle as Paul's had been, 'The point is, Anson, that even if the numbers are off by a factor of as much as two or three hundred percent, there can only be a few thousand dominant-level Entities on this planet altogether. Which brings up the question of a campaign of attrition aimed against them, a program of steady assassination that will in time eliminate the entire – '

'*Assassination?*' the Colonel cried, aghast. He came up out of his chair like a rocket.

'Guerrilla warfare, yes,' Bacon said. 'As I've said, a campaign of attrition. Picking them off one by one with sniper attacks, until – '

'Wait a second,' said the Colonel. 'Just wait.' He was trembling, suddenly. Suddenly unsteady on his feet. He started to sway and clamped his fingers down hard into Anse's shoulder. 'I don't like the direction in which we're heading, here. Does any of you seriously think we're anywhere near ready to begin a program of -of – '

He began to falter. They were all looking at him, and they seemed uneasy. He had the hazy impression that this was not the first time these matters had come up.

No matter. He had to get it all out. He heard some faint muttering, but he kept on going.

'Let's leave out of the discussion for the moment,' the Colonel said, summoning from some half-forgotten reserve the strength to continue, 'the fact that nobody, so far as we know for certain, has ever managed to assassinate as many as one Entity, and here we are talking of knocking the whole bunch of them off, bang bang bang. Maybe we should call for opinions from Generals Brackenridge and Comstock before we get any deeper into this.'

'Brackenridge and Comstock are both dead, dad,' Anse said in what was becoming the universally kindly, condescending way of addressing him today.

'Don't you think I'm aware of that? Died in the Plague, both of them, and the Plague, I remind you, is something that the Entities called down on us in reprisal for that Denver laser attack, which for all we ever knew achieved nothing anyway. Now you want to get some snipers out there who'll start shooting down the whole population of Entities one at a time in the streets, without stopping to consider what they would do to us if we killed even a single one of them? I fought that notion then, and I'm going to fight it again today. It's much too soon to try any such thing. If they killed off half the world's population the last time, what will they do now?'

'They won't kill us all off, Anson,' said someone on the far side. Hastings, Hal Faulkenburg, one of those. 'The last time, when they sent the Plague, it was as a warning to us not to try any more funny business. And we haven't. But they won't kill us off like that again, even if we do take another whack at them. They need us too much. We're their labor supply. They'll get nasty, sure. But they won't get *that* nasty.'

'How can you know that?' the Colonel demanded.

'I don't. But a second round of the Plague would just about exterminate us all. I don't think that's what they want. That's a calculated risk, I agree. But *we* can kill all of *them*. Only nine hundred, Paul says, maybe a thousand? One by one, we'll get the whole bunch of them, and when they're gone we're a free planet again. It's high time we got under way. If not now, when?'

'There's a whole planet of them somewhere,' said the Colonel. 'We knock off a few, and they'll send some more.'

'From forty light-years away, or wherever their world is? That'll take time.' This was definitely Faulkenburg speaking now, a rancher from Santa Maria, slab-jawed, cold-eyed, vehement. 'Meanwhile we'll get ourselves ready for their next visit. And when they arrive –'

'Craziness,' the Colonel said hollowly, and subsided into his seat. 'Absolute lunacy. You don't understand the first thing about our true situation.'

He was quivering with anger. A pounding pulsation hammered at his left temple. The room had grown very silent, a silence that had a peculiar, almost electric, intensity.

Then it was broken by a voice from the other side of the room: 'I ask you, Anson –' The Colonel looked across. Cantelli, it was. 'I ask you, sir: what kind of resistance movement do you think we have here, if we don't ever dare to resist?'

'Hear! Hear!' That was Faulkenburg again.

The Colonel began to reply, but then he realized he was not sure of his answer, though he knew there had to be a good one. He said nothing.

'He's always been a pacifist at heart, really,' someone murmured. The voice was distant, indistinct. The Colonel could not tell who it might belong to. 'Hates the Entities, but hates fighting even more. And doesn't even see the contradictions in his own words. What kind of soldier is that?'

No, the Colonel roared, though no sound came from him. *Not so. Not so.*

'He had all the right training,' said someone else. 'But he was in Vietnam. That changes you, losing a war.'

'I don't think it's that,' came a third voice. 'It's just that he's so old. All the fight's gone out of him.'

Were they, he wondered, actually saying these things, right out loud in his very presence? Or was he simply imagining them?

'Hey, wait just one goddamned second!' the Colonel cried, trying once more to get to his feet and not quite succeeding. He felt a hand on his wrist. Then another. Anse and Ronnie, flanking him.

'Dad –' Anse said, that same soft, gentle, infuriatingly condescending tone. 'A little fresh air, maybe? That always perks a person up, don't you think?'

Outside, again. The warm springtime sun, the lush green hills. A little fresh air, yes. Always a good idea. Perks a person up.

The Colonel's head was spinning. He felt very shaky.

'Just take it easy, dad. Everything'll be all right in a minute.'

That was Ronnie. A fine boy, Ronnie. Just as solid as Anse, nowadays, maybe even more so. Got off to a bad beginning in life, but had come around wonderfully in the last few years. Of course, it was Peggy who had been the making of him. Settled him down, straightened him out.

'Don't fret over me. I'll be okay,' the Colonel said. 'You go back inside, Ron. Vote my proxy at the meeting. Keep hammering away at the reprisal issue.'

'Right. Right. Here – you sit right here, dad –'

His mind seemed to be clearing, a little.

A disheartening business, in there. He recognized the sound of blind determination in the face of all logic when he heard it. The old, old story: they saw the light at the end of the tunnel, or thought they did. And so they *would*, the Colonel knew, make the Denver mistake a second time, no matter what arguments he raised. And would produce the catastrophic Denver result again, too.

And yet, and yet, Cantelli had a point: How could they call themselves a Resistance, if they never resisted? Why these endless, useless meetings? What were they waiting for? When were they going to strike? Was it not their goal to rid the world of these mysterious invaders, who, like thieves coming in the night, had stolen all point and purpose from human existence without offering a syllable of explanation?

Yes. That *was* the goal. We have to kill them all and reclaim our world.

And, if so, why let any more time go by before beginning the struggle? Were we getting any stronger as the years went by? Were the Entities growing weaker?

A hummingbird shot past him, a brilliant flash of green and red, not much bigger than a butterfly. Two hawks were circling far overhead, dark swooping things high up against the blinding brightness of the sky. A couple of small children had emerged from somewhere, a boy and a girl, and stood staring in silence at him. Six or seven years old: the Colonel was confused for a moment about who they were, mistaking them for Paul and Helena, until he reminded himself that Paul and Helena had long since entered into adulthood. This boy here was his youngest grandson, Ronnie's boy. The latest model Anson Carmichael: the fifth to bear that name, he was.

And the girl? Jill, was she, Anse's daughter? No. Too young for that. This had to be Paul's daughter, the Colonel supposed. What was her name? Cassandra? Samantha? Something fancy like that.

'The thing is,' the Colonel said, as though picking up a conversation they had broken off only a little while before, 'that you must never forget that Americans were free people once, and when you grow up and have children of your own you'll need to teach them that.'

'Just Americans?' the boy asked, the young Anson.

'No, others too. Not everyone. Some peoples never knew what freedom was. But we did. Americans are all we can think about now, I guess. The others will have to get free on their own.'

They were looking at him strangely, big-eyed, bewildered. Didn't have a clue about the meaning of what he was saying. He wasn't any too sure himself that it made any sense.

'I don't really know how it's going to come about,' he went on. 'But we must never forget that it *has* to come about, someday, somehow. There has to be a way, but we haven't discovered it yet. And meanwhile, while we're biding our time, you mustn't let the concept of liberty be forgotten, you children. We have to remember who and what we once were. Do you hear me?'

Blank looks of incomprehension. They did not understand, he was certain of that. Too young, perhaps? No. No. They ought to be old enough to grasp these ideas. He certainly had, when he was their age and his father was explaining to him the reasons why the country had gone to war in Korea. But these two had never known the world to be anything other than this. They had nothing to compare it with, no yardstick by which to measure the notion of 'freedom'. And so, as time went along and the ones who remembered the old kind of world gave way to these children, that notion would be lost forever.

Would it? Would it, really?

If no one ever lifted a finger against the Entities, then, yes, it would. Something had to be done. Something. Something. But what?

Right now there was nothing they could do. He had said so many times: *The world is the toy of the Entities. They are omnipotent and we are weak.* And so the situation was likely to remain, until somehow – he could not say how – we were able to change things. Then, when we had bided our time long enough, when we were ready to strike, we would strike, and we would prevail.

Wasn't that so?

*   *   *

You could still see the ghostly lettering over the front door of the former restaurant, if you knew what to look for, the pale greenish outlines of the words that once had been painted there in bright gold: KHAN's MOGUL PALACE. The old swinging sign that had dangled above the door was still lying out back, too, in a clutter of cracked basins and discarded stewpots and broken crockery.

But the restaurant itself was gone, long gone, a victim of the Great Plague, as was poor sad Haleem Khan himself, the ever-weary little brown-skinned man who in ten years had somehow saved five thousand pounds from his salary as a dishwasher at the Lion and Unicorn Hotel and had used that, back when England had a queen and Elizabeth was her name, as the seed money for the unpretentious little restaurant that was going to rescue him and his family from utter hopeless poverty. Four days after the Plague had hit Salisbury, Haleem was dead. But if the Plague hadn't killed him, the tuberculosis that he was already harboring probably would have done the job soon enough. Or else simply the shock and disgrace and grief of his daughter Yasmeena's ghastly death in childbirth two weeks earlier, at Christmastime, in an upstairs room of the restaurant, while bringing into the world the bastard child of the long-legged English boy, Richie Burke, the future traitor, the future quisling.

Haleem's other daughter, the little girl Leila, had died in the Plague also, three months after her father and two days before what would have been her sixth birthday. As for Yasmeena's older brother, Khalid, he was already two years gone by then, beaten to death late one Saturday night during the time known as the Troubles by a gang of long-haired yobs who had set forth in fine English wrath, determined to vent their resentment over the conquest of the Earth by doing a lively spot of Paki-bashing in the town streets.

Which left, of all the family, only Aissha, Haleem's hardy and tireless second wife. She came down with the Plague, too, but she was one of the lucky ones, one of those who managed to fend the affliction off and survive – for whatever that was worth – into the new and transformed and diminished world. But she could hardly run the restaurant alone, and in any case, with three quarters of the population of Salisbury dead in the Plague, there was no longer much need for a Pakistani restaurant there.

Aissha found other things to do. She went on living in a couple of rooms of the now gradually decaying building that had housed the restaurant, and supported herself, in this era when national currencies had ceased to mean much and strange new sorts of money circulated in the land, by a variety of improvised means. She did housecleaning and laundry for those people who still had need of such services. She cooked meals for elderly folks too feeble to cook for themselves. Now and then, when her number came up in the labor lottery, she put in time at a factory that the Entities had established just outside town, weaving little strands of colored wire together to make incomprehensibly complex mechanisms whose nature and purpose were never disclosed to her.

And when there was no such work of any of those kinds available, Aissha would make herself available to the lorry-drivers who passed through Salisbury, spreading her powerful muscular thighs in return for meal certificates or corporate scrip or barter units or whichever other of the new versions of money they would pay her in. That was not something she would have chosen to do, if she had had her choices. But she would not have chosen to have the invasion of the Entities, for that matter, nor her husband's early death and Leila's and Khalid's, nor Yasmeena's miserable lonely ordeal in the upstairs room, but she had not been consulted about any of those things, either. Aissha needed to eat in order to survive; and so she sold herself, when she had to, to the lorry-drivers, and that was that.

As for why survival mattered, why she bothered at all to care about surviving in a world that had lost all meaning and just about all hope, it was in part because survival for the sake of survival was in her genes, and – mostly – because she wasn't alone in the world. Out of the wreckage of her family she had been left with a child to look after – her grandchild, her dead stepdaughter's baby, Khalid Haleem Burke, the child of shame. Khalid Haleem Burke had survived the Plague too. It was one of the ugly little ironies of the epidemic that the angered Entities had released upon the world in retribution for the Denver laser attack that children less than six months old generally did not contract it. Which created a huge population of healthy but parentless babes.

He was healthy, all right, was Khalid Haleem Burke. Through every deprivation of those dreary years, the food shortages and the fuel shortages and the little outbreaks of diseases that once had been thought to be nearly extinct, he grew taller and straighter and stronger all the time. He had his mother's wiry strength and his father's long legs and dancer's grace. And he was lovely to behold. His skin was tawny golden-brown, his eyes were a glittering blue-green, and his hair, glossy and thick and curly, was a wonderful bronze color, a magnificent Eurasian hue. Amidst all the sadness and loss of Aissha's life, he was the one glorious beacon that lit the darkness for her.

There were no real schools, not any more. Aissha taught little Khalid herself, as best she could. She hadn't had much schooling herself, but she could read and write, and showed him how, and begged or borrowed books for him wherever she might. She found a woman who understood arithmetic, and scrubbed her floors for her in return for Khalid's lessons. There was an old man at the south end of town who had the Koran by heart, and Aissha, though she was not a strongly religious woman herself, sent Khalid to him once a week for instruction in Islam. The boy was, after all, half Moslem. Aissha felt no responsibility for the Christian part of him, but she did not want to let him go into the world unaware that there was – somewhere, *somewhere*! – a god known as Allah, a god of justice and compassion and mercy, to whom obedience was owed, and that he would, like all people, ultimately come to stand before that god upon the Day of Judgment.

'And the Entities?' Khalid asked her. He was six, then. 'Will they be judged by Allah too?'

'The Entities are not people. They are jinn.'

'Did Allah make them?'

'Allah made all things in heaven and on Earth. He made us out of potter's clay and the jinn out of smokeless fire.'

'But the Entities have brought evil upon us. Why would Allah make evil things, if He is a merciful god?'

'The Entities,' Aissha said uncomfortably, aware that wiser heads than hers had grappled in vain with that question, *'do* evil. But they are not evil themselves. They are merely the instruments of Allah.'

'Who has sent them to us to do evil,' said Khalid. 'What kind of god is that, who sends evil among His own people, Aissha?'

She was getting beyond her depth in this conversation, but she was patient with him. 'No one understands Allah's ways, Khalid. He is the One God and we are nothing before him. If He had reason to send the Entities to us, they were good reasons, and we have no right to question them.' *And also to send sickness,* she thought, *and hunger, and death, and the English boys who killed your uncle Khalid in the street, and even the English boy who put you into your mother's belly and then ran away. Allah sent all of those into the world, too.* But then she reminded herself that if Richie Burke had not crept secretly into this house to sleep with Yasmeena, this beautiful child would not be standing here before her at this moment. And so good sometimes could come forth from evil. Who were we to demand reasons from Allah? Perhaps even the Entities had been sent here, ultimately, for our own good.

Perhaps.

Of Khalid's father, there was no news all this while. He was supposed to have run off to join the army that was fighting the Entities; but Aissha had never heard that there was any such army, anywhere in the world.

Then, not long after Khalid's seventh birthday, when he returned in mid-afternoon from his Thursday Koran lesson at the house of old Iskander Mustafa Ali, he found an unknown white man sitting in the room with his grandmother, a man with a great untidy mass of light-colored curling hair and a lean, angular, almost fleshless face with two cold, harsh blue-green eyes looking out from it as though out of a mask. His skin was so white that Khalid wondered whether he had any blood in his body. It was almost like chalk. The strange white man was sitting in his grandmother's own armchair, and his grandmother was looking very edgy and strange, a way Khalid had never seen her look before, with glistening beads of sweat along her forehead and her lips clamped together in a tight thin line.

The white man said, leaning back in the chair and crossing his legs, which were the longest legs Khalid had ever seen, 'Do you know who I am, boy?'

'How would he know?' his grandmother said.

The white man looked toward Aissha and said, 'Let me do this, if you don't mind.' And then, to Khalid: 'Come over here, boy. Stand in front of me. Well, now, aren't we the little beauty? What's your name, boy?'

'Khalid.'

'Khalid. Who named you that?'

'My mother. She's dead now. It was my uncle's name. He's dead too.'

'Devil of a lot of people are dead who used to be alive, all right. Well, Khalid, my name is Richie.'

'Richie,' Khalid said, in a very small voice, because he had already begun to understand this conversation.

'Richie, yes. Have you ever heard of a person named Richie? Richie *Burke*.'

'My – father.' In an even smaller voice.

'Right you are! The grand prize for that lad! Not only handsome but smart, too! Well, what would one expect, eh? – Here I be, boy, your long-lost father! Come here and give your long-lost father a kiss.'

Khalid glanced uncertainly toward Aissha. Her face was still shiny with sweat, and very pale. She looked sick. After a moment she nodded, a tiny nod.

He took half a step forward and the man who was his father caught him by the wrist and gathered him roughly in, pulling him inward and pressing him up against him, not for an actual kiss but for what was only a rubbing of cheeks. The grinding contact with that hard, stubbly cheek was painful for Khalid.

'There, boy. I've come back, do you see? I've been away seven worm-eaten miserable years, but now I'm back, and I'm going to live with you and be your father. You can call me "dad".'

Khalid stared, stunned.

'Go on. Do it. Say, "I'm so very glad that you've come back, dad".'

'Dad,' Khalid said uneasily.

'The rest of it too, if you please.'

'I'm so very glad –' He halted.

'That I've come back.'

'That you've come back –'

'*Dad.*'

Khalid hesitated. 'Dad,' he said.

'There's a good boy! It'll come easier to you after a while. Tell me, did you ever think about me while you were growing up, boy?'

Khalid glanced toward Aissha again. She nodded surreptitiously.

Huskily he said, 'Now and then, yes.'

'Only now and then? That's all?'

'Well, hardly anybody has a father. But sometimes I met someone who did, and then I thought of you. I wondered where you were. Aissha said you were off fighting the Entities. Is that where you were, dad? Did you fight them? Did you kill any of them?'

'Don't ask stupid questions. Tell me, boy: do you go by the name of Burke or Khan?'

'Burke. Khalid Haleem Burke.'

'Call me "*sir*" when you're not calling me "*dad*". Say, "Khalid Haleem Burke, sir".'

'Khalid Haleem Burke, sir. Dad.'

'One or the other. Not both.' Richie Burke rose from the chair, unfolding himself as though in sections, up and up and up. He was enormously tall, very thin. His slenderness accentuated his great height. Khalid, though tall for his age, felt dwarfed beside him. The thought came to him that this man was not his father at all, not even a man, but some sort of demon, rather, a jinni, a jinni that had been let out of its bottle, as in the story that Iskander Mustafa Ali had told him. He kept that thought to himself. 'Good,' Richie Burke said. 'Khalid Haleem Burke. I like that. Son should have his father's name. But not the Khalid Haleem part. From now on your name is – ah – Kendall. Ken for short.'

'Khalid was my –'

' – uncle's name, yes. Well, your uncle is dead. Practically everybody is dead, Kenny. Kendall Burke, good English name. Kendall *Hamilton* Burke, same initials, even, only English. Is that all right, boy? What a pretty one you are, Kenny! I'll teach you a thing or two, I will. I'll make a man out of you.'

Here I be, boy, your long-lost father!

Khalid had never known what it meant to have a father, nor ever given the idea much examination. He had never known hatred before, either, because Aissha was a fundamentally calm, stable, accepting person, too steady in her soul to waste time or valuable energy hating anything, and Khalid had taken after her in that. But Richie Burke, who taught Khalid what it meant to have a father, made him aware of what it was like to hate, also.

Richie moved into the bedroom that had been Aissha's, sending Aissha off to sleep in what had once been Yasmeena's room. It had long since gone to rack and ruin, but they cleaned it up, some, chasing the spiders out and taping oilcloth over the missing window-panes and nailing down a couple of floor-boards that had popped up out of their proper places. She carried her clothes-cabinet in there by herself, and set up on it the framed photographs of her dead family that she had kept in her former bedroom, and draped two of her old saris that she never wore any more over the bleak places on the wall where the paint had flaked away.

It was stranger than strange, having Richie living with them. It was a total upheaval, a dismaying invasion by an alien life-form, in some ways as shocking in its impact as the arrival of the Entities had been.

He was gone most of the day. He worked in the nearby town of Winchester, driving back and forth in a small brown pre-Conquest automobile. Winchester was a place where Khalid had never been, though his mother had, to purchase the pills that were meant to abort him. Khalid had never been far from Salisbury, not even to Stonehenge, which now was a center of Entity activity anyway, and not a tourist sight. Few people in Salisbury traveled anywhere these days. Not many had automobiles, because of the difficulty of obtaining petrol, but Richie never seemed to have any problem about that.

Sometimes Khalid wondered what sort of work his father did in Winchester; but he asked about it only once. The words were barely out of his mouth when his father's long arm came snaking around and struck him across the face, splitting his lower lip and sending a dribble of blood down his chin.

Khalid staggered back, astounded. No one had ever hit him before. It had not occurred to him that anyone would.

'You must never ask that again!' his father said, looming mountain-high above him. His cold eyes were even colder, now, in his fury. 'What I do in Winchester is no business of yours, nor anyone else's, do you hear me, boy? It is my own private affair. My own – private – affair.'

Khalid rubbed his cut lip and peered at his father in bewilderment. The pain of the slap had not been so great; but the surprise of it, the shock – that was still reverberating through his consciousness. And went on reverberating for a long while thereafter.

He never asked about his father's work again, no. But he was hit again, more than once, indeed with fair regularity. Hitting was Richie's way of expressing irritation. And it was difficult to predict what sort of thing might irritate him. Any sort of intrusion on his father's privacy, though, seemed to do it. Once, while talking with his father in his bedroom, telling him about a bloody fight between two boys that he had witnessed in town, Khalid unthinkingly put his hand on the guitar that Richie always kept leaning against his wall beside his bed, giving it only a single strum, something that he had occasionally wanted to do for months; and instantly, hardly before the twanging note had died away, Richie unleashed his arm and knocked Khalid back against the wall. 'You keep your filthy fingers off that instrument, boy!' Richie said; and after that Khalid did. Another time Richie struck him for leafing through a book he had left on the kitchen table, that had pictures of naked women in it; and another time, it was for staring too long at Richie as he stood before the mirror in the morning, shaving. So Khalid learned to keep his distance from his father; but still he found himself getting slapped for this reason and that, and sometimes for no reason at all. The blows were rarely as hard as the first one had been, and never ever created in him that same sense of shock. But they were blows, all the same. He stored them all up in some secret receptacle of his soul.

Occasionally Richie hit Aissha, too – when dinner was late, or when she put mutton curry on the table too often, or when it seemed to him that she had contradicted him about something. That was more of a shock to Khalid than getting slapped himself, that anyone should dare to lift his hand to Aissha. The first time it happened, which occurred while they were eating dinner, a big carving knife was lying on the table near Khalid, and he might well have reached for it had Aissha not, in the midst of her own fury and humiliation and pain, sent Khalid a message with her furious blazing eyes that he absolutely was not to do any such thing. And so he controlled himself, then and any time afterward when Richie hit her. It was a skill that Khalid had, controlling himself – one that in some circuitous way he must have inherited from the ever-patient, all-enduring grandparents whom he had never known and the long line of oppressed Asian peasants from whom they descended. Living with Richie in the house gave Khalid daily opportunity to develop that skill to a fine art.

Richie did not seem to have many friends, at least not friends who visited the house. Khalid knew of only three.

There was a man named Arch who sometimes came, an older man with greasy ringlets of hair that fell from a big bald spot on the top of his head. He always brought a bottle of whiskey, and he and Richie would sit in Richie's room with the door closed, talking in low tones or singing raucous songs. Khalid would find the empty whiskey bottle the following morning, lying on the hallway floor. He kept them, setting them up in a row amidst the restaurant debris behind the house, though he did not know why.

The only other man who came was Syd, who had a flat nose and amazingly thick fingers, and gave off such a bad smell that Khalid was able to detect it in the house the next day. Once, when Syd was there, Richie emerged from his room and called to Aissha, and she went in there and shut the door behind her and was still in there when Khalid went to sleep. He never asked her about that, what had gone on while she was in Richie's room. Some instinct told him that he would rather not know.

There was also a woman: Wendy, her name was, tall and gaunt and very plain, with a long face like a horse's and very bad skin, and stringy tangles of reddish hair. She came once in a while for dinner, and Richie always specified that Aissha was to prepare an English dinner that night, lamb or roast beef, none of your spicy Paki curries tonight, if you please. After they ate, Richie and Wendy would go into Richie's room and not emerge again that evening, and the sounds of the guitar would be heard, and laughter, and then low cries and moans and grunts.

One time in the middle of the night when Wendy was there, Khalid got up to go to the bathroom just at the time she did, and encountered her in the hallway, stark naked in the moonlight, a long white ghostly figure. He had never seen a woman naked until this moment, not a real one, only the pictures in Richie's magazine; but he looked up at her calmly, with that deep abiding steadiness in the face of any sort of surprise that he had mastered so well since the advent of Richie. Coolly he surveyed her, his eyes rising from the long thin legs that went up and up and up from the floor and halting for a moment at the curious triangular thatch of woolly hair at the base of her flat belly, and from there his gaze mounted to the round little breasts set high and far apart on her chest, and at last came to her face, which, in the moonlight had unexpectedly taken on a sort of handsomeness if not actual comeliness, though before this Wendy had always seemed to him to be tremendously ugly. She didn't seem displeased at being seen like this. She smiled and winked at him, and ran her hand almost coquettishly through her straggly hair, and blew him a kiss as she drifted on past him toward the bathroom. It was the only time that anyone associated with Richie had ever been nice to him: had even appeared to notice him at all.

But life with Richie was not entirely horrid. There were some good aspects.

One of them was simply being close to so much strength and energy: what Khalid might have called *virility*, if he had known there was any such word. He had spent all his short life thus far among people who kept their heads down and went soldiering along obediently, people like patient plodding Aissha, who took what came to her and never complained, and shriveled old Iskander Mustafa Ali, who understood that Allah determined all things and one had no choice but to comply, and the quiet, tight-lipped English people of Salisbury, who had lived through the Conquest and the Great Silence and the Troubles and the Plague and were prepared to be very, very English about whatever horror was coming next.

Richie was different, though. Richie hadn't a shred of passivity in him. 'We shape our lives the way we want them to be, boy,' he would say again and again. 'We write our own scripts. It's all just a bloody television show, don't you see that, Kenny-boy?'

That was a startling novelty to Khalid: that you might actually have any control over your own destiny, that you could say 'no' to this and 'yes' to that and 'not right now' to this other thing, and that if there was something you wanted, you could simply reach out and take it. There was nothing Khalid wanted. But the *idea* that he might even have it, if only he could figure out what it was, was fascinating to him.

Then, too, for all of Richie's roughness of manner, his quickness to curse you or kick out at you or slap you when he had had a little too much to drink, he did have an affectionate side, even a charming one. He often sat with them and played his guitar, and taught them the words of songs, and encouraged them to sing along with them, though Khalid had no idea what the songs were about and Aissha did not seem to know either. It was fun, all the same, the singing; and Khalid had known very little fun. Richie was proud of Khalid's good looks and agile, athletic grace, also, and would praise him for them, something which no one had ever done before, not even Aissha. Even though Khalid understood in some way that Richie was only praising himself, really, he was grateful for that.

Richie took him out behind the building and showed him how to throw and catch a ball. How to kick one, too, a different kind of ball. And sometimes there were cricket matches in a field at the edge of town; and when Richie played in these, which he occasionally did, he brought Khalid along to watch. Later, at home, he showed Richie how to hold the bat, how to guard a wicket.

Then there were the drives in the car. These were rare, a great privilege. But sometimes, of a sunny Sunday, Richie would say, 'Let's take the old flivver for a spin, eh, Kenny, lad?' And off they would go into the green countryside, usually no special destination in mind, only driving up and down the quiet lanes, Khalid gawking in wonder at this new world beyond the town. It made his head whirl in a good way, as he came to understand that the world actually did go on and on past the boundaries of Salisbury, and was full of marvels and splendors.

So, though at no point did he stop hating Richie, he could see at least some mitigating benefits that had come from his presence in their home. Not many. Some.

Once Richie took him to Stonehenge. Or as near to it as it was possible now for humans to go. It was the year Khalid turned ten: a special birthday treat.

'Do you see it out there in the plain, boy? Those big stones? Built by a bunch of prehistoric buggers who painted themselves blue and danced widdershins in the night. Do you know what "widdershins" means, boy? No, neither do I. But they did it, whatever it was. Danced around naked with their thingummies jiggling around, and then at midnight they'd sacrifice a virgin on the big altar stone. Long, long ago. Thousands of years. – Come on, let's get out and have a look.'

Khalid stared. Huge gray slabs, set out in two facing rows flanking smaller slabs of blue stone set in a three-cornered pattern, and a big stone standing upright in the middle. And some other stones lying sideways on top of a few of the gray ones. A transparent curtain of flickering reddish-green light surrounded the whole thing, rising from hidden vents in the ground to nearly twice the height of a man. Why would anyone have wanted to build such a thing? It all seemed like a tremendous waste of time.

'Of course, you understand this isn't what it looked like back then. When the Entities came, they changed the whole business around from what it always was, buggered it all up. Got laborers out here to move every single stone. And they put in the gaudy lighting effects, too. Never used to be lights, certainly not that kind. You walk through those lights, you die, just like a mosquito flying through a candle flame. Those stones there, they were set in a circle originally, and those blue ones there – hey, now, lad, look what we have! You ever see an Entity before, Ken?'

Actually, Khalid had: twice. But never this close. The first one had been right in the middle of the town at noontime, standing outside the entrance of the cathedral cool as you please, as though it happened to be in the mood to go to church: a giant purple thing with orange spots and big yellow eyes. But Aissha had put her hand over his face before he could get a good look, and had pulled him quickly down the street that led away from the cathedral, dragging him along as fast as he was able to could go. Khalid had been about five then. He dreamed of the Entity for months thereafter. The second time, a year later, he had been with friends, playing within sight of the main highway, when a strange vehicle came down the road, an Entity car that floated on air instead of riding on wheels, and two Entities were standing in it, looking right out at them for a moment as they went floating by. Khalid saw only the tops of their heads that time: their eyes again, a sort of a curving beak below, a great V-shaped slash of a mouth, like a frog's. He was fascinated by them. Repelled, too, because they were so bizarre, these strange alien beings, these enemies of mankind, and he knew he was supposed to loathe and disdain them. But fascinated. Fascinated. He wished he had been able to see them better.

Now, though, he had a clear view of the creatures, three of them. They had emerged from what looked like a door that was set right in the ground, out on the far side of the ancient monument, and were strolling casually among the great stones like lords or ladies inspecting their estate, paying no heed whatever to the tall man and the small boy standing beside the car parked just outside the fiery barrier. It amazed Khalid, watching them teeter around on the little ropy legs that supported their immense tubular bodies, that they were able to keep their balance, that they didn't simply topple forward and fall with a crash.

It amazed him, too, how beautiful they were. He had suspected that from his earlier glances, but now their glory fell upon him with full impact.

The luminous golden-orange spots on the glassy, gleaming purple skin – like fire, those spots were. And the huge eyes, so bright, so keen: you could read the strength of their minds in them, the power of their souls. Their gaze engulfed you in a flood of light. Even the air about the Entities partook of their beauty, glowing with a liquid turquoise radiance.

'There they be, boy. Our lords and masters. You ever see anything so bloody hideous?'

'Hideous?'

'They ain't pretty, isn't that right?'

Khalid made a noncommittal noise. Richie was in a good mood; he always was, on these Sunday excursions. But Khalid knew only too well the penalty for contradicting him in anything. So he looked upon the Entities in silence, lost in wonder, awed by the glory of these strange gigantic creatures, never voicing a syllable of his admiration for their elegance and majesty.

Expansively Richie said, 'You heard correctly, you know, when they told you that when I left Salisbury just before you were born, it was to go off and join an army that meant to fight them. There was nothing I wanted more than to kill Entities, nothing. Christ Eternal, did I ever hate those creepy bastards! Coming in like they did, taking our world away. But I got to my senses pretty fast, let me tell you. I listened to the plans the underground army people had for throwing off the Entity yoke, and I had to laugh! I had to *laugh*! I could see right away that there wasn't a hope in hell of it. This was even before they put the Great Plague upon us, you understand. I knew. I damn well knew, I did. They're as powerful as gods. You want to fight against a bunch of gods, lots of luck to you. So I quit the underground then and there. I still hate the bastards, mind you, make no mistake about that, but I know it's foolish even to dream about overthrowing them. You just have to fashion your accommodation with them, that's all there is. You just have to make your peace within yourself and let them have their way. Because anything else is a fool's own folly.'

Khalid listened. What Richie was saying made sense. Khalid

understood about not wanting to fight against gods. He understood also how it was possible to hate someone and yet go on unprotestingly living with him.

'Is it all right, letting them see us like this?' he asked. 'Aissha says that sometimes when they see you, they reach out from their chests with the tongues that they have there and snatch you up, and they take you inside their buildings and do horrible things to you there.'

Richie laughed harshly. 'It's been known to happen. But they won't touch Richie Burke, lad, and they won't touch the son of Richie Burke at Richie Burke's side. I guarantee you that. We're absolutely safe.'

Khalid did not ask why that should be. He hoped it was true, that was all.

Two days afterward, while he was coming back from the market with a packet of lamb for dinner, he was set upon by two boys and a girl, all of them about his age or a year or two older, whom he knew only in the vaguest way. They formed themselves into a loose ring just beyond his reach and began to chant in a high-pitched, nasal way: '*Quisling, quisling, your father is a quisling!*'

'What's that you call him?'

'Quisling.'

'He is not.'

'He is! He is! *Quisling, quisling, your father is a quisling!*'

Khalid had no idea what a quisling was. But no one was going to call his father names. Much as he hated Richie, he knew he could not allow that. It was something Richie had taught him: *Defend yourself against scorn, boy, at all times.* He meant against those who might be rude to Khalid because he was part Pakistani; but Khalid had experienced very little of that. Was a quisling someone who was English but had had a child with a Pakistani woman? Perhaps that was it. Why would these children care, though? Why would anyone?

'*Quisling, quisling –*'

Khalid threw down his package and lunged at the closest boy, who darted away. He caught the girl by the arm, but he would not hit a girl, and so he simply shoved her into the other boy, who went spinning up against the side of the market building. Khalid pounced on him there, holding him close to the wall with one hand and furiously hitting him with the other.

His two companions seemed unwilling to intervene. But they went on chanting, from a safe distance, more nasally than ever.

'*Quis-ling, quis-ling, your fa-ther is a quis-ling!*'

'Stop that!' Khalid cried. 'You have no right!' He punctuated his words with blows. The boy he was holding was bleeding, now, his nose, the side of his mouth. He looked terrified.

'*Quis-ling, quis-ling –*'

They would not stop, and neither would Khalid. But then he felt a hand seizing him by the back of his neck, a big adult hand, and he was yanked backward and thrust against the market wall himself. A vast meaty man, a navvy, from the looks of him, loomed over Khalid. 'What do you think you're doing, you dirty Paki garbage? You'll kill the boy!'

'He said my father was a quisling!'

'Well, then, he probably is. Get on with you, now, boy! Get on with you!'

He gave Khalid one last hard shove, and spat and walked away. Khalid looked sullenly around for his three tormentors, but they had run off already. They had taken the packet of lamb with them, too.

That night, while Aissha was improvising something for dinner out of yesterday's rice and some elderly chicken, Khalid asked her what a quisling was. She spun around on him as though he had cursed Allah to her ears. Her face all ablaze with a ferocity he had not seen in it before, she said, 'Never use that word in this house, Khalid. Never! Never!' And that was all the explanation she would give. Khalid had to learn, on his own, what a quisling was; and when he did, which was soon thereafter, he understood why his father had been unafraid, that day at Stonehenge when they stood outside that curtain of light and looked upon the Entities who were strolling among the giant stones. And also why those three children had mocked him in the street. *You just have to fashion your accommodation with them, that's all there is.* Yes. Yes. Yes. To fashion your accommodation.

* * *

The Colonel sat on the ranch-house porch, rocking, rocking, rocking. Afternoon shadows were gathering. The day was growing a little cool. He realized that he might have been dozing again. Paul's young daughter seemed to have wandered off, but the other child, little Anson, was still with him, gazing solemnly at him as though wondering how anybody who looked so old could continue to find the strength to breathe.

Then Ronnie appeared from within, and instantly the boy went running toward him. Ronnie swept him off his feet, tossed him high, caught him and tossed him again. The boy squealed with pleasure. The Colonel was pleased, too. He loved to watch Ronnie playing with his son. He loved the idea that Ronnie *had* a son at all, that he had married a fine woman like Peggy, that he had settled down. He had changed so much, had Ronnie, since the Conquest. Given up his bad old ways, become so responsible. The one good thing to come out of the whole dreary event, the Colonel thought.

Putting the boy down and turning toward him, now, Ronnie said, 'Well, dad, the meeting's over, and you'll be happy to hear how things turned out.'

'The meeting?'

'The Resistance Committee meeting, yes,' said Ronnie gently.

'Yes, of course. What other meeting would it have been? – You don't think I've gone senile yet, do you, boy? No, don't answer that. Tell me about the meeting.'

'We just finished taking the vote. It went your way.'

'The vote.' He tried to remember what they had been discussing in there.

His mind was like molasses. Currents of thoughts stirred slowly, sullenly, within it. There were days when he still recognized himself to be Colonel Anson Carmichael III, USA, Ret. Anson Carmichael Ph.D *Professor* Anson Carmichael, the distinguished authority on Southeast Asian linguistics and the thought processes of non-western cultures. This was not one of those days. There were other days, days like this one, when he was barely capable of making himself believe that he once had been an alert, forceful, intelligent man. Such days came more and more often now.

'The vote,' Ronnie said. 'On the campaign of attrition, the proposed sniper program.'

'Of course. – They voted it down?' The Colonel remembered now. 'I can't believe it. What changed their minds?'

'Just as the discussion was getting toward the vote, and indeed it looked mighty like the vote would be in favor of a program of ambushing Entities wherever we caught one going around by itself, Doug came out with some new information that he'd been sitting on all afternoon, the way he sometimes likes to do. Stuff that he had pulled in from an on-line operation working out of Vancouver, which got it from those Seattle hackers just before the borgmanns spilled the beans on them.' Ronnie paused, giving him a doubtful look. 'You're following all this, aren't you, dad?'

'I'm with you. Go on. This Vancouver information –'

'Well, it looks to be pretty much impossible, trying any sort of sniper attacks on Entities. Apparently there *have* been sniper attempts already, at least three of them, one in the southern United States, one in France, one somewhere else that I forget. They flopped, all three. The snipers never even managed to get off a single shot. The Entities have some kind of mental power, a mind-field that surrounds them and scans for hostile thought-emanations, and when the field detects anybody nearby who might be planning to do anything nasty to them, they just reach out and give him the Push, extra hard, and the sniper falls over dead. It's happened every time.'

'What's the range of this mind-field?'

'Nobody knows. Wide enough to pick up the mental broadcasts of any sniper who might get within shooting range, evidently.'

'Mental telepathy too,' the Colonel said. He closed his eyes for a moment, shook his head slowly. 'They must have *animals* on their planet that are more evolved than we are. Pets, even. – So Doug dumped all this out into the Committee meeting, and that killed the attrition plan right then and there?'

'It was tabled. Between the mind-field thing and the whole reprisal issue, we decided that there was no sense in attempting anything against them right now. Everybody but Faulkenburg agreed, and sooner or later he came around too. Before we can launch any sort of hostile action, we need to gather more information, a lot more, about how their minds work. At present we know practically nothing. If there was some way we could neutralize that mind-field, for example –'

'Right,' the Colonel said. He chuckled. His own mind was as clear now as it had been in days. 'The Santa Claus approach to coping with the problem, eh? Maybe he'll bring us a mind-field neutralizer next Christmas. Or maybe he won't. At any rate, I'm glad the vote went the way it did. I was worried, for a while. Everybody seemed in such a hurry to kill the Entities off, all of a sudden, and not a reason in the world for a rational person to think that it could be done. I thought we were done for. I thought you were all going to shoot us clear over the brink.'

Late that night, as Ronnie was moving through the back wing of the building turning off the lights, he caught sight of Anse sitting by himself in one of the small rooms off the library. There was a bottle in front of him on a little table. There usually was a bottle somewhere close by Anse, these days. A damned shame, Ronnie thought, the way Anse had gone back on the stuff after breaking his leg. Anse had worked so hard for so many years to keep his boozing under control. And now. Look at him, Ronnie thought sadly. Look at him.

'Little nightcap, bro?' Anse called.

'Sure,' Ronnie said. Why the hell not? 'What are we drinking?'

'Grappa.'

'Grappa,' Ronnie repeated, glancing away and wincing. 'Well, sure, Anse. Sure.' It was a sort of Italian brandy, very harsh, not much to his taste, really. They had a case of it, one of the stranger things in the weird loot they had brought back from that deserted warehouse downtown. Anse would drink anything, though.

Anse poured. 'Say when, bro.'

'When,' said Ronnie, quickly.

Solemnly he clinked glasses with his brother and took a shallow sip. If only to be sociable. He didn't like to see Anse drinking alone. It was ironic, he thought, how the Colonel had always looked upon Anse as a pillar of stability and dependability and virtue, and on him as some kind of wild, disreputable high-living heathen, when in fact Anse was a deeply closeted drunk who had spent his whole adult life struggling desperately against his craving for the sauce and he, for all his high-life tastes and fast-lane companions, had never had the slightest problem with it.

Anse drained his glass and set it down. He picked up the half-empty bottle and stared at it a long while, as though the deepest secrets of the universe were inscribed on its label. When the silence started to drag a little Ronnie said, 'Everything all right, bro?'

'Fine. Fine.'

'But it isn't, is it?'

'What do you think?'

'I don't think anything,' Ronnie said. 'It's been a long day. I don't like to think after ten in the evening. Sometimes I call it quits even earlier than that. – What's eating you now, Anse? The old man? He'll be okay. Not what he once was, but which one of us is? We aren't immortal, you know. But he brightened up plenty when I told him how the vote had turned out today.'

'Have some more?'

'Thanks, no. I'm still working on this.'

'Mind if I?'

Ronnie shrugged. Anse filled his glass practically to the brim.

'This fucking meeting,' Anse said in a low, somber tone, when he had put another goodly slug of the grappa away. 'This whole fucking Resistance, Ronnie.'

'What about it?'

'What a sham! What a miserable idiotic sham! We hold these meetings, and all we're doing is making empty gestures. Spinning our wheels, don't you see? Appointing committees, making studies, cooking up grand plans, sending e-mail about those grand plans to people just as helpless as we are all around the world. That's a Resistance? Are the Entities giving ground before our valiant onslaughts? Is the liberation of Earth practically within our grasp, do you think? Are we doing the slightest fucking thing, really, to achieve it? – There isn't any Resistance, not really. We're just pretending that there is.'

'As long as we go on pretending,' Ronnie said, 'we keep the idea of being free alive. You've heard the Colonel say that a million times. Once we give up even the pretense, we're slaves forever.'

'You really believe that shit, bro?'

Some grappa was needed before replying to that one. Ronnie tried to gulp the stuff without tasting it. 'Yes,' he said, fixing his gaze squarely on Anse's squinting bloodshot eyes. 'Yes, bro, I really do. I don't think it's shit at all.'

Anse laughed. 'You sound so amazingly sincere.'

'I *am* sincere, Anse.'

'Right. Right. You say that very sincerely, too. – You're still a con man at heart, aren't you, bro? Always were, always will be. And very good at it.'

'Watch it, Anse.'

'Am I saying anything other than the truth, bro? You can tell me that you believe the old man's bullshit, sure, but don't ask me to start believing yours, not this late in the game. – Here. Here. Have some more grappa. Do you some good. Oil up your sincerity glands a little more for the next sucker, right?'

He extended the bottle toward Ronnie, who peered at it for perhaps ten seconds while trying to gain control over the anger that was surging upward in him, anger at Anse's drunken mocking accusations and the partial truths that lay not very far beneath their surface, at the Colonel's deterioration, at his own growing sense of mortality as the years went along, at the continued presence of the Entities in the world. At everything. Then, as Anse pushed the grappa bottle even closer, thrusting it practically into his face, Ronnie slapped at it with a hard backhand blow, knocking it out of Anse's hand. The bottle struck Anse across the lip and chin and went bouncing to the floor. A stream of grappa came spilling forth. Anse grunted in fury and burst from his chair, clawing at Ronnie with one hand and trying to swing with the other.

Ronnie pressed one hand against the middle of Anse's chest to hold him at bay and tried to push him back into his chair. Anse, eyes bright now with rage, growled and swung again, with the same futility as before. Ronnie shoved hard. Anse went toppling backward and sat down heavily, just as Peggy came scurrying into the room.

'Hey! Hey, guys! What is this?'

Ronnie looked shamefacedly toward his wife. He could feel his face growing hot with embarrassment. All his anger was gone, now. 'We were discussing today's meeting, is all.'

'I'll bet you were.' She scooped the fallen grappa bottle up, sniffed at it disgustedly, tossed it into a wastebasket. She gave him a withering look. 'Yes, you ought to blush, Ron. Like little boys, the two of you. Little boys who've found their way into their father's liquor closet.'

'It's a little more complicated than that, Peg.'

'Sure it is. Sure.' Then she turned away from him, toward Anse, who sat now with his head bowed, hands covering his face. 'Hey,' she said. 'What's this, Anse?'

He was crying. Great blubbering racking sobs were coming from him. Peggy put an arm around his shoulder and bent close to him, while signalling fiercely with her other hand for Ronnie to get himself out of the room.

'Hey,' Peggy said softly. '*Hey*, now, Anse!'

Once or twice a month, more often if he could manage to scrape up the gas, Steve Gannett descended the mountainside from the ranch and made his way down the battered and dilapidated highway that was Route 101 as far as the city of Ventura, where Lisa would be waiting for him downtown, near the San Buenaventura Mission. Then they would continue on together in her car along the Pacific Coast Highway, past the abandoned Point Mugu Naval Air Station and on into Mugu State Park itself. They had a special place there, a secluded woodsy grove up in the hilly inland part, where they could make love. That was the deal, that he drove as far as Ventura and Lisa would drive the rest of the way. That was only fair, considering the current tight gasoline quotas.

It still amazed Steve that he had a steady girl at all. He had been such a lumpy, ungainly, nerdy kid, fat and awkward, good for very little except working with computers, at which he was very good indeed. Like his father Doug, he had never fitted very well into the Carmichael family, that tribe of crisp, strong, hard, cold-eyed people. Even when they were weak – the way the

Colonel was weak, now, getting so old and vague, or Anse was weak, hitting the bottle whenever he thought nobody was looking – they were still somehow strong. They would give you a look with their blue Carmichael eyes that said, *We come from a long line of soldiers. We understand what the word 'discipline' means. And you are fat and sloppy and lazy, and the only thing you know how to do is fool around with computers.* Even his twin cousins Mike and Charlie had given him that look, and they were only little boys.

But Steve was half Carmichael himself, and by the time he had been living at the ranch a few years that part of his heritage had at last started to show. The outdoor life, the fresh mountain air, the need for everyone to put in some hours of hard manual labor every day, had done the trick. Gradually, very gradually, the baby fat had burned away. Gradually his coordination had improved and he had learned how to run without falling on his face, how to climb a tree, how to drive a car. He would always be chunkier and less agile than his cousins, his hair would always be floppy and unruly and his shirt-tails would always have a way of working their way out of his pants, and his eyes would never be icy Carmichael blue, but always that mousy Gannett brown. Still and all, by the year he turned fifteen he had shaped up in a way that surprised him immensely.

The first real sign that he might actually be going to have a life came when Anse's daughter Jill allowed him to take some sexual liberties with her.

He was sixteen then, and still hideously unsure of himself. She was two years younger, a slim leggy blonde like her mother Carole, handsome, athletic, lively. It would not have occurred to Steve that anything might happen between them. Why would such a gorgeous girl – and one who was his cousin, as well – be interested in *him*? She had never given the slightest sign of caring for him: had, in fact, always been cool toward him, remote. He was just her nerdy cousin Steve, which is to say, nobody in particular, simply someone who happened to live at the ranch. But then, one hot summer day when he was far up the mountain by himself, in a sheltered rocky place out beyond the apple orchard where he liked to come and sit and think, Jill appeared suddenly out of nowhere and said, 'I followed you. I wanted to see where you went when you went off by yourself. Do you mind if I sit down here?'

'Suit yourself.'

'It's pretty up here,' she said. 'Quiet. Real private. What a great view!'

That she had any curiosity about him at all, that she would give even a faint damn about where he might go when he went off by himself, astounded and bewildered him. She settled down beside him on the flat slab of rock from which he could see practically the entire valley. Her proximity was unsettling. All she wore was a halter and a pair of shorts, and a sweet, musky odor of perspiration was coming from her after the steep climb.

Steve had no idea what to say to her. He said nothing.

Abruptly she said, after a time, 'You can touch me, if you like, you know.'

'Touch you?'

'If you like.'

His eyes widened. What was this? Was she serious? Cautiously, as if inspecting an unexploded land mine, he put his hand to her bare knee, gripped it lightly with his fingertips a moment, and then, hearing no objections, moved his hand upward along her long smooth thigh, scarcely allowing himself to draw a breath. He had never felt anything so smooth. He reached the cuff of her shorts and paused there, doubting that his fingers would reach very far beyond that point. And in any case he was afraid to risk the attempt.

'Not my leg,' she said, sounding a little annoyed.

Steve looked up at her. Thunderstruck, he saw that she had opened the clasp of her halter. It slid down to her waist. She had lovely breasts, white as milk, that thrust out straight in front of her. He had seen them before, spying on her one night last summer through her window, but that had been from fifty yards away. He stared now, goggle-eyed, astonished. Jill was looking at him expectantly. He wriggled closer to her on the rock and slipped his right arm around her, bringing his hand up so that it cupped the smooth taut undercurve of her right breast. She made a little hissing sound of pleasure. He gripped a little tighter. He did not dare touch the hard little nipple, fearing it might be tender, fearing he might hurt her. Nor did he try to kiss her or do anything else, though his whole body felt ready to explode with desire.

They sat there that way for a long while. He sensed that she might be as terrified as he was, as confused about what the next move ought to be. And finally she said, shrugging his hand away and primly pulling the fallen halter back into place, 'I'd better go now.'

'Do you have to?'

'I think it's a good idea. But we'll do this again.'

They did. They made appointments to go up to the high outcropping together, elaborate schemes for traversing the routes from opposite sides of the hill. They progressed in easy stages to the full exploration of her body, and then his, and then, one utterly astounding autumn morning, to his sliding himself inside her for a few seconds of gasping excitement followed by a headlong tumble into explosive ecstasy, and then a longer, less frenzied, repetition of the act twenty minutes later.

They did it five or six more times that season, and on a dozen or so very widely scattered occasions over the next couple of years, always at her instigation, never at his. Then they stopped.

The risks were becoming too great. It wasn't hard to imagine what the Colonel would say or do, or her father, or his, if she turned up pregnant. Of course, they could always get married; but they had both heard dire stories about the evils of marriage between cousins, and in any case Steve had no great yearning to be married to Jill. He didn't love her, so far as he comprehended that word, nor did he even feel much affection for her, only gratitude for the sense of confidence in his own maleness that she had given him.

He was disappointed when it ended, but he had never expected it to last anyway. He understood, by then, what had led Jill to him in the first place. It wasn't that she found him attractive – oh, no, hardly that. But the hormones had begun to flow freely through her ripening body, and he was all there was for her at the ranch, the only male under forty other than her brothers and baby Anson. He had always sensed that she was merely using him, that she felt nothing whatever for him. He was convenient, that was all. Almost anyone else would have served in his place. That she had wonderfully transformed his own sorry life by giving her luscious self to him was incidental. It had probably never occurred to her that she was doing any such thing.

Not very flattering to consider; but still, still, whatever her motives, the fact remained that they had done it, that she had met his needs even while he was meeting hers, that she had ushered him into manhood on that hill and he would always be grateful for that.

What Jill had awakened in him, however, could not easily be put back to sleep. Steve began to rove the countryside beyond the ranch, searching for a mate. Everyone in the family understood what he was doing, and no one objected, though he used a lot of precious gasoline doing it. Of all the cousins in his generation – he, Jill, Mike, Charlie, Cassandra, Ron's son Anson – he was the first one reaching adulthood. The only way to avoid inbreeding on the mountaintop was for the clan members to look outward.

But it was definitely inconvenient that when he did find a girl, she was one that lived all the way down the road in Ventura. The pickings were slim along the depopulated coast, though, and even the new and more confident Steve Gannett was not exactly an expert lady-killer. He could hardly come swaggering into some little nearby place like Summerland or Carpinteria, where there might be no more than five or six single girls anyway, and coolly announce that he, the great Steverino, was holding auditions for a mate. So he roved farther and farther afield. And even so he had no luck finding anybody.

Then he met Lisa Clive – not in his travels through the territory but in a way that was much more appropriate to his nature: through the on-line channels, which were open, more or less regularly and reliably, all up and down the coast now. She called herself 'Guinevere', which Steve's Uncle Ron told him was a name out of a famous old story. 'Call yourself Lancelot,' Ron advised. 'You'll get her attention.' He did. They courted at long distance for six months, exchanging quips, programming queries, little fragments of carefully veiled autobiography. Of course, she could have been any age, any sex, behind the line-name that she used. But something authentically youthful and female and definitely pleasing seemed to come through to Steve. He warily let her know, ultimately, that he lived in the vicinity of Santa Barbara and would like to meet her if she were anywhere nearby. She told him that she lived down the coast from him, but not as far as Los Angeles. They agreed to meet in Ventura, outside the Mission, which he supposed would be about halfway between their homes. He was wrong about that: Ventura was actually the place where she lived.

She said she was twenty-four, which was three years older than he was. He lied and told her, as they strolled together along the highway fronting the ocean, that he was twenty-four also; later he learned that she was actually twenty-six, but by then their ages didn't matter. She was pleasant-looking, not at all beautiful the way Jill was beautiful, but certainly attractive. A little on the heavy side, maybe? Well, so was he. She had straight, soft brown hair, a round cheerful face, full lips, a snub nose. Her eyes were bright, alert, warm, friendly. And brown. After all those years spent among the blue-eyed Carmichaels he could love her for the color of her eyes alone.

She lived, she said, with her father and two brothers at the south end of town. In one way or another they all worked for the telephone company, she told him, doing programming work. She seemed not to want to go into details, and he didn't press her. His own father, Steve said, had been a programmer himself before the Conquest, and he allowed as how he himself was pretty skilled in that area too. He showed her his wrist implant. She had one also. He told her that his family now lived by raising crops on the land of his grandfather, a retired army officer. About the Carmichaels' Resistance activities he said nothing, naturally.

He was hesitant about making any sort of physical overtures, and in the end she had to take the initiative, just as Jill had. A kiss goodbye was the best he had managed, after three meetings; but on the fourth, a warm midsummer day, Lisa suggested a visit to a park that she was fond of. It was Point Mugu State Park, farther down the coast. The route took them past several Entity installations, great shining silo-like things along the tops of the hills that flanked the coast road, and then they turned off into the park, he driving and she navigating, and wound up in a secluded oak grove that Steve suspected was a place she had visited more than once before. The ground was thickly carpeted with last year's fallen leaves and a dense layer of leaf-mold beneath; the air was fragrant with the sweet musky odor of natural decay.

They kissed. Her tongue slipped between his lips. She pressed herself very close. She slowly moved her hips from side to side. She led him easily onward, step by step, until he needed no further leading.

Her breasts were heavier than Jill's, and softer, and subject to the laws of gravity in a way that Jill's did not yet seem to be. Her belly was more rounded, her thighs were fuller, her arms and legs shorter, making Jill seem almost boyish in comparison, and when she opened herself to him she held her legs in a different way from Jill, her knees drawn up practically to her chest. All that seemed strange and fascinating to Steve, at first; but then he stopped noticing, stopped comparing. And very soon Lisa became the norm of womanhood for him, the only true yardstick of love. The things he had done with Jill became mere fading memories, odd adolescent amusements, episodes out of ancient history.

They made love every time they were together. She seemed as hungry for it as he was.

They talked, too, before, afterward: talked computers, talked programs, talked of contacts they had sporadically succeeded in making with hackers in the farthest reaches of the conquered world. Put their implants together and exchanged little data tricks. She taught him some things he had never known an implant could do, and he taught her a few. The silent assumption emerged between them that before long they would meet each other's families and begin to plan their life together. But as the relationship moved on into its sixth month, its seventh, its eighth, they never actually got around to bringing each other home for introductions. What they did, mainly, was to meet outside the Mission, drive down to Mugu, into the oak grove, lie down together on the carpet of fallen leaves.

On a day in early spring she said, apropos of nothing at all, 'Have you heard that they're building a wall around Los Angeles?'

'On the freeways, you mean?' He knew about the concrete-block wall that cut Highway 101 in half, a little way beyond Thousand Oaks.

'Not just the roads. Everywhere. A huge wall clear around the whole city.'

'You aren't serious!'

'No? You want to see?'

He had not been any closer to Los Angeles than this park itself since the day, ten years before, that his father and mother had thrown in their lot with the old Colonel at the mountaintop ranch. There was no occasion ever to go there. These days you needed to get an entry permit from LACON, the administrative body that ran the city on behalf of the Entities, for one thing. Besides, the place was said to have become a huge teeming slum, ugly and dangerous; and such contact as was necessary to maintain with Resistance operatives there could be and was maintained via on-line means, safe enough so long as proper coding precautions were observed.

But a wall around all of Los Angeles, if the Entities were really constructing such a thing: that was news, that was something that they needed to know about back at the ranch. The existing limitations on entry and departure were purely bureaucratic ones, a matter of documents and electronic checkpoints. An actual tangible wall would be a surprising new development in the ongoing tightening of Entity control of human life. He wondered why no word of it had reached them from Nat Jackman or one of the other Resistance agents within the city.

'Show me,' Steve said.

Lisa drove. It was a slow, difficult business. They had to take all mountain roads, because of the long-standing blockage on Highway 101 and some new problem on the Pacific Coast Highway just before Malibu, a rock slide during a recent rainy spell that had never been cleared away. She was forced to turn inland at Mulholland Highway, and then to wiggle interminably onward along one narrow potholed road after another, going through sparsely inhabited high country that was rapidly reverting to a primitive state, until at last they emerged onto Highway 101 beyond the Agoura end of the zone where it had been walled off. Steve wondered why the Entities were bothering to have Los Angeles itself surrounded by a wall, when it was this difficult of access already.

'The new wall cuts in at Topanga Canyon Boulevard,' Lisa said, but that name meant nothing to him. They were traveling eastward through steep, hilly countryside along a wide freeway in a relatively good state of repair. There was practically no traffic. He could see that this once had been a heavily populated region. The crumbling ruins of sprawling shopping malls and large residential subdivisions were still apparent everywhere, on both sides of the road.

Just before an exit that was marked Calabasas Parkway Lisa braked suddenly, startling him.

'Oops: sorry. Checkpoint up ahead. I almost forgot.'

'Checkpoint?'

'Nothing to worry about. I've got the password.'

A ramshackle array of wooden sawhorses blocked the freeway before them. A couple of LACON Highway Patrol officers were sitting by the side of the road. As Lisa drew up, one of them wandered out and held a scanner out toward her. She rolled her window down and pressed her implant against its sensor plate. A green light flashed, and the patrolman waved them onward, through the zigzagging assemblage of sawhorses and back onto the open freeway. A routine affair.

'Now,' Lisa said, some minutes later. 'Look there.'

She pointed ahead. And he saw the new wall, rising beyond and below them, where the subsidiary highway labeled Topanga Canyon Boulevard ran at right angles to their freeway.

It was made of square concrete blocks, like the pair that cut a big section out of Highway 101 behind them from Thousand Oaks to Agoura. But this wall didn't simply close off the hundred-foot width of the freeway, as the other ones did. It was a great long dinosaur of a thing that stretched as far as the eye could see, up and down the land. It came curving down out of the region to the northeast, which was or at least once had been a densely occupied suburb, and not only crossed the highway but continued on south of it, disappearing in a gently bending arc that appeared to head on down to the coast.

The wall looked to be about a dozen feet high, Steve thought, judging its height by the size of the men in the work crews bustling about it. It wasn't as easy to guess how thick it was, but it appeared to be seriously substantial, even deeper than it was high: an astoundingly massive barrier, far thicker than any imaginable wall would need to be.

She said, 'It gets to the coast near Pacific Palisades, and runs right down the middle of the Pacific Coast Highway to somewhere around Redondo Beach. Then it turns inland, and goes on eastward past Long Beach, where it peters out. But I hear that they plan to extend it back northward along the route of the Long Beach Freeway until it reaches to around Pasadena, and then they'll close the circuit. It's really only just in the beginning stages, you know. Especially what you see here. There are places off to the north of here where it's already two and three times as high as this section of it in front of us.'

Steve whistled. 'But what's it all *for*? The Entities have us where they want us already, haven't they? Why put in so much effort building a stupid enormous wall around Los Angeles?'

'It isn't *their* effort that's being put in,' Lisa said, and laughed. 'Anyway, who understands anything about what the Entities want? They don't explain anything, you know. They just give a Push, and we do what we're Pushed to do, and that's all there is to it. You know that.'

'Yes. Yes, I do.'

He sat there with her for a long while, numbed by the incomprehensible magnitude of the vast project that was under way before them. Hundreds of workers, swarming about the wall like so many ants, were hard at work lifting new blocks into place with mighty cranes, squaring them off, mortaring them. How high was the wall ultimately going to get? Twenty feet? Thirty? And forty or fifty feet deep? Why? *Why*?

There wasn't enough time for them to go to their secluded grove in the park that day, not if Steve hoped to get back to the ranch at any reasonable hour. But they made love anyway, in the car, twisted around crazily, Lisa's legs splayed up over the back seat as they parked in a turnout along Mulholland – a frenzied, breathless, uncomfortable coupling, but it was unthinkable for him to go home without their having done it. He reached the ranch at ten that evening, rumpled, tired, a little depressed. He had never come back from a day with Lisa depressed before.

As Steve put together a late dinner for himself, his uncle Ron appeared, winked, salaciously pumped his fisted arm back and forth, and said, 'Hey, boy, that was a long day you put in, gone by dawn, back after dark. You do the old razzmatazz a couple of extra times today?'

Steve reddened. 'Come *on*, Ron. Let me be.' But he couldn't help being amused and flattered. Secretly it pleased him that Ron would talk to him this way, one man to another, tacitly acknowledging the fact that his fat, nerdy little nephew Steve had made the transition into manhood.

He had decided some time ago that the jaunty, somehow slightly disreputable Uncle Ron was his favorite member of the family. He had heard, of course, that Ron had been pretty wild when he was younger, involved in all sorts of dodgy and probably illicit financial deals and maneuvers back in the days before the Entities came. But there was no sign that he was involved in any of that stuff now, such of it as might still be possible to carry on.

So far as Steve could see, Ron was the real center of the family: keen-witted and hard-working, a dedicated Resistance leader, probably the true king-pin of the whole operation. In theory Anse was in command now, by direct succession from the aging, increasingly feeble Colonel, who still held the official rank of chairman. But Anse drank. Ronnie *worked*. He was the one who was constantly in touch, thanks to the on-line skills of his brother-in-law Doug and his cousin Paul and his nephew Steve, with Resistance people all around the world, coordinating their findings, keeping everything moving along, as well as anyone could, toward the distant ultimate goal of human liberation. And he was good company, too, Steve thought. So different from the brooding Anse and his own glum, humorless father Doug.

Steve said, grinning up from his soup, 'Did you know they're building a wall all the way around Los Angeles?'

'Been some rumors about that, yes.'

'They're true. I saw it. Lisa took me there. Through the mountains to the far side of the Highway 101 blockade, and then down the highway to where they're doing the construction work. The new wall crosses 101 at a place called Topanga Canyon Boulevard. It's a real monster. You can't believe the size of it, Ron, the height, the width, the way it goes on and on and on.'

Ron's chilly blue eyes were studying him shrewdly.

'There's a LACON checkpoint, isn't there, between Agoura and Calabasas. How were you able to get through it, fella?'

'You know about that?' Steve asked. 'Then you even know about the wall, don't you? And not just from rumors.'

Ron shrugged. 'We try to keep on top of things. We have people out there moving around all the time. – How did you get through the Calabasas checkpoint, Steve?'

'Lisa had the password software. She put her implant right to the highway patrolman's scanner, and –'

'She *what*?' His whole face tightened up. A vein popped into sudden prominence on his forehead.

'Gave the password with her implant. Jesus, Ron, you look absolutely appalled!'

'She lives in Ventura, your girlfriend, right?'

'That's right.'

'All existing entry permits to Los Angeles for Ventura County people and beyond were revoked by LACON a couple of months ago. Except for those people living in the outer counties who work for the Entities and might have reason to commute into the city, and members of their families.'

'Except for – people who work for –'

'My God,' Ron said. Steve felt those eyes of his cutting into him in a way that was almost impossible to bear. 'You know what kind of a girlfriend you've got, boy? You've got yourself a quisling. And she's a computer nut too, right? A real borgmann, I bet. From a whole family of quislings and borgmanns. Oh, kiddo, kiddo, kiddo, what have you done? What have you done?

*   *   *

It was after the time that Richie beat Aissha so severely, and then did worse than that – violated her, raped her – that Khalid definitely decided that he was going to kill an Entity.

Not Richie. An Entity.

It was a turning point in Khalid's relationship with his father, and indeed in Khalid's whole life, and in the life of any number of other citizens of Salisbury, Wiltshire, England, that time when Richie hurt Aissha so. Richie had been treating Aissha badly all along, of course. He treated *everyone* badly. He had moved into her house and had taken possession of it as though it were his own. He regarded her as a servant, there purely to do his bidding, and woe betide her if she failed to meet his expectations. She cooked; she cleaned the house; Khalid understood now that sometimes, at his whim, Richie would make her come into his bedroom to amuse him or his friend Syd or both of them together. And there was never a word of complaint out of her. She did as he wished; she showed no sign of anger or even resentment; she had given herself over entirely to the will of Allah. Khalid, who had found no convincing evidence of Allah's existence, had not. But he had learned the art of accepting the unacceptable from Aissha. He knew better than to try to change what was unchangeable. So he lived with his hatred of Richie, and that was merely a fact of daily existence, like the fact that rain did not fall upward.

Now, though, Richie had gone too far.

Coming home plainly drunk, red-faced, enraged over something, muttering to himself. Greeting Aissha with a growling curse, Khalid with a stinging slap. No apparent reason for either. Demanding his dinner early. Getting it, not liking what he got. Aissha offering mild explanations of why beef had not been available today. Richie shouting that beef bloody well *should* have been available to the household of Richie Burke.

So far, just normal Richie behavior when Richie was having a bad day. Even sweeping the serving-bowl of curried mutton off the table, sending it shattering, thick oily brown sauce splattering everywhere, fell within the normal Richie range.

But then, Aissha saying softly, despondently, looking down at what had been her prettiest remaining sari now spotted in twenty places, 'You have stained my clothing.' And Richie going over the top. Erupting. Berserk. Wrath out of all measure to the offense, if offense there had been.

Leaping at her, bellowing, shaking her, slapping her. Punching her, even. In the face. In the chest. Seizing the sari at her midriff, ripping it away, tearing it in shreds, crumpling them and hurling them at her. Aissha backing away from him, trembling, eyes bright with fear, dabbing at the blood that seeped from her cut lower lip with one hand, spreading the other one out to cover herself at the thighs.

Khalid staring, not knowing what to do, horrified, furious.

Richie yelling. 'I'll stain you, I will! I'll give you a sodding stain!' Grabbing her by the wrist, pulling away what remained of her clothing, stripping her all but naked right there in the dining room. Khalid covering his face. His own grandmother, forty years old, decent, respectable, naked before him: how could he look? And yet how could he tolerate what was happening? Richie dragging her out of the room, now, toward his bedroom, not troubling even to close the door. Hurling her down on his bed, falling on top of her. Grunting like a pig, a pig, a pig, a pig.

I must not permit this.

Khalid's breast surged with hatred: a cold hatred, almost dispassionate. The man was inhuman, a jinni. Some jinn were harmless, some were evil; but Richie was surely of the evil kind, a demon.

His father. An evil jinni.

But what did that make him? What? What? What? What?

Khalid found himself going into the room after them, against all prohibitions, despite all risks. Seeing Richie plunked between Aissha's legs, his shirt pulled up, his trousers pulled down, his bare buttocks pumping in the air. And Aissha staring upward past Richie's shoulder at the frozen Khalid in the doorway, her face a rigid mask of horror and shame: gesturing to him, a repeated brushing movement of her hand through the air, telling him to go away, to get out of the room, not to watch, not to intervene in any way.

He ran from the house and crouched cowering amid the rubble in the rear yard, the old stewpots and broken jugs and his own collection of Arch's empty whiskey bottles. When he returned, an hour later, Richie was in his room, chopping malevolently at the strings of his guitar, singing tunelessly in a low, boozy voice. Aissha was dressed again, moving about in a slow, downcast way, cleaning up the mess in the dining room. Sobbing softly. Saying nothing, not even looking at Khalid as he entered. A sticking-plaster on her lip. Her cheeks looked puffy and bruised. There seemed to be a wall around her. She was sealed away inside herself, sealed from all the world, even from him.

'I will kill him,' Khalid said quietly to her.

'No. That you will not do.' Her voice was deep and remote, a voice from the bottom of the sea.

Aissha gave him a little to eat, a cold chapati and some of yesterday's rice, and sent him to his room. He lay awake for hours, listening to the sounds of the house, Richie's endless drunken droning song, Aissha's barely audible sobs. In the morning nobody said anything about anything.

Khalid understood that it was impossible for him to kill his own father, however much he hated him. But Richie had to be punished for what he had done. And so, to punish him, Khalid was going to kill an Entity.

The Entities were a different matter. They were fair game.

For some time now, on his better days, Richie had been taking Khalid along with him as he drove through the countryside, doing his quisling tasks, gathering information that the Entities wanted to know and turning it over to them by some process that Khalid could not even begin to understand, and by this time Khalid had seen Entities on so many different occasions that he had grown quite accustomed to being in their presence.

And had no fear of them. To most people, apparently, Entities were scary things, ghastly alien monsters, evil, strange; but to Khalid they still were, as they always had been, creatures of enormous beauty. Beautiful the way a god would be beautiful. How could you be frightened by anything so beautiful? How could you be frightened of a god?

They didn't ever appear to notice him at all. Richie would go up to one of them and stand before it, and some kind of transaction would take place. While that was going on, Khalid simply stood to one side, looking at the Entity, studying it, lost in admiration of its beauty. Richie offered no explanations of these meetings and Khalid never asked.

The Entities grew more beautiful in his eyes every time he saw one. They were beautiful beyond belief. He could almost have worshipped them. It seemed to him that Richie felt the same way about them: that he was caught in their spell, that he would gladly fall down before them and bow his forehead to the ground.

And so.

I will kill one of them, Khalid thought.

Because they are so beautiful. Because my father, who works for them, must love them almost as much as he loves himself, and I will kill the thing he loves. He says he hates them, but I think it is not so: I think he loves them, and that is why he works for them. Or else he loves them and hates them both. He may feel the same way about himself. But I see the light that comes into his eyes when he looks upon them.

So I will kill one, yes. Because by killing one of them I will be killing some part of *him*. And maybe there will be some other value in my doing it, besides.

IV

Twenty-Two Years
from Now

These years, the years of alien rule, had been good years for Karl-Heinrich Borgmann. When he was sixteen, living out his dark and lonely adolescent days, he had wanted prestige, power, fame. He was twenty-nine now, and he had them all.

Prestige, certainly.

He knew more about the Entities' communications systems, and probably about the Entities themselves, than anyone else on Earth. That was a widely known fact. Everyone in Prague knew it; perhaps everyone on the planet. He was the master communicator, the conduit through whom the Entities spoke to the people of the world. He was the Maharajah of Data. He was Borgmann the borgmann. There was prestige in that, certainly. You had to respect someone who had achieved what he had achieved, however you might feel about the morality of the achievement.

And power. He had that too, *in excelsis*.

From his glistening office on the top floor of the majestic riverfront building that had once been Prague's Museum of Decorative Arts, he could connect with the Entity net at fifty different points around the world: he, and only he, knew the way in, knew how to insert himself in their data banks, how to swim through the surging currents of those rivers of alien computation. Anyone in the world who wanted to make contact with the Entities for whatever reason, to file a petition, to enroll in their service, to request information from them, had to go through his office, his interface. The Borgmann interface: he had slapped his own name right on it for all to see.

Power, yes. He was, in a way, the master of life and death, here. What he understood, and hardly anyone else did, was that the Entities paid essentially no attention to all those petitions and requests and even the offers of service. They were above all that, mysteriously drifting through levels far beyond human ken. It was he who dealt with most of these people's urgent requests, passing them along to the Entities for decisions that probably would never be made, or, often, interposing his own decisions on the assumption that the decrees he issued were approximately what the Entities would have chosen to do if only they had deigned to pay attention to any of the applications. He who proposed and disposed, he who assigned, transferred, rearranged, reorganized. Whole population sectors were uprooted and moved about on his say-so. Huge public-works projects came into being because he believed that the Entities desired them to exist. Was that not power? Supreme power? Was he not the Entities' viceroy on Earth?

And fame –

Ah. A touchy matter, that. There was fame and then there was fame. Certainly the inventor of the Borgmann interface was world-famous. But Karl-Heinrich knew quite well that his fame was not entirely a positive thing. He was aware that his name had become a common noun, now, in the popular speech of every land: *borgmann*. And what it meant, that word, was 'traitor'. What it meant, that word, was 'judas'.

Well, he could do nothing about that. He was what he was; he had done what he had done. He had no regrets. He had meant no harm. It had all been an intellectual game for him, opening the interface between human computational systems and those of the aliens. A test of his abilities, which he had triumphantly passed. If he had not done it, someone else would have. And if he had never even been born, the world would have been no worse off than it now was. Borgmann or no Borgmann, the Entities still would be here; still would rule, in their unfathomable, almost random way; still would be arranging and rearranging the conquered world in whatever ways they found amusing. He had merely facilitated things a little.

And here he was in this magnificent office paneled with the rarest of exotic woods brought in at infinite expense from the rain forests of South America, up here on top of this wonderful old French Renaissance Revival building, sitting here with a billion koruna worth of state-of-the-art computer hardware of his own design all around him, and the museum's own spectacular collection of glassware and ceramics and silver serving dishes and nineteenth-century furniture still in place behind him in the surrounding hallways.

Karl-Heinrich rarely bothered to look at those things, indeed knew very little about most of them, but they were there for his amusement whenever he felt like strolling amongst them. He had had some of the paintings brought down from the National Gallery on Hradcany hill too, a Holbein and a Cranach and that sexy *Suicide of Lucretia* by Vouet; and his lavish Art Nouveau penthouse apartment a few blocks away was equally satisfactorily decorated with the national art, Renoir, Gauguin, Picasso, Braque. Why not? No one was allowed to go to the museum any more anyway, because it was on the castle grounds, where the Entity command compound was; and did they actually expect him to live in an apartment with bare walls?

Transferring the paintings had been a matter of a few simple keystrokes. Transferring some woman he fancied to his bed was just as easy. A work requisition had to be put through; that was all. The work involved service in the office of Karl-Heinrich Borgmann. You got the order, and you went, no questions asked, though you were only too well aware of what the 'service' entailed. Because the alternative would surely be a lot worse: transfer to a work camp in Antarctica, transfer to sewer-sweeping duty in Novosibirsk, transfer to a latrine-cleaning job at a medical clinic in the middle of Africa. Or, if not you, then something equally terrible for your aged mother, your beloved babe, your husband, your cat.

Karl-Heinrich had not forgotten those evenings, ten years ago, eleven, twelve, when he had wandered disconsolate through the dark streets of Prague, gazing with insatiable longing at the girls he saw walking just ahead of him, or the ones sitting with their beaus in brightly lit cafés, or those standing before their mirrors in third-floor apartments. All of them as inaccessible to him as the inhabitants of alien worlds, those girls were. Then.

Well, he had access to them now. A long procession of them had marched through his bedroom in his years as Borgmann the borgmann. Starting with the girls he had lusted after in school, those of them that had survived the Great Plague: Jarmila and Magda, Eva, Jana, Jaroslava and Ludmila, the other Eva with the flat face and the wonderful bosom, and Osvalda, Vera, Ivana, Maria. Zuzana of the fiery hair. Bozena of the fiery temper. Milada. Jirina. Milena. He had had a long list to work his way through. Glorious Stepanka, alas, had died; he requisitioned her sister Katrina instead. And then Anna, Sophia, Theresa, Josefa. The other Milada, the tall one; the other Ludmila, the short one. And both Martinas. Some came with hatred in their eyes, some came in sullen indifference, some saw his bed as their gateway to special privilege. But they all came. What choice did they have?

Oh, yes, and Barbro Ekelund, too. One of the very first, even before Jarmila and Magda and Eva and the rest. The Swedish girl, the one for whom he had invented the myth of being able to tap into the Entity computers, the spontaneous boast that had been the beginning of all this for him. Barbro of the long slender limbs, the unexpectedly full breasts, the golden hair, the sea-green eyes.

'Why am I here?' she had asked, the first time he requisitioned her.

'Because I love you.'

'You don't even know me. We've never met.'

'Oh, we have, we have. It was in August last year, in the Stare Mesto. You forgot.'

'August. The Stare Mesto.' A blank look.

'And then again at Christmastime. In the street. I wanted to buy you a coffee, but you were too busy.'

'I'm sorry. I don't remember.'

'No. You don't remember. But I do. Please, now, your clothes. Take them off.'

'What?'

'Please. Right now.' He was seventeen, then. Still new at this. Had had only four women up till that point, counting the first, and he had had to pay for that one, and she had been very stupid and smelled of garlic.

'Let me leave here,' she had said. 'I don't want to undress for you.'

'Ah, no, you will have to,' he said. 'Look.' And he went to his computer, and from it came an official labor-requisition form, Barbro Ekelund of Dusni Street, Prague, assigned to hospital orderly duty, the Center for Communicable Diseases, Bucharest, Romania, effective three days hence. It seemed quite authentic. It was quite authentic.

'Am I supposed to believe that this is real?' she asked.

'You should. When you get home today, you'll find that your residence permit has been revoked and your ticket for Bucharest is waiting for you at the station.'

'No. No.'

'Strip, then, please,' he said. 'I love you. I want you.'

So she yielded, because she knew now that she had to. Their lovemaking was chilly and far from wonderful, but he had expected nothing much better. Afterward he revoked her transfer order; and, because he was still new at this then and had some residual human feelings of guilt still in his system, he wrote new orders for her that allowed her a year's entry privileges at the swimming facilities in Modrany, and a season pass for two to the opera house, and extra food coupons for her and her family. She offered him the most rudimentary of thanks for these things, and did not take the trouble of concealing from him the shudder that ran through her as she was dressing to leave.

He had her come back five or six more times. But it was never any good between them, and by then Karl-Heinrich had found others with whom it *was* good, or who at least were able to make him think so; and so he left her in peace after that. At least he had had her, though. That was why he had given himself over to the Entities in the first place, so that he might have Barbro Ekelund; and Karl-Heinrich Borgmann was the sort of person who followed through on his intentions.

Now it was a dozen years later, an August day again, sunny, warm – sweltering, even; and on his screen was the information that a certain Barbro Ekelund was downstairs, desiring to see him, a matter of personal importance that would be of great interest to him.

Could it be? The very same one? It must. How many other

Swedes could there be in Prague, after all? And with that very name.

Visitors here were unusual, except for those people whom Karl-Heinrich summoned to him, and he certainly had not summoned her. Their encounters of long ago had been too bleak, too chilly; he did not look back on them with sentimental fondness or longing. She was nothing more than a phantom out of his past, a wandering ghost. He leaned toward the mouthpiece of his servo and began to order her to be sent away, but cut himself off after half a syllable. Curiosity gnawed at him. Why not see her? For old times' sake despite everything, a reunion with an artifact of his unhappy adolescence. There was nothing to be afraid of. Surely her resentment had died away, after all this time. And she was so close to having been the first woman he had ever possessed: the temptation to see what she looked like today overmastered him.

He told the servo to send her up, and activated the security spy-eyes mounted in his walls, just in case. No one, nothing, could get within his safety perimeter while the security field was on. It was a reasonable precaution for a man in his position to take.

She had changed, had changed a great deal.

Still slender and fair, yes, the golden hair, the sea-green eyes. Still quite tall, of course, taller than he. But her radiant Nordic beauty had faded. Something was gone: the ski-slope freshness, the midnight-sun glow. Little lines at the corners of her eyes, along the sides of her mouth. The splendid shining hair somewhat dulled. Well, she was thirty, now, maybe thirty-one: still young, still quite attractive, actually, but these had been hard years for most people.

'Karl-Heinrich,' she said. Her voice was calm, neutral. She seemed actually to be smiling, though the smile was a distant one. 'It's been a long time, hasn't it? You've done well for yourself.' She gestured broadly, taking in the paneled office, the river view, the array of computer equipment, the wealth of national artistic treasures all about him.

'And you?' he said, more or less automatically. 'How have you been, Barbro?' His own tone sounded unfamiliar to him, oddly cozy. As though they were old friends, as though she were not merely some stranger whose body he had used five or six times, under compulsion, a dozen years before.

A little sigh. 'Not as good as I would wish, to speak the truth,' she said. 'Did you get my letter, Karl-Heinrich?'

'I'm sorry, I don't recall.' He never read his mail, *never*. It was always full of angry screeds, execrations, denunciations, threats.

'It was a request for assistance. A special thing, something only you would really understand.'

His face turned bleak. He realized that he had made a terrible mistake, letting a petitioner get in here to see him in person. He had to get rid of her.

But she was already pulling documents out, unfolding papers in front of him. 'I have a son,' she said. 'Ten years old. You would admire him. He is wonderful with computers, the way you must have been when you were growing up. He knows everything about everything that has to do with them. Gustav, his name is. Look, I have his picture here. A handsome boy.'

He waved it away. 'Listen, Barbro, I'm not in need of any protégés, if that's what you came here to –'

'No. There is a terrible problem. He has been transferred to a work camp in Canada. The order came through last week. Somewhere far in the north, where it is cold all the time, a place where they cut trees down for paper mills. Tell me, Karl-Heinrich, why would they want to send a boy of not even eleven years to a logging camp? Not to work with the computers. It is a straight manual-labor requisition. He will die there. It is surely a mistake.'

'Errors do get made, yes. A lot of these things are purely random.' He saw where this was heading.

He was right.

'Save him,' she said. 'I remember how you wrote out transfer orders for me, long ago. And then changed them. You can do anything. Save my boy, I beg you. I beg you. I'll make it worth your while.'

She was looking at him in a stricken way, eyes fixed, every muscle of her face rigid.

In a low, crooning voice she said, 'I will do anything for you, Karl-Heinrich. You wanted me as a lover, once. I held myself back from you, then, I would not allow myself to please you, but I will be your lover now. Your slave. I will kiss your feet. I will perform any act you ask of me. The most intimate things, whatever you desire. For as long as you want me, I am yours. Just save him, that I beg of you. You are the only one that can.'

She was wearing, on this humid summer day, a white blouse, a short blue skirt. As she spoke she was unbuttoning herself, tossing one garment after another to the floor. The pale heavy mounds of her breasts rose into view. They were glistening with perspiration. Her nostrils flared; her lips drew back in what apparently was meant as a hungry, seductive smile.

I will be your slave. How could she have known? His very fantasy, of so many years ago!

He was beginning to develop a headache. *Save my boy. I beg you I will be your slave.*

Karl-Heinrich didn't want Barbro Ekelund to be his slave, not any more. He didn't want Barbro Ekelund at all. He had yearned for her long ago, yes, desperately, when he was sixteen, and he had her, for whatever that had been worth, and that was that; she was history, she was an archival fact in his memory, and nothing else. He was no longer sixteen. He had no desire for ongoing relationships. He wanted no sentimental reunions with figures out of his past. He was content simply to call women up by computer almost at random, new ones all the time; have them come to him, briefly serve him, disappear forever from his life.

All those troublesome human entanglements, those messy little snarls of dependency and whatnot, that any sort of true personal transaction involved: he had tried to avoid them all his life, had kept himself as far above the worldly fray as any Entity, and yet from time to time he seemed to find himself becoming ensnarled in them anyway, this one wanting a favor, that one, offering some sort of quid pro quo as though he needed one, people pretending they were his friends, his lovers. He had no friends. There was no one he loved. There was, he knew, no one who loved him. That was satisfactory to him. There was nothing Karl-

Heinrich Borgmann needed that he could not simply reach out and take.

Even so, he thought. Be merciful for once. This woman meant something to you for a little while, a long time ago. Give her what she wants, do what needs to be done to save her son, then tell her to put her clothes on and get out of here.

She was naked now. Wriggling provocatively before him, offering him in a way that would have made him delirious with delight many years ago, but which seemed only absurd to him, now. And in another moment she would step within the security perimeter. 'Watch out,' he said. 'My desk area is guarded. If you get any closer, you'll trip the barrier screen. It'll knock you cold.'

Too late.

'Oh!' she cried, a little gasp. And flung up her arms, and went spinning backward.

She had touched the security field, it seemed – at least the fringe of it – and had had a jolt from it. She recoiled from it dramatically. Karl-Heinrich watched her stagger and lurch and crumple and go tumbling to the floor, landing with a hard thump in the middle of the room. There she pulled herself instantly into a little ball, face down in a huddled sobbing heap, her forehead grinding into the ancient Persian carpet from the museum. This was the first time Karl-Heinrich had seen anyone encounter the field. Its effect was even more powerful than he had expected. To his dismay she seemed now to be going into hysterics, her whole body jerking convulsively, her breath coming in wild gulping gasps. That was annoying; annoying and yet somehow sad, too. That she should suffer so.

He wondered what to do. He stood over her, staring down at her twitching naked form, seeing her now as he had seen her in that illicit spy-eye view of all those years ago, the fleshy white buttocks, the slim pale back, the delicate tracery of her spine.

For all his earlier indifference, a surprising touch of desire arose in him now, even in the midst of her agony. Because of it, perhaps. Her vulnerability, her misery, her utter pitifulness; but also that smooth taut rump heaving there, the lovely slender legs coiling beneath her. He knelt beside her and let his hand rest lightly on her shoulder. Her skin was hot, as though she was feverish.

'Look, there's really no problem,' he said gently. 'I'll get you your son back, Barbro. Don't carry on like that. Don't.'

Moans came from her. This was almost like a seizure. He knew that he should send for help.

She was trying to say something. He could not make out the words, and leaned closer still. Her long arms were splayed out wide, the left hand drumming in torment on the floor, the other one clutching at the air with quivering fingers. Then, suddenly, she was turning, rolling over to face him, jerking and twitching no longer, and there was a ceramic knife in that outstretched hand, arriving there as though by magic – pulled out of thin air? Out of her pile of discarded garments? – and, utterly calm and poised, she rose toward him in a single smooth movement and thrust the blade with extreme force, with astonishing strength, deep into his lower abdomen.

Pulled it upward. Brought it ripping like an irresistible force through his internal organs until it came clinking up against the cage of his ribs.

He grunted and clasped his hands to the gaping wound. He could barely cover it with his ten outspread fingers. Surprisingly, there was no pain yet, only a dull sense of shock. She rolled backward from him and sprang to her feet, looming over him like a naked avenging demon.

'I have no son,' she said vindictively, biting off the edges of the words, as his eyes began to dim.

Karl-Heinrich nodded. Blood was spouting from him, covering the Persian carpet with a pool of blood. He attempted to tell the servo to send help, but he found himself unable to make a sound. His mouth opened and closed, opened and closed, in soft furry silence. In any case what good would calling for help do? He could feel himself already dying. His strength was leaving him with every spurt. Eyesight growing blurry, inner systems shutting down. He was finished, a dead man at twenty-nine. He was surprised how little he cared. Perhaps that was what dying was like.

So they had caught up with him at last.

How odd that she would be the one. How appropriate.

'I've dreamed of this for twelve years,' the lovely assassin said. 'We all have. What joy it is to see you like this now, Borgmann.' And said again, this time making the name sound like the curse it had become: '*Borgmann.*'

Yes. Of course. That was *borgmann*, no capital letter.

She had killed him, all right.

But there was consolation all the same, he told himself. He would die famous. His very name was part of the language now; that he knew; that knowledge he hugged lovingly close to himself as his life dwindled away. He would be dead in a few moments more, but his name – ah, his name – that would be immortal, that would march on through human history forever. *Borgmann . . . borgmann . . . borgmann.*

The baby was a girl. Steve and Lisa named her Sabrina Amanda Gannett. Everyone at the ranch came around to go *ooh* and *ahh* and *kitchy-koo*, as the cultural norms demanded.

But there was an enormous amount of muddle and turmoil before things got to that point, of course.

First there was the awkward business of Lisa's family's quisling affiliations for Steve to deal with. So far as his uncle Ron was concerned, that was a simple matter. 'You have to dump her, boy, that's all there is to it. Carmichaels just can't hang out with quislings. They just *can't*. – Don't give me that stricken expression, my friend. Out of all the pussy there is for you to find in California, why did you have to wind up with one of *them*?'

That, though, was Ron, who was cool and smooth and handsome and who over the years had had any number of girlfriends, dozens of them, maybe hundreds, and at least a couple of wives too, before meeting up with Peggy and deciding to mend his wandering ways. Easy enough for him to say: *dump her*. What would someone as magnetic and charming as Ron understand, really, about poor pasty-faced Steve Gannett, who didn't know how to keep his own shirt-tails tucked in and whose entire sex life up till the time he had met Lisa had consisted of serving as an animated dildo for his heartless cousin Jill? Did Ron think that it would really be so easy for him to toss Lisa back into the pool and find himself another girlfriend just like that, half an hour later?

Besides, he *loved* Lisa. She was important to him in a way that nobody ever had been before. He lived for their meetings, their trips to Point Mugu Park, their delicious sweaty grapplings on that carpet of fallen leaves beneath the oak trees. He couldn't imagine life without her. Nor did he see how he could bring himself to discard her, the way Jill had discarded him.

How, though, was he going to work all this out?

'I've got to see you,' he told her, a couple of days after their visit to the Topanga Canyon Boulevard construction site. 'Right away. It's essential.' But he didn't have the ghost of an idea of what he was going to say to her.

He drove blindly southward at top velocity over the battered coastal highway, giving no heed to potholes, cracks, dips and curves, and other such trifling obstacles. When he got to Mission San Buenaventura, Lisa was waiting out in front, sitting in her car. She smiled pleasantly as he approached, just as though this were one of their ordinary dates, though it was so soon after their last meeting that she should have suspected something. That cheery, expectant smile of hers made everything just that much worse. She opened the door on the passenger side for him and he slipped in beside her, but when she began to start the engine he caught her by the wrist and stopped her.

'No, let's not go down to the park. Let's just stay here and talk, okay?'

She looked startled. 'Is something wrong?'

'Plenty's wrong, yes,' he said, allowing the words to come out without pausing to form them in his mind. 'I've been thinking, Lisa. About how we got through the checkpoint, and all. How you happened to have the password, when practically all the LACON entry permits for Los Angeles have been revoked.' He could hardly bear to look straight at her. He had to force himself; and, even so, his gaze kept sliding away from her eyes toward her cheek or her chin. Surprisingly, she seemed very calm, staring steadily back at him, even when he let the next string of words come blurting forth: 'Lisa, the only way you could have had that passport would be if you're a quisling, isn't that so? Or know someone who is?'

'That's an ugly word, quisling.'

'Well, collaborator, then. Is that any better?'

She shrugged. She was still strangely calm, though now her face seemed a little flushed. 'My father works for the telephone company, and so do my brothers, and so do I. You know that.'

'Doing what?'

'You know that too. Programming.'

'And the phone company: what's its relationship to LACON?'

'LACON controls all communications networks in and around the Los Angeles Basin, from Long Beach to Ventura. Certainly you would know that.'

'So someone who works for the telephone company in this county actually works for LACON, isn't that so?'

'You might say so, yes.'

'And therefore,' said Steve, with a sense that he was pitching himself off the edge of a high cliff, 'you and your family work for LACON, and, since LACON is the human administrative arm of the alien occupying powers, therefore you all can be regarded as quis – as collaborators. Yes?'

'Why are you grilling me like this, Steve?' Not at all indignant. Merely prompting him to speak the next line. As though she had expected this conversation to come, sooner or later.

'I have to know these things.'

'Well, you *do* know them, now. Like thousands and thousands of other people, my family earns its living by supplying services to the beings that happen to rule our planet. I don't see anything wrong with that, really. It's just our job. If we didn't do it, somebody else would, and the Entities would still be here, only my family and I would have a much harder time keeping things together. If you have any problem with that, you ought to say so right now.'

'I do have a problem with it. I'm with the Resistance.'

'I know that, Steve.'

'You do?'

'You're part of the Carmichael family. Your mother is old

Colonel Carmichael's daughter. You live up on top of that mountain behind Santa Barbara.'

He blinked at her, amazed.

'How do you know all that?'

'You think you're the only one who knows how to trace back a communications line? I'm with the phone company, remember.'

'So you knew all along,' he said, lost now in bewilderment. 'Practically from the start, you were aware that I'm Resistance, and it didn't bother you, even though you're a qu –'

'Don't say that word again.'

'Someone who's willing to work for *them*.'

'Someone who sees no sensible alternatives, Steve. They've been here, what, fifteen years, now? What has your Resistance accomplished in all that time? A lot of talk, is all. And meanwhile the Entities are as much in control as the day they turned all the power off, and they've taken over every aspect of our lives.'

'With the help of people like –'

'So? What's the alternative? They're here. They run things. They own us. We aren't going to kick them out, not ever. That's a fact of life. So we need to get on with our lives, to do our jobs, whatever our jobs might be.' She was looking at him in a level, uncompromising way, forcing him toward telling her whatever it was that he had come down here to tell her today. But he had not known, setting out that morning, what that was going to be.

Suddenly he knew it now. He let himself say it. The words came rolling from him like a sentence of death.

'We can't go on seeing each other, Lisa. That's all there is to it. Your family and mine, they're just incompatible. We work to overthrow the Entities and you work to make things easier for them.'

She met his feverish stare unblinkingly. 'And why should that matter?'

'It does. It simply does. We have our family traditions, and they're pretty stiff stuff. You ought to see my grandfather, the Colonel. He's getting a little senile, maybe, but he has flashes when he's his old self, and then he makes the grandest speeches about liberty, freedom, the need never to forget what we were before the Entities came.'

'I agree with that. I think it's important to remember what it was like to be free.'

'He means it, though.'

'So do I. But there's nothing we can do about it. We can't turn time backwards. The Entities own the world and nothing we do is going to change that.'

They were getting nowhere. He felt as though he were breaking in half.

'There's no sense arguing about it,' he said. 'All I know is that I don't see how we can go on, your family collaborating, mine resisting. There couldn't ever be any contact between the families. How could we have any life together, like that?'

'I don't know,' she said. 'But there's one thing I ought to tell you, Steve –'

'Oh, Jesus, Lisa! You're not –'

Pregnant, yes. The old business of the Capulets and the Montagues, but with one extra little devastating twist.

Her self-possession now disintegrated. So did his, such as it was. She began to cry, and he pulled her head against his chest and he began to cry too, and the astonishing thought came to him of the brown-eyed child that was sprouting in her belly, and of the improbability that so hopeless a nerd as he had been had actually fathered a baby; and he knew beyond doubt that he loved this woman and meant to marry her and stand beside her, no matter what.

But that took some doing. He returned to the ranch and called Ron aside and told him of this newest development; and Ron, pensive and somber and not at all jaunty now, told him to sit tight and went off to talk to his sister Rosalie. Who after a time called Steve to her, and quizzed him extensively about his entire relationship with Lisa, not so much the sex part as the emotional part, his feelings, his intentions.

He amazed himself with the forthrightness, the directness, the sheer *adulthood* of his own responses. No hemming, no hawing, no subterfuges, no standing on one leg and then the other. He came right out and said he loved Lisa. He told his mother that it made him terribly happy to know that there was going to be a child. He said that he had no intention of abandoning her.

'You'll stick by her even if you have to leave the ranch?'

'Why would I let that interfere?' he asked.

She seemed oddly pleased to hear that. But then she was quiet for a long while. Her face grew sad. 'What a sorry mess this is, Steve. What a mess.'

There were whispered family conferences all week long. His mother and her two brothers; the three of them and his father; Steve with Ron again, with Anse, with his mother, with Paul, with Peggy. He sensed that Ron, who had told him so bluntly and uncompromisingly to rid himself of Lisa, was coming around to a more sympathetic position, perhaps under some pressure from Peggy; that his mother was of several minds about the problem, though more on his side than not; that Anse seemed mainly angry at being troubled by so complicated a business as this. During this time, Steve was forbidden to engage in any communications operations on behalf of the Resistance. Was forbidden, indeed, to go anywhere near a computer. Which cut him off from communication with Lisa. Just to make certain, his father wrote a blocking command into the system that guaranteed he could not have access to it; and Steve, good as he was, knew he could not countermand a block written by Doug. Not that he would dare, not in this situation.

He wondered what was going through Lisa's mind. He had promised her, as they parted in Ventura, that he would work something out with his family. But what? What?

It was the longest week of his life. He spent it roaming the hillside, sitting for long hours on the rocky outcropping where Jill once had followed him and made use of him. That seemed a million years ago. Jill now paid almost no attention to him at all. If she had any inkling of the pickle he was in, she gave no indication of it to him, though he overheard her giggling with her brothers Charlie and Mike, and was sure that it was his situation that they were giggling over.

Finally Ron came to him and said, 'The Colonel wants to talk to you.'

The Colonel was frail, now. He had grown very thin and had a tremor in his hands, and used a walking-stick when he moved about. But he moved about infrequently; he spent most of his time these days sitting quietly in his chair near the edge of the patio, looking out over the valley, with a lap-robe spread across him except on the very warmest days.

'Sir?' Steve said, and stood before him and waited.

The Colonel's eyes, at least, had lost none of their old force. He studied Steve for an intolerably long time, staring, staring, while Steve drew himself up as straight as he knew how to hold himself, and waited. And waited.

And at last the Colonel spoke. 'Well, boy. Is it true that you're going to sell us out to the Entities?'

It was a monstrous question; but there was something in his eyes that told Steve that it was not to be taken too seriously. Or so Steve hoped.

'No, sir. It's not true in the slightest, and I hope no one has been telling you anything of the kind.'

'She *is* a quisling, isn't she, though? She and her whole family?'

'Yes, sir.'

'You knew that when you became involved with her?'

'No, sir. Not even remotely. I didn't realize it until the other day, when she got us through a LACON checkpoint with a password that she shouldn't have been able to have.'

'Ah. But she was aware all along that you were a Carmichael?'

'Evidently so.'

'And consorted with you for the sake of infiltrating the ranch and betraying us to the Entities, do you think?'

'No, sir. Absolutely not. It's not really a secret that this is a Resistance headquarters, you know, sir. I think even the Entities must be aware of that. But in any case, there was never a word out of Lisa that indicated to me that she had any such dark intentions.'

'Ah. Then it was just an innocent little romantic thing, what went on between you and her?'

Steve reddened. 'In truth, not all that innocent, sir, I would have to admit.'

The Colonel said, chuckling, 'So I've been given to understand. When is the baby due?'

'Around six months from now.'

'And then what?'

'What do you mean, sir?'

'I mean, do you leave the ranch to live with her, then, or are we supposed to take her in here?'

Flustered, Steve said, 'Why, I don't know, sir. It's up to the family to decide, not to me.'

'And if the family tells you that you're to give up the woman and the baby and never see either one of them again?'

The fierce old blue eyes drilled deep.

After a moment's silence Steve said, 'I don't think I would go along with that, sir.'

'You love her that much?'

'I love her, yes. And I have a responsibility to the child.'

'Indeed. That you do. – So you would go to live among quislings if need be, eh? But would they take you in, do you think, knowing that you were an agent of the Resistance?'

Steve moistened his lips. 'What if we were to take Lisa in, instead?'

'To spy on us, you mean?'

'I don't mean that at all. It's just a job for her, working for them. She doesn't see it as working for the Entities at all, just for the phone company, which is an arm of LACON, which of course is the Entity puppet administration down there. There's nothing ideological about her. She doesn't like having the Entities here any more than we do. She just doesn't see what we can do about it, so she does her job and doesn't think about such things. If she came here, she'd have no further contact with the other side.'

'Including her father? Her brothers?'

'I suppose she'd speak with them, visit them sometimes, maybe. But there's no reason in the world why she would reveal anything about ranch activities to them or anyone else.'

'And so you ask us – infatuated as you are, blinded by love – to accept a spy into our midst simply because you've managed to make her pregnant,' said the Colonel. 'Do I have it right?'

Steve had a sense of having being played with throughout the entire interview. It seemed to him that the Colonel, kindly though he had been during most of this, had been testing him, primarily, trying to see how he reacted under pressure. Taking this position and that one, now sympathetic, now hostile, poking at him here, poking at him there, making harsh assumptions, raising damning hypotheses, checking things out from all angles. But plainly the old man's mind was already made up, and not in his favor. How could he possibly allow a girl from a quisling family into the ranch?

There was no point in being diplomatic any longer, Steve saw.

Taking a deep breath, he said, 'No, sir, you *don't* have it right. I may be infatuated, yes, but I think I know her pretty well, and I don't see her as a danger to us in any way. I ask you to take her in because she's going to bring the next member of this family into the world, and this is where she belongs, because I belong here, and I want my wife and child to be here with me. If they don't belong here, I don't either. And I'm prepared to leave the ranch forever if that's what I have to do.'

The Colonel did not reply. His face was expressionless, unreadable. It was as though Steve had not spoken at all.

And the silence extended itself to an unendurable length. Steve wondered if he had gone too far, had offended the stern old warrior with his bluntness and dealt a fatal blow to his case. Then he started to wonder whether the old man had simply fallen asleep with his eyes open.

'Well, then,' the Colonel said, at last, his face coming to life, even something like a twinkle entering the stern chilly eyes. 'If that's how it is, do you mind if we have Ron meet with her and get some sort of reading on her before we make a final decision about her coming here?'

Steve gasped. 'You'll allow her into the ranch, then?'

'If Ron thinks that we should, yes. Yes, I will.'

'Oh, sir! Oh! Oh, sir, sir, sir – ! '

'Easy, boy. Nothing's been settled yet, you know.'

'But it'll work out. I know that it will. Ron's going to see right away what kind of a person she is. He'll love her. You all will. – And I want to tell you here and now, grandfather, that if the baby is a boy, we're naming him for you. There'll be one more Anson at the ranch: Anson Gannett, this one will be. Anson *Carmichael* Gannett. That's a promise, grandfather.'

*   *   *

The baby, though, was a girl. Sabrina Amanda Gannett, then, after Lisa's mother and grandmother. The next one was a girl, too, two years later, and they named her Irene, for the Colonel's long-dead wife, the grandmother whom Steve had never known. Anson Carmichael Gannett didn't get himself born for another three years, coming into the world finally by a neat coincidence on the Colonel's 83rd birthday, which occurred in the twenty-first year after the Conquest. 'You're going to be the greatest computer genius of all time,' Steve told the new baby, as he lay red-faced and gurgling, two hours old, in his weary mother's arms. 'And a shining hero of the Resistance, too.'

Those would turn out to be pretty accurate prophecies. But not quite in the ways that Steve was expecting.

Richie Burke said, 'Look at this goddamned thing, will you, Ken? Isn't it the goddamnedest fantastic piece of shit anyone ever imagined?'

They were in what had once been the main dining room of the old defunct restaurant. It was early afternoon. Aissha was elsewhere, Khalid had no idea where. His father was holding something that seemed something like a rifle, or perhaps a highly streamlined shotgun, but it was like no rifle or shotgun he had ever seen. It was a long, slender tube of greenish-blue metal with a broad flaring muzzle and what might have been some type of gunsight mounted midway down the barrel and a curious sort of computerized trigger arrangement on the stock. A one-of-a-kind sort of thing, custom made, a home inventor's pride and joy.

'Is it a weapon, would you say?'

'A weapon? A weapon? What the bloody hell do you think it is, boy? It's a fucking Entity-killing gun! Which I confiscated this very day from a nest of conspirators over Warminster way. The whole batch of them are under lock and key this very minute, thank you very much, and I've brought Exhibit A home for safe keeping. Have a good look, lad. Ever seen anything so diabolical?'

Khalid realized that Richie was actually going to let him handle it. He took it with enormous care, letting it rest on both his outstretched palms. The barrel was cool and very smooth, the gun lighter than he had expected it to be.

'How does it work, then?'

'Pick it up. Sight along it. You know how it's done. Just like an ordinary gunsight.'

Khalid put it to his shoulder, right there in the room. Aimed at the fireplace. Peered along the barrel.

A few inches of the fireplace were visible in the crosshairs, in the most minute detail. Keen magnification, wonderful optics. Touch the right stud, now, and the whole side of the house would be blown out, was that it? Khalid ran his hand along the butt.

'There's a safety on it,' Richie said. 'The little red button. There. That. Mind you don't hit it by accident. What we have here, boy, is nothing less than a rocket-powered grenade gun. A bomb-throwing machine, virtually. You wouldn't believe it, because it's so skinny, but what it hurls is a very graceful little projectile that will explode with almost incredible force and cause an extraordinary amount of damage, altogether extraordinary. I know because I tried it. It was amazing, seeing what that thing could do.'

'Is it loaded now?'

'Oh, yes, yes, you bet your little brown rump it is! Loaded and ready! An absolutely diabolical Entity-killing machine, the product of months and months of loving work by a little band of desperados with marvelous mechanical skills. As stupid as they come, though, for all their skills. – Here, boy, let me have that thing before you set it off somehow.'

Khalid handed it over.

'Why stupid?' he asked. 'It seems very well made.'

'I said they were skillful. This is a goddamned triumph of miniaturization, this little cannon. But what makes them think they could kill an Entity at all? Don't they imagine anyone's ever tried? Can't be done, Ken, boy. Nobody ever has, nobody ever will.'

Unable to take his eyes from the gun, Khalid said obligingly, 'And why is that, sir?'

'Because they're bloody unkillable!'

'Even with something like this? Almost incredible force, you said, sir. An extraordinary amount of damage.'

'It would fucking well blow an Entity to smithereens, it would, if you could ever hit one with it. Ah, but the trick is to succeed in firing your shot, boy! Which cannot be done. Even as you're taking your aim, they're reading your bloody mind, that's what they do. They know exactly what you're up to, because they look into our minds the way we would look into a book. They pick up all your nasty little unfriendly thoughts about them. And then – bam! – they give you the bloody Push, and you're done for, piff paff poof. We know of four cases, at least. Attempted Entity assassination. Trying to take a shot as an Entity went by. Found the bodies, the weapons, just so much trash by the roadside.' Richie ran his hands up and down the gun, fondling it almost lovingly. ' – This gun here, it's got an unusually great range, terrific sight, will fire upon the target from an enormous distance. Still wouldn't work, I wager you. They can do their telepathy on you from three hundred yards away. Maybe five hundred. Who knows, maybe a thousand. Still, a damned good thing that we broke this ring up in time. Just in case they could have pulled it off somehow.'

'It would be bad if an Entity was killed, is that it?' Khalid asked.

Richie guffawed. 'Bad? Bad? It would be a bloody cata-strophe. You know what they did, the one time anybody managed to damage them in any way? No, how in hell would you know? It was right around the moment you were getting born. Some buggerly American idiots launched a laser attack from space on an Entity building. Maybe killed a few, maybe didn't, but the Entities paid us back by letting loose a plague on us that wiped out damn near half the people in the world. Right here in Salisbury they were keeling over like flies. Had it myself. Thought I'd die. Damned well hoped I *would*, I felt so bad. Then I arose from my bed of pain and threw it off. But we don't want to risk bringing down another plague, do we, now? Or any other sort of miserable punishment that they might choose to inflict. Because they certainly will inflict one. One thing that has been clear from the beginning is that our masters will take no shit from us, no, lad, not one solitary molecule of shit.'

He crossed the room and unfastened the door of the cabinet that had held Khan's Mogul Palace's meager stock of wine in the long-gone era when this building had been a licensed restaurant. Thrusting the weapon inside, Richie said, 'This is where it's going to spend the night. You will make no reference to its presence when Aissha gets back. I'm expecting Arch to come here tonight, and you will make no reference to it to him, either. It is a top secret item, do you hear me? I show it to you because I love you, boy, and because I want you to know that your father has saved the world this day from a terrible disaster, but I don't want a shred of what I have shared with you just now to reach the ears of another human being. Or another inhuman being for that matter. Is that clear, boy? Is it?'

'I will not say a word,' said Khalid.

And said none. But thought quite a few.

All during the evening, as Arch and Richie made their methodical way through Arch's latest bottle of rare pre-Conquest whiskey, salvaged from some vast horde found by the greatest of good luck in a Southampton storehouse, Khalid clutched to his own bosom the knowledge that there was, right there in that cabinet, a device that was capable of blowing the head off an Entity, if only one could manage to get within firing range without announcing one's lethal intentions.

Was there a way of achieving that? Khalid had no idea.

But perhaps the range of this device was greater than the range of the Entities' mind-reading capacities. Or perhaps not. Was it worth the gamble? Perhaps it was. Or perhaps not.

Aissha went to her room soon after dinner, once she and Khalid had cleared away the dinner dishes. She said little these days, kept mainly to herself, drifted through her life like a sleepwalker. Richie had not laid a violent hand on her again, since that savage evening several years back, but Khalid understood that she still harbored the pain of his humiliation of her, that in some ways she had never really recovered from what Richie had done to her that night. Nor had Khalid.

He hovered in the hall, listening to the sounds from his father's room until he felt certain that Arch and Richie had succeeded in drinking themselves into their customary stupor. Ear to the door: silence. A faint snore or two, maybe.

He forced himself to wait another ten minutes. Still quiet in there. Delicately he pushed the door, already slightly ajar, another few inches open. Peered cautiously within.

Richie slumped head down at the table, clutching in one hand a glass that still had a little whiskey in it, cradling his guitar between his chest and knee with the other. Arch on the floor opposite him, head dangling to one side, eyes closed, limbs sprawled every which way. Snoring, both of them. Snoring. Snoring. Snoring.

Good. Let them sleep very soundly.

Khalid took the Entity-killing gun now from the cabinet. Caressed its satiny barrel. It was an elegant thing, this weapon. He admired its design. He had an artist's eye for form and texture and color, did Khalid: some fugitive gene out of forgotten antiquity miraculously surfacing in him after a dormancy of centuries, the eye of a Gandharan sculptor, of a Rajput architect, a Gujerati miniaturist coming to the fore in him after passing through all those generations of the peasantry. Lately he had begun doing little sketches, making some carvings. Hiding everything away so that Richie would not find it. That was the sort of thing that might offend Richie, his taking up such piffling pastimes. Sports, drinking, driving around: those were proper amusements for a man.

On one of his good days last year Richie had brought a bicycle home for him: a startling gift, for bicycles were rarities nowadays, none having been available, let alone manufactured, in England in ages. Where Richie had obtained it, from whom, with what brutality, Khalid did not like to think. But he loved his bike. Rode long hours through the countryside on it, every chance he had. It was his freedom; it was his wings. He went outside now, carrying the grenade gun, and carefully strapped it to the bicycle's basket.

He had waited nearly three years for this moment to make itself possible.

Nearly every night nowadays, Khalid knew, one could usually see Entities traveling about on the road between Salisbury and Stonehenge, one or two of them at a time, riding in those cars of theirs that floated a little way above the ground on cushions of air. Stonehenge was a major center of Entity activities nowadays and there were more and more of them in the vicinity all the time. Perhaps there would be one out there this night, he thought. It was worth the chance: he would not get a second opportunity with this captured gun that his father had brought home.

About halfway out to Stonehenge there was a place on the plain where he could have a good view of the road from a little copse several hundred yards away. Khalid had no illusion that hiding in the copse would protect him from the mind-searching capacities the Entities were said to have. If they could detect him at all, the fact that he was standing in the shadow of a leafy tree would not make the slightest difference. But it was a place to wait, on this bright moonlit night. It was a place where he could feel alone, unwatched.

He went to it. He waited there.

He listened to night-noises. An owl; the rustling of the breeze through the trees; some small nocturnal animal scrabbling in the underbrush.

He was utterly calm.

Khalid had studied calmness all his life, with his grandmother Aissha as his tutor. From his earliest days he had watched her stolid acceptance of poverty, of shame, of hunger, of loss, of all kinds of pain. He had seen her handling the intrusion of Richie Burke into her household and her life with philosophical detachment, with stoic patience. To her it was all the will of Allah, not to be questioned. Allah was less real to Khalid than He was to Aissha, but Khalid had drawn from her her infinite patience and tranquility, at least, if not her faith in God. Perhaps he might find his way to God later on. At any rate, he had long ago learned from Aissha that yielding to anguish was useless, that inner peace was the only key to endurance, that everything must be done calmly, unemotionally, because the alternative was a life of unending chaos and suffering. And so he had come to understand from her that it was possible even to hate someone in a calm, unemotional way. And had contrived thus to live calmly, day by day, with the father whom he loathed.

For the Entities he felt no loathing at all. Far from it. He had never known a world without them, the vanished world where humans had been masters of their own destinies. The Entities, for him, were an innate aspect of life, simply *there*, as were hills and trees, the moon, or the owl who roved the night above him now, cruising for squirrels or rabbits. And they were very beautiful to behold, like the moon, like an owl moving silently overhead, like a massive chestnut tree.

He waited, and the hours passed, and in his calm way he began to realize that he might not get his chance tonight, for he knew he needed to be home and in his bed before Richie awakened and could find him and the weapon gone. Another hour, two at most, that was all he could risk out here.

Then he saw turquoise light on the highway, and knew that an Entity vehicle was approaching, coming from the direction of Salisbury. It pulled into view a moment later, carrying two of the creatures standing serenely upright, side by side, in their strange wagon that floated on a cushion of air.

Khalid beheld it in wonder and awe. And once again marveled, as ever, at the elegance of these Entities, their grace, their luminescent splendor.

How beautiful you are! Oh, yes. Yes.

They moved past him on their curious cart as though traveling on a river of light, and it seemed to him, dispassionately studying the one on the side closer to him, that what he beheld here was surely a jinni of the jinn: Allah's creature, a thing made of smokeless fire, a separate creation. Which none the less must in the end stand before Allah in judgment, even as we.

How beautiful. How beautiful.

I love you.

He loved it, yes. For its crystalline beauty. A jinni? No, it was a higher sort of being than that; it was an angel. It was a being of pure light – of cool clear fire, without smoke. He was lost in rapt admiration of its angelic perfection.

Loving it, admiring it, even worshipping it, Khalid calmly lifted the grenade gun to his shoulder, calmly aimed, calmly stared through the gun-sight. Saw the Entity, distant as it was, transfixed perfectly in the crosshairs. Calmly he released the safety, as Richie had inadvertently showed him how to do. Calmly put his finger to the firing stud.

His soul was filled all the while with love for the beautiful creature before him as – calmly, calmly, calmly – he pressed the stud. He heard a whooshing sound and felt the weapon kicking back against his shoulder with astonishing force, sending him thudding into a tree behind him and for a moment knocking the breath from him; and an instant later the left side of the beautiful creature's head exploded into a cascading fountain of flame, a shower of radiant fragments. A greenish-red mist of what must be alien blood appeared and went spreading outward into the air.

The stricken Entity swayed and fell backward, dropping out of sight on the floor of the wagon.

In that same moment the second Entity, the one that was riding on the far side, underwent so tremendous a convulsion that Khalid wondered if he had managed to kill it, too, with that single shot. It stumbled forward, then back, and crashed against the railing of the wagon with such violence that Khalid imagined he could hear the thump. Its great tubular body writhed and shook, and seemed even to change color, the purple hue deepening almost to black for an instant and the orange spots becoming a fiery red. At so great a distance it was hard to be sure, but Khalid thought, also, that its leathery hide was rippling and puckering as if in a demonstration of almost unendurable pain.

It must be feeling the agony of its companion's death, he realized. Watching the Entity lurch around blindly on the platform of the wagon in what had to be terrible pain, Khalid's soul flooded with compassion for the creature, and sorrow, and love. It was unthinkable to fire again. He had never had any intention of killing more than one; but in any case he knew that he was no more capable of firing a shot at this stricken survivor now than he would be of firing at Aissha.

During all this time the wagon had been moving silently

onward as though nothing had happened; and in a moment more it turned the bend in the road and was gone from Khalid's sight, down the road that led toward Stonehenge.

He stood for a while watching the place where the vehicle had been when he had fired the fatal shot. There was nothing there now, no sign that anything had occurred. *Had* anything occurred? Khalid felt neither satisfaction nor grief nor fear nor, really, any emotion of any other sort. His mind was all but blank. He made a point of keeping it that way, knowing he was as good as dead if he relaxed his control even for a fraction of a second.

Strapping the gun to the bicycle basket again, he pedaled quietly back toward home. It was well past midnight; there was no one at all on the road. At the house, all was as it had been; Arch's car parked in front, the front lights still on, Richie and Arch snoring away in Richie's room.

Only now, safely home, did Khalid at last allow himself the luxury of letting the jubilant thought cross his mind, just for a moment, that had been flickering at the threshold of his consciousness for an hour:

Got you, Richie! Got you, you bastard!

He returned the grenade gun to the cabinet and went to bed, and was asleep almost instantly, and slept soundly until the first bird-song of dawn.

In the tremendous uproar that swept Salisbury the next day, with Entity vehicles everywhere and platoons of the glossy balloon-like aliens that everybody called Spooks going from house to house, it was Khalid himself who provided the key clue to the mystery of the assassination that had occurred in the night.

'You know, I think it might have been my father who did it,' he said almost casually, in town, outside the market, to a boy named Thomas whom he knew in a glancing sort of way. 'He came home yesterday with a strange sort of big gun. Said it was for killing Entities with, and put it away in a cabinet in our front room.'

Thomas would not believe that Khalid's father was capable of such a gigantic act of heroism as assassinating an Entity. No, no, no, Khalid argued eagerly, in a tone of utter and sublime disingenuousness: he did it, I know he did it, he's always talked of wanting to kill one of them one of these days, and now he has.

He has?

Always his greatest dream, yes, indeed.

Well, then –

Yes. Khalid moved along. So did Thomas. Khalid took care to go nowhere near the house all that morning. The last person he wanted to see was Richie. But he was safe in that regard. By noon Thomas evidently had spread the tale of Khalid Burke's wild boast about the town with great effectiveness, because word came traveling through the streets around that time that a detachment of Spooks had gone to Khalid's house and had taken Richie Burke away.

'What about my grandmother?' Khalid asked. 'She wasn't arrested too, was she?'

'No, it was just him,' he was told. 'Billy Cavendish saw them taking him, and he was all by himself. Yelling and screaming, he was, the whole time, like a man being hauled away to be hanged.'

Khalid never saw his father again.

During the course of the general reprisals that followed the killing, the entire population of Salisbury and five adjacent towns was rounded up and transported to walled detention camps near Portsmouth. A good many of the deportees were executed within the next few days, seemingly by random selection, no pattern being evident in the choosing of those who were put to death. At the beginning of the following week the survivors were sent on from Portsmouth to other places, some of them quite remote, in various parts of the world.

Khalid was not among those executed. He was merely sent very far away.

He felt no guilt over having survived the death-lottery while others around him were being slain for his murderous act. He had trained himself since childhood to feel very little indeed, even while aiming a rifle at one of Earth's beautiful and magnificent masters. Besides, what affair was it of his, that some of these people were dying and he was allowed to live? Everyone died, some sooner, some later. Aissha would have said that what was happening was the will of Allah. Khalid more simply put it that the Entities did as they pleased, always, and knew that it was folly to ponder their motives.

Aissha was not available to discuss these matters with. He was separated from her before reaching Portsmouth and Khalid never saw her again, either. From that day on it was necessary for him to make his way in the world on his own.

He was not quite thirteen years old.

Ron Carmichael said, trotting up toward the main house along the grassy path from the gray stone building that was the Resistance communications center, 'Where's my father? Has anyone seen the Colonel?' The despatch from London was in his hand.

'On the patio,' Jill called to him. She was descending the same path, on her way down to the vegetable garden with a pail for tomatoes. 'In his rocking chair, as usual.'

'No. I can see the patio from here. He's not there.'

'Well, he was five minutes ago. It's not my fault if he isn't there now, is it? Man gets up and moves around sometimes, you know.'

He gave her a scowling look as they passed each other, and she stuck her tongue out at him. She was such a sour bitch, was his pretty niece. Of course, what she needed was a man, he knew. Getting on into her twenties and still sleeping alone, and even her dorky cousin Steve married now and about to be a father – it made no sense, Ron thought.

Time for Jill to find someone, yes. Ted Quarles had been asking about her just the other day, at the last meeting of the Resistance committee. Of course that was a little odd, Ted being at least twenty years her senior, maybe more. And Jill had never given him so much as a glance. But these were odd times.

The first person Ron encountered within the house was his older daughter, Leslyn. 'Do you know where Grandpa is?' he asked her. 'He's not on the porch.'

'Mommy's with him. In his room.'

'Is something wrong?'

But the little girl had already gone skipping away. Ron wasted no time calling her back. Hurrying through the maze of slate-floored corridors, he made his way to his father's bedroom, at the back of the house with a grand view of the mountain wall above the ranch, and found him sitting up in bed, wearing his pajamas and bathrobe and a red muffler about his throat. He seemed pallid and weary and very old. Peggy was with him.

'What's going on?' he asked her.

'He was feeling chilly, that's all. I brought him inside.'

'Chilly? It's a bright sunny morning out there! Practically like summer.'

'Not for me,' the Colonel said, smiling faintly. 'For me it's starting to be very, very late in autumn, Ronnie, going on winter very fast. But your lovely lady is taking good care of me. Giving me my medicine, and all.' He patted Peggy affectionately on the back of one hand. 'I don't know what I'd do without her. What I *would* have done without her, these many years.'

'Mike and Charlie have been all the way up to Monterey and back,' Peggy said, looking up from the bedside at Ron. 'They found a whole new supply of the Colonel's pills in a store up there. They brought a girl back with them, too, a very nice one. Eloise, her name is. You'll be impressed.'

Ron blinked a couple of times. '*A* girl? What are they going to do, share her? Even if they *are* twins, I don't see how they can seriously propose –'

Laughing, the Colonel said, 'You've become stuffier than Anse, do you know that, Ronnie? "*I don't see how they can seriously propose* –" My God, boy, they aren't *marrying* her! She's just a house guest! You sound like you're fifty years old.'

'I *am* fifty,' Ron said. 'Will be in another couple of months, anyway.' He paced restively around the room, clutching the Net message from London, wondering if he ought to bother his obviously ailing father with this startling news now. He decided after a moment that he should; that the Colonel would not have had it any other way.

And in any case the Colonel had already guessed.

'Is there news?' he asked, with a glance at the crumpled grayish sheet in Ron's hand.

'Yes. Pretty amazing stuff, as a matter of fact. An Entity has been assassinated in the English town of Salisbury. Paul just picked up the story on a Net link.'

The Colonel, nestling back against his mound of pillows and giving Ron a slow, steady, unflustered look, said quietly, as though Ron had announced that word had just arrived via the Net of the second coming of Christ, 'Just how reliable is this report, boy?'

'Very. Paul says, unimpeachable authority, London Resistance network, Martin Bartlett himself.'

'An Entity. Killed.' The Colonel considered that. 'How?'

'A single shot on a lonely road, late at night. Hidden sniper, using some sort of home-made grenade-firing rifle.'

'The very plan that Faulkenburg and Cantelli and some of the others were so hot to put into being two or three years ago, and which we ultimately voted down because it was impossible to kill Entities that way anyhow, because of the telepathic screening field. Now someone has gone and done it, you tell me? How? How? We all agreed it couldn't be done.'

'Well,' Ron said, 'somebody found a way, somehow.'

The Colonel considered that for a time, too. He sat back, there among his framed diplomas and military memorabilia and innumerable photographs of his dead wife and his dead brothers and his sons and daughters and growing tribe of grandchildren, and he seemed to vanish into the labyrinth of his own thoughts and lose his way in there.

Then he said, 'There's really only one way that would work, isn't there? Getting around the telepathy, I mean. The assassin would have to be like some sort of machine, practically – somebody with no more emotion and feeling than an android. Someone completely stolid and unexcitable. Someone who could wait there by the roadside holding that rifle and never for a moment let his mind dwell on the notion that he was going to strike a great blow for the liberation of mankind, or for that matter that he was about to murder an intelligent creature. Or any other sort of thought that might possibly attract the attention of the Entity who was going to be his victim.'

'A total moron,' Ronnie suggested. 'Or an utter sociopath.'

'Well, yes. That might work, if you could teach a moron to use a rifle, or if you found a sociopath who didn't get some kind of sick kick out of the anticipation of firing that shot. But there are other possibilities, you know.'

'Such as?'

'In Vietnam,' said the Colonel, 'we ran across them all the time: absolutely impassive people who did the goddamnedest bloody things without batting an eye. An old woman who looked like your grandmother's grandmother who would come up to you and placidly toss a bomb in your car. Or a sweet little six-year-old boy putting a knife into you in the marketplace. People who would kill or maim or mutilate you without pausing to think about what they were about to do and without feeling a gnat's worth of animosity for you as they did it. Or remorse afterward. Half the time they blew themselves up right along with you, and the likelihood that that was going to happen didn't faze them either. Perhaps it never even entered their minds. They just went ahead and did what they'd been told to do. An Entity mind-field might not be any defense against somebody like that.'

'It's hard for me to imagine a mentality like that.'

'Not for me,' the Colonel said. 'I saw just that kind of mentality in action at very close range indeed. Then I spent much of my academic career studying it. I even taught about it, remember? Way back in the Pleistocene? Professor of non-western psychology.' He shook his head. 'So they've actually killed one. Well, well, well. – What about reprisals, now?'

'They've cleaned out half a dozen towns in the vicinity, London says.'

'Cleaned them out? What does that mean?'

'Rounded up every person. Taken them away somewhere.'

'And killed them?'

'Not clear,' Ronnie said. 'I doubt that anything nice is going to happen to them, though.'

The Colonel nodded. 'That's it, then? Purely local reprisal? No worldwide plagues, no major power shutoffs?'

'So far, no.'

'So far,' said the Colonel. 'We can only pray.'

Ronnie approached his father's bedside. 'Well, at any rate, that's the news. I thought you'd like to know, and now you do. Now you tell me: how are you feeling?'

'Old. Tired.'

'That's all? Nothing in particular hurting you?'

'Old and tired, that's all. So far. Of course, the Entities haven't let any plagues loose yet, either, so far.'

He and Peggy went into the hallway. 'Do you think he's dying?' he asked her.

'He's been dying for a long time, very very slowly. But I think he's still got some distance to go. He's tougher than you think he is, Ron.'

'Maybe so. But I hate to watch him crumbling like this. You have no idea what he was like when we were young, Peg. The way he stood, the way he walked, the way he held himself. Such an amazing man, absolutely fearless, absolutely honorable, always strong when you needed him to be strong. And always *right*. That was the astounding thing. I'd argue with him about something I had done, you know, trying to justify myself and feeling that I had made out a good case for myself, and he'd say three or four quiet words and I'd know that I had no case at all. Not that I would admit it, not then. – Christ, I'll hate to lose him, Peggy!'

'He's not going to die yet, Ron. I know that.'

'*Who* isn't going to die?' said Anse, lumbering up out of one of the side corridors. He came to a halt alongside them, breathing hard, leaning on his cane. There was the faint sweet odor of whiskey about him, even now, well before noon. His bad leg had grown much more troublesome lately. '*Him*, you mean?' Anse asked, nodding toward the closed door of the Colonel's bedroom.

'Who else?'

'He'll live to be a hundred,' Anse said. 'I'll go before he does. Honestly, Ron.'

He probably would, Ron thought. Anse was fifty-six and appeared to be at least ten years older. His face was gray and bloated, his no longer intense eyes were lost in deep shadows, his shoulders now were rounded and slumped. All that was new. He didn't seem as tall as he once had been. And he had lost some weight. Anse had always been a fine, sturdy man, not at all beefy – Ron was the beefy brother – but with plenty of muscle and flesh on him. Now he was visibly shrinking, sagging, diminishing. Some of it was the booze, Ron knew. Some of it was simply age. And some of it was, no doubt, that mysterious dark cloud of disappointment and discontent that had surrounded Anse for so long. The big brother who somehow had not gone on to become head of the family.

'Come off it, Anse,' Ron said, with as much sincerity as he could muster. 'There's nothing wrong with you that a new left leg wouldn't fix.'

'Which I could probably have gotten,' Anse said, 'but for the fucking Entities. – Hey, Paul says a story's come in that they've actually succeeded in killing one, over in England. What are the chances that it's true?'

'No reason to think it isn't.'

'Is this the beginning, then? The counterattack?'

'I doubt that very much,' said Ron. 'We don't have a lot of details about how they managed it. But dad's got a theory that it would take a very special kind of assassin to bring it off – somebody with essentially no emotions at all, somebody who's practically an android. It would be hard to put together a whole army of people like that.'

'We could train them.'

'We could, yes,' Ron said. 'It would take quite a bit of time. Let me give it some thought, okay?'

'Was he happy about the killing?'

'He wondered about the reprisals, mostly. But yes, yes, he was happy about it. I suppose. He didn't come right out and say that he was.'

'He wants them eradicated from the Earth once we're properly ready to do the job,' said Anse. 'That's always been his goal underneath it all, even when they were saying that he had turned pacifist, even when they were hinting he had gone soft in the head. You know that. And now it's the one thing keeping him alive – the hope that he'll stick around long enough to see them completely wiped out.'

'Well, he isn't going to. Nor you, nor me. But we can always hope. And you know, bro, he's never been anything *but* a pacifist. He hates war. Always has. And his idea of preventing war is to constantly be prepared to fight one. – Ah, he's some guy, isn't he? They broke the mold when they made him, let me tell you. I hate to see him fading away like this. I hate it more than I can say.'

It was an oddly valedictory conversation, Ron thought. They were telling each other things, now, that both of them had known since they were children. But it was as though they needed to get these things said one more time before it was too late to say them at all.

Ron suspected he knew what was going to be said next – he could already see the moist gleam of emotion coming into Anse's eyes, could already hear the heavy throbbing chords of the symphonic accompaniment – and, sure enough, out the words came, a moment later:

'What really gets to me is when you talk about how much you care for him, bro. You know, there were all those years when you and he weren't speaking to each other, and I thought you really despised him. But I was wrong about that, wasn't I?' *Now Anse will take my hand fervently between both of his. Yes, like that.* 'One more thing, bro. I want to tell you, if I haven't already done so, how glad I am that in the course of time you did shape up the way that you have, how proud I am that you could be capable of changing so much, to make your peace with our dad and come here and be so much of a comfort to him. You worked out all right, in the long run. I confess I was surprised.'

'Thank you, I guess.'

'Especially when I – didn't – work out so well.'

'That was a surprise too,' Ron said, having quickly decided that there was no point in offering any contradiction.

'Well, it shouldn't have been,' said Anse, in a tone that was almost without expression. 'It just wasn't in me to do any better. It really wasn't. No matter what he expected of me. I tried, but – well, you know how it's been with me, bro –'

'Of course I know,' said Ron vaguely, and returned the squeeze; and Anse gave him a blurrily affectionate look and went limping off toward the front of the house.

'That was very touching,' Peggy said. 'He loves you very much.'

'I suppose he does. He's drunk, Peg.'

'Even so. He meant what he said.'

Ron glowered at her. 'Yes. Yes. But I loathe it when people tell me how much I've changed, how glad they are that I'm not the mean selfish son-of-a-bitch I used to be. I loathe it. I *haven't* changed. You know what I mean? I'm simply doing things in this region of my life that I hadn't felt like making time for before. Like moving to the ranch. Like marrying a woman like you, like settling down and raising a family. Like agreeing with my father instead of automatically opposing him all the time. Like assuming certain responsibililties that extend beyond my own skin. But I'm still living within that skin, Peg. My behavior may have changed, but *I* haven't. I've always made the sort of choices that make sense to me – they're just different sorts of choices now, that's all. And it makes me mad as hell when people, especially my own brother, patronize me by telling me that it's wonderful that I'm not as shitty as I once was. Do you follow what I'm saying?'

It was a long speech. Peggy was staring at him in what looked like dismay.

'Am I running off at the mouth?' he asked.

'Well –'

'Hey, forget it,' he said, reaching out and stroking her cheek. 'I'm very worried about my father, is all. And about Anse, for that matter. How fragile they're both getting. How much Anse drinks. Both of them getting ready to die.'

'No,' said Peggy. 'Don't say that.'

'It's true. Wouldn't surprise me if Anse goes first, either.' Ron shook his head. 'Poor old Anse. Always trying to turn himself into the Colonel, and never able to. And burning himself out trying. Because nobody possibly could be the Colonel except the Colonel. Anse didn't have the Colonel's intelligence or dedication or discipline, but he forced himself to pretend that he did. At least I had the good sense not even to try.'

'Is Anse really that sick?'

'Sick? I don't know if he's sick, no. But he's done for, Peg. All these years trying to run a Resistance, trying to find some way to beat the Entities because the Colonel thinks we should, although there *isn't* any way and Anse has had to live in perpetual simmering rage inside because he's been trying to accomplish the impossible. His whole life has gone by, trying to accomplish things he wasn't meant to do, things that maybe couldn't even have been done. Burned him out.' Ron shrugged. 'I wonder if I'll get like that when my turn comes: shrunken, frail, defeated-looking? No. No, I won't, will I? I'm a different kind. Nothing in common but the blue eyes.'

Was that really true? he wondered.

There was noise, suddenly, down the hall, a clattering, some whoops. Mike and Charlie appeared, Anse's boys, taller now than their father, taller even than him. Seventeen years old. Blue Carmichael eyes, light-hued Carmichael hair. They had a girl with them: the one from Monterey, it must be. Looked to be a year or two older than they were.

'Hey, Uncle Ron! Aunt Peg! Want you to meet Eloise!'

That was Charlie, the one with the unmarked face. The brothers had had a terrible fight when they were about nine, and Mike had come out of it with that angry red scar down his cheek. Ron had often thought it was very considerate of Charlie to have marked his brother like that. They were, otherwise, the most identical twins he had ever seen, altogether alike in movement, stance, voice, patterns of thought.

Eloise was dark-haired, pretty, vivacious: sharp cheekbones, tiny nose, full lips, lively eyes. Leggy below and full on top. Very nice indeed. Ancient lustful reflexes stirred for an instant in Ron. *She is only a child*, he told himself sternly. *And to her, you are simply some uninteresting old man.*

'Eloise Mitchell – our uncle, Ronald Carmichael – Peggy, our aunt –'

'Pleased,' she said. Her eyes were sparkling. Impressive, yes. 'It's so beautiful here! I've never been this far south before. I love this part of the coast. I never want to go home!'

'She isn't going to,' Charlie said. And Mike winked and laughed.

Then they were off, running down the hall, heading for the sunlight and warmth outside the old stone house.

'I'll be damned,' Ron said. 'Do you think they *are* sharing her?'

'That isn't any of your business,' Peggy told him. 'The younger generation does as it pleases. Just as we did.'

'The younger generation, yes. And we're the stuffy old geezers now. There's the world's future rising up before our eyes. Charlie. Mike. Eloise.'

'And our Anson and Leslyn and Heather and Tony. Cassandra and Julie and Mark. And now Steve's baby soon too.'

'The future, crowding in on the present all the time. While the past makes ready to clear out. Been like that for a long while, hasn't it, Peg? And not going to change now, I guess.'

V

Twenty-Nine Years
from Now

Khalid was at work in the cluttered corner of the dormitory that he used as his studio, carving a statuette from a bar of soap, when Litvak came in and said, 'Start packing, guys. We're all being transported again.'

Litvak was the communications-net man in the group, the one with the implant jack who knew how to rig the house telephone to pick information off the Entity net. He was the dormitory's borgmann, in a manner of speaking: a borgmann in reverse who spied on the Entities rather than working for them, a compact diminutive Israeli with an oddly triangular head, very broad through the forehead and tapering downward to a sharp little pointed chin. It was an interesting head. Khalid had sculpted portraits of him several times.

Khalid didn't look up. He was fashioning a miniature figure of Parvati, the Hindu goddess: high tapering headdress, exaggerated breasts, benign expression of utter tranquility. Lately he had been carving the entire Hindu pantheon, after Litvak had pulled photos of them out of some forgotten archive of the old Net. Krishna, Shiva, Ganesha, Vishnu, Brahma: the whole lot of them. Aissha probably wouldn't have approved of his making statuettes of Hindu gods and goddesses – for that matter, a good Muslim should not be making graven images at all – but it was seven years since he had last seen Aissha. Aissha was ancient history to him, like Krishna and Shiva and Vishnu, or Richie Burke. Khalid was a grown man now and he did as he pleased.

From across the room the Bulgarian, Dimiter, said, 'Are we going to be split up, do you think?'

'What do you suppose, dummy?' Litvak asked tartly. 'You think they find us so charming as a group that they're going to keep us together for the rest of eternity?'

There were eight of them in this sector of the transportee dormitory, five men, three women, tossed together higgledy-piggledy by the random-scoop arrangements that the Entities seemed to favor. They had been together fourteen months, now, which was the longest period Khalid had stayed with any group of transportees. The dormitory, the whole prison camp, was located somewhere along the Turkish coast – 'just north of Bodrum,' Litvak had said, though where Bodrum was, or, for that matter Turkey itself, was something not very clear to Khalid. It was a pretty place, anyhow, warm sunny weather most of the year, dry brown hills running down to the coastal plain, a beautiful blue ocean, a scattering of islands just off shore. Before this place he had been in central Spain for eleven months, and in Austria for seven or eight, and in Norway for close to a year, and before that – well, he no longer remembered where he had been before that. The Entities liked to keep their prisoners on the move.

It was a long while since he had been housed with anyone from the vicinity of Salisbury. Not that that mattered greatly to him, since there was no one in Salisbury for whom he had cared in any special way except Aissha and old Iskander Mustafa Ali, and he had no idea where Aissha might be and Iskander Mustafa Ali surely was dead by this time. In the beginning, in the camp at Portsmouth, most of his fellow prisoners had been people from Salisbury or one of the neighboring towns, but by now, after five or six (or was it seven?) changes of detention center, he no longer lived with anyone from England at all. Apparently there were many people throughout the world, not just his own English neighbors, who had displeased the Entities in some manner and now were subjected to this constant rotation from one prison camp to another.

In Khalid's group there was, aside from Litvak and Dimiter, a Canadian woman named Francine Webster, and a man from Poland named Krzysztof, and a perpetually sulky Irish girl, Carlotta, and Genevieve from the south of France, and a small, dark-skinned man from somewhere in North Africa whose name Khalid had never managed to catch, though he had not tried very hard. They all got along reasonably well together. The North

African man spoke only French and Arabic; everybody else in the group spoke English, some better than others, and Genevieve translated for the North African whenever it was necessary. Khalid had little interest in getting to know his roommates, since they were almost certainly temporary. He found jittery little Litvak amusing, and the hearty, good-humored Krzysztof was pleasant company, and he liked the warm, motherly Francine Webster. The others didn't matter. On several occasions he had slept with Francine Webster and also with Genevieve, because there was no privacy in the dormitory nor much remaining sense of individual boundaries, and nearly everybody in the group slept in a casual way with nearly everybody else now and then, and Khalid had discovered, during the years of his imprisoned adolescence, that he was not without sexual drive. But the sexual part of things had made little impact on him either, other than pure physical release.

He went on with his sculpting, and offered no comments about the impending transfer, and three days later, just as Litvak had predicted, they were all ordered to report to Room 107 of the detention center's administration sector. In Room 107, which was a large hall entirely unfurnished except for an empty bookcase and a three-legged chair, they were left by themselves to stand for close to an hour before someone came in, asked them their names, and, referring to a sheet of brown paper in his hand, brusquely said, 'You, you, and you, Room 103. You and you, Room 106. You, you, you, Room 109. And make it snappy.'

Khalid, Krzysztof, and the North African were the ones who were sent to room 109. They went there quickly. No time was spent on offering farewells to the other five, for they all knew that they now were disappearing from each other's lives forever.

Room 109, which was mysteriously distant from Room 107, was much smaller than 107 but just about as sparsely furnished. A picture-frame that held no picture hung on the left-hand wall; on the floor against the wall opposite it stood a large green ceramic flower-vase with no flowers in it; there was a bare desk in front of the far wall, facing the door. Seated behind the desk was a petite round-faced woman who looked to be about sixty. Her dark eyes, which seemed to be set very far apart, had an odd glittery gleam, and her hair, which had probably once been jet black, was dramatically streaked with jagged zones of white, like flashes of lightning cutting across the night.

Glancing at a paper she was holding, she said, looking at the Pole, 'Are you Kr – Kyz – Kzyz – Kryz –' She could not get her tongue around the letters of his name. But she seemed amused rather than irritated.

'Krzysztof,' he said. 'Kryzsztof Michalski.'

'Michalski, yes. And that first name again?'

'Krzysztof.'

'Ah. *Christoph*. I get it now. All right: Christoph Michalski. Polish name, right?' She grinned. 'A lot easier to say it than to read it.' Khalid was surprised at how chatty she was. Most of these quisling bureaucrats were chilly and abrupt. But she had what sounded to him like an American accent. Perhaps her being American had something to do with that. 'And which one of you is Khalid Haleem Burke?' the woman asked.

'I am.'

She gave him a long slow look, frowning a little. Khalid stared right back.

'And then you,' she said, turning now toward the North African, 'must be – ah – Mulay ben Dlimi.'

'*Oui*.'

'What kind of name is that, Mulay ben Dlimi?'

'*Oui*,' the North African said again.

'He doesn't understand English,' said Khalid. 'He's from North Africa.'

The woman nodded. 'A real international group. All right, Christoph, Khalid, Mulay. I think you know the deal. You're going to be transported again, day after tomorrow. Or possibly even tomorrow, if the paperwork gets done in time. Pack your stuff and be ready to leave your quarters as soon as you're called.'

'Can you tell us,' Krzysztov said, 'where we're going to be sent this time?'

She smiled. 'The good old U.S. of A., this time. Las Vegas, Nevada. Do any of you know how to play blackjack?'

*   *   *

The transport plane once had been a commercial airliner, long, long ago, in the days when the citizens of the countries of Earth still moved about freely from one place to another on journeys of business or pleasure and there were such things called airlines to carry them. Khalid had not known that era at first hand, but he had heard tales of it. This plane, whose painted hull was faded and even rusted in places, still bore an inscription identifying it as belonging to British Airways. For Khalid, stepping aboard it was in a little way like returning to England. He was not sure how he felt about that.

But the airplane wasn't England. It was only a long metal tube with blotchy gray walls and scars on the floor to mark the places where the seats had been ripped out. Bare mattresses had replaced the seats. There was no place to sit; one could only walk about or lie down. Long bars had been soldered to the walls above the windows, something to grab if the flight turned turbulent. Threadbare curtains divided the passenger compartment into several sub-compartments.

For Khalid there was nothing new about any of this. All the planes that had carried him from one detention camp to another had been much like this one. This one seemed bigger, that was all. But that was because they were going to the United States, a lengthy journey that must require a larger plane. He had only the vaguest idea where the United States might be, but he knew that it was very far from where they were now.

The small woman who had met with them in Room 109 was aboard the plane, supervising the departure arrangements. Khalid assumed that she would leave once everybody who was being transported had been checked off the master list, but, no, she stayed on the plane after the check-off was complete and the doors were closed. That was unusual. The detention-center officials did not normally accompany the transported prisoners to their destinations. But perhaps she wasn't actually staying. He watched her disappear through the curtain that separated Khalid's sector of the plane from the zone up front where the official personnel were, and wondered if there might be some other door up there through which she might leave before the plane took off. In a curious way he hoped there wasn't. He liked her. She was an amusing woman, lively and irreverent, not at all like any of the other quisling officials with whom he had come in contact in his seven years of internment.

Khalid was pleased to see, not long after the plane had taken off, that she was still on board. She emerged from the front compartment, walking carefully in the steeply climbing plane, and halted when she reached the mattress where Khalid and the North African man were sitting.

'May I join you?' she asked.

'You need to ask permission, do you?' said Khalid.

'A little politeness never hurts.'

He shrugged. She spiraled down next to him, lowering herself to the floor in a quick, graceful way that belied her age, and folded herself up opposite him on the mattress with her legs crossed neatly, ankles to knees.

'You're Khalid, is that right?'

'Yes.'

'My name is Cindy. You're very pretty, Khalid, do you know that? I love the tawny color of your skin. Like a lion's, it is. And that crop of dense bushy hair.' When he offered no reply, she said, 'You're an artist, I understand.'

'I make things, yes.'

'I made things once, too. And I was also pretty, once, for that matter.'

She smiled and winked at him, rendering Khalid somehow a co-conspirator in the agreement that she had once been pretty. It hadn't occurred to him before this that she might have been an attractive woman once upon a time, but now, taking a close look at her, he saw that it was quite possible that she had been: a small and energetic person, trimly built, with delicate features and those bright, bright eyes. Her smile was still very appealing. And the wink. He liked that wink. She was definitely unlike any quisling he had ever encountered. With his artist's eye he edited out the grooves and wrinkles that her sixty years had carved in her face, restored the darkness and glossiness of her hair, gave her skin the freshness of youth. Yes, he thought. No doubt quite pretty thirty or forty years ago.

'What are you, Khalid?' she said. 'Some sort of Indian? At least in part.'

'Pakistani. My mother was.'

'And your father?'

'English. A white man. I never knew him. He was a quisling, people told me.'

'*I'm* a quisling.'

'Lots of people are quislings,' Khalid said. 'It makes no difference to me.'

'Well,' she said. And said nothing further for a while, simply sat there crosslegged, her eyes looking into his as though she were studying him. Khalid looked back amiably. He was afraid of nothing and nobody. Let her stare, if she wanted to.

Then she said, 'Are you angry about something?'

'Angry? Me? What is there to be angry about? I never get angry at all.'

'On the contrary. I think you're angry all the time.'

'You are certainly free to think that.'

'You seem very calm,' she said. 'That's one of the things that makes you so interesting, how cool you are, how you just shrug within yourself at everything that happens to you and around you. It's the first thing anyone would notice about you. But that kind of calmness can sometimes be a mask for seething anger. You could have a volcano inside you that you don't want to allow to erupt, and so you keep a lid on it a hundred percent of the time. A hundred *twenty* percent of the time. What do you think of that theory, Khalid?'

'Aissha, who raised me like a mother because my mother died when I was born, taught me to accept the will of Allah in whatever form it might manifest itself. Which I have done.'

'A very wise philosophy. Islam: the word itself means "absolute submission", right? Surrendering yourself to God. I've studied these things, you know. – Who was Aissha?'

'My mother's mother. Her stepmother, really. She was like a mother to me. A very good woman.'

'Undoubtedly she was. And I think you're a very, very angry man.'

'You are certainly free to think that,' said Khalid again.

* * *

Half an hour later, as Khalid sat by the window peering incuriously out at the vast island-dotted blue sea that stretched before him, she came back again and once more asked if she might sit down with him. Such politeness on the part of administrators puzzled him, but he beckoned her with an open palm to do as she pleased. She slipped with wonderful ease again into the crosslegged position.

With a nod toward Mulay ben Dlimi, who sat with his back against the wall of the plane, eyes veiled as though he were in a trance, she said, 'Does he really not understand English?'

'He never appeared to. We had a woman in our group who spoke to him in French. He didn't ever say a word to any of the rest of us.'

'Sometimes people understand a language but still don't want to speak it.'

'I suppose that's so,' said Khalid.

She inclined her torso toward the North African and said, 'Do you know any English at all?'

He glanced blankly at her, then off into space again.

'Not even a word?' she asked.

Still no response.

Smiling pleasantly, she said, in a polite conversational tone, 'Your mother was a whore in the marketplace, Mulay ben Dlimi. Your father fucked camels. You yourself are the grandson of a pig.'

Mulay ben Dlimi shook his head mildly. He went on staring into space.

'You really don't understand me even a bit, do you?' said Cindy. 'Or else you've got yourself under even tighter control than Khalid, here. Well, God bless you, Mulay ben Dlimi. I guess it's safe for me to say anything I want in front of you.' She turned back to Khalid. 'Well, now. Let's get down to business. Would you ever do anything that's against the law?'

'What law do you mean? What law is there in this world?'

'Other than Allah's, you mean?'

'Other than that, yes. What law is there?' he asked again.

In a low voice she said, leaning close to his ear, 'Listen carefully to me. I'm tired of working for them, Khalid. I've been their loyal handmaiden for twenty-odd years and that's about enough. When they first arrived I thought it was a miraculous thing that they had come to Earth, and it could have been, but it didn't work out right. They didn't share any of their greatness with us. They simply *used* us, and never even told us what they were using us *for*. Also they promised me to show me their world, you know. But they didn't deliver. They were going to take me there as an ambassador from Earth: I'm sure that's what they were telling me with their minds. They didn't, though. They lied to me, or else I was imagining everything and I was lying to myself. Well, either way, to hell with them, Khalid. I don't want to be their quisling any more.'

'Why are you telling me this?' he asked.

'What do you know about the geography of the United States?'

'Nothing whatever. It is a very big country very far away, that's all I know.'

'Nevada,' she said, 'which is the place where we're heading, is a dry empty useless place where nobody in his right mind would want to live. But it's right next door to California, and California is where I come from. I want to go home, Khalid.'

'Yes. I suppose you do. How does this concern me?'

'I come from the city of Los Angeles. You've heard of Los Angeles? Good. – It's about three hundred miles, I would guess, from Las Vegas, Nevada, to Los Angeles. Most of the way, it's pretty bleak country. A desert, actually. One woman traveling alone, those three hundred miles, might run into problems. Even a tough old dame like me. You see where this might concern you?'

'No. I am in permanent detention.'

'A situation that could be reversed by a simple recoding of your registration. I could do that for you, just as I arranged to put myself aboard this plane. We could leave the detention compound together and no one would say a word. And you would accompany me to Los Angeles.'

'I see. And then I would be free, once I was in Los Angeles?'

'Free as a bird, Khalid.'

'Yes. But in detention they give me a place to sleep and food to eat. In Los Angeles, a place where I know no one, where I will understand nothing –'

'It's beautiful there. Warm all year round, and flowers blooming everywhere. The people are friendly. And I'd help you. I'd see that things went well for you there. – Look, we won't be getting to the States for a couple of days. Think about it, Khalid, between now and then.'

He thought about it. They flew from Turkey to Italy, stopping there to refuel, in Rome, and they refueled again in Paris, and then they stopped in Iceland, and after that came a long dreamlike time of flying over a land of ice and snow, until they landed again somewhere in Canada. These were only names to Khalid. Los Angeles was only a name, too. He rotated all these names in his mind, and from time to time he slept, and once in a while he pondered the quisling woman Cindy's offer.

It occurred to him that it might all be a trick of some kind, a trap, but then he asked himself what purpose they would have in snaring him, when he was already their prisoner and they could do anything they wished with him anyway. Then, later, he found himself wondering whether he should ask her if they could take Krzysztof with them too, because Krzysztof was a cheerful, good-hearted man, and Khalid was fond of him, as much as he was capable of being fond of anyone, and, besides, the sturdy Krzysztof might be a useful person to have with them on the journey across that desert. And, wondering that, he realized that he had somehow managed to make his decision without noticing that he had.

'I can't take him, no,' Cindy said. 'I can't risk getting two of you free. If you won't come, I'll ask him. But it can only be one or the other of you.'

'Well, then,' Khalid said. 'So be it.'

He regretted leaving Krzysztof behind: as much as he was capable of regretting anything, at any rate. But that was how it had to be, was it not? And so that was how it would be.

Nevada was the ugliest place he had ever seen or even imagined, a nightmare land so different from green and pleasant England that he could almost believe he was on some other planet. It seemed as though no rain had fallen here for five hundred years.

Turkey had been hot and dry, too, but in Turkey there were farms everywhere, and the ocean nearby, and trees on the hills. Here there seemed to be only sand and rocks and dust, and occasional gnarly shrubs, and dark twisted little mountains farther back that had no vegetation on them at all. And the heat came down out of the sky like a metal weight, pressing down, pressing, pressing, pressing.

The city where their long plane journey had ended, Las Vegas, was ugly too, but at least its ugliness was of a kind that amused the eye, no two buildings alike, one resembling an Egyptian pyramid and one a Roman palace and others like structures out of strange dreams or fantasies, and everything of such colossal size. Khalid would have preferred to remain longer in Las Vegas, to make a few sketches of those peculiar buildings that would fix them more firmly in his memory. But he and Cindy were out of Las Vegas almost as soon as they arrived, heading off together into the grim, terrible desert that surrounded it.

She had, somehow, arranged to get the use of a car to take them to Los Angeles. 'You are being transferred now from the Las Vegas detention center to one in Barstow, California,' she explained. 'I have been assigned to deliver you to Barstow. It's all been quite legally recorded in the archives. A friend in Leipzig who knows his way around the Entity computer net set it all up for me.'

The car looked ancient. It probably was: pre-Conquest, even. Its sides were dented and its silvery paint had flaked away in a hundred places, showing red rusty patches beneath, and it leaned badly on the left side, drooping so visibly that Khalid wondered whether the rim of the frame would strike the ground when the car moved.

'Can you drive?' Cindy asked, as they loaded their meager luggage into the car.

'No.'

'Of course you can't. Where would you have learned to drive? How old were you, anyway, when they put you in detention?'

'Not quite thirteen.'

'And that was how long ago? Eight years? Ten?'

'Seven. I'll be twenty-one on December 25th.'

'A Christmas baby. How nice. Everybody singing to celebrate your birthday. "Si-lent night, ho-o-ly night – "'

'Yes, very nice,' he said bitterly. 'My birthdays were all extremely happy ones. We would gather around our Christmas tree, my mother and father and my brothers and sisters and I, and we would sing the Christmas songs, and we would give each other wonderful presents.'

'Really?'

'Oh, yes. There were some happy times.'

'Wait a second,' she said. 'You told me on the plane that your mother died in childbirth and you never knew your father, and you were raised by your grandmother.'

'Yes. And I also told you then that I was Muslim.'

She laughed. 'You were just trying to see if I was paying attention.'

'No,' he said. 'I was just saying what came into my mind.'

'What an odd duck you are, Khalid!'

'Duck?'

'Never mind. An expression.' She unlocked the car's doors and signalled for him to get in. He entered on the left-hand side, as he always had when he went out driving with Richie, and was surprised to find himself confronted by the steering wheel. It had been on the other side in Richie's car: he was sure of that.

'American cars are different,' Cindy said. 'At least you've been in a car before, I see. Even if you don't know how to drive one.'

'I would go driving sometimes in my father's car. On Sundays he would take me to places like Stonehenge.'

She looked at him sharply. 'You never knew your father, you said.'

'I lied.'

'Oh. Oh. Oh. You play a lot of head games, don't you, Khalid?'

'There was one thing I said that was true. I hated him.'

'For being a quisling? You said that he was. Was that part true?'

'He was one, but that was of no importance to me. I hated him because he treated Aissha badly. And, sometimes, me. He was probably bad to my mother, too. What does any of this matter now, though? The past is far away.'

'But not forgotten, I see.' She put the key into the ignition and turned it. The engine sputtered, coughed, caught, failed, sputtered again and this time came to life. Noisily the car moved forward through the detention compound. Cindy flashed her identification at the gate, the guard waved, and off they went.

They were out in the desert almost immediately.

For a time neither of them said anything. Khalid was too appalled by the hideous landscape all around him to speak; and Cindy, who was so small she could barely see over the top of the steering wheel, was concentrating intently on her driving. The surface of the road was a bad one, cratered and cracked in a million places, and the car, venerable ruin that it was, unceasingly groaned and grumbled, jouncing and jiggling them in merciless fashion and occasionally emitting ominous knocking noises as though getting ready to explode. He looked over at her and saw her sitting with her shoulders tensely hunched, biting down on her lower lip, gripping the wheel with all her strength as though to keep the car from skittering off into the sandy wasteland beyond the pavement's edge.

'The speed limit on this freeway used to be seventy miles an hour. In kilometers that's – what, a hundred ten? A hundred twenty? Something like that. And we all used to drive it at eighty or eighty-five – miles an hour, I mean – when I was a kid. Of course you'd have to be crazy to do that now. Assuming this car was capable of it, which it isn't. It's probably older than you are. It's the kind that people had to use until just a few years before the Conquest, the sort you have to operate manually, because it doesn't have a computer brain and won't understand spoken commands. An antique. And definitely coming to the end of its days, too. But we'll make it to L.A., one way or another. On foot, if we have to.'

'If you are supposed to be delivering me to a place called Barstow,' Khalid said, 'how can we continue on to Los Angeles? Won't they wonder about us when we don't show up at this Barstow?'

'No reason why they should. We're going to die in an auto accident tomorrow, before we ever get to Barstow.'

'Excuse me?'

'The accident's already programmed into the computer. My
pal in Leipzig fed it in. A crackerjack pardoner, he is. Do you
know what a pardoner is, Khalid?'

'No.'

'Pardoners are very clever hackers. They're something like
borgmanns, except they do their hacking on our behalf instead
of the Entities'. They cut into the Entity net and make revisions
in the records. If you've been transferred someplace you don't
want to go, for example, it's possible to get a pardoner to undo
the transfer. For a price, of course. What has been programmed
in here by my pardoner friend is that Agent C. Carmichael, transporting Detainee K. Burke, met with an unfortunate freeway
accident on the 18th of this month, which is to say, tomorrow,
ten miles north of Barstow while driving south on Interstate 15.
She lost control of her manually-operated vehicle and crashed
into a roadside barrier. The car was totally demolished and she
and the passenger were killed. Their bodies were cremated by
local authorities.'

'She met with this accident tomorrow, you say?'

'When tomorrow comes up on the computer net, the accident
will come up with it. So I use the past tense. It's already in there
waiting to activate itself. Agent C. Carmichael will be removed
from the system. So will Detainee K. Burke. We will vanish as
though we never existed. Since the car will also no longer exist
any official scanner that happens to pick up its license plate
as we continue on will most likely assume that the reading is
erroneous. Once we're in L.A., I'll arrange to obtain a new license
for the car, just to be on the safe side. – Are you getting hungry
yet?'

'Yes.'

'So am I. Let's do something about it.'

They stopped at a woebegone highway café in the middle of
nowhere, where the heat outside the car closed around them like
a great fist. She bought a dinner of sorts for them both simply
by showing her I.D. card. It was terrible food, some sort of card-
boardy and tasteless grilled meat on a bun and a cold bubbling

drink, but Khalid was used to terrible food of all sorts by this time.

Onward, again, through the sandy emptiness. There was very little traffic. None at all going in the direction they were traveling; perhaps one car every half hour going the other way. Whenever they passed someone, Cindy kept her eyes fixed rigidly on the road ahead, and Khalid noticed that the drivers of the other cars never looked toward them, either.

The road was climbing, and good-sized mountains were visible all around them now, bigger than he had ever seen before. But the landscape was still as ugly as ever, rocky and sandy, not much vegetation and most of that stunted and gnarled. At one point Cindy said, as they went flashing past a sign by the edge of the road, 'We're in California now, Khalid. Or what used to be California when this country still had such things as separate states. When there were still such things as countries.' He imagined palm trees and soft breezes. Not so. Everything was just as ugly here as it had been on the Nevada side of the line.

'Getting dark,' Cindy announced, an hour later. 'The driving's going to get tougher. These old crates are a lot of work to operate on a bad road. So I'm going to pull off and rest for a little while before we try to go further. You're sure you don't know how to drive?'

'Would you like me to try?'

'Maybe not, I think. Just stay awake, keep watch, let me know if you see anything strange.'

She left the freeway at the next exit and brought the car to a halt just off the road. Pushing her seat back until it was practically horizontal, she reclined against it, closed her eyes, and seemed to fall asleep almost at once.

Khalid watched her for a while. There was a look of great peace on her face.

She was, he thought, an unusual woman, very much in control of herself at all times, self-assured, confident. A very capable person. Possessing much inner serenity, of that he was certain. Inner serenity was something Khalid admired very much. He had worked very hard to attain it himself, and he had, he believed, succeeded; surely he would never have been able to kill that Entity without it.

Or *did* he have it? What had she said, on the plane? *I think you're angry all the time.* A seething volcano inside him, she said, with a tight lid clamped down on it to keep it from erupting. Was that true? He didn't know. He always *felt* calm; but perhaps, somewhere deep down inside, he was really raging with red-hot fury, killing Richie Burke a hundred times a day, killing all those who had made his life such a misery ever since the moment when he had understood that his mother was gone and his father was a monster and the world was under the control of bizarre, bewildering creatures who ruled, so it seemed, purely by whim and savage caprice.

Perhaps so. He didn't choose to look within and see.

But he was sure that there were no hidden volcanoes in this woman Cindy. She seemed to take life as it came, easily, day by day; very likely always had. Khalid wanted to know more about her, who she was, what her existence had been like before the Entities came, why she had become a quisling, all of that. But probably he would never ask. He was not used to asking people such things about themselves.

He left the car, walked around a little, glanced up at the moon and stars as night settled in. It was very quiet here, and with the coming of darkness the day's blistering warmth was fleeing into the thin desert air. Already it had become quite cool. There were scrabbling sounds somewhere nearby: animals, he supposed. Lions? Tigers? Did they have such things in California? This was a wild land, fierce and harsh. It made England seem very placid. He sat on the ground beside the car and watched shooting stars go streaking across the black dome overhead.

'Khalid?' Cindy called, after a time. 'You out there? What are you doing?'

'Just looking at the sky,' he said.

She had rested enough, she told him. He got back in, and they drove onward. Some time during the night they came to the exit for Barstow.

'We died ten miles back,' she said. 'It was all over so fast we never knew what was happening.'

*   *   *

A little before dawn, as they were descending a long gentle curve in a hilly part of the route, Khalid saw the turquoise lights of an Entity transport convoy far below, making its way uphill toward them. Cindy did not appear to notice.

'Entities,' he said, after a moment.

'Where?'

'That light down there.'

'Where? Where? Oh. *Shit!* Sharp eyes you have. – Who would expect them to be driving around in a place like this in the middle of the night? But of course, why wouldn't they?' She swerved the car roughly to the left and brought it to a screeching halt on the outer margin of the freeway.

He frowned at her. 'What are you doing?'

'Come on. Get out and let's run for it. We've got to hide in that ravine until they go past.'

'Why is that?'

'Come *on*,' she said. She was anything but serene now. 'We're supposed to be dead! If they detect us, and decide to check out our I.D. –'

'They will pay no attention to us, I think.'

'How do you know? Oh, Jesus, Jesus, you *idiot!*' She could not wait any longer. She made a furious snorting sound and leaped from the car, plunging off straight away into the steep brushy drop alongside the highway. Khalid remained where he was. He watched her dwindle into the darkness until the angle of the ravine hid her from his sight; and then he leaned back against the head-rest of his seat and waited for the Entity transport to approach.

He wondered whether they would notice him, sitting here in a parked car by the side of a dark road in an empty landscape, and whether they would care. Could they reach into his mind and see that he was Khalid Haleem Burke, who had died in an accident some hours earlier on this road, on the other side of the city called Barstow? Would they know anything about the supposed accident without consulting their computer net? Why would they bother? Why would they care?

Perhaps, he thought, they would look into his mind as they went past and discover that he was the person who had killed a member of their species seven years ago on the highway between

Salisbury and Stonehenge. In that case he had made a mistake, very likely, by remaining here, staying within range of their telepathy, instead of running off into the underbrush with Cindy.

The image blossomed in his mind of that night long ago on the road to Stonehenge, the beautiful angelic creature standing in the transport wagon, the gun, the crosshairs, the head perfectly targeted. Squeezing the trigger, seeing the angel's head burst apart, the bright fountain of flame, the radiant fragments flying outward, the greenish-red cloud of alien blood swiftly expanding into the air. The other Entity going into that frantic convulsion as its companion's spirit went whirling out into the darkness. He was as good as dead, Khalid knew, if the Entities detected that image as they passed by.

He pushed it aside. He emptied his mind entirely. He sealed it off from intruders with iron bands.

I am no one at all. I am not here.

Glimmers of turquoise light now ascended heavenward right in front of him. The transport had almost reached the top of the hill. Khalid waited for it in utter tranquility.

He was not there. There was no one at all in the car.

Three aliens rode in the transport: one of the big ones who were the Entities, and two of the lesser kind, the Spooks. Khalid ignored the Spooks and fixed his eyes in wonder on the Entity, enraptured as always by its magical gleaming beauty. His soul went out to it in love and admiration. If they had stopped and asked him to give them the world, he would have given it to them. But of course they already owned it.

He wondered why, as he watched the convoy go by, he had never become a quisling, if he admired the Entities so much. But the answer came just as quickly. He had no desire to serve them, only to worship their beauty. It was an esthetic thing. A sunrise was beautiful too, or a snow-capped mountain, or a lake that reflected the red glow of the end of day. But one did not enroll in the service of a mountain or a lake or a sunrise simply because one thought it was beautiful.

He let the time slide along: five minutes, ten. Then he left the car and called down to Cindy, in the ravine, 'They're gone, now. You can come back.'

A faint, distant reply came to him: 'Are you sure?'

'I sat here and watched them go by.'

It was a while before she reappeared. At last she came scrambling up out of the brush, out of breath and looking very rumpled and flustered and flushed. Collapsing down next to him in the car, she said, between deep gulps of air, 'They – didn't bother – you – at all?'

'No. Went right by, paid no attention. I told you that they wouldn't. I wasn't there.'

'It was crazy to take the chance.'

'Maybe I'm crazy,' Khalid said cheerfully, as she started the car and pulled back out onto the freeway.

'I don't think you are,' she said, after a moment. 'Why did you do it?'

'To be able to look at them,' he told her, in absolute sincerity. 'They are so beautiful, Cindy. They are like magical creatures to me. Jinn. Angels.'

She swiveled around in her seat and gave him a long strange look. 'You really are something unusual, Khalid.'

He made no answer to that. What could he say?

After another lengthy silent stretch she said, 'I lost my cool back there, I guess. There wasn't any real reason why they'd have stopped to interrogate us, was there?'

'No.'

'But I was afraid. A quisling and a detainee out driving together on an empty road late at night, well beyond the city that I was supposed to be taking you to, and both our I.D.s already invalidated on the master net because we've been reported as dead – we'd have been in a mess. I panicked.'

A little way farther onward she said, breaking the next silence into which they had slipped, 'Exactly what was it that you did, Khalid, to get yourself interned in the first place?'

He hesitated not at all. 'I killed an Entity.'

'You *what*?'

'In England, outside Salisbury. The one that was shot along the side of a road. I did it, with a special kind of gun that I took from my father. They collected everyone in the five towns closest to the place of the killing and executed some of us and sent the rest of us into the prison camps.'

She laughed, in a way that told him she hadn't for a moment believed him. 'What a wild sense of humor you have, Khalid.'

'Oh, no,' he said. 'I have no sense of humor whatever.'

Now morning had come and they were out of the desert and among a scattering of towns – a few cities, even, a little later on –and there was some traffic on the road. 'That's San Bernardino,' she said. 'Redlands is that place over down there. We're about an hour's drive from Los Angeles, I'd say.'

He saw palm trees now, huge and strange against the brightening sky. Other plants and trees that he could not identify, spiky, odd. Low buildings with roofs of red tiles. Cindy drove with exaggerated precision, so much so that the cars behind her honked their horns at her to get her to move along. To Khalid she said, 'Got to be very careful not to get into any accidents here. If a highway patrolman wanted to see my identification, we'd be cooked.'

They came to a place where they switched from one freeway to another. 'This is called the San Bernardino Freeway,' Cindy explained. 'It takes us westward, through Ontario, Covina, towns like that, toward the San Gabriel Valley and on into Los Angeles itself. The one we were on goes down through Riverside toward San Diego.'

'Ah,' he said knowingly, as though these names meant something to him.

'It's over twenty years since I was last in L.A. God knows how much it's changed in all that time. But what I figure on doing is driving straight out to the coast. Siegfried gave me the name of a friend of his, too, who lives in Malibu. I'll try to track him down and maybe he can plug me into the local communications channels. I had a lot of friends out in that part of town once, Santa Monica, Venice, Topanga. Some of them must still be alive and living in the vicinity. Siegfried's buddy can help me find them. And get me a new license plate, too, and new I.D. for us both.'

'Siegfried?'

'My hacker friend from Leipzig.'

'The pardoner.'

'Yes. The pardoner.'

'Ah,' said Khalid.

The freeway was huge here, so many lanes wide that he could scarcely believe it. The traffic, though heavier than he had seen anywhere else, was swallowed up in its vastness. But Cindy assured him that in the old days this freeway had been busy all day and all night, thousands of cars choking it all the time. In the old days, that was.

A little way farther on they came to an immense yellow sign stretching across all the lanes, high overhead, that said, FREE-WAY ENDS IN FIVE MILES.

'Huh?' Cindy said. 'We're only in Rosemead! Nowhere near Los Angeles yet. Are they telling me I'm going to have to do all the rest of it on surface streets? How the hell am I supposed to find my way through all these little towns on surface streets?'

'What are surface streets?' Khalid asked, but she had already pulled off the freeway and into a dilapidated service station just at the exit. It looked deserted; but then a stubbly-faced man in stained overalls appeared from behind the pumps. Jumping from the car, Cindy trotted over to him. A long conference ensued, with much pointing and waving of arms. When she returned to the car she had a stunned, disbelieving look on her face.

'There's a wall,' she told Khalid, in a tone of awe. 'A great humongous *wall*, all around Los Angeles!'

'Is that something new?'

'New? Damned right it's new! He says it's sky-high and runs clear around the whole place, with gates every five or six miles. Nobody gets in or out of the city without giving a password to the gatekeeper. *Nobody*.'

'You have your official identification number,' Khalid said.

'I've been dead since late last night, remember? I give the gatekeeper my number and we'll both be in detention five minutes later.'

'What about your pardoner friend's friend? Can't he get you a new identification pass?'

'He's in there, on the other side of the wall,' Cindy said. 'I've got to be able to get to him before he can do anything for me. There's no way I can reach him from out here.'

'You could hook into the computer net and reach him that way,' Khalid suggested.

'With what?' She held forth her arms, wrists turned upward. 'I don't have an implant. Never bothered with them. Do you? No, of course you don't. What am I supposed to do, send him a postcard?' She pressed her fingertips against her eyes. 'Let me think a minute. Shit! *Shit!* A wall around the entire city. Who the hell could have imagined *that?*'

In silence Khalid watched her think.

'One possibility,' she said eventually. 'A long shot. Santa Barbara.'

'Yes?' he said, if only to encourage her.

'That's a little city a couple of hours north of L.A. They can't have run the goddamned wall that far up. I used to have a relative up there, my husband's older brother. Retired army colonel, he was. Had a big ranch on a mountain above the town. I was there a couple of times long ago. He never cared for me very much, the Colonel. I wasn't his kind of person, I suppose. Still, I don't think he'd turn me away.'

Her husband. She had said nothing about a husband until this moment.

'The Colonel! Haven't thought of him in a million years,' Cindy said. 'He'd be – I don't know – eighty, ninety years old by now. But he'd still be there. I'd bet on it. Man was made out of leather and steel; I can't imagine him ever dying. If he did, well, one of his children or grandchildren probably would be living there. Somebody would be, anyway, some member of the family. They might take us in. It's worth a try. I don't know what else to do.'

'What about your husband?' Khalid asked. 'Where is he?'

'Dead, I think. I heard once that he died the day the Entities arrived. Cracked up his plane while on firefighting duty, something like that. A sweet man, he was. Sweet Mike. I really loved him.' She laughed. 'Not that I can even remember exactly what he looked like, now. Except his eyes. Blue eyes that saw right into you. The Colonel had eyes like that, too. So did his kids.

They all did. The whole tribe. – Well, what do you say, my friend? Shall we try for Santa Barbara?'

She returned to the freeway and continued along it, past more signs warning that it was ending, until in another few minutes the wall came into view before them.

'Joseph Mary Jesus,' Cindy said. 'Will you look at that thing?'

It was impressive, all right. It was a solid gray mass of big concrete blocks extending off to the left and right as far as Khalid could see, rising about as high as Salisbury Cathedral. The wall was pierced, where the freeway ran into it, by an arched gateway, deep and dark. A long line of cars was strung out in front of it. They were passing within very slowly, one by one. Occasionally an eastbound car would emerge from the other lane of the gate and drive off onto the freeway.

Cindy turned off the freeway to a city street, a wide boulevard lined by shabby little shops that looked mostly to be out of business, and began following the line of the wall northward. It seemed impossible for her to get over her astonishment at its height and bulk. She kept muttering to herself, shaking her head, now and then whistling in wonderment as some particularly lofty section of it appeared before them. There were places where the pattern of the streets forced them a few blocks away from the wall, but it was always visible off to their left, rearing up high over the two- and three-story buildings that seemed to be all there were in this district, and she returned to its proximity whenever she could.

She said very little to him. The struggle to find her way through these unfamiliar neighborhoods seemed to be exhausting her.

'This is incredible,' she said, toward mid-morning, as they churned on and on through a series of towns all packed very close together, some of them much more attractive than others. 'The immensity of it. The amount of labor that must have been poured into it. What sheep we've become! Build a wall all the way around Los Angeles, they tell us – they don't even say it, they just give you a little Push – and right away you get ten thousand men out there building them a wall. Raise food for us! And we do. Put enormous incomprehensible machines together for us. Yes. Yes. They've *domesticated* us. A whole planet of sheep, is what we are now. A planet of slaves. And the damnedest thing is that we don't lift a finger to undo it all. – Did you really kill that Entity?'

'Do you think that I did?'

'I think you might have, yes. Whoever did it, though, it's the only time anyone ever succeeded at it.' She leaned forward, squinting at a faded highway sign, pockmarked as though someone had used it for target practice. 'I remember the day it happened. For five minutes the Entities all went crazy. Jumping around like they'd been given a high-voltage jolt. Then they calmed down. Some wild day, that was. I was at the Vienna center, then. Like a circus, that day. And then we found out what had happened, that somebody had actually knocked one of them off, back in England. It hit me very hard, personally, when I heard that. I was, like, totally shocked. A terrible, terrible crime, I thought. I was still in love with them, then.'

The conversation was making Khalid uncomfortable. 'Are we near Los Angeles yet?' he asked.

'This is all Los Angeles, more or less. These were independent towns, but everything was really Los Angeles except they called themselves separate towns. The actual official Los Angeles is all on the far side of the wall, though. Maybe twenty miles away.'

You could tell when you were leaving one little city and entering another, because the street lamps were different and so were the houses, one city having splendid mansions and the very next one very small half-ruined ones. But there was a certain sameness to everything, beneath it all: the huge glossy-leaved trees, the lush gardens that even the smallest and poorest houses had, the low buildings and the bright eye of the sun blasting down onto everything. There were mountains just up ahead, stupendous ones, looking right down onto all these little towns. They had snow on their summits, though it was as warm as a summer day down here.

Cindy called off all the names of the cities to him as they passed through them, as if giving him a geography lesson. 'Pasadena,' she said. 'Glendale. Burbank. That's Los Angeles down there, to our left.'

They had turned, now, and were heading west, toward the sun, driving on a freeway again. The wall was quite distant from them along this part of the route, though later on they came near it again, and, later still, they were forced off the freeway into another region of what she called surface streets. The terrain here was flat and monotonous and the streets were long and straight.

'We're very close to the place where the Entities made their first landing,' Cindy told him. 'I hurried right to the spot, that morning. I had to see them. I was in love with the whole idea that the space people had come. I gave myself to them. Offered my services: the very first quisling, I guess. Not that I saw myself as a traitor, you understand, just an ambassador, a bridge between the species. But they let me down. They just shuffled me around from one job to another all those years while I waited for them to put me aboard a ship going to their home world. And finally I realized that they never would. – Look, Khalid, you can just about manage to see the wall again in that valley to our left, all the way down there, curving off toward the Pacific. But we're outside it now. We should have clear sailing all the way to Santa Barbara.'

And they did. But when they got there, late in the day, they found the town practically deserted, whole neighborhoods abandoned, block after block of handsome stucco-walled tiled buildings that had fallen into ruin. 'I can't believe this,' she said, over and over. 'This beautiful little city. Everybody must have just walked away from it! Or been taken away.' Pointing toward the lofty mountains rising behind the oceanfront plain on which the city stood, she said, 'Use those sharp eyes of yours. Can you see any houses up there?'

'Some, yes.'

'Signs that they're inhabited?'

'My eyes aren't that sharp,' he said.

But Santa Barbara wasn't wholly desolate. After driving around for a time Cindy found three short, swarthy-looking men standing together on a street corner in what must once have been the main commercial sector. She rolled down her car window and spoke to them in a language Khalid did not understand; one of them answered her, very briefly, and she spoke again, at great length this time, and they smiled and conferred with one another, and then the one who had answered before began to gesture toward the mountains and to indicate with movements of his hands and wrists a series of twisting, turning roads that would take her up there.

'What language was that?' Khalid asked, when they were moving again.

'Spanish.'

'Is that the language they speak in California?'

'In this part,' she said. 'Now, at any rate. He says the ranch is still there, that we just keep going up and up and up and eventually we'll come to the gate. He also said they wouldn't let us in. But maybe he's wrong.'

It was Cassandra, on duty in the children's compound, who was the one that heard the distant honking: three long honks, then a short one, then three more. She picked up the phone and called down to the ranch house. A voice that was either her husband's or her husband's twin brother's answered. Cassandra was better at telling Mike and Charlie's voices apart than anyone, but even she had trouble sometimes.

'Mike?' she said, guessing.

'No, Charlie. What's up?'

'Someone at the gate. We expecting anybody?'

She could hear Charlie asking someone, perhaps Ron. Then he said, 'No, nobody that we know of. Why don't you run up there and take a look, and call me back? You're closer to the gate than anybody else, where you are.'

'I'm six months pregnant and I'm not going to run anywhere,' said Cassandra tartly. 'And I'm in the kiddie house with Irene and Andy and La-La and Jane and Cheryl. And Sabrina, too. Besides, I don't have a gun. You find somebody else to go, you hear?'

Charlie was muttering something angry-sounding when Cassandra put down the receiver. Not my problem, she thought. The ranch was crawling with small kids and right this moment it was her job to look after them. Let Charlie find someone else to trot up to the gate: Jill, or Lisa, or Mark. Anybody. Or do it himself.

Some minutes went by. There was more honking.

Then she saw her young cousin Anson go jogging by, carrying the shotgun that was always carried by anyone who went to meet unexpected callers at the gate. His face was set in that clenched, rigid way that it always took on when one of the older men gave him a job to do. Anson was a terribly *responsible* kind of kid. Rain or shine, you could always get him to jump to it.

Well, problem solved, Cassandra thought, and went back to changing little Andy's diaper.

'Yes?' Anson said, peeping through the bars of the gate at the strangers. The shotgun dangled casually from his hand, but he could bring it up into position in an instant. He was sixteen, tall and strapping, ready for anything.

These people didn't seem very threatening, though. A thin, tired-faced little woman about his mother's age, or even a few years older; and an unusual-looking man in his twenties, very tall and slender, with huge blue-green eyes and darkish skin and an enormous mop of shining curly hair that was not quite red, not quite brown.

The woman said, 'My name is Cindy Carmichael. I was Mike Carmichael's wife, long long ago. This is Khalid, who's been traveling with me. We have no place to stay and we wonder if you can take us in.'

'Mike Carmichael's wife,' Anson said, frowning. That was confusing. Mike Carmichael was his cousin's name; but Cassandra was Mike's wife, and in any case this woman was old enough to be Mike's grandmother. She had to be talking about some other Mike Carmichael, in some other era.

She seemed to understand the problem. 'Colonel Carmichael's brother, he was. He's dead now. – You're a Carmichael yourself, aren't you? I can tell by the eyes. And the way you stand. What's your name?'

'Anson, ma'am.' And added: 'Carmichael, yes.'

'That was the Colonel's name, Anson. And he had a son by that name too. Anse, they called him. Are you Anse's boy?'

'No, ma'am. Ron's.'

'Are you, now? Ron's boy. So he's a family man these days. I suppose a lot of things have changed. – Let me think: that would make you Anson the Fifth, right? Just like in a royal dynasty.'

'The Fifth, yes, ma'am.'

'Well, hello, Anson the Fifth. I'm Cindy the First. Can we come in, please? We've been traveling a long way.'

'You wait here,' Anson said. 'I'll go and see.'

He jogged down to the main house. Charlie, Steve, and Paul were there, sitting at a table in the chart room with a sheaf of printouts spread out in front of them. 'There's a strange woman at the gate,' Anson told them. 'And somebody foreign-looking with her, a man. She says she's a Carmichael. Was married to a brother of the Colonel named Mike, once upon a time. I don't know who the man is at all. She seems to know a lot about the family. – Did the Colonel ever have a brother named Mike?'

'Not that I know of,' Charlie said. 'Before my time, if he did.' Steve merely shrugged. But Paul said, 'How old is she? Older than I am, would you say?'

'I'd say so. Older even than Uncle Ron, maybe. About Aunt Rosalie's age, maybe.'

'She tell you her name?'

'Cindy, she said.'

Paul's eyes grew very wide. 'I'll be damned.'

'So you surely will, cousin,' said Ron, entering the room just then. 'What's going on?'

'You aren't going to believe this. But apparently the ambassador from outer space has returned, and she's waiting at the gate. Cindy, I mean. Mike's wife Cindy. How about that?'

So the whole place was a kind of Carmichael commune now, the Colonel's entire family living together on the hilltop. Cindy hadn't expected that. That was a whole lot of Carmichaels, counting in the kids, and all. She felt a little outnumbered.

It was amazing to see them all again, these people who for a few years had been her kinfolk, after a manner of speaking, so many years ago. Not that Cindy had ever been particularly close to any of them, back in her free-wheeling old Los Angeles days. Taking their cue from the formidable old Colonel, they had never really allowed her into the family circle, except perhaps for Mike's nephew Anse, who had treated her politely enough. To the others she was just Mike's crazy hippie wife, who dressed funny and talked funny and thought funny, and they had made it pretty clear that they wanted very little, if anything, to do with her. Which had basically been okay with Cindy. They had their lives; she and Mike had had theirs.

But that was then and this was now, and Mike was long gone and the world had changed beyond anybody's ability to imagine, and she had changed too, and so had they. And these people were the closest thing to family that she had left. She could not let them reject her now.

'I can't tell you how glad I am to be here, to be back among the Carmichaels again. Or to be among the Carmichaels for the first time, really. I never was much of a family person back in the old days, was I? But I'd like to be, now. I really would.'

They were gawking at her as though an Entity, or perhaps a Spook, had wandered somehow into their house on the mountainside and was standing in their midst.

Cindy looked right back at them. Her gaze traveled around the room. She summoned up what she could remember of them.

Ronnie. That one had to be Ronnie, there in the middle of the group. He seemed to be running things, now. That was odd, Ronnie being in charge. She remembered sly Ronnie as a wild man, a trickster, a plunger, an operator, always on the outside in family stuff. If anything he had been more of the black sheep of the family than she. But here he was, now, fifty years old, fifty-five, maybe, big and solid, grown very stocky with the years, his blond hair now almost white, and you could see immediately that he had changed inwardly too, in some fundamental way, that he had grown stronger, steadier, transformed himself colossally in these twenty-odd years. He had never looked *serious*, in the old days. Now he did.

Next to him was his sister, Rosalie. A nice-looking woman then, Cindy remembered, and she had aged very well indeed, tall, stately, controlled. She had to be around sixty but she seemed younger. Cindy recalled Mike telling her that Rosalie had been a big problem when she was a girl – drugs, a great deal of screwing around – but all that was far behind her now. She had married some fat nerdy guy, a computer man, and become a reformed character overnight. That must be him with her, Cindy thought: that big bald doughy-faced fellow. She didn't remember his name.

And that one – the stringy-looking blonde woman – she must be Anse's wife. A suburban-mom type back then, somewhat high strung. Cindy had found her to be of absolutely no interest. Another name forgotten.

The younger man – he was Paul, wasn't he? Mike's other brother's son. Pleasant young fellow, science professor at some college south of L.A. Figured to be forty-five or so, now. Cindy recalled that he had had a sister. She didn't seem to be here now.

As for the others, four of them were kids in their middle or late twenties, and the other, the teenager, was Ron's kid, who had met them at the gate. The rest were probably Anse's children, or Paul's. They all looked more or less alike, except for one, clearly the oldest, who was heavyset and brown-eyed and balding already, with only the faintest traces of Carmichael about him. The son of Rosalie and her computer guy, Cindy supposed. There would be time to sort the others out later. The remaining person was a woman in her late forties who was standing just alongside Ron. The late-fortyish woman seemed vaguely familiar to Cindy but plainly was no Carmichael, not with those dark eyes and that smallish, fine-boned frame. Ronnie's wife, most likely.

She said, as she completed her survey, 'And the Colonel? What about him? Could he still be alive?'

'Could be and is,' Ronnie said. 'Almost eighty-five and very feeble, and I don't think he'll be with us much longer. He's going to be damned surprised to see you.'

'And not very pleased, I bet. I'm sure you know he never thought very highly of me. Perhaps for good reasons.'

'He'll be glad to see you now. You're his closest link with his brother Mike, you know. He spends most of his time in the past these days. Of course, he doesn't have much future.'

Cindy nodded. 'And there's somebody else missing. Your brother Anse.'

'Dead,' Ronnie said. 'Four years back.'

'I'm so sorry. He was a fine man.'

'He was, yes. But he had a lot of trouble with drinking, his later years. Anse wanted so much to be as strong and good as the Colonel, you know, but he never quite managed it. Nobody could have. But Anse just wouldn't forgive himself for being human.'

Was there anyone else from the old days that she should ask about? Cindy didn't think so. She glanced toward Khalid, wondering what he was making out of all this. But Khalid appeared utterly placid. As though his brain had gone off on a voyage to Mars.

The late-fortyish woman standing near Ronnie said cheerily, 'I guess you don't recognize me, do you, Cindy? But of course we were only together for a very few hours.'

'We were? When was that? I'm sorry.'

'On the Entity spaceship, after the Porter Ranch landing. We were in the same group of prisoners.' A warm smile. 'Margaret Gabrielson. Peggy. I came here to work for the Colonel, and later I married Ron. No reason why you would remember me.'

No. There wasn't. Cindy didn't.

'You were very distinctive. I've never forgotten: the beads, the sandals, the big earrings. They let most of us go that afternoon, but you volunteered to stay with the aliens. You said they were going to take you to their planet.'

'That's what I thought. But they never did,' Cindy said. 'I worked for them all those years, doing whatever they wanted me to do, running detainee centers for them, transporting prisoners around, waiting for them to make good on their promise. But it didn't happen. After a while I began to wonder if they had ever promised it. By now I've decided that it was all my own delusion.'

'You're a quisling, then?' Ronnie asked. 'Are you aware that this is a major center of the Resistance?'

'*Was* a quisling,' she said. 'Not any longer. I was working at a detention center on the Turkish coast when I realized I had wasted twenty years playing footsie with the Entities for nothing. They hadn't come here to turn our world into a paradise, which is what I used to believe. They had come here to enslave us. So

I wanted out; I wanted to go home. I arranged for a pardoner I know in Germany to have me shipped out to the States, escorting a batch of prisoners to Nevada, and he rewrote my personnel code to say that I had been killed in an auto accident between Vegas and Barstow while driving this young man to his next detention camp. That's why he's here. The pardoner rewrote *his* code too. We're permanent vanishees, now. When we got to L.A., I discovered that there's a wall around the place. No way for us to get in, because we don't officially exist any more.'

'So then you had the notion of coming here.'

'Yes. What else could I do? But if you don't want me, just say so, and I'll take off. My name is Carmichael, though. I was a member of this family once, your uncle's wife. I loved him very much and he loved me. And I'm not about to interfere with any of your Resistance activities. If anything, I can help with them. I can tell you a lot of stuff about the Entities that you may not know.'

Ronnie was eyeing her reflectively.

'Let's go talk to the Colonel,' he said.

Khalid watched her go from the room, followed by most of the others. Only a few of the younger ones remained with him: two men who were obviously twin brothers, though one had a long red scar on his face, and the tense, earnest, boyish-looking one, plainly related to the twins, who had met them at the gate with the shotgun in his hand. And also a girl who looked like a female version of the two brothers, tall and lean and blonde, with those icy blue eyes that almost everyone around here seemed to have. The rest of her seemed icy too: she was as cool and remote as the sky. But very beautiful.

The brother with the scar said, to the other one, 'We'd better move along, Charlie. We're supposed to be fixing the main irrigation pump.'

'Right.' To the boy with the shotgun Charlie said, 'Can you manage things here on your own, Anson?'

'Don't worry about me. I know what to do.'

'If he does anything peculiar, you let him have it right in the gut, you hear me, Anson?'

'Go on, Charlie,' Anson said stiffly, gesturing toward the door with the shotgun. 'Go fix the goddamned pump. I told you, I know what to do.'

The twins went out. Khalid stood patiently where he had been standing all along, calm as ever, letting time flow past him. The tall blonde girl was looking at him intently. There was a detachment in her curiosity, a kind of aloof scientific fascination. She was studying him as though he were some new kind of life-form. Khalid found that oddly appealing. He sensed that she and he might be similar in certain interesting ways, behind their wholly different exteriors.

She let a moment or two go by. Then she said to the boy, 'You run along now, Anson. Let me have the gun.'

Anson seemed startled. He is so very earnest, Khalid thought. Takes himself very seriously. 'I can't do that, Jill!'

'Sure you can. You think I don't know how to use a shotgun? I was shooting rabbits on this mountain while you were still shitting in your diapers. Give it here. Run along.'

'Hey, I don't know if –'

'*Go*, now,' she said, taking the gun from him and pointing with her thumb toward the door. She had not raised her voice at all throughout the entire interchange; but Anson, looking bewildered and cowed, went shuffling from the room as though she had struck him in the face with a whip.

'Hello,' the girl said to Khalid. Only the two of them were left in the room, now.

'Hello.'

Her eyes were fixed steadily on him. Almost without blinking. The thought came to him suddenly that he would like to see her without her clothes. He wanted to know whether the triangle at her loins was as golden as the hair on her head. He found himself imagining what it would be like to run his hand up her long, smooth thighs.

'I'm Jill,' she said. 'What's your name?'

'Khalid.'

'Khalid. What kind of name is that?'

'An Islamic name. I was named for my uncle. I was born in England, but my mother was of Pakistani descent.'

'Pakistani, eh? And what may that be?'

'Pakistanis are people who come from Pakistan. That's a country near India.'

'Ah-hah. India. I know about India. Elephants and tigers and rubies. I read a book about India once.' She waggled the gun around in a careless, easy way. 'You have interesting eyes, Khalid.'

'Thank you.'

'Do all Pakistanis look like you?'

'My father was English,' he said. 'He was very tall, and so am I. Pakistanis aren't usually this tall. And they have darker skin than I have, and brown eyes. I hated him.'

'Because he had the wrong color eyes?'

'His eyes did not matter to me.'

Hers were staring right into his. Those blue, blue eyes.

She said, 'You were in Entity detention, that woman said. What did you do to get yourself detained?'

'I'll tell you that some other time.'

'Not now?'

'Not now, no.'

She ran her hand along the barrel of the shotgun, stroking it lovingly, as though she just might be thinking of ordering him at gunpoint to tell him what the crime was that he had committed. He remembered how he had stroked the grenade gun, the night he had killed the Entity. But he doubted that she would shoot him; and he did not intend to tell her anything about that now, no matter what kind of threats she made. Later, maybe. Not now.

She said, 'You're very mysterious, aren't you, Khalid. Who are you, I wonder?'

'No one in particular.'

'Neither am I,' she said.

The Colonel looked to be about two hundred years old, Cindy thought. There didn't seem to be anything left of him but those outrageous eyes of his, blue as glaciers, sharp as lasers.

He was in bed, propped up on a bunch of pillows. He had a visible tremor of some kind, and his face was haggard and deathly pale, and from the look of his shoulders and chest he weighed about eighty pounds. His famous shock of silvery hair had thinned to mere wisps.

All around him, on both night-tables and on the wall, were dozens and dozens of family photographs, some two-dimensional and some in three, along with all manner of official-looking framed documents, military honors and such. Cindy spotted the photo of Mike at once. It leaped out instantly from everything else: Mike as she remembered him, a vigorous handsome man in his fifties, out in the New Mexico desert standing next to that little plane he had loved so much, the Cessna.

'Cindy,' the Colonel said, beckoning with a claw-like palsied hand. 'Come here. Closer. Closer.' Faint and papery as it was, it was still unmistakably the voice of the Colonel. She could never have forgotten that voice. When the Colonel said something, however mildly, it was an *order*. 'You really are Cindy, are you?'

'Really. Truly.'

'How amazing. I didn't ever imagine that I'd see you again. You went to the aliens' planet, did you?'

'No. That was just a pipe dream. They just kept me, all those years. Put me to work, moving me around from this compound to that, one administrative job and another. Eventually I decided to escape.'

'And come here?'

'Not at all. I had no way of knowing I'd find anyone here. I went to L.A. But I couldn't get in, so I took a chance and came up here. This was my last resort.'

'You know that Mike is long dead, don't you?'

'I know that, yes.'

'And Anse, too. You remember Anse? My older son?'

'Of course I remember him.'

'My turn's next. I've already lived ten years too long, at the very least. Thirty, maybe. But it's just about over for me, now. I broke my hip last week. You don't recover from that, not at my age. I've had enough, anyway.'

'I never thought I'd hear you say anything like that.'

'You mean that I sound like a quitter? No. That's not it. I'm not giving up, exactly. I'm just going away. There's no preventing it, is there? We aren't designed to live forever. We outlive our own time, we outlive our friends, if we're really unlucky we outlive our children, and then we go. It's all right.' He managed a sort of smile. 'I'm glad you came here, Cindy.'

'You are? Really?'

'I never understood you, you know. And I guess you never understood me. But we're family, all the same. My brother's wife: how could I not love you? You can't expect everybody around you to be just like yourself. Take Mike, for instance –'

He began to cough. Ronnie, who had been standing to one side in silence, stepped forward quickly, snatching up a glass of water from a nearby table and offering it to him. Quietly he said, 'You may be over-exerting yourself, dad.'

'No. No. All I'm doing is making a little speech.' The Colonel drank deeply, let his eyes droop shut for a moment, opened them and turned them on Cindy again. 'As I was saying: Mike. A martyr, I used to think, to all the cockeyed ideas that went running through American life since we went to war in Vietnam. The things he did. Quit the Air Force, ran off to L.A., married a hippie, went out to the desert a lot to hide himself away and meditate. I didn't approve. But what business was it of mine? He was what he was. He was already himself when he was six years old, and what he was was something different from me.'

Another deep drink of water.

'Anse. Tried his best to be someone like me. Failed at it. Burned himself out and died young. Ronnie. Rosalie. Problems, problems, problems. If my own children are this crazy, I thought, what must the rest of the world be like? One big lunatic asylum, with me stranded in it. And that was before the Entities came, even. But I was wrong. I just wanted everybody to be as stiff and stern as me, because that's how I thought people should be. Carmichaels, anyway. Warriors, dedicated to the cause of righteousness and decency.' A soft chuckle came from him. 'Well, the Entities showed us a thing or two, didn't they? The good, the bad, the indifferent – we all got conquered the same day, and lived unhappily ever after.'

'*You* never got conquered, dad,' Ronnie said.

'Is that how it seems to you? Well, maybe. Maybe.' The old man had not released his grip on Cindy's hand. He said, 'You lived among the Entities all this time, you say? So you must know a thing or two about them. Do they have any flaws, do you think? An Achilles' heel somewhere that will let us defeat them, ultimately?'

'I wouldn't say I saw anything like that, no.'

'No. No. They're perfect superbeings. They're just like gods. Can that be so? I suppose it is. But I wanted to go on resisting, all the same. Keeping the *idea* of resistance alive, anyway. The memory of what it had been like to live in a free world. Maybe we never even *did* live in a free world, anyway. God knows I heard plenty of that stuff during the Vietnam time, how the evil multinational corporations actually were the ones who ran everything, or some little group of secret political masters, conspiracies, lies. That nothing was what it seemed to be on the surface. All our supposed democratic freedoms just illusions designed to keep people from understanding the truth. America really a totalitarian state like all the rest. I never believed any of that. But even so, even if I was naive all my life, I want to think it's possible for the America that I used to think existed to exist again, regardless of whether it ever did the first time around. Are you following me? That it can all be reborn, that we can come out from under these slave-master Entities, that we can repair ourselves somehow and live as we were meant to live. Call it faith in the ultimate providence of God, I guess. Call it –' He paused and winked at her. 'Some speech, eh, Cindy? The old man's farewell address. I've just about run out of steam, though. Are you going to live here with us from now on?'

'I want to.'

'Good. Welcome home.' For once the fierce eyes softened a little. 'I love you, Cindy. It's taken me thirty years to get around to being able to say that, and I guess the world had to be conquered by aliens, first, and Mike to die, and a lot of other wild stuff to happen. But I love you. That's all I want to say. I love you.'

'And I love you,' she said softly. 'I always did. I just didn't know it, I guess.'

VI

Forty Years
from Now

It was eleven years after Khalid and Cindy had come to the ranch, and ten since he had married Jill, when he finally revealed to anyone what it was that he had done to warrant being put into detention by the Entities.

Eleven years.

And thirty-three since the Conquest; and the ranch still floated above the suffering world like an island in mid-air, sacrosanct. Somewhere out there were the impregnable compounds of the Entities – within which the conquering creatures from another world went about the unfathomable activities requisite to an occupation of the conquered planet, an occupation that now had lasted a full third of a century without let-up or explanation; and, somewhere out there, labor gangs working under conditions amounting to slavery were building huge walls around all of Earth's major cities, and doing, at the behest of human task-masters who took their orders from the aliens, all manner of other things whose purpose no one could comprehend. And somewhere out there, too, there were prison camps in which thousands or hundreds of thousands of people who had broken some mystifying and inexplicable regulation that had been decreed by Earth's starborn monarchs were capriciously and randomly detained.

Here, meanwhile, were the Carmichaels up above the world. It was rare for any of them to leave their mountain home any longer. The ranch's confines were much less confining, now; the Carmichael domain had spread outward and to some degree downward into the depopulated hillsides all about them. They spent their days raising tomatoes and corn and sheep and pigs and squadrons of new Carmichael babies. The making of babies was, in fact, a primary occupation there. The place swarmed with them, one generation tumbling fast upon its predecessor. And also, like some machine that has been set blindly into motion without any means of halting, going through the unending motions of running a Resistance that consisted mainly of sending strings of resolute and inspiring e-mail to other groups of Resisters all over the world. The Entities, inscrutable as ever, must surely must have known what was going on up there, but they stayed their hand.

The Carmichaels lived in such utter isolation that when some stranger, some spy, broke into their walled domain a few years after Khalid's arrival there, it was an altogether astounding event, an unprecedented foray of reality into their charmed sphere. Charlie found him quickly and killed him and all was as it had been, once again. And the world went on, for the unconquered Carmichaels on their mountainside and for the conquered hosts below.

Eleven years. For Khalid they went by in a moment.

By then, the Carmichaels had just about forgotten the whole subject of Khalid's detention. Khalid lived among them like a Martian among humans, he and the almost equally Martian Jill, in an isolated cabin of their own that he and Mike and Anson had constructed for them beyond the vegetable garden, and there Khalid spent his days fashioning sculptures large and small out of stone or clay or pieces of wood, and drew sketches, and taught himself how to grind pigments into paint and how to paint with them; and he and Jill raised their tribe of eerily beautiful children there, and no one, not even Khalid, ever thought much about Khalid's mysterious past. The past was not a place Khalid cared to visit. It held no fond memories. He preferred to live one moment at a time, looking neither forward nor back.

The pasts of other people impinged on him all the time, though, because it was just a short way from his cabin to the ranch's graveyard, off in a gravelly little rock-walled natural enclosure, a sort of box canyon, just to the left of the vegetable patch. Khalid went there often to sit among the dead people and look outward, thinking about nothing at all.

The view from the graveyard was ideal for that purpose. The

little box canyon opened at its downslope end into a larger side canyon on the mountain's western face, canted not toward the city of Santa Barbara but toward the next mountain in the series that ran parallel to the coastline. So you could sit there with your back against the steep mountain face and look right out into blue sky and wheeling hawks, with little else in your line of sight except the distant gray-brown bulk of the next mountain over, the one that bordered the ranch on the west.

Gravestones sprouted like toadstools all around him here, but that was all right. The dead were no more frightening to Khalid than the living. And in any case he had known very few of these people.

The biggest and most elaborate of the stones belonged to the grave of Colonel Anson Carmichael III, 1943–2027. There always were fresh flowers on that grave, every day of the year. Khalid understood that the Colonel had been the patriarch of this community. He had died a day or two after Khalid's arrival here. Khalid had never laid eyes on him.

Nor on Captain Anson Carmichael IV, 1964–2024. They loved that name Anson here. The settlement was full of them. Ron Carmichael's oldest son was an Anson; so was Steve Gannett's boy, though everyone called him 'Andy'. And Khalid thought there might be others. There were so many children that it was hard to keep track. At Jill's insistence Khalid had even given the name to one of his own sons: Rasheed Anson Burke, he was. This one in the grave before him had been known as 'Anse': the oldest son of the illustrious Colonel, dead before his own father. A sad story, evidently, but no one had ever told Khalid the details of it. Jill, although she had been Anse's daughter, never talked of him.

Jill's mother was buried next to her husband: Carole Martinson Carmichael, 1969–2034. Khalid remembered her as a thin, pallid, downcast woman, a worn and ragged version of her beautiful daughter. She had never had much to say. Khalid had carved the headstone himself, with two winged angels on it within an elaborate wreath. Jill had requested that. Just back of the graves of Anse and Carole was the grave of someone named Helena Carmichael Boyce, 1979–2021 – Khalid had no idea who she had been – and, not far from hers, the resting place of Jill's first husband, the mysterious Theodore Quarles, 1975–2023, called 'Ted'.

All Khalid knew about Theodore Quarles was that he had been many years older than Jill, that they had lived together as man and wife for about a year, that he had been killed in a rockslide during a stormy winter. He was another one of whom Jill never spoke; but that too was all right. Khalid had no interest in knowing any more about Theodore Quarles than he already did, which was the mere fact of his existence.

Then there were the graves of various children of the family who had died young in this little mountainside village that had no doctor. Five, six, seven headstones, small ones all in a row. These usually had flowers on them too. But there were never any flowers on the next grave over, that of the nameless intruder, perhaps a quisling spy, whom Charlie had killed six or seven years back after discovering him prowling around in the computer shack. Ron had insisted that he be given a proper burial, though there was a hot argument about it, Charlie and Ron going at it for hour after hour until young Anson managed to calm them down. That grave had only a crude marker on it. It was up against the side wall of the little canyon and no one ever went near it.

Also toward that side of the cemetery there were two gravestones that Khalid had erected himself, a couple of years ago. He hadn't asked anyone's permission, had just gone ahead and done it. Why not? He lived here too. He was entitled.

One of them marked Aissha's grave. Of course, Khalid had no definite knowledge that she was dead. But he had no particular reason to think she was alive, either, and he wanted her to be commemorated here somehow. She was the only person in the universe who had ever meant anything to him. So he carved a fine stone for her, with intricate patterns of interwoven scrollwork all along it. Everything abstract: no graven images for devout Aissha. And wrote in bold letters right in the middle, *AISSHA KHAN*. With a few lines from the Koran below, lines in English, because Khalid had forgotten most of the little Arabic that

Iskander Mustafa Ali had managed to teach him: *Praise be to Allah, Lord of the Universe. You alone we worship, and to You alone we turn for help.* No dates. He knew no dates to put there.

The other gravestone that Khalid put up had simpler ornamentation and a shorter inscription:

YASMEENA
Mother of Khalid

Leaving the last names off. He loathed his own; and even if Yasmeena had been married to Richie Burke, which Khalid doubted, he didn't want that name on her stone. He could have called her 'Yasmeena Khan.' But it seemed wrong for mother and son to have different last names, so he left both off. And also no dates. Khalid knew when she had died, because it was the day of his own birth, but he wasn't sure how old she had been then. Young, that was all he knew. What did such things matter, anyway? The only thing that mattered was that she was remembered.

Jill, watching him carve Yasmeena's stone, said, 'And will you make one for your father, too?'

'No. Not for him.'

He was visiting the graves of Aissha and Yasmeena on a bright day in the middle of one of those long, endless-seeming sun-drenched summers that came to the ranch in February or March of every year and stayed until November or December, when Jill unexpectedly appeared at the downslope side of the burying-ground, where the entrance was. One of the children was with her, the girl Khalifa, who was five.

'You're praying,' Jill said. 'I interrupted you.'

'No. I'm all done.'

Every Friday Khalid came here and spoke some words from the Koran over the two graves, words that he had tried to resurrect from his memories of his long-ago lessons in Salisbury with Iskander Mustafa Ali. *On the day when the first and second blasts of the Trumpet are heard,* Khalid would say, *all hearts shall be filled with terror, and all eyes shall stare with awe.* And then he would say: *When the sky is torn asunder, when the stars scatter and the oceans roll together, when the graves are thrown about, then each soul shall know what it has done and what it has failed to do. And then: On that day some will have beaming faces, smiling and joyful, for they will live in Paradise. And on that day the faces of others will be veiled with darkness and covered with dust.* He could remember no more than that, and he knew that he had jumbled these lines together from different sections; but they were the best he could manage, and he believed that Allah would accept them from him, even though you were not supposed to alter a single word of the scripture, because this was the best he could do and Allah did not demand from you more than was possible.

Jill was barefoot and wore only a strip of blue fabric around her waist and another over her breasts. Khalifa wore nothing at all. Cloth was getting hard to come by, these days, and clothing wore out all too quickly; and in warm weather the small children went naked and most of the younger adult Carmichaels wore very little. Jill, at forty, still thought of herself as a younger Carmichael, and, even though she had borne five children and showed the signs of that, her long, slender frame had the look of youth about it yet.

'What is it?' Khalid asked. It had to be something unusual to bring her here while he was at his prayers. Above all else he and Jill respected each other's privacy.

'Khalifa says she saw an Entity.'

Well, that was certainly something unusual, Khalid thought. He glanced at the child. She didn't seem particularly upset. Quite calm, in fact.

'An Entity, eh? And where did this happen?'

'By the wading pond, she says. The Entity got into the pond with her and splashed around. It played with her and talked with her a long time. Then it took her in its arms and went with her on a trip into the sky and brought her back.'

'You believe that this happened?' Khalid asked.

Jill shrugged. 'Not necessarily. But how would I know whether it happened or not? I thought you should know. What if they're beginning to snoop around here?'

'Yes. I suppose.'

Jill was like that: she made no judgments, she drew no conclusions. She drifted through life like a Spook, rarely touching the ground. Sometimes she and Khalid went for days at a time without speaking to each other, though all was peaceful between them, and they would turn to each other in bed every night during such times as naturally and passionately as they always did. In eleven years together Khalid had never attempted to penetrate her inner thoughts, nor she his. They respected each other's privacy, yes. Two of a kind, they were.

He knelt beside the little girl and said gently, 'You saw an Entity, eh?'

'Yes. It took me flying into space.'

Khalifa was the most beautiful of his five striking children: angelic, even. She combined in herself the best of Jill's fair-skinned fair-haired beauty and his own more exotic hybrid traits. Her limbs were long, already arguing for extraordinary height; her hair was shimmering golden fleece, with an underglow of bronze; her eyes were his gem-like blue-green; her pellucid skin had some subtle trace of his tawniness to it, a subcutaneous ruddy gleam like that of burnished copper.

He said, 'What did it look like, this Entity?'

'It was a little like a lion,' she said, 'and a little like a camel. It had shining wings and a long snaky tail. It was pink all over and very tall.'

'How tall?'

'As tall as you are. Maybe even a little taller.'

Her eyes were wide and solemn and sincere. But this had to be a fable. There were no Entities that looked like that. Unless some new kind had recently arrived on Earth, of course.

'Were you afraid?' Khalid asked.

'A little. It was sort of scary, I suppose. But it said it wouldn't hurt me if I kept quiet. It just wanted to play with me, it said.'

'Play?'

'We played splashing games, and we danced around in the pond. It asked me my name and the names of my mommy and my daddy, and a lot of other things that I don't remember. Then it took me flying. We went up to the moon and back. I saw the castles and rivers on the moon. It said that it would come back on my birthday and take me flying again.'

'To the moon?'

'To the moon, and Mars, and lots of other places.'

Khalid nodded. For a moment or two he studied Khalifa's angelic countenance, marveling at the teeming fantasies behind that small smooth forehead. Then he said: 'How do you know anything about lions and camels?'

The briefest of hesitation. 'Andy told me about them.'

Andy. Now it made sense. Her twelve-year-old cousin Andy, Steve and Lisa's son, was a gushing fountain of uncontrolled imagination. Too clever for his own good, that boy, forever making his magic with computers, bringing forth all sorts of unheard-of trickery. And something diabolical in his eyes, even back when he was only a baby.

'Andy told you?' Khalid said.

'He showed me pictures of them on the screen of his machine. And told me stories about them. Andy tells me lots of stories.'

'Ah,' Khalid said. He shot a glance at Jill. – 'Does Andy tell you stories about Entities too?' he asked the girl.

'Sometimes.'

'Did he tell you this one?'

'Oh, no. This one really happened!'

'To you, or to Andy?'

'To me! To me!' Indignantly. She gave him a petulant, even angry, look, as though annoyed that he would doubt her. But then, abruptly, things changed. An expression of uncertainty, or perhaps fear, appeared on the child's face. Her lower lip trembled. She was on the edge of tears. – 'I wasn't supposed to tell you. I shouldn't have. The only one I told was Mommy, and she told you. But the Entity told me not to say anything to anybody about what had happened, or it would kill me. It isn't going to kill me, is it, Khalid?'

He smiled. 'No, child. That won't happen.'

'I'm scared.' The tears were showing, now.

'No. No. Nothing's going to kill you. Listen to me, Khalifa: if this so-called Entity or any other kind of creature comes back here and bothers you again, you tell me about it right away and I'll kill *it*. I've already killed one Entity in my life and I can do it again. So there isn't a thing for you to be afraid of.'

'*Would* you kill an Entity?' she asked.

'If it tried to bother you, yes,' said Khalid. 'In a flash, I would.' He pulled her to him, lifted her, hugged her, set her gently down. Patted her on her bare little rump, told her once more not to worry about the Entity, sent her on her way.

To Jill he said, 'That boy Andy is all mischief. I need to talk to him about not filling the girl's head with nonsense.'

She was looking at him strangely.

'Did I say something wrong?' he asked.

'Andy's not the only one filling her head with nonsense, I think. Why did you tell her that thing about your killing an Entity once?'

'That wasn't nonsense. It's true.'

'Come on, Khalid.'

'What do you think I did that got me into Entity detention? You remember, I was an escaped detainee when I came here?' Jill was looking at him as though he had begun to speak in an unknown language. But, Khalid thought, it was time he had told her of this. More than time. He went on, 'An Entity was shot dead once on a country road in England, years and years ago. I'm the one that shot it. But they had no way of knowing that, so everybody in my part of England was rounded up and killed, or put into the camps. The only one I ever told was Cindy. I'm not sure that she believed me.' Jill was still staring. 'What's the matter?' he asked. 'Don't you believe that I could have done something like that?'

She was very slow to answer.

'Yes,' she said, eventually. 'Yes, I think you could.'

He found Andy exactly where he expected to find him, on a bench outside the computer shack, tinkering with one of his portable computers. The boy, like his father, like his grandfather, seemed to eat and breathe and live computers, and probably wrote programs while he was sleeping, too.

'Andy?'

'Just a minute, Khalid.'

'I need to talk to you.'

'Just a *minute*!'

Calmly Khalid reached down and pushed a button on Andy's computer. The screen went dark. The boy gave him a fiery look and leaped to his feet, fists balled. He was big for his age, very well developed, but Khalid stood poised, ready to deal with any attack. Not that he would hit Andy – that would be too much like Richie, hitting a twelve-year-old boy – but he would restrain him, if he had to, until the boy's fit of temper had passed.

Andy got control of himself quickly enough, though. Sourly he said, 'You shouldn't have done that, Khalid. You might have spoiled what I was writing.'

'When an adult tells you to pay attention, you pay attention,' Khalid said. 'That is the rule here. You will not ignore me when I tell you I wish to speak with you. What were you doing? Eavesdropping on the secret conversations of the Entities?'

Andy's fury dropped away. Smirking cheekily, he said, 'You wish.'

The boy was naked. That bothered Khalid. Andy might be only twelve, but his body was already that of a man; he should cover himself. Khalid disliked the idea that this naked man-child should have been playing with his naked little daughter, telling her fantastic fables.

He said, 'I hear from Khalifa that you make up very interesting stories about new kinds of Entities. In particular one that looks something like a lion and something like a camel.'

'What's so bad about that?'

'This is true, then?'

'Sure. I show the kids all sorts of graphics.'

'Show me,' said Khalid.

Andy turned the computer back on. Instantly four lines of bright lettering edged with flames blazed forth on the screen:

PRIVATE PROPERTY OF
ANSON CARMICHAEL GANNETT.
KEEP YOUR FUCKING HANDS OFF!
THIS MEANS YOU!!!

He hit a key, and another one, and another one, and a vivid picture began to take form on the screen. A mythical beast of some sort, it seemed. A camel's long comic face, a lion's ferocious claws, an eagle's splendid wings. A long curling serpentine tale. Andy filled in the details quickly, until the image on the screen seemed almost three-dimensional. Ready to jump out of the computer and dance around before them. It turned its head from side to side, it grinned at them, it leered, it glowered, it showed a set of gleaming fangs that no camel had ever possessed.

How had the boy done that? Khalid knew almost nothing about computers. It seemed like magic to Khalid, black magic. The work of a jinni: one of the evil ones. The work of a demon.

'What is this creature?' Khalid asked.

'A griffin. I found it in a mythology text. I put the camel's head on myself, just for fun.'

'And told Khalifa that it was an Entity?'

'Uh-uh. That was strictly her idea. I was just showing her graphics. Did she tell you I called it an Entity?'

'She said she *saw* an Entity, that it visited her and played with her and took her on a flight to the moon. And plenty of other crazy stuff. But she also said you'd been showing her lots of things like this on your computer.'

'And if I have?' Andy asked. 'What's the problem, Khalid?'

'She's just a little girl. She hasn't yet learned how to sort out reality from fantasy. Don't mix her up, Andy.'

'I'm not supposed to tell her stories, you're saying?'

'Don't mix up her head, is what I'm saying. – And put some clothes on. You're too old to be running around with everything you have showing.'

Quickly Khalid walked away. It troubled him to be giving angry orders to young people. It brought buried memories of ancient ugliness back to life.

But this boy, Andy – someone needed to impose some discipline on him. Khalid knew that he was not the one; but someone should. He was too wild, too defiant. You could see the rebelliousness growing in him from week to week. He was good with computers, yes: wonderful with computers, miraculous. But Khalid saw the wildness in him, and was puzzled that no one else did. Even now, Andy did mainly as he pleased; what would he be like later on? The first Carmichael quisling? The family's first borgmann?   *   *   *

Close to a year went by before the story Khalid had told Jill had any repercussions whatever. That he had ever said a word to her about having killed that Entity was something that had all but passed from his mind.

He was carving a statue of Jill out of a slab of red manzanita wood, the latest in a series of such statues that he had made over the years. Little gatherings of them stood arrayed around the cabin in groups of three and four, congregations of Jills. Jill standing and Jill kneeling and Jill running, caught in mid-stride with her long hair flowing out behind her, and Jill stretched out with her elbow on the ground and her head resting on her fist; Jill with a baby in the crook of each arm; Jill asleep. She was nude in all of them. And she looked exactly alike in every one, always the youthful Jill of Khalid's first days at the ranch, with the smooth unlined face and the flat belly and the high taut breasts. Even though he had her pose for each new statue, he depicted her only as she had been, not as she now was.

She had noticed that, after a time, and had remarked on it. 'That is how I will always see you,' he explained. She went on posing for him nevertheless, though even he knew that there was really no need, not if all he was doing was carving statues of the Jill within his mind.

She was posing for him on a mild, humid spring morning when Tony came to him, Ron Carmichael's younger son, a big, brawny, easy-going boy in his late teens with a lion's mane of golden hair down to his shoulders. He gave only the most perfunctory of glances to the naked Jill, who stood with her arms outstretched and her head turned to the sky as if she were about to take wing. Everyone who passed by Khalid's cabin was accustomed to seeing Jill posing.

Khalid glanced up. Tony said, 'My brother would like to talk with you. He's in the chart room.'

'Yes. Right away,' Khalid said, and set about the task of putting his chisels back in their chest.

The chart room was a big, airy room in the main house, the largest in the series of rooms in the wing that stretched off to the left of the dining room. The Colonel, long ago, had bedecked its mahogany-paneled walls with an extensive collection of military

maps and charts from the time of the Vietnam War, framed topo-
graphic plans of battlefields and city maps and harbor charts,
out of which bizarre unfamiliar names that must once have been
terribly important came leaping, boldly underlined in red: Hai-
phong, Cam Ranh, Phan Rang, Pleiku, Khe Sanh, Ia Drang, Bin
Dinh, Hue. The room had a fine strategic feel to it and at some
time late in the Colonel's life Ron Carmichael had made it the
central planning headquarters for the Resistance. A direct telephone line that Steve and Lisa Gannett had wired up connected
it with the communications center out back.

There was a pack of Carmichaels in the chart room when
Khalid entered. They were sitting side by side behind the big
curving leather-topped desk in the middle of the floor, like an
assembly of judges, and they were all looking at him with peculiar intensity, the way they might look at some mythological
monster that had wandered into the room.

Three of them were Carmichaels, anyway: Mike, the more
pleasant of Jill's two brothers, and Mike's cousins Leslyn and
Anson, two of Ron's children. Steve Gannett was there also: some
kind of Carmichael, Khalid knew, but not as Carmichael as the
others, too plump, too bald, wrong color eyes. Khalid did not
always bother to keep his sense of the relationships among all
these people straight in his head. Fate had decreed that he should
live among them, even marry one and have children by her; but
none of that meant that he would ever feel like a true member
of the family.

Anson was at the center of the group. Khalid understood that
in recent months Anson had come to be in charge of things, now
that his father Ron was beginning to grow old. Not quite thirty
yet, was Anson, younger than Mike and Charlie and their sister
Jill, younger considerably than Steve. But he was plainly the
boss now, the Carmichael of Carmichaels, the one who had the
strength to command, the one who always took opportunity into
his hands. Anson was a tall wide-faced man with very pale skin
and a great thick swoop of coarse yellow hair that fell down low
across his forehead. And, of course, those rock-drill eyes that all
these Carmichaels inevitably were born with. He had always
struck Khalid as being very tightly wound – too tightly wound,

perhaps, and perhaps also brittle at the core, so that it would not take very much to make him snap in half.

Anson said, 'Jill told me something extremely strange about you last night, Khalid. I was up practically all night thinking about it.'

'Yes?' Khalid said, noncommittal as ever.

'What she said was that you had told her, some time back, that the thing you had been sent into detention for was the killing of that Entity who was assassinated on a highway in England fifteen or twenty years ago.'

'Yes,' Khalid said.

'Yes what?'

'Yes, I did it. I am the one.'

Anson's penetrating eyes rested unblinkingly on him. But Khalid was not afraid of anyone's eyes.

'And never said a word about it to anyone?' Anson said.

'Cindy knows. I told her years ago, when I first knew her, before we ever came to this place.'

'Yes. I asked her last night, and she confirms that you made that claim to her, while the two of you were driving down from Nevada. She wasn't sure then whether to take you seriously. She still isn't.'

'I was serious,' Khalid said. 'I was the one who did it.'

'But never saw fit to mention it here. Why was that?'

'Why should I have talked about it? It was not a matter that ever came up in ordinary conversation. It is something I did one night a long time ago, when I was still a child, for reasons that were of concern to me on that night alone, and it is not important to me now.'

'Did it ever occur to you, Khalid,' Mike Carmichael said, 'that it might be important to us?'

Khalid shrugged.

Anson said, 'What made you come out with it to Jill, after all this time, then?'

'What I said is something that I said to my daughter Khalifa, not to Jill. Khalifa imagined that an Entity of a strange sort had come here to the ranch and played with her, and then made threats to her if she said anything about what had happened –

this is something that your son Andy put into her mind,' Khalid said, looking coolly at Steve – 'and when I heard this tale I told the child to have no fear, that I would protect her as a father should, that I had killed an Entity once and I would do it again, if need be. Then Jill asked me if I had really done such a thing. And so I told her the story.'

Leslyn Carmichael, a young slender woman who looked to Khalid disturbingly like the Jill of ten years before, said, 'The Entities are capable of reading minds and defending themselves against attacks before the attack can even be made. That's why nobody's ever been able to kill one, except for that one incident in England all those years ago. How is it that you were able to do what no one else can manage to do, Khalid?'

'When the Entity came along the road in its wagon, there was nothing in my mind to cause it alarm. I felt no hatred for it, I felt no enmity. I allowed none of those things into my mind. Entities are very beautiful to me, and I love beautiful things. I was feeling love for that one, for its beauty, even as I picked up the rifle and shot it. If it had looked into my mind as it approached, all it would have seen was my love.'

'You can do that?' Anson said. 'You can turn off everything in your mind that you don't want to be there?'

'I could then. Perhaps I still can.'

'Is that how you avoided being blamed for the killing afterward?' Leslyn asked. 'You blanked all knowledge of the murder from your mind, so the Entity interrogators couldn't detect it in there?'

'There were no Entity interrogators. They simply gave the order for everyone in our town to be gathered together and punished, as if we all were guilty. Human troops under Entity orders gathered us together. My mind would not have been open to them.'

There was some silence then, as all these Carmichaels contemplated what Khalid had said. He watched them, seeing in their faces that they were weighing his words, testing them for plausibility.

Believe me or don't believe me, as you wish. It makes no difference to me.

But it seemed as if they did believe him.

'Come over here, Khalid,' Anson said, indicating the leather-topped desk. 'I want to show you something.'

The desk had papers spread out all over it. They were computer printouts, full of jagged lines, diagrams, graphs. Khalid looked down at them without comprehension, without interest.

Anson said, 'We've been collecting these reports for five or six years, now. What they are is an analysis of the movements of high-caste Entity personnel between cities, as well as we've been able to track them. These dotted lines here, these are transit vectors, the patterns of movement. They represent elite Entity figures, traveling from place to place. Look. Here. Here. Here. This cluster here.' He pointed to groups of lines and dots.

'Yes,' Khalid said, meaning nothing at all.

'We've noticed, over the years, certain patterns within the patterns, a flow of Entities in and out of specific places, sometimes gathering in relatively great numbers in such places. Los Angeles is one of those places. London is another. Istanbul, Turkey, is a third.'

Anson glanced toward him in that taut way of his, as though expecting some reaction. Khalid said nothing.

'It's become evident, or so we think,' Anson went on, 'that these three cities are the main command centers of the Entities, their capitals on Earth, and that Los Angeles is probably the capital of capitals for them. You may be aware that the wall around Los Angeles is higher and thicker than the wall around any other city. There may be some significance in that. – Well, Khalid, we jump now to our big hypothesis. Not only is Los Angeles very likely the main city, but it may contain a supreme figure, the commander-in-chief of all the Entities. What we have begun to call Entity Prime.'

Another wary glance at Khalid. Again Khalid offered no reaction. What was there for him to say?

Anson went on, 'We think – we guess, we suspect, we believe – that all the Entities might be linked in some telepathic way to Entity Prime, and that they make regular pilgrimages to the site where Prime is located for some reason that we don't understand,

ut which may have to do with their own biological processes,
or their mental processes. A communion of some sort, maybe.
As though they renew themselves somehow by going to see
Prime. And that is Los Angeles, although there's certain second-
ary evidence that it could be London or Istanbul instead.'

'You know this?' said Khalid doubtfully.

'Just a hypothesis,' said Leslyn. 'But maybe a pretty good one.'

Khalid nodded. He wondered why they were bothering him
with these matters.

'Like the queen bee who rules the hive,' said Mike.

'Ah,' said Khalid. 'The queen bee.'

Anson said, 'Not necessarily female, of course. Not necessarily
anything. But suppose, now, that we were able to *locate* Prime –
track him down, find him wherever they've got him hidden away
in Los Angeles, or maybe in London or Istanbul. If we did that,
and could get an assassin in to kill him, what effect would that
have on the rest of the Entities, do you think?'

At last Khalid could provide something worthwhile. 'When I
killed the one in Salisbury,' he said, 'the one next to him in the
wagon went into convulsions. I thought for a moment I might
have shot that one too, though I didn't. So their minds may be
linked just as you say.'

'You see? You see?' cried Anson triumphantly. 'We start to get
confirmation! Why the hell didn't you *tell* us this stuff, Khalid?
You shoot one and the other one on the wagon has convulsions!
I'll bet they all did, all around the world, right on up to Prime!'

'We need to check on this,' Steve said. 'Find out, from as many
sources we can, whether anyone observed unusual behavior
among the Entities at the time of the Salisbury killing.'

Anson nodded. 'Right. And if there was some kind of general
worldwide Entity freakout as a result of the death of one relatively unimportant member of their species – then if we could
somehow manage to find and kill Prime – well, Khalid, do you
see where we're heading?'

Khalid looked down at the maze of papers spread out all over
the leather-topped desk.

'Of course. That you want to kill Prime.'

'More specifically, that we want *you* to kill Prime!'

'Me?' He laughed. 'Oh, no, Anson.'

'No?'

'No. That is not a thing I would want to do. Oh, no, Anson No.'

That seemed to stun them. It knocked the wind right out of them Anson's pale face turned bright red with anger, and Mike said something under his breath to Leslyn, and Steve muttered something to Leslyn also.

Then Leslyn, who was sitting just at Khalid's elbow, looked up at him and said, 'Why wouldn't you? You're the one person qualified to do it.'

'But I have no reason to do it. Killing Prime, if there is such a thing as Prime, is nothing to me.'

'Are you afraid?' Mike asked.

'Not at all. I would probably die in the attempt, and I would not want that to happen, because I have small children whom love, and I want them to have a father. But I am not afraid, no What I am is indifferent.'

'To what?'

'To the project of killing Entities. It is true that I killed that Entity when I was a boy, but I did it for special reasons that were of importance only to myself. Those reasons have been satisfied Killing Entities is your project, not mine.'

'Don't you want to see them driven from the world?' Steve Gannett asked him.

'They can keep the world forever, so far as I am concerned, replied Khalid evenly. 'Who rules the world is not my concern From what I understand, there was never much happiness in it even before the Entities came, at least not for my family. Those people are all dead, now, the family I had in England. I never knew them anyway, except for one. But now I have children of my own. I find happiness in them. For the first time in my life I have tasted happiness. The thing that I want is to stay here and raise my children. Not to go into a city I do not know and try to kill some strange being that means nothing to me. Perhaps would return alive from that, more likely not. But why should take the risk? What is there for me to gain?'

'Khalid –' Anson said.

'Was I not sufficiently clear? I tried to express myself very clearly indeed.'

Stymied. Khalid seemed as alien to them as the Entities themselves.

They sent him from the room. He went back to his cabin, opened his tool chest, asked Jill to resume her pose. Of what had taken place in the chart room he said nothing at all. His children fluttered around him, Khalifa, Rasheed, Yasmeena, Aissha, Haleem, naked, lovely. Khalid's heart swelled with joy at the sight of them. Allah was good; Allah had brought him to this mountain, had given him the strange and beautiful Jill, had caused these children of his to be born to her. After much suffering his life had begun at last to blossom. Why should he surrender it for these people's foolish project?

'Get me Tony,' Anson said, when Khalid was gone.

His conversation with his brother was brief. Tony had never been a deep thinker, nor was he a man of many words. He was eight years younger than Anson and had always held him in the deepest reverence. Loved him; feared him; looked up to him. Would do anything for him. Even this, Anson hoped.

He explained to Tony what was at stake, and what would be needed to bring it off.

'I'm going to give it a try,' Anson said. 'It's my responsibility.'

'Is that how you see it? Well, then.'

'That's how I see it, yes. But the first one who goes down there may not bring it off. If I don't succeed in killing Prime, will you agree to be the next one to take a whack at the job?'

'Sure,' Tony replied immediately. He seemed hardly even to give the matter any consideration. The difficulties, the risk. No frowns furrowed Tony's broad, amiable, clear-eyed face. 'Why not? Whatever you say, Anson. You're the boss.'

'It won't be that simple. It could involve months of special training. Years, maybe.'

'You're the boss,' Tony said.

*   *   *

A little while later, as Khalid was finishing his morning's work, Anson came to him. He looked even more tightly wound than usual, lips clamped tightly, eyebrows furrowed. They stood together outside the building, amidst the carved array of naked wooden Jills, and Anson said, 'You told us just now that you were indifferent to the whole idea of killing Entities. That you were indifferent to it, apparently, even as you went about killing one.'

'Yes. This is so.'

'Do you think you could instruct somebody in that kind of indifference, Khalid? That way you have of wiping your mind clean of anything that might arouse an Entity's defenses?'

'I could try, I suppose. I think it would not work. You have to be born to it, I think.'

'Perhaps not. Perhaps it could be taught.'

'Perhaps,' said Khalid.

'Could you try to teach *me*?'

That startled Khalid, that Anson would want to propose himself for what was surely would be a suicide mission. Khalid could almost understand that sort of dedication to a task: in the abstract, at least. But Anson was the father of a large family, as Khalid was. Six, seven children already, Anson had, and still young himself, a few years younger even than Khalid. Year after year children came out of Raven, the plump little broad-hipped wife whom Anson had found for himself over in the ranch-hand compound, with unvarying regularity. You could always tell when spring had arrived, because Raven was having her annual baby. Did Anson not want the joy of watching those children grow up? Was it worth losing all that for the sake of a foolhardy attempt to kill some monstrous being from another world?

This was a pointless discussion, though. 'You would never learn it,' Khalid said. 'You have the wrong kind of mind. You could never be indifferent to anything.'

'Try me anyway.'

'I will not. It would be a waste of your time and mine.'

'What a stubborn bastard you are, Khalid!'

'Yes. Yes, I suppose I am that.'

He waited for Anson to go away. But Anson remained right

here, looking at him, frowning, chewing on his lower lip, visibly calculating things. A moment or two went by; and then he said, 'Well, then, Khalid, what about my brother Tony? He's told me that he'd be willing.'

'Tony,' Khalid repeated. The big stupid one, yes. He was a different story, that one. 'I suppose I could try it, with Tony,' Khalid said. 'It probably would not work even for him, because I think it is a thing that you must learn from childhood, and even if he did learn, and he went to destroy the Entity, I think he would perish in the attempt. I think they would see through him no matter how well he is trained, and they would kill him. Which is something for you to consider. But I could try to teach him, yes. If that is what you want.'

VII

Forty-Seven Years
from Now

Toward dawn, bleary-eyed and going foggy in the head after sitting in front of seven computer screens all night long, Steve Gannett decided he had had enough. He was going to be fifty next year, a little old for pulling all-nighters. He looked up at the blond-haired boy who had just entered the communications center with a breakfast tray for him and said, 'Martin, have you seen my son Andy around yet this morning?'

'I'm Frank, sir.'

'Sorry. Frank.' All of Anson's goddamned kids looked alike. This one's voice, he realized, had already begun to break, which would put him at about thirteen, which would make him Frank. Martin was only around eleven. Steve looked groggily into the tray and said again, 'Well, tell me, Frank, is Andy up yet?'

'I don't know, sir. I haven't seen him. – My father sent me to ask you for a progress report.'

'Minimal, tell him.'

'Minimum?'

'Close. *Minimal* is what I said. It means "very little". It means "just about goddamn none", as a matter of fact. Tell him that I didn't get anywhere worth speaking of, but I do see one possible new approach to the problem, and I'm going to ask Andy to explore it this morning. Tell him that. And then, Frank, go look for Andy and tell him to get himself over here lickety-split.'

'Lickety-split?'

'"Extremely quickly" is what that phrase means.'

Jesus Christ, Steve thought. The language is rotting away before my very eyes.

Anson, looking out the chart room's open window half an hour later, saw Steve go trudging like a weary bullock across the lawn toward the Gannett family compound, and called out to him: 'Hey, cousin! Cousin! Got a minute to spare for me?'

Yawning, Steve said, 'Just about that much, I guess.' There was very little enthusiasm in his voice.

He came trudging over and peered in through the window. A light early-season rain had begun to fall, but Steve was standing out there as though unable to perceive that that was happening.

Anson said, 'No. Come on inside. This may take a minute and a half, maybe even two, and you're going to get soaked if you stay out there.'

'I would really like to get some sleep, Anson.'

'Just give me a little of your time first, cousin,' Anson said, a little less affably this time, his tone verging on what his father described as the Colonel-voice. Anson, who had been sixteen when the Colonel died, had only the vaguest of recollections of his grandfather's special tone of command. But apparently he had inherited it.

'So?' Steve said, when he was in the chart room, letting droplets of water fall to the rug in front of Anson's leather-topped desk.

'So Frank tells me you say you've found some new approach to the Prime problem. Can you tell me what it is?'

'It's not a new approach, exactly. It's the approach to a new approach. What it is is, I think I've hacked into the entrance to Karl-Heinrich Borgmann's private archives.'

'*The* Borgmann?'

'The very one. Our own special latter-day Judas himself.'

'He's been dead for ages. You mean his archives still exist?'

'Listen, can we discuss this after I've had some sleep, Anson?'

'Just let me have a moment more. We're approaching a kind of crisis point in the Prime project and I need to keep myself on top of all the data. Tell me about this Borgmann thing insofar as it may impact the hunt for Prime. I assume that that's the angle, right? Some link to Prime in the Borgmann files?'

Steve nodded. He looked about ready to fall down. Anson wondered charitably whether he might be pushing the man too hard. He expected top-flight performance from everyone, the way his father had, the way the old Colonel had before him.

Carmichael-grade performance. But Steve Gannett was only half Carmichael, a bald, soft-bellied, bearish middle-aged man who had been up all night.

There were things Anson needed to know, though. Now.

Steve said, 'Borgmann was assassinated twenty-five years back. In Prague, which is a city in the middle of Europe that has been the site of a major Entity headquarters just about from the beginning. We know that he was hooked right into the main Entity computer net for at least ten years prior to his death, doing so with the knowledge and permission of the Entities, but also perhaps in some illicit way too. That would be true to what we know about Borgmann, that he'd have been spying on the very people he was working for. We also know, from what we've heard from people who dealt with the actual Borgmann in the period between the Conquest and his murder, that he was the sort of person who never deleted a file, who squirreled every goddamned thing away in the most anal-retentive way you could imagine.'

'Anal-retentive?' Anson said.

'It means retentive, okay? Just a fancy way of saying it.' Steve seemed to sway, and his eyes began to close for a moment. 'Don't interrupt me, okay? Okay? – What you need to know, Anson, is that we've always thought Borgmann's archives are still there somewhere, maybe buried down deep in the Prague mainframe in a secret cache that he was able to conceal even from the Entities, and it's widely believed that if they exist, they would be full of critical information about how the minds of the Entities work. Highly explosive stuff, so it's thought. Just about every hacker in the world has been looking for Borgmann's data practically since the day he died. The quest for the Holy Grail, so to speak. And with pretty much the same degree of success.'

Anson started to ask another question, and cut himself off. Steve's speech frequently was laced with cryptic references out of the world culture that had vanished, that world of books and plays and music, of history and literature, which Steve had been just old enough to experience, to some degree, before it disappeared; but Anson reminded himself that he probably did not need to find out just now what the Holy Grail was.

Steve said, 'As you know, I devoted this night past to yet one more goddamn heroic eight-hour attempt to link up all the data we've been able to compile about every major nexus of Entity intelligence, create an overlay, get some kind of confirmation of the theory that we've been playing with, for God only knows how long, that Prime is situated in downtown Los Angeles. Well, I failed. Again. But in the course of failing I think I stumbled over something peculiar in the data conduit linking Prague, Vienna, and Budapest that might just have Karl-Heinrich Borgmann's personal paw prints on it. *Might*. It's a locked door and I don't know what's behind it and I don't know how to pick the lock, either. But it's the first hopeful thing I've come upon in five years.'

'If you can't pick the lock, who can?'

'Andy can,' Steve said. 'He's very likely the only hacker in the world who could do it. He's the best there is, even if I say so myself. That's not paternal pride speaking, Anson. God knows I'm not very proud of Andy. But he can do magic with a data chain. It's just the truth.'

'Okay. Let's get him on it, then!'

'Sure,' said Steve. 'I sent your boy Frank out just now to find Andy and bring him to me. Frank reports that Andy left the ranch at four in the morning and took off for parts unknown. Frank got this bit of information from Eloise's girl La-La, who saw him go, and who unbeknownst to the rest of us has apparently has been indulging in some kind of romance with Andy for the past six months and who, incidentally, revealed to your son Frank this morning that she's pregnant, presumably by Andy. She thinks that's why he took off. She also doesn't think he plans to come back. He took his two favorite computers with him and apparently spent all of last evening downloading all his files into them.'

'The little son of a bitch,' Anson said. 'Begging your pardon, Steve. Well, we've just got to find him and haul his sneaky ass back here, then.'

'Find Andy?' Steve guffawed. 'Nobody's going to find Andy unless he feels like being found. It would be easier to find Entity Prime. *Now* can I go to sleep, Anson?'

*   *   *

We're approaching a kind of crisis point in the Prime project.

That was what he had told Steve, a little to his own surprise, for he had not quite articulated the situation that way before, even to himself. But yes, yes, indeed, Anson thought. A crisis. A time to make bold decisions and act on them. He realized now that he had been thinking of the situation that way for several weeks. But he was beginning to suspect that the whole dire thing was taking place within the arena of his own mind.

It had been building up in him for years. He knew that, now. That sense of himself as Anson the Entity-Killer, the man who finally would drive the alien bastards from the planet, the shining hero who would give Earth back to itself. He couldn't remember a time when he hadn't thought it was his destiny to be the one who brought the task to culmination.

But three times now in these recent weeks something very strange had come over him: a dizzying intensification of that ambition, a frantic passion for it, a wild hunger to get on with the job, strike now, strike hard. A passion that possessed him beyond all reasoning – that became, for the five or ten minutes that it held him in its grip, utterly uncontrollable. At such times he could feel the pressure beating against his skull, hammering against it from within as though there were some creature in there trying to get out.

It was a little scary. Passionate impatience is not the hallmark of a great military commander.

Perhaps, he thought, I should have a little talk with my father.

Ron, who was nearly seventy and not in the best of health, had inherited the Colonel's old bedroom, as was fitting for the patriarch of the family. Anson found him there now, sitting up in bed amidst a pile of ancient books and magazines, yellowing rarities from the Colonel's crumbling library of twentieth-century reading matter. He looked poorly, pale and peaked.

Cassandra was with him: the Carmichael community doctor, Cassandra was, self-trained out of the Colonel's books and such medical texts as Paul or Doug or Steve had been able to extricate from the remnants of the pre-Conquest computer net. She did her best, and sometimes seemed like a miracle-worker; but it

always was a sobering thing to find the busy Cassandra in a sick
person's room, because it usually meant that the patient had
taken a turn for the worse. That was how it had been six months
before, when Anson's wife Raven, having gone through one preg-
nancy too many, had died, exhausted, from some very minor
infection a few weeks after giving birth to their eighth child.
Cassandra had done her best then, too. Had even seemed hopeful,
for a time. But Anson had realized from the outset that nothing
could save the worn-out Raven. He had pretty much the same
feeling here.

'Your father is a man of iron,' she said at once, almost defiantly,
before Anson could say anything at all. 'He'll be up and around
and chopping down trees with a single blow of the axe by this
time tomorrow. I guarantee it.'

'Don't believe her, boy,' Ron said, winking. 'I'm a goner, and
that's the truth. You can tell Khalid to get started carving the
stone. And tell him to make it a damned good one, too. "Ronald
Jeffrey Carmichael", and remember that you spell "Jeffrey" with
just seven letters, J-E-F-F-R-E-Y, born the twelfth of April, 1971,
died the sixteenth of –'

'Today's the fourteenth already, dad. You should have given
him a little more notice.' Turning to Cassandra, Anson said, 'Am
I interrupting something important? Or can you excuse us for a
little while?'

She smiled pleasantly and went from the room.

'How sick are you, really?' Anson asked bluntly, when Cassandra was gone.

'I feel pretty shitty. But I don't think I'm actually dying
just yet, although I wish Cassie had some clearer idea of what's
really going on in my midsection. – Is there some problem,
Anson?'

'I'm itching to make a move on Prime. That's the problem.'

'You mean you've succeeded in discovering Prime's hiding-
place at last? Then why is that a problem? Go in there and get
him!'

'We *haven't* discovered it. We don't know any more than we
did five years ago. The Los Angeles theory is still top of the list,
but it's still only a theory. The problem is that I don't want to

wait any longer. My patience has just about run itself out.'

'And Tony? Is he getting impatient too? All in a sweat to make a strike in the dark, is he? Willing to go in there without knowing exactly where he's supposed to go?'

'He'll do whatever I tell him to do. Khalid's got him all charged up. He's like a bomb waiting to go off.'

'Like a bomb,' Ron said. 'Waiting to go off. Ah. *Ah.*' He seemed almost amused. There was a curiously skeptical expression on his face, a smile that was not entirely a smile.

Anson said nothing, simply met Ron's gaze stare for stare and waited. It was an awkward moment. There was a streak of playfulness, of quicksilver unpredictability, in his father that he had never been able to deal with.

Then Ron said gravely, 'Let me get this straight. We've been planning this attack for years and years, training our assassin with an eye to sending him in as soon as we've pinned down the precise location of Prime, and now we have the assassin ready but we still don't have the location, and you want to send him in *anyway*? Today? Tomorrow? Isn't this a little premature, boy? Do we even know for sure that Prime actually exists, let alone where he is?'

Like scalpel thrusts, they were. The hotheaded young leader's idiocy neatly laid bare, just as Anson had feared and expected and even hoped it would be. He felt his cheeks flaming. It became all that he could manage to keep his eyes on Ron's. He felt his headache beginning to get going.

Lamely he said, 'The pressure's been rising inside me for weeks, dad. Longer, maybe. I get the feeling that I'm letting the whole world down by holding Tony back this long. And then my head starts pounding. It's pounding now.'

'Take an aspirin, then. Take two. We've still got plenty on hand.'

Anson recoiled as though he had been struck.

But Ron didn't seem to notice. He was wearing that strange smile again. 'Listen, Anson, the Entities have been here for forty years. We've all been holding ourselves back, all this time. Except for the suicidally addlebrained laser strike that brought the Great Plague down on us before you were born, and Khalid's uniquely successful and perhaps unduplicatable one-man attack, we haven't lifted a finger against them in all that time. Your grandfather grew old and died, miserable because the world had been enslaved by these aliens but only too well aware that it would be dumb to try any hostile action before we understood what we were doing. Your Uncle Anse sat stewing on this very mountain decade after decade, drinking himself silly for the same reason. I've held things together pretty well, I suppose, but I'm not going to last forever either, and don't you think I'd like to see the Entities on the run before I check out? So we've all had our little lesson in patience to learn. You're what, thirty-five years old?'

'Thirty-four.'

'Thirty-four. By that age you should have learned how to keep yourself from flying off the handle.'

'I don't think I am flying off the handle. But what I'm afraid of is that Tony's training will lose its edge if we hold him back much longer. We've been winding him up for this project for the past seven years. He could be getting over-trained by now.'

'Fine. So first thing tomorrow you'll send him into L.A. with a gun on each hip and a belt full of grenades around his waist, and he'll walk up to the first Entity he sees and say, "Pardon me, sir, can you give me Prime's address?" Is that how you imagine it? If you don't know where your target is, where do you throw your bomb?'

'I've thought of all these things.'

'And you still want to send him? Tony's your brother. It isn't as though you've got lots of others. Are you really ready to have him get killed?'

'He's a Carmichael, dad. He's understood the risks from the beginning.'

Ron made a groaning sound. 'A Carmichael! A Carmichael! My God, Anson, do I have to listen to that bullshit right to the end of my days? What does being a Carmichael mean, anyway? Disapproving of your own children's behavior, like the Colonel, and cutting them out of your life for years at a time? Twisting yourself inside out for the sake of an ideal and obliterating yourself with drink so you can go on living with yourself, the way

Anse did? Or winding up like the Colonel's brother Mike, maybe, the one who got himself into such a bind over his notions of proper behavior that he went and found himself a hero's death the day the Entities landed? Is it your notion that Tony's supposed to go waltzing to his certain death on a crazy mission simply because he had the bad luck to be born into a family of fanatic disciplinarians and hyper-achievers?'

Anson peered at him, horrified. These were words he had never expected to hear, and they came crashing into him with stunning impact. Ron was red-faced and trembling, practically apoplectic. But after a moment he became a little calmer.

He said, once more smiling in that bemused way, 'Well, well, well, listen to the old guy rant and rave! All that sound and fury. – Look here, Anson, I know you want to be the general who launches the victorious counteroffensive against the dread invaders. We all wanted that, and maybe you'll actually be the one. But don't waste Tony so soon, all right? Can't you hang on at least until you've got some decent idea of where Prime may be? Aren't Steve and Andy still trying to work out some kind of precise pinpointing?'

'Steve has been doing just that, yes. With occasional help from Andy, whenever Andy can be bothered. They're pretty sure that L.A.'s the place where Prime is stashed away, probably downtown, but they can't get it any more precise than that. And now Steve tells me, though, that he's hit a wall. He thinks Andy's the only hacker good enough to get beyond the blockage. But Andy's gone.'

'Gone?'

'Skipped out in the night, last night. Something about getting La-La pregnant and not wanting to stay around.'

'No! The miserable little bastard!'

'We'll try to find him and bring him back. But we don't even know where to begin looking for him.'

'Well, figure it out. Catch him and yank him home and sit him down in the communications room until he tells you exactly where Prime is, which part of town, what building. And *then* send in Tony. Not before, not until you know the location right down to the street address. Okay?'

Anson rubbed his right temple. Was the pounding subsiding a little in there? Perhaps. A little, anyway. A little.

He said, 'You think sending him now is really crazy, then?'

'I sure do, boy.'

'That's what I needed you to tell me.'

Khalid said, pointing toward the hawk that came riding up over the crest of the mountain on the wind from the sea, 'You see the bird, there? Kill it.'

Unhesitatingly Tony raised his rifle, sighting and aiming and pulling the trigger all in one smooth unhurried continuous process. The hawk, black against the blue shield of the sky, exploded into a flurry of scattering feathers and began to plummet toward the bare stony meadow in which they stood.

Tony was perfect, Khalid thought. He was a magnificent machine. A machine of Khalid's own creation, flawless, the finest thing he had ever shaped. A superbly crafted mechanism.

'Very nice shot. Now you, Rasheed.'

The slender boy with amber-toned skin at Khalid's side lifted his gun and shot without seeming even to aim. The bullet caught the falling hawk squarely in the chest and knocked it spinning off on a new trajectory that sent it over to their left, down into the dark impenetrable tangle of chaparral that ran just below the summit.

Khalid gave the boy an approving smile. He was fourteen now, already shoulder-high to his long-legged father, a superb marksman. Khalid often took him along on these back-country training sessions with Tony. He loved the sight of him, his wiry athletic form, his luminous intelligent green eyes, his corona of coppery hair. Rasheed too was perfect, in a different way from Tony. His perfection was not that of a machine but of a person. It was wonderful to have made a boy like Rasheed. Rasheed was the boy Khalid might have been, if only things had gone otherwise for him when he was young. Rasheed was Khalid's second chance at life.

To Tony, Khalid said, 'And what do you feel, killing the bird?'

'It was a good shot. I'm pleased when I shoot that well.'

'And the bird? What do you think about the bird?'

'Why should I think about the bird? The bird was nothing to me.'

It was just before dawn when Andy reached Los Angeles. The first thing he did, after letting himself through the wall at the Santa Monica gate with the LACON credentials that he had whipped up for himself the week before, was to jack himself into a public-access terminal that he located at Wilshire and Fifth. He needed to update his map of the city. He might be staying here quite some time, several months at the very least, and Andy knew that the information about this place that was already in his files was almost certainly out of date. They kept changing the street patterns around all the time, he had heard, closing off some streets that had been perfectly good transit arteries for a hundred years, opening new ones where there had never been any before. But everything seemed pretty much as he remembered it.

He hit the access code for Sammo Borracho's e-mail slot and said, 'It's Megabyte, good buddy. I'm down here to stay, and planning to set up in business. Be so kind as to patch me on to Mary Canary, okay?'

This was Andy's fourth visit to Los Angeles. The first time, about seven years back, he had sneaked down here with Tony and Charlie's son Nick, using Charlie's little car, which Andy had made available to them by emulating the code for the car's ignition software. Tony and Nick, who were both around nineteen then, had wanted to go to the city to find girls, which were of lesser interest to Andy then, he being not quite thirteen. But neither Tony nor Nick was worth a damn as a hacker, and the deal was that they had to take Andy along with them in return for his liberating the car for them.

Girls, Andy discovered on that trip, were more interesting than he had suspected. Los Angeles was full of them – it was a gigantic city, bigger than Andy had ever imagined, easily two or three hundred thousand people living there, maybe even more – and Tony and Nick were both the kind of big, good-looking guys who latched on to girls very quickly. The ones they found, in a part of Los Angeles that was called Van Nuys, were sixteen

The Alien Years

years old and named Kandi and Darleen. Kandi had red hair and Darleen's was dyed a sort of green. They seemed very stupid, even dumber than the ones at the ranch. Nick and Tony didn't seem bothered by that, though, and when Andy gave the matter a little thought, he couldn't find any reason why they should be, considering what it was that they had come here for.

'You want one too, don't you?' Tony asked Andy, grinning broadly. This was back in the era when Tony still seemed like a human being to Andy, a few months before Khalid had started teaching him Khalid's crazy philosophy, which so far as Andy was concerned had transformed Tony into an android, pretty much. 'Darlene's got a kid sister. She'll show you a thing or two, if you like.'

'Sure,' said Andy, after only a fraction of a moment's hesitation.

Darleen's sister's name was Delayne. He told her he was fifteen. Delayne seemed exactly like Darleen, except that she was two years younger and about twice as stupid. She had a room of her own, a mattress on the floor, girl-clutter everywhere, photographs of long-ago movie stars tacked up all over the wall.

Andy didn't care how dumb she was. It wasn't her mind that he was interested in communing with. He winked and gave her what he hoped was a torrid look.

'Oh, you want to play?' she asked, batting her eyes at him. 'Well, come here, then.'

Within the past year Andy had accessed a dozen pre-Conquest porno videos that he had found cached in somebody's Net library in Sacramento, and so he had an approximate idea of how to go about things, but it turned out to be a little more complicated than it seemed on video. Still, he thought that he had conducted himself creditably. And apparently he had. 'You were okay, for your first time,' Delayne told him afterward. 'Truly truly, I tell you. Not bad at all.' He hadn't fooled her in the least, but she hadn't let that be a problem. Which lifted her considerably in his estimation. Perhaps, he decided, she wasn't quite as stupid as he thought.

He made his second trip to L.A. a year and a half later, when he had grown bored with trying out the things Delayne had shown him on various cousins at the ranch. Jane and Ansonia and Cheryl were willing to play, but La-La wasn't, and La-La, who was two years older than Andy was, was the only one who held much appeal for him, because she was smart and tough, because she had the same kind of sharp edge on her that her father Charlie did. Since La-La didn't seem to want to be cooperative, and fooling around with Jane and Ansonia and Cheryl was a little like molesting the sheep, Andy went off to try to find Delayne.

This time he went alone, borrowing his father's car, which was a much newer model than Charlie's, the voice-actuated kind. 'Los Angeles,' Andy said, in a deep, authoritative tone, and it took him to Los Angeles. Like a magic carpet, practically. He found Darleen, but not Delayne, because Delayne had been caught in some infraction and reassigned to a labor gang working out of Ukiah, which was somewhere far upstate. Darleen, though, was willing enough to spend a day or two playing with him. Apparently she was as bored with her regular life as Andy was with his, and he was like a Christmas treat for her.

She took him around the city, giving him a good taste of its immensity. The place was made up, Andy realized, of a whole string of little cities pasted together into one gigantic one. And as he heard their names – Sherman Oaks, Van Nuys, Studio City, West Hollywood – he began to put together in his mind a more tangible sense of the physical location of some of the hackers with whom he had dealt with by e-mail over the past few years.

They knew him as Megabyte Monster, alias Mickey Megabyte. He knew them as Teddy Spaghetti of Sherman Oaks, Nicko Nihil of Van Nuys, Green Hornet of Santa Monica, Sammo Borracho of Culver City, Ding-Dong 666 of West L.A. While driving around with Darleen, Andy jacked in at a series of widely separated access points and let them know he was in the vicinity. 'Down here for a couple of days visiting a girl I know,' he told them. And waited to see what they had to say. Not much, is what they had to say. No immediate invitations to come around for face-to-face, eye-to-eye. You had to be careful, though, making eye-to-eye with other hackers whom you knew only electronically. They might not be quite the people you thought they were. Some could be stooges for LACON, or even for the Entities, happy to turn you in for the sake of getting patted on the head. Some could be predators. Some could be bozos.

But Andy felt them out, and they felt him out, and the time came when he decided it was safe to meet Sammo Borracho of Culver City, as a first move. Sammo Borracho's on-line persona was quick and clever, and nevertheless he was always ready to acknowledge Andy's superiority as a data-thrower. 'You know how to get to Culver City?' Andy asked Darleen.

'All the way down there?' She wrinkled her nose. 'What for?'

'Somebody there I need to talk to, face-face. But I can find it myself, if you don't want to bother showing me how to –'

'No, I'll go. It's just straight down Sepulveda, anyway, miles and miles and miles. We can do a little of it on the freeway, but the road's a wreck south of the Santa Monica interchange.'

The trip took more than an hour, through an assortment of neighborhoods, some of them burned out. Sammo Borracho had always come on like a big fat drunken Mexican in his e-mail, but in person he was small, pale, wiry, a little twitchy, with an implant jack in each arm and lines of little purple tattoos across his cheeks. Not drunken, not Mexican, and no more than a couple of years older than Andy. Andy and Darleen met him, as arranged, at a swivelball parlor in the shadow of the ruined San Diego Freeway. From the way he kept staring at Darleen, Andy figured that he hadn't been laid in at least three years. Or ever.

'I thought you'd be older,' Sammo Borracho told him.

'I thought you'd be, too.'

He told Sammo Borracho he was nineteen, winking at Darleen to keep quiet, because she thought he was only seventeen. He was, in fact, fourteen and a half. Sammo Borracho said he was twenty-three. Andy figured that was at least a six-year upgrading. 'You live in San Francisco, right?' Sammo Borracho asked him.

'Right.'

'Never been there. I hear it's freezing cold all the time.'

'It's not so bad,' said Andy, who had never been there either. 'But I'm getting tired of it.'

'Thinking of moving down here, are you?'

'Another year, year or two, maybe.'

'Let me know,' Sammo Borracho said. 'I've got connections. Couple of pardoners I know. Been doing a little pardoning work myself, and I could probably get some for you, if you were interested.'

'I could be,' Andy said.

'Pardoners?' said Darleen, eyes going wide. 'You know some *pardoners*?'

'Why?' said Sammo Borracho. 'You need a deal?'

Andy and Darleen and Sammo Borracho spent the night together at Sammo Borracho's place at the eastern edge of Culver City. That was something new, for Andy. And, in its way, pretty interesting.

'Whenever you come down to stay,' Sammo Borracho told him in the morning, 'you just let me know, guy. I'll set things up the way you want. Just say the word.'

The third trip was two years after that, when word reached Andy that new interface upgrades had been invented that would fit his kind of implant jack, upgrades that had double the biofiltering capacity of the old-fashioned sort. That caught his attention. It wasn't often that some new technological improvement came along, any more, and you wanted to keep as much bio-originated crud out of your implant as you could. The manufacture of mobile androids had been the last big breakthrough, five years back, and that had been worked out in quisling laboratories under Entity auspices. The new interface was good old free-lance human ingenuity at work.

It turned out that there were only two places where Andy could have the upgrade installed: in the old Silicon Valley that was just south of San Francisco, or Los Angeles. He remembered what Sammo Borracho had said about the weather in San Francisco. Andy didn't like cold weather at all; and it was time, perhaps, to check in with Darleen once again. He swiped his father's car without much difficulty and went to Los Angeles.

Darleen wasn't living in the Valley any more. Andy tracked her down, after some quick work with access codes that let him look into the LACON residential-permit files, in Culver City, living with Sammo Borracho. Delayne had been pardoned out of the Ukiah labor camp and she was living there too. Sammo Borracho seemed to be one very happy hacker indeed.

You owe me one, pal, Andy thought.

'You finally moving south, then?' Sammo Borracho asked him, looking just a bit uneasy about that possibility, as though he might be thinking that Andy intended to reclaim one or both of the girls.

'Not yet, man. I'm just here on a holiday. Thought I'd get me one of the new bio interfaces, too. You know an installer?'

'Sure,' Sammo Borracho said, not taking any trouble at all to hide his relief that that was all that Andy wanted.

Andy got his interface upgrade put in in downtown L.A. Sammo Borracho's installer was a little hunchbacked guy with a soft, crooning voice and eagle eyes, who did the whole thing freehand, no calipers, no microscope. Sammo Borracho let Andy borrow Delayne for a couple of nights, too. When that started to get old he went back to the ranch.

'Any time you want to come down here and set yourself up writing pardons, man, just let me know,' said Sammo Borracho, as usual, as Andy was getting ready to leave.

And now he was in the big city once more and ready to set up shop. He was done with ranch life. Ultimately La-La had come across, sure. Had come across big time, in fact, six months of wild nights, plenty of fun. Too much fun, because she was knocked up, now, and talking about marrying him and having lots of kids. Which was not exactly Andy's idea of what the next few years ought to hold for Andy. Goodbye, La-La. Goodbye, Rancho Carmichael. Andy's on his way into the big bad world.

Sammo Borracho had moved to Venice, which was a town right along the ocean, narrow streets and weird old houses, just down the road from Santa Monica. He had put a little meat on his bones and had had his dumb tattoos removed and all in all he looked sleek and prosperous and happy. His house was a nice place just a couple of blocks from the water, lots of sunlight and breezes and three rooms full of impressive-looking hardware, and he had a nice red-haired live-in playmate named Linda, too, long and lean as a whippet. Sammo Borracho didn't say a word about Darleen or Delayne, and Andy didn't ask. Darleen and Delayne were history, apparently. Sammo Borracho was on his way in the world too, it seemed.

'You'll need your own territory,' Sammo Borracho told him. 'Somewhere out east of La Brea, I imagine. We've already got enough pardoners working the West Side. As you know, the territorial allotments are done by Mary Canary. I'll hook you along to Mary and she'll take care of things.'

Mary Canary, Andy soon discovered, was as female as Sammo Borracho was Mexican. Andy had a brief on-line discussion with 'her' and they arranged to meet in Beverly Hills at the place where Santa Monica Boulevard crossed Wilshire, and when he got there he found a dark-haired greasy-skinned man of about forty, nearly as wide as he was tall, waiting there for him with a blue Los Angeles Dodgers baseball cap on his head, turned back to front. The turned-around Dodger cap was the identification signal Andy had been told to look for.

'I know who you are,' said Mary Canary right away. His voice was deep and full of gravel, a tough voice, a movie-gangster voice. 'I just want you to realize that. If you mess around, you'll be shipped back to your family's cozy little hideaway in Santa Barbara in several pieces.'

'I'm from San Francisco, not Santa Barbara,' Andy said.

'Sure you are. San Francisco: I accept that. Only I'd like you to understand that I'm aware it isn't true. Now let's get down to business.'

There was a formally organized guild of pardoners, it seemed, and Mary Canary was one of the guildmasters. Andy, having been vouched for by Sammo Borracho and being also widely known by reputation to various other Los Angeles guild members, was welcome to join. His territory, Mary Canary told him, would be bounded by Beverly Boulevard on the north and Olympic Boulevard on the south, and would run from Crenshaw Boulevard in the west to Normandie Avenue in the east. That sounded like a sizable chunk of turf, although Andy suspected that it was somewhat less than the most lucrative area around.

Within his territory he was free to solicit as much pardoning work as he dared. The guild would give him all the basic know-how he would need to perform basic pardoning operations, and the rest was up to him. In return, he would pay the guild a commission of thirty percent of his first year's gross earnings, and fifteen percent each year thereafter. In perpetuity, said Mary Canary.

'Don't try to finagle,' Mary Canary warned him. 'I know how good you are, believe me. But our guys aren't such dopes themselves, and the one thing we don't tolerate is a hacker trying to subvert revenues. Play it straight, pay what's due, is what I most strenuously advise.'

And gave Andy a long, slow look that very explicitly said, *We are quite aware of your hacking skills, Mr Andy Gannett, and therefore we will be keeping our eyes on you. So you just better not mess around.*

Andy didn't intend to mess around. Not right away, anyway.

On a cold, windy day three weeks after Andy's departure for Los Angeles, one of those bleak mid-winter days when the ranch was being buffeted by a wild storm that had burst howling out of Alaska and gone rampaging right down the entire West Coast looking for Mexico, Cassandra walked without knocking, an hour before dawn, into the austere, monastic little bedroom where Anson Carmichael had spent his nights since Raven's death. 'You'd better come now,' she told him. 'Your father's going fast.'

Anson was awake instantly. A surge of surprise ran through him, and some anger. Accusingly he said, 'You told me that he'd be okay!'

'Well, I was wrong.'

They hurried down the hallways. The wind outside was heading toward gale force and hail was scrabbling against the windows.

Ron was sitting up in bed and seemed still to be conscious, but Anson could see right away that something had changed just in the past twelve hours. It was as if his father's facial muscles were relinquishing their grasp. His face looked strangely smooth and soft, now, as though the lines that time had carved in it had vanished in the night. His eyes had an oddly unfocused look; and he was smiling, as always, but the smile appeared to be sliding downward on the left side of his mouth. His hands were resting languidly on the bedcovers on either side of him in an eerie way: he could almost be posing for his own funerary monument. Anson could not push aside the distinct feeling that he was looking upon someone who was poised between worlds.

'Anson?' Ron said faintly.

'Here I am, dad.'

His own voice sounded inappropriately calm to him. But what am I supposed to do? Anson wondered. Wail and shriek? Rend my hair? Rip my clothing?

Something that might have been a chuckle came from his father. 'Funny thing,' Ron said, very softly. Anson had to strain to hear him. 'I was such a baddie that I thought I'd live forever. I was really, really bad. It's the *good* who are supposed to die young.'

'You aren't dying, dad!'

'Sure I am. I'm dead up to the knees already, and it's moving north very goddamned fast. Much to my surprise, but what can you do? When your time comes, it comes. Let's not pretend otherwise, boy.' A pause. 'Listen to me, Anson. It's all yours, now. You're the man: the Carmichael of the hour. Of the era. The new Colonel, you are. And you'll be the one who finally brings the thing off, won't you?' Again a pause. A frown, of sorts. He was entering some new place. 'Because – the Entities – the Entities – look, I tried, Anse – I goddamn well tried –'

Anson's eyes went wide. Ron had never called him 'Anse'. Who was he talking to?

'The Entities –'

Yet another pause. A very long one.

'I'm listening, dad.'

That smile. Those eyes.

That pause that did not end.

'Dad?'

'He isn't going to say anything else, Anson,' Cassandra told him quietly.

I tried, Anse – I goddamn well tried –

Khalid carved a magnificent stone almost overnight. Anson made sure that he spelled *Jeffrey* correctly. They all stood together in the cemetery – it was still raining, the day of his burial – and Rosalie said a few words about her brother, and Paul spoke, and Peggy, and then Anson, who got as far as saying, 'He was a lot better man than he thought he was,' and bit his lip and picked up the shovel.

A fog of grief hung over Anson for days. The subtraction of Ron from his life left him in a weirdly free-floating state, unchecked as he was, now, by Ron's constant presence, his wisdom, his graceful witty spirit, his poise and balance. The loss was tremendous and irrevocable.

But then, though the sense of mourning did not recede, a new feeling began to take hold of him, a strange sense of liberation. It was as if he had been imprisoned all these years, encased within Ron's complex, lively, mercurial self. He – sober-sided, earnest, even plodding – had never felt himself to be the fiery Ron's equal in any way. But now Ron was gone. Anson no longer needed to fear the disapproval of that active, unpredictable mind. He could do anything he wanted, now.

Anything. And what he wanted was to drive the Entities from the world.

The words of his dying father echoed in his mind:

– *The Entities – the Entities –*

– *You'll be the one who finally brings the thing off – you'll be the one –*

– *The one – the one –*

Anson played with those words, moved them this way and that, stood them upside down and rightside up again. *The one.* *The one.* Both Ron and the Colonel, he thought – and Anse too, in a way – had lived all those years waiting, suspended in maddening inaction, dreaming of a world without the Entities but unwilling, for one reason or another, to give the order for the launching of a counterattack. But now *he* was in command. The Carmichael of the era, Ron had said. Was he to live a life of waiting too? To go through the slow cycle of the years up here on this mountain, looking forever toward the perfect time to strike? There would *never* be a perfect time. They must simply choose a time, be it perfect or not, and at long last begin to lash back at the conquerors.

There was no one to hold him back, any more. That was a little frightening, but, yes, it was liberating, too. Ron's death seemed to him to be a signal to act.

He found himself wondering if this was some kind of manic overreaction to his father's death.

No, Anson decided. *No.* It was simply that the time had come to make the big move.

The pounding in his head was starting again. That terrible pressure, the furious knuckles knocking from within. This is the time, it seemed to be saying. This is the time. This is the time.

If not now, when?

When?

Anson waited two weeks after the funeral.

On a bright, crisp morning he came striding into the chart room. 'All right,' he said, looking about the room at Steve and Charlie and Paul and Peggy and Mike. 'I think that the right moment to get things started has arrived. I'm sending Tony down to L.A. to take out Prime.'

Nobody said a word against it. Nobody dared. This was Anson's party all the way. He had that look in his eye, the look that came over him when something started throbbing inside his head, that unanswerable something that told him to get on with the job of saving the world.

Down there in Los Angeles, Andy was in business in a big way, or at least semi-big. Mickey Megabyte, ace pardoner. It beat sitting around the ranch listening to the sheep go baa.

He found a little apartment right in the middle of his district, just south of Wilshire, and for the first two days sat there wondering how people who needed a pardoner's services were going to know how to find him. But they knew. It wasn't necessary for him to beat the bushes for jobs. In his first week he did four pardoning deals, splicing himself neatly and expertly into the system to reverse a driver's-licence cancellation for a man who lived on Country Club Drive, to cancel a mystifying denial of a marriage permit for a couple from Koreatown, to arrange a visit to relatives in New Mexico for someone who had arbitrarily been refused exit passage from Los Angeles – the Entities were getting tighter and tighter about letting people move about from place to place, God only knew why, but who ever had any answers to questions about Entity policies? – and to maneuver a promotion and a raise for a LACON highway patrolman who was raising two families at opposite ends of the city.

That last one was pushing things a little, doing a hack for a LACON man, but the fellow came to Andy with valid documentation from Mary Canary saying it was safe to take on the job, and Andy risked it. It worked out. So did the others. Everybody paid promptly and Andy obediently flipped his commissions over to the guild right away and all was well.

So: the pardoning career of Mickey Megabyte had begun. Easy money for not very much work. He would begin to yearn for something more challenging after a while, he knew. But Andy didn't expect to spend his life at this, after all. It was his plan to pile up bank accounts for himself all around the continent and then write himself an exit ticket that would let him get out of L.A. and see a little of the world.

After the fourth pardon came a surprise, though. Someone from Mary Canary's staff dropped around and said to him, 'You like to do things a little too well, don't you, kid?'

'What?'

'Didn't anybody tell you? You can't make every fucking pardon you write a perfect one. You do that all the time, you're bound to attract the attention of the Entities, and that's not something you really want to do, is it? Or anything that we would want you to do.'

Andy didn't get it. 'I'm supposed to write bad pardons some of the time, is that what you're saying? Pardons that don't go through?'

'Right. Some of them, anyway. I know, I know, it's a professional thing with you. You have a rep to maintain and you want to look good. But don't look *too* good, you know what I mean? For your own sake. And also it makes everybody else look bad, because nobody else does perfect work. Once word gets around town about you, customers will start coming in here from other districts, and you can see the problem with that. So flub a few, Mickey. Stiff a client, now and then, okay? For your own sake. Okay? Okay?'

That was hard, being expected to do less than perfect work. It went against his nature to do an incompetent hack. But he'd have to write a couple of stiffs before long, he supposed, just to keep the guild guys happy.

At the beginning of the second week a woman came to him who wanted a transfer to San Diego. Nice-looking woman, twenty-eight, maybe thirty years old, job in the LACON judiciary wing, had some reason for wanting to change towns but couldn't swing the transfer arrangements. Tessa, her name was. Fluffy red hair, full red lips, pleasant smile, good figure. Nice. He had always had a thing for older women.

Andy was uneasy about having so many LACON people coming to him for pardons. But this one had the right letter of recommendation too.

He started setting up the hack for her.

Then he said, thinking about the fluffy red hair, the good figure, the week and a half he had just spent sleeping alone in this strange new town, 'You know, Tessa, I've got an idea. Suppose I write a transfer for *both* of us, for Florida, or maybe Mexico. Mexico would be nice, wouldn't it? Cuernavaca, Acapulco, somewhere down there in the sun.' A sudden wild impulse. But what the hell: nothing ventured, nothing gained. 'We could have a nice little holiday together, okay? And when we came back you'd go to San Diego, or wherever you wanted, and –'

Andy could see her reaction right away, and it wasn't a good one.

'Please,' she said, very cool and crisp, no pleasant smile at all, now. Glowering at him, in fact. 'They told me you were a professional. Making passes at the customers isn't very professional.'

'Sorry,' Andy said. 'Maybe I got a little carried away.'

'San Diego is what I want, yes? And solo, if you don't mind.'

'Right, Tessa. Right.'

She was still giving him that scowling look, as though he had unzipped himself in front of her, or worse. Suddenly he was

angry. Perhaps he had let himself get carried away, yes. A little
out of line, yes. But she didn't have to look at him that way, did
she? Did she? It was offensive, being scowled at like that, just
because he had stepped a little out of line.

He was supposed to write a few pardons that didn't work out,
Mary Canary's guy had told him. Screw up his code a little, once
in a while, get things just a tiny bit wrong.

All right, he thought. Let this one be the first. What the hell.
What the hell. He wrote her an exit permit for San Diego. And
put just the littlest little bug in it, down near the end, that invalidated the whole thing top to bottom. It was a *very* little bug, not
even an entire line of code. It would do the trick, though. Teach
her a lesson, too. He didn't like it when people glowered at him
like that.

Mark, Paul Carmichael's oldest son, drove Tony down to Los
Angeles from the ranch, taking the back road eastward through
Fillmore and Castaic to the place where it met the remnants of
Interstate 5, and heading south from there. Steve Gannett had
determined that the most likely location of Prime's sanctuary was
in the northeastern sector of the city, bounded by the Hollywood
Freeway on the north, the Harbor Freeway on the west, the city
wall on the east, and Vernon Boulevard on the south.

Within that zone, Steve said, the highest-probability location
for the site itself was right in the heart of the old downtown
business district. He had all sorts of figures, based on Entity
transit vector observations, that proved to his own satisfaction,
at least, that a certain building two blocks south of the old Civic
Center was the place. Mark delivered him, therefore, to the East
Valley gate of the wall, where Burbank met Glendale, which was
as close as he could get to downtown. There Mark would wait,
for days, if necessary, while Tony entered the city on foot and
made his steady way toward the designated target area.

'Give me a ping,' Mark said, as Tony got out of the car.

Tony grinned and held up his arm. 'Ping,' he said. 'Ping. Ping.
Ping. Ping.'

'There you are,' Mark said. 'Right on the screen where you
belong.'

They had put an implant in Tony's forearm, one that had a directional locator built into it. One of the best implant men in San Francisco had designed it and come down to the ranch to install it, and Lisa Gannett had programmed it to broadcast its signal right into the city telephone lines. Wherever Tony went, they would be able to follow him. Mark could trace him from the car; Steve or Lisa could track him from the ranch's communications center.

'Well, now,' Mark said. 'All set to get going, are you, then?'

'Ping,' said Tony again, and moved off in the direction of the wall.

Mark watched him go. Tony didn't look back. He walked quickly and steadily toward the gate. When he reached it, he put his implant over the gatekeeper node and let it read the access code that Lisa had written for him.

The gate opened. Tony entered Los Angeles. It was a few minutes past midnight. His big moment was unfolding at last.

He was ready for it. More than ready: Tony was ripe.

He was carrying, in his backpack, a small explosive device powerful enough to take out half a dozen square blocks of the city. All he had to do now was find the building where Steve thought Prime might be hidden, affix the bomb to its side, walk quickly away, and send the signal to the ranch, the single blurt of apparently meaningless digital information that would tell them they could detonate at will.

Khalid had spent close to seven years training him for this, emptying out whatever had been inside Tony's soul before and replacing it with a sense of serene dedication to unthinking action. And, so they all hoped, Tony was completely and properly programmed now. He would go about his tasks in Los Angeles the way a broom goes about sweeping away fallen leaves scattered along a walk, giving no more thought to what he had come here to do, or what the consequences of a successful mission might be, than the broom gives to the leaves or the walk.

'He's inside the wall,' Mark said, over the car phone. 'On his way.'

'He's inside the wall,' Steve said at the ranch, pointing to the yellow dot of light on the screen, and to the red one. 'That's

Mark, sitting in the car just outside the wall,' he said. 'And that one's Tony.'

'And now we wait, I guess,' said Anson. 'But is his mind blank enough, I wonder? Can you just trot right in there and stick a bomb on a building without thinking at all about what you're doing?'

Steve looked up from the screen. 'I know what Khalid would say to that. Everything is in the hands of Allah, Khalid would say.'

'Everything is,' said Anson.

In the darkness of the city Tony plodded on, south and south and south, past looming silent freeways, past gigantic empty office buildings, dead and dark, that were left over from an era that now seemed prehistoric. The computer in his forearm made little soft noises. Steve was guiding him from Santa Barbara, following his progress on the screen and moving him from street to street like the machine he was. A sound like *this* meant to turn left. A sound like *that*, right. Eventually he might hear a tone that sounded like *this this this*, and then he was to take the little package from his backpack and stick it to the wall of the building that was just in front of him. After which he was supposed to move swiftly away from the site, going back in the direction from which he had just come.

The streets were practically deserted, here. Occasionally a car went by; occasionally, one of the floating wagons of the Entities, with a glowing figure or two standing upright in it. Tony glanced at them incuriously. Curiosity was a luxury he had long ago relinquished.

Turn left at this corner. Yes. Right at the next one. Yes. Straight ahead, now, ten blocks, until the mighty pillars of an elevated freeway blocked his way. Steve, far away, directed him with tiny sounds toward an underpass that went between the freeway's elephantine legs, taking him beneath the roadbed and across to the far side. Onward. Onward. Onward.

Mark, in the car outside the wall, followed the pings coming from Tony's implant as they converted themselves into splashes of light on the screen on his dashboard. Steve, at the ranch, monitored them also. Anson stood beside him, watching the screen.

'You know,' Anson said hoarsely, breaking a long silence about four in the morning, 'this can't possibly work.'

'What?' Steve said.

Startled, he glanced up from his equipment. Sweat was streaming down Anson's face, giving him a glossy, waxen look. His eyes were bulging. Knotted-up muscles were writhing along his jaw-line. Altogether he looked very strange.

Anson said, 'The problem is that the basic idea is wrong. I see that now. It's complete madness to imagine that we could decapitate the entire Entity operation just by knocking off the top Entity. Steve, I've sent Tony down there to die for nothing.'

'Maybe you ought to get some rest. It doesn't take two of us to do this.'

'Listen to me, Steve. This is all a huge mistake.'

'For Christ's sake, Anson! Have you lost your mind? You've been behind the project from the start. It's a hell of a time for you to be saying stuff like this. Anyway, Tony's going to be all right.'

'Will he?'

'Look, here: he's moving along very smoothly, past the Civic Center already, closing in on the building that I think is Prime's, nicely going about his job, and there's no sign of any intercept. If they knew he had a bomb on him this close to Prime, they'd have stopped him by now, wouldn't they? Five more minutes and it'll be done. And once we kill Prime, they'll all go bonkers from the shock. You know that, Anson. Their minds are all hooked together.'

'Are you sure of that? What do we know, really? We don't even know that Prime exists in the first place. If Prime isn't in that building, it might not matter to them that Tony's armed. And even if Prime does exist and is sitting right there, and even if they are all hooked together telepathically, how can we be sure what'll happen if we kill him? Other than terrible reprisals, that is? We're assuming that they'll just lie down and weep, once Prime's dead. What if they don't?'

Steve ran his hand in anguish through what was left of his hair. The man seemed to be having a breakdown right before his eyes.

'Cut it out, Anson, will you? It's very late in the game to be spouting crap like this.'

'But *is* it such crap? The way it looks to me, all of a sudden, is that in my godawful impatience to do something big, I've done something very, very dumb. Which my father and my grand-father before me had the common sense not to try. – Call him back, Steve.'

'Huh?'

'Get him out of there.'

'Jesus, he's practically at the site now, Anson. Maybe half a block away, looks like. Maybe less than that.'

'I don't care. Turn him around. That's an order.'

Steve pointed to the screen. 'He *has* turned around. You see those bleeps of light? He's signalling that he's already placed the explosive. Leaving the scene, heading for safe ground. So the thing's done. In five minutes or so I can detonate. No sense not doing it, now that the bomb's been planted.'

Anson was silent. He put his hands to the sides of his head and rubbed them.

'All right,' he said, though the words came from him with a reluctance that was only too obvious. 'Go ahead and detonate, then.'

Tony heard the sound rising through the air behind him, an odd kind of hissing first, then a thud, then the first part of the boom, then the main part of it, very loud. Painfully loud, even. His ears tingled. A hot breeze went rushing past him. He walked quickly on. Something must have exploded, he thought. Yes. Something must have exploded. There has been an explosion back there. And now he had to return to the wall and go through the gate and find Mark and go home. Yes.

But there were figures, suddenly, standing in his way. Human figures, three, four, five of them, wearing gray LACON uniforms. They seemed to have sprung right from the pavement before him, as though they had been following him all this time, waiting for the moment for making themselves known.

'Sir?' one of them said, too politely. 'May I see your identification, sir?'

'He's off the screen,' Mark said, from the car outside the wall. 'I don't know what happened.'

'The bomb went off, didn't it?' said Steve.

'It went off, all right. I could hear it from here.'

'He's off my screen too. Could he have been caught up in the explosion?'

'Looked to me like he was well clear of the site when it blew,' Mark said.

'Me too. But where –'

'Hold it, Steve. Entity wagon going by just now. Three of them in it.'

'Behaving crazily? Signs of shock?'

'Absolutely normal,' Mark said. 'I think I better begin getting myself out of here.'

Steve looked toward Anson. 'You hear all that?'

'Yes.'

'Entity wagon going by. No sign of unusual behavior. I think the site we blew might not have been the right one.'

Anson nodded wearily. 'And Tony?' he asked.

'Off the screen. Allah only knows.'

In the three days after Andy had written the self-canceling pardon for the woman with fluffy red hair, he wrote five legitimate ones for other people who were in various sorts of trouble. He figured that was about the right proportion to keep the guild happy, one stiff per every five or six legits.

He wondered what had befallen her when she showed up at the wall and presented her dandy little exit permit, the one he had written that granted her the right to change her residence to San Diego. The gatekeeper would disagree. And then? Off to a labor camp for trying to use a phony permit, most likely. What a pity, Tessa. But no pardoner ever offered guarantees. They all made that clear right up front. You hired a pardoner, you had to understand that there were certain risks, both for you and the pardoner. And it wasn't as if the customers had any recourse, did they? You couldn't hire somebody to do illegal work for you and then complain about the quality of the job. Pardoners didn't give refunds to dissatisfied customers.

Poor Ms Tessa, he thought. Poor, poor Tessa.

He put her out of his mind. Her problems were not his problem. She was just a job that hadn't worked out.

Not long after the Tessa event, Andy decided that it was time to begin raking off a little of his fees from the top. Mary Canary and his gang didn't need quite that much out of him, he figured. A little here, a little there: it could mount up very nicely.

Soon, though, he began to see signs that they might be tapping in on him, checking on his figures. Did they suspect something, or was this just a routine check? He didn't know. He wrote a cute little cancel that would keep them in the dark. But also he decided that he had had enough of Los Angeles for the time being. He didn't love the place much. It was time to move along, maybe. Phoenix? New Orleans? Acapulco?

Someplace warm, at any rate. Andy had never liked cold weather.

At the ranch, Anson waited for a sign that the explosion in Los Angeles had had some effect on things.

What kind of reprisal would there be – arrests, plagues, disruptions of electrical service? – and when would it come? The Entities were certainly going to send mankind a message, now, to the effect that it was unacceptable to set off bombs in the middle of a major Entity administrative district.

There did not seem to have been any reprisal.

Anson waited for it for weeks. Waited. Waited.

But nothing happened. The world went on as before. Tony did not reappear, nor could he be traced via the Net; but that was no surprise. And otherwise everything was as it had been.

Thinking about Tony was almost unbearable for him. Sickening waves of guilt came sweeping through him, dizzying him, giving him attacks of the staggers, whenever he allowed himself to dwell on his brother's probable fate.

Anson couldn't understand how it had been possible for him to act on so little information – or how he could so coolly have let his brother go to his death. 'I should have gone myself,' he said over and over. 'I should never have let him take the risk.'

'The Entities wouldn't have allowed you to get within ten miles of Prime,' Steve told him. 'You'd have been broadcasting your intentions every step of the way.'

And Khalid said, 'You were not someone who could have done it, Anson. Tony was the one to go. Not you. Never you.'

Gradually Anson came to admit the truth of that, though not before his brooding had reached such a pitch of despondency that Steve and Mike and Cassandra had seriously discussed the desirability of keeping him on suicide watch. Things never came to that; but the dark cloud that had settled on Anson did not seem ever to lift, either.

The great puzzle now was why had there been no response to the bombing. What were the Entities up to? Anson had no answer to that.

It was almost as if they were mocking him, refusing to strike back. Saying to him, *We know what you were trying to do, but we don't give a damn. We have nothing to fear from insects like you. We are too far above you even to be angry. We are everything and you are nothing.*

Or perhaps not. Perhaps it was nothing at all like that.

The thing about aliens, Anson reminded himself, is that they are *alien*. Whatever we think we understand about them is wrong. We will never understand them. Never. Never. Never.

Never.

VIII

Fifty-Two Years
from Now

'Key Sixteen, Housing Omicron Kappa, aleph sub-one,' Andy said to the software on duty at the Alhambra gate of the Los Angeles Wall.

He didn't generally expect software to be suspicious. This wasn't even very smart software. It was working off some great biochips – he could feel them jigging and pulsing as the electron stream flowed through them – but the software itself was just a kludge. Typical gatekeeper stuff, Andy thought.

He stood waiting as the picoseconds went ticking away by the millions.

'Name, please,' the gatekeeper said, what could have been a century later, in its kludgy robotic gatekeeper voice.

'John Doe. Beta Pi Upsilon l04324x.'

He extended his wrist. A moment for implant check. Tick tick tick tick. Then came confirmation. Once more Andy had bamboozled a keeper. The gate opened. He walked into Los Angeles.

As easy as Beta Pi.

He had forgotten how truly vast the wall that encircled Los Angeles was. Every city had its wall, but this one was something special: a hundred, maybe a hundred fifty feet thick, easily. Its gates were more like tunnels. The total mass of it was awesome. The expenditure of human energy that went into building it – muscle and sweat, sweat and muscle – must have been phenomenal, he thought. Considering that the wall ran completely around the L.A. basin from the San Gabriel Valley to the San Fernando Valley and then over the mountains and down the coast and back the far side past Long Beach, and that it was at least sixty feet high and all that distance deep. That was something to think about, a wall that size. So much sweat, so much toil. Not his own personal sweat and toil, of course, but still – still –

What were they for, all these walls?

To remind us, Andy told himself, that we are all slaves nowadays. You can't ignore the walls. You can't pretend they aren't there. *We made you build them*, is what they say, *and don't you ever forget that.*

Just within the wall Andy caught sight of a few Entities walking around right out in the street, preoccupied as usual with their own mystifying business and paying no attention to the humans in the vicinity. These were high-caste ones, the boss critters, the kind with the luminous orange spots along their sides. Andy gave them plenty of room. They had a way sometimes, he knew, of picking a human up with those long elastic tongues, like a frog snapping up a fly, and letting him dangle in mid-air while they studied him with those saucer-sized yellow eyes. Old Cindy, back at the ranch, had told tales of being snatched up that way right at the beginning of the Conquest.

Andy didn't think he would care for that. You didn't get hurt, apparently, but it wasn't dignified to be dangled in mid-air by something that looks like a fifteen-foot-high purple squid standing on the tips of its tentacles.

His first project after entering the city was to find himself a car. He had driven in from Arizona that morning in quite a decent late-model Buick that he had picked up in Tucson, plenty of power and style, but by now he expected that there were alerts out for it everywhere and it didn't seem wise to try to bring it through the wall. So, with great regret, he had left it parked out there and gone in on foot.

On Valley Boulevard about two blocks in from the wall he came upon a late-model Toshiba El Dorado that looked pretty good to him. He matched frequencies with its lock and slipped inside and took about ninety seconds to reprogram its drive control to his personal metabolic cues. The previous owner, he thought, must have been fat as a hippo and probably diabetic: her glycogen index was absurd and her phosphines were wild.

'Pershing Square,' he told the car.

It had nice capacity, maybe 90 megabytes. It turned south right away and found the old freeway and drove off toward downtown. Andy figured he'd set up shop in the middle of things, work two or three quick pardons to keep his edge sharp, get himself a hotel room, a meal, maybe hire some companionship. And then think about the next move. Stay in L.A. a week or so, no more than that. Then head out to Hawaii, maybe. Or down to South America. Meanwhile, L.A. wasn't such a bad place to be, this time of year. It was the middle of winter, yes, but the Los Angeles winter was a joke: that golden sun, those warm breezes coming down the canyons. Andy was glad to be back in the big town at last, at least for a little while, after five years roving the boondocks.

A couple of miles east of the big downtown interchange, traffic suddenly began to back up. Maybe an accident ahead, maybe a roadblock: no way of knowing until he was there. Andy told the Toshiba to get off the freeway.

Slipping through roadblocks could have its scary aspects and even under favorable conditions called for a lot of hard work. He preferred not to deal with them. He knew that he probably could fool any kind of software at a roadblock and certainly any human cop, but why bother if you didn't have to?

After some zigging and zagging, heading basically in the general direction of the downtown towers, he asked the car where he was.

The screen lit up. Alameda near Banning, it said. Right at the edge of downtown, looked like. He had the car drop him at Spring Street, a couple of blocks from Pershing Square. 'Pick me up at 1830 hours,' Andy told it. 'Corner of – umm – Sixth and Hill.' It went away to park itself and he headed for the Square to peddle some pardons.

It wasn't Andy's plan to check in with the Mary Canary syndicate. They wouldn't welcome him very warmly, and in any case he was planning to be in town only a short while, too short for them to be able to track him down, so why split the fees with them? He'd be gone before they ever knew he was here.

He didn't need their help, anyway. It wasn't hard for a good free-lance pardoner to find buyers. You could see the need in their eyes: the tightly controlled anger, the smoldering resentment at whatever it was that the mindless, indifferent Entity-controlled bureaucracy had done to them. And something else, something intangible, a certain sense of having a shred or two of inner integrity left, that told you right away that here was a customer, which meant somebody willing to risk a lot to regain some measure of freedom. Andy was in business within fifteen minutes.

The first one was an aging surfer sort, barrel chest and that sun-bleached look. Surfing, once such a big thing along the coast, was pretty much extinct, Andy knew. The Entities hadn't allowed it for ten, perhaps fifteen years – they had their plankton seines just off shore from Santa Barbara to San Diego, gulping in the marine nutrients that seemed to be their main food, and any beach boy who tried to take a whack at the waves out there would be chewed right up.

But this guy must have been one hell of a performer in his day. The way he moved through the park, making little balancing moves as if he needed to compensate for the irregularities of the Earth's rotation, it was easy to see what an athlete he had been. He sat down next to Andy and began working on his lunch. Thick forearms, gnarled hands. A wall-laborer, most likely. Muscles knotting in his cheeks: the anger, forever simmering just below boil.

Andy got him talking, after a while. A surfer, yes. At least forty years old, and lost in the far-away and gone. He began sighing about legendary beaches where the waves were tubes and they came pumping end to end. 'Trestle Beach,' he murmured. 'That's north of San Onofre. You had to sneak through Camp Pendleton, the old LACON training base. Sometimes the LACON guards would open fire, just warning shots. Or Hollister Ranch, up by Santa Barbara.' His blue eyes got misty. 'Huntington Beach. Oxnard. I got everywhere, man.' He flexed his huge fingers. 'Now these fucking Entity hodads own the shore. Can you believe it? They own it. And I'm pulling wall, my second time around, seven days a week for the next ten years.'

'Ten?' Andy said. 'That's a shitty deal.'

'You know anyone who doesn't have a shitty deal?'

'Some,' he said. 'They buy their way out.'

'Yeah. Sure.'

'It can be done, you know.'

The surfer gave him a careful look. That was sensible, Andy thought. You never knew who might be a quisling. Collaborators and spies were everywhere. An amazing number of people loved working for the Entities.

'It can?' the surfer asked.

'All it takes is money,' Andy said.

'And a pardoner.'

'That's right.'

'One you can trust.'

Andy shrugged. 'There are pardoners and then there are pardoners. You've got to go on faith, man.'

'Yeah,' the surfer said. Then, after a while: 'I heard of a guy, he bought a three-year pardon and wall passage thrown in. Went up north, caught a krill trawler, wound up in Australia, right out there on the Reef. Nobody's ever going to find him there. He's out of the system. Right out of the fucking system. What do you think that would have cost him?'

'About twenty grand,' Andy said.

'Hey, that's a sharp guess!'

'No guess.'

'Oh?' Another careful look. 'You don't sound local.'

'I'm not. Just visiting.'

'That's still the price? Twenty grand?'

'I can't do anything about supplying krill trawlers. You'd be on your own once you were outside the wall.'

'Twenty grand just to get through the wall?'

'And a seven-year labor exemption.'

'I pulled ten,' he said.

'I can't get you off a ten. It's not in the configuration, you follow? It would draw too much attention if I tried to nix you out of a ten-year term. But seven would work. You'd still owe them three when the exemption was up, but you could get so far from here in seven years that they'd lose you forever. You could goddamned swim to Australia in that much time. Come in low, below Sydney, no seines there.'

'You know a hell of a lot.'

'My business to know,' Andy said. 'You want me to run an asset check on you?'

'I'm worth seventeen five. Fifteen hundred real, the rest collat. What can I get for seventeen five?'

'Just what I said. Through the wall, and seven years' exemption.'

'A bargain rate, hey?'

'I take what I can get,' Andy said. 'You have an implant?'

'Yep.'

'Okay. Give me your wrist. And don't worry. This part is read-only.'

He keyed the surfer's data implant and patched his own in. The surfer had fifteen hundred in the bank and a collateral rating of sixteen thou, exactly as he claimed. They eyed each other very carefully now. This was a highly illegal transaction. The surfer had no way of knowing whether Andy was a quisling or not, but Andy couldn't be sure of the surfer, either.

'You can do it right here in the park?' the surfer asked.

'You bet. Lean back, close your eyes, make like you're snoozing in the sun. The deal is that I take a thousand of the cash now and you transfer five thou of the collateral bucks to me, straight labor-debenture deal. When you get through the wall I get the other five hundred cash and five thou more on sweat security. The rest you pay off at three thou a year plus interest, wherever you are, quarterly key-ins. I'll program the whole thing, including beep reminders on payment dates. It's up to you to make your travel arrangements, remember. I can do pardons and wall transits but I'm not a goddamned travel agent. Are we on?'

The surfer put his head back and closed his eyes.

'Go ahead,' he said.

It was fingertip stuff, straight circuit emulation, Andy's standard hack. He picked up all his identification codes, carried them into Central, found the man's records. He seemed real, nothing more or less than he had claimed. Sure enough, he had drawn a lulu of a labor tax, ten years on the wall. Andy wrote him a pardon good for the first seven of that. Then he gave him a wall-transit pass, which meant writing in a new skills class for him, programmer third grade. The guy didn't think like a programmer and he didn't look like a programmer, but the wall software wasn't going to figure that out.

With these moves Andy had made him a member of the human elite, the relative handful who were free to go in and out of the walled cities as they wished. In return for these little favors he signed over the surfer's entire life savings to various accounts of his, payable as arranged, part now, part later. The surfer wasn't worth a nickel any more, but he was a free man. That wasn't such a terrible trade-off, was it?

And it was a valid pardon, too. Andy didn't intend to write any stiffs while he was here. The guild might require its pardoners to write the occasional stiff, but he wasn't working with the guild just now. And though Andy could understand the need to fudge up a pardon now and then if you were going to work the same territory for any prolonged period, he had never cared for the idea of doing it. It was offensive to his professional pride. He didn't plan to be in town long enough, anyway, this time around, for anybody – the Entities, their human puppets, or, for that matter, the guild itself – to be unduly disturbed by the skill with which he was practicing his trade.

The next one was a tiny Japanese woman, the classic style, sleek, fragile, doll-like. Crying in big wild gulps that Andy thought might break her in half, while a gray-haired older man in a shabby blue business suit – her grandfather, perhaps – was trying to comfort her. Public crying was a good indicator, Andy knew, that someone was in bad Entity trouble. 'Maybe I can help,' he said, and they were both so distraught that they didn't even bother to be suspicious.

He was her father-in-law, not her grandfather. The husband was dead, killed by burglars the year before. There were two small kids. Now she had received her new labor-tax ticket. She had been afraid they were going to send her out to work on the wall, which of course wasn't likely to happen: the assignments were pretty random, but they seemed rarely to be crazy, and what use would a ninety-pound girl be in hauling stone blocks around?

The father-in-law, though, had some friends who were in the know, and they managed to bring up the hidden encoding on her ticket. The computers hadn't sent her to the wall, no. They had sent her to Area Five. That was bad news. And they had given her a TTD classification. Even worse.

'The wall would have been better,' the old man said. 'They'd see, right away, she wasn't strong enough for heavy work, and they'd find something else, something she could do. But Area Five? Who ever comes back from that?'

'So you know what Area Five is, do you?' Andy said, surprised.

'The medical experiment place. And this mark here, TTD. I know what that stands for too.'

She began to moan again. Andy couldn't really blame her. TTD meant Test To Destruction. So far as he understood the TTD program, it had to do with a need the Entities felt for finding out how much physical labor humans were really capable of doing. The only reliable way to discover that, apparently, was to put a sampling of the populace through tests that showed where the endurance limits lay.

'I will die,' the woman wailed. 'My babies! My babies!'

'Do you know what a pardoner is?' Andy asked the father-in-law.

Which produced a quick excited response: sharp intake of breath, eyes going bright, head nodding vehemently. And just as quickly the excitement faded, giving way to bleakness, help-lessness, despair.

'They all cheat you,' he said.

'Not all.'

'Who can say? They take your money, they give you nothing.'

'You know that isn't true. Sometimes things don't work out, sure. It isn't an exact science. But everybody can tell you stories of pardons that came through.'

'Maybe. Maybe,' the old man said. The woman sobbed quietly. 'You know of such a person?'

'For three thousand dollars,' Andy said quietly, 'I can take the

TTD off her ticket. For five I can write an exemption from service that'll be good until her children are in high school.'

He wondered why he was being so tender-hearted. A fifty percent discount, and he hadn't even run an asset check. For all he knew the father-in-law was a millionaire. But no, if that was so he'd have been off long ago cutting a deal for a pardon for her, then, and not sitting around like this, weeping and wailing in Pershing Square.

The old man gave Andy a long, deep, appraising look. Peasant shrewdness coming to the surface.

'How can we be sure you'll do what you say you'll do?' he asked.

Andy might have told him that he was the king of his profession, the best of all pardoners, a genius hacker with the truly magic touch. Who could slip into any data network there was and get it to dance to his tune. That would have been nothing more than the truth. But all he said was that the man would have to make up his own mind, that Andy couldn't offer any affidavits or guarantees, that he was available if they wanted him and otherwise it was all the same to him if she preferred to stick with her TTD ticket.

They went off and conferred for a couple of minutes. When they came back, the old man silently rolled up his sleeve and presented his implant. Andy keyed his credit balance: thirty thou or so, not bad. He transferred eight of it to his accounts, half to Seattle, the rest to Honolulu. Then he took the woman's wrist, which was about two of his fingers thick, and got into her implant and wrote her the pardon that would save her life.

'Go on,' Andy said. 'Home. Your kids are waiting for their lunch.'

Her eyes glowed. 'If I could only thank you somehow –'

'I've already banked my fee. Go. If you ever see me again, don't say hello.'

'This will work?' the old man asked.

'You say you have friends who know things. Wait seven days, then tell the data bank that she's lost her ticket. When you get the new one, ask your pals to decode it for you. You'll see. It'll be all right.'

He didn't seem convinced. Andy suspected the man was more than half sure that he had just been swindled out of one fourth of his life's savings. The hatred in his eyes was all too visible. But in a week he would find out that Andy really had saved his daughter-in-law's life, and then he would rush down to the Square to tell Andy how sorry he was that he had had such terrible feelings toward him. Only by that time Andy expected to be somewhere else far away.

They shuffled out the east side of the park, pausing a couple of times to look back over their shoulders at Andy as if they thought he was going to transform them into pillars of salt the moment their backs were turned. Then they were gone.

In short order Andy had earned enough now to get him through his week in L.A. But he stuck around the park anyway, hoping for a little more. That proved to be a mistake.

The next customer was Little Mr Invisible, the sort of man no one would ever notice in a crowd, gray on gray, thinning hair, mild bland apologetic smile. But his eyes had a shine. He and Andy struck up a conversation and very quickly they were jockeying around trying to find out things about each other. He told Andy he was from the Silver Lake neighborhood. That conveyed very little to Andy. Said that he had come down here to see someone at the big LACON building on Figueroa Street. All right: probably an appeals case. Andy smelled a deal.

Then the gray little man wanted to know where Andy was from – Santa Monica? West L.A.? Andy wondered if people had a different kind of accent on that side of town. 'I'm a traveling man,' he said. 'Hate to stay in one place.' True enough. 'Came in from Utah last night. Wyoming before that.' Not true, either one. 'Maybe on to New York, next.'

The little man looked at Andy as though he had said he was planning a voyage to Jupiter.

He knew now, though, that Andy had wall-transit clearance, or else that he had some way of getting it when he wanted it, or at least was willing to claim openly that he did. Which was as good as Andy's advertising that he was something special. That was what the little man was looking to find out, obviously.

In no time at all they were down to basics.

The little gray man said that he had drawn a new labor ticket, six years at the salt-field reclamation site out back of Mono Lake. Bad news, bad, bad, bad. People died like mayflies out there, Andy had heard. What he wanted, naturally, was a transfer to something softer, like Operations & Maintenance, and it had to be within the walls, preferably in one of the districts out by the ocean where the air was cool and clear.

'Sure,' Andy said. 'I can do that.'

Andy quoted him a price and the little man accepted without a quiver.

'Let's have your wrist,' Andy said.

The little man held out his right hand, palm upward. His implant access was a pale yellow plaque, mounted in the usual place but rounder than the standard kind and of a slightly smoother texture. Andy didn't see any great significance in that. As he had done so many times before, he put his own arm over the other's, wrist to wrist, access to access.

Their biocomputers made contact.

The moment that they did, the little man came at him like a storm, and instantly Andy knew, from the strength of the signal that was hitting him, that he was up against something special and very possibly in trouble; that he had been hustled, in fact. This colorless little man hadn't been trying to buy a pardon at all. What he had been looking for, Andy realized, was a data duel. Mr Macho behind the bland smile, out to show the new boy in town a few of his tricks.

It was a long, long time since Andy had ever been involved in something like this. Dueling was adolescent stuff. But back in Andy's dueling days no hacker had ever mastered him in a one-on-one anywhere. Not a one, ever. Nor was this one going to. Andy felt sorry for him, but not very much.

He shot Andy a bunch of fast stuff, cryptic but easy, just by way of finding out Andy's parameters. Andy caught it and stored it and laid an interrupt on him and took over the dialog. His turn to do the testing, now. He wanted the other man to begin to see who he was fooling around with.

But just as Andy began to execute, the other man put an

interrupt on *him*. That was a new experience. Andy stared at him
with some respect.

Usually any hacker anywhere would recognize Andy's signal
in the first thirty seconds, and that would be enough to finish
the interchange. He would know that there was no point in continuing. But this one either hadn't been able to identify Andy or
just didn't care, and so he had come right back with his interrupt.
Andy found that amazing. The stuff the little man began laying
on Andy next was pretty amazing too.

He went right to work, energetically trying to scramble Andy's
architecture. Reams of stuff came flying at Andy up in the heavy
megabyte zone.

– *jspike. dbltag. nslice. dzcnt.*

Andy gave it right back, twice as hard.

– *maxfrq. minpau. spktot. jspike.*

But the other hacker didn't mind at all.

– *maxdz. spktim. falter. nslice.*

– *frqsum. eburst.*

– *iburst.*

– *prebst.*

– *nobrst.*

Mexican standoff. The gray little man was still smiling. Not
even a trace of sweat on his forehead. There was something eerie
about him, Andy thought, something new and strange.

This is some kind of borgmann hacker, he realized suddenly.
Working for the Entities, roving the city, looking to make trouble
for freelancers like me.

Good as the man was, and he was plenty good, Andy despised
him for that. There was just enough Carmichael blood in his
veins for Andy to know which side he was on in the Entity-
human struggle. A borgmann – now, that was something
truly disgusting. Using your hacking skills to help *them* – no.
No. A filthy business. Andy wanted to short him. He wanted
to burn him out. He had never hated anyone so much in his
life.

But Andy couldn't do a thing with him.

That baffled him. He was the Data King, he was the Megabyte
Monster. All these years he had gone floating back and forth

across a world in chains, blithely riding the data stream, picking every lock he came across. And now this nobody was tying him in knots. Whatever Andy gave him, he parried; and what came back from him was getting increasingly bizarre. The little man was working with an algorithm Andy had never seen before and was having major trouble solving. After a little while he couldn't even figure out what was being done to him, let alone what he was going to do to cancel it. It was getting so he could barely execute. The little man was forcing him inexorably toward a wetware crash.

'Who the fuck are you?' Andy yelled, furious.

The little man laughed in Andy's face.

And kept pouring it on. He was threatening the integrity of Andy's implant, going at him down on the microcosmic level, attacking the molecules themselves. Fiddling around with electron shells, reversing charges and mucking up valences, clogging his gates, turning his circuits to soup. The computer that had been implanted in Andy's body was nothing but a lot of organic chemistry, after all. So was his brain. If he kept this up the biocomputer would go, and the brain to which it was linked would follow.

This wasn't a sporting contest. This was murder.

Andy reached for the reserves, throwing up all the defensive blockages he could invent. Things he had never had to use in his life; but they were there when he needed them, and they did slow his opponent down. For a moment he was able to halt the onslaught and even push the other man back a little, giving himself the breathing space to set up a few offensive combinations of his own. But before he could get them running, the little man shut Andy down once more and started to drive him toward crashville all over again. The guy was unbelievable.

Andy blocked him. He came back again. Andy hit him hard and the little man threw the punch into some other neural channel altogether and it went fizzling away.

Andy hit him again, harder. Again his thrust was blocked.

Then the little man hit Andy with a force that was far beyond anything he had used before, enough to send him reeling and staggering. Andy was about three nanoseconds from the edge of the abyss when he managed, but by no more than a whisker and a half, to pull himself back.

Groggily, he began to set up a new combination. But even as he did it, he was reading the tone of the other man's data, and what Andy was getting was absolute cool confidence. The little man was waiting for him. He was ready for anything Andy could throw. He was in that realm of utter certainty that lies beyond mere self-confidence.

What it was coming down to was this, Andy saw. He was able to keep the little man from ruining him, but only just barely, and he wasn't able to lay a glove on him at all. And the little man seemed to have infinite resources behind him. Andy didn't worry him. The fellow was tireless. He didn't appear to degrade at all. He just took all Andy could give and kept throwing new stuff at him, coming at him from six sides at once.

Now Andy understood for the first time what it must have felt like for all the hackers he had beaten over the years. Some of them must have felt pretty cocky, he supposed, until they had run into him. It costs more to lose when you think you're good. When you *know* you're good. People like that, when they lose, they have to reprogram their whole sense of their relation to the universe.

He had two choices now. He could go on fighting until the little man wore him down and crashed him. Or he could give up right now. Those were the real only choices he had.

In the end, Andy thought, everything always comes down to that, doesn't it? Two choices: yes or no, on or off, one or zero.

He took a deep breath. He was looking straight into chaos.

'All right,' he said. 'I'm beaten. I quit.' Words he had never thought he would hear himself say.

He wrenched his wrist free of his opponent's implant, trembled, swayed, went toppling down on the ground.

A minute later five LACON cops sprang out of nowhere and jumped him and trussed him up like a turkey and hauled him away, with his implant arm sticking out of the package and a security lock wrapped around his wrist, as if they were afraid he was going to start pulling data right out of the air.

*   *   *

Steve Gannett said, coming out on the patio where Anson was sitting in the Colonel's old chair, 'Look at this, will you, Anson?'

He put a long sheet of glossy green paper into Anson's hand. Anson stared at it uncomprehendingly. It was all arrows and squiggles, Greek letters, a lot of indecipherable computer nonsense.

'You know that I don't understand this goddamned stuff,' Anson said sharply. He realized it was wrong to speak to Steve that way; but his patience grew thinner every day. Anson was thirty-nine years old and felt like fifty. He had been full of big plans, once, when he was young and full of juice and certain that he would be the one to free the world from its serenely tyrannical alien overlords; but everything had gone awry, leaving him with a chilly hollow zone within him that was gradually expanding and expanding and expanding until it seemed to him that there was very little of Anson left around it. For years, now – ever since the failure of the great Prime expedition – he had lived a life that felt as though it had neither past nor future. There was only the endless gray present. He schemed no schemes, dreamed no dreams. 'What am I looking at, here?'

'Andy's fingerprints, I think.'

'His fingerprints?'

'His on-line coding profile. His personal touch. You could compare it to a person's fingerprints, yes. Or his handwriting. I think this is Andy's.'

'Truly? Where'd you get it from?'

'It came out of Los Angeles, picked up by a random line scan by one of our stringers down there. It's new. If he's there, he must have gone back there quite recently.'

Anson examined the printout again. Arrows and squiggles, still. A hopeless maze. Something was beginning to throb within him that he had not felt in years, but he forced it back. He shrugged and said, 'What makes you think this is Andy's?'

'Intuition, maybe. I've been looking for him for five years, and by now I think I know what to expect. This sheet yells "Andy" to me, somehow. He used to use codes like these when he was a kid. I remember his explaining them to me, but I never had a clue about what he was trying to say. That was when he was ten, eleven years old. I have a feeling he's started falling back on this stuff in the time that he's been on the run. Reverting to his own private lingo. We've gone back in and set up a trace for it, and now we see that whoever's been using it has been moving steadily westward across the country all year, Florida, Louisiana, Texas, Arizona. And now L.A. The hacker whose codes these are is working as a pardoner down there right this minute. A free-lancer, operating outside the guild, from the looks of things. I'm sure it's Andy.'

Anson looked up into his cousin's round, sincere, pudgy face. There was an expression of complete conviction on it. Anson was surprised to find himself swept by a sudden rush of admiration, even love, for him.

Steve was fifteen years his senior and should have been the leader of the clan by now. But Steve had never wanted to be a leader. He wanted only to keep on plugging away at the things that mattered to him, sitting there in the communications center all day and half the night, pulling in data from everywhere in the world. Whereas he himself –

The throbbing inside him was growing stronger, now. It would not be suppressed.

'Tell me this,' Anson said. 'Do you think you actually could track him down, on the basis of this stuff?'

'That I can't say. Andy's very, very tricky, you know. I hardly need to tell you. He moves around fast. Simply picking up his trail gives us no guarantee that we could catch up with him. But we can try.'

'We can try, yes. Christ, let's give it a try, all right? Find him, bring him here, put him to use. That crazy mutant son of yours.'

'Mutant?'

'A wild man. Undisciplined, amoral, self-centered, ego-maniacal – where did he get that stuff from, Steve? From you? From Lisa? I doubt it. And certainly not from the fraction of him that's Carmichael. So he has to be a mutant. A mutant, yes. With enormous special skills for which we happen to have a great need. A _gigantic_ need. If only he would deign to employ them on our behalf.'

Steve said nothing. Anson wondered what Steve was thinking;

but he had no reading, none at all. His mild chubby face was utterly blank. The silence stretched uncomfortably, and stretched some more, until it became unbearable. Anson rose and walked to the edge of the patio, gripping the rail and staring out into the great green gorge below. And found himself beginning to tremble.

He knew what had happened. The grand old ambition had started suddenly to rise up in him again, the glorious dream of leading a successful crusade against the aliens, striking down Prime and shattering their dominion with a single blow. Ever since Tony's ill-fated trip to Los Angeles, Anson had had all that locked away in some storage vault of his soul. But now it had broken loose, somehow; and with it, now, came fear, doubt, dark gloom, an agonizing shaft of fresh guilt over the way he had sent Tony foolishly to his death – a whole host of pessimistic self-accusing bleaknesses.

He stood there, taking deep, slow breaths, trying to calm himself as he looked out into the tangled post-Conquest wilderness that had grown up, over the years, between the ranch and the town down there. And a strange vision suddenly went swirling through his mind.

He saw a domed building that looked like a beehive, but of white marble: a shrine, a temple, a sanctuary. A sanctuary, yes. Prime lay within it. Prime was a great bloated pallid sluglike thing, thirty feet long, encased in mechanisms that supplied it with nutrients.

And now Anson saw a human figure approaching that dome: an enigmatic figure, slender, calm, faceless. It might almost be an android. Andy Gannett, sitting before his terminal with a diabolical look in his eyes, was guiding it by remote control, furiously feeding it data that he had pulled out of the sealed archive of Karl-Heinrich Borgmann. The faceless assassin stood before the door of the sanctuary, now, and Andy gave it mysterious digital commands that it transmitted to the sanctuary's gatekeeper, and instantly the door slid open, revealing another beyond and another, and another, until at last the faceless killer stood within the sacred hiding-place of Prime itself –

Raising a weapon. Calmly firing. Prime bathed in blue flame. Sizzling, charring, blackening.

And in that same moment the Entities everywhere on Earth magically shriveling, withering, dying – the sun rising the next day on a world set free –

Anson looked back toward Steve, who was leaning against the wall of the house, watching Anson in an oddly placid way. Anson managed a pale smile and said, 'You know, don't you, that I haven't given much of a shit about the whole Resistance thing since Tony died? That I've just been going through the motions?'

'Yes. I know that, Anson.'

'This might change things, though. If you could only find your damn renegade mutant genius son, finally. And if you can make him crack open the Borgmann archive. And if the Borgmann stuff should give us some clue to the nature and whereabouts of Prime. And if we can then insert a properly programmed killer who –'

'I'd say that's a hell of a lot of ifs.'

'It is, isn't it, cousin? Maybe we should just forget the whole thing. What do you say? Let's wrap up the Resistance once and for all, acknowledge that the world is going to belong to the Entities until the end of time, shut down the entire underground network that you and Doug and Paul spent the last thirty years putting together, and just go on peacefully sitting on our asses up here, living our quiet little lives the way we've been living them all along. What do you say, Steve? Shall we give up the tired old pretense of a Resistance at last?'

'Is that what you want, Anson?'

'No. Not really.'

'Neither do I. Let me see what I can do about finding Andy.'

Where they took him, wrapped and trussed as he was, was LACON headquarters on Figueroa Street, the ninety-story tower of black marble that was the home of the puppet city government. They sat him against the wall in a cavernous, brightly lit hallway and left him there for what seemed like a day and a half, though he supposed it was really no more than an hour or so. Andy didn't give a damn. He was numb. They could have put him in a cesspool and he wouldn't have cared. He wasn't physically damaged – his automatic internal circuit check was still running and it came up green – but the humiliation was so intense that he felt crashed. He felt destroyed. The only thing he wanted to know now was the name of the hacker who had done it to him.

He had heard a lot about the Figueroa Street building. It had ceilings about twenty feet high everywhere, so that there would be room for Entities to move around. Voices reverberated in those vast open spaces like echoes in a cavern. As he sat there he could feel inchoate streams of blurred sounds going lalloping back and forth all around him, above, below, fore, aft. He wanted to hide from them. His brain felt raw. He had never taken such a pounding in his life.

Now and then a couple of mammoth Entities would come rumbling through the hall, tiptoeing on their tentacles in that weirdly dainty mincing way of theirs. With them came a little entourage of humans, bustling along on every side of them like tiny courtiers hovering around members of some exalted nobility. Nobody paid any attention to Andy. He was just a piece of furniture lying there against the wall.

Then some LACON people returned, different ones from before.

'Is this the pardoner, over here?' someone asked.

'That one, yeah.'

'She wants to see him now.'

'You think we should fix him up a little first?'

'She said now.'

A hand at Andy's shoulder, rocking him gently. Lifting him. Hands working busily, undoing the wrappings that bound his legs together, but leaving his arms still strapped up. They let him take a couple of wobbly steps. He glared at them as he worked to get the kinks out of his thigh muscles.

'All right, fellow. Come along now: it's interview time. And remember, don't make any trouble or you'll get hurt.'

He let them shuffle him down the hall and through a gigantic doorway and into an immense office that had a ceiling high enough to provide an Entity with all the room it could possibly want. He didn't say a word. There weren't any Entities in the office, just a woman in a black robe, sitting behind a wide desk down at the far end, about a mile away from him. In that colossal room, it looked like a toy desk. She looked like a toy woman. The LACONs pushed him into a chair near the door and left him alone with her. Trussed up like that, he didn't pose much of a risk.

'Are you John Doe?' she asked.

'Do you think I am?'

'That's the name you gave upon entry to the city.'

'I give lots of names as I travel around. John Smith, Richard Roe, Joe Blow. It doesn't matter much to the gate software what name I give.'

'Because you've gimmicked the gate?' She paused. 'I should tell you, this is a court of inquiry.'

'You already know everything I could tell you. Your borgmann hacker's been swimming around in my brain.'

'Please,' she said. 'This'll be easier if you cooperate. The accusations against you include illegal entry, illegal seizure of a vehicle, and illegal interfacing activity – specifically, selling pardons. Do you have a statement?'

'No.'

'You deny that you're a pardoner?'

'I don't deny, I don't affirm. What's the goddamned use?'

She rose and came out from behind the desk and very slowly walked toward to him, pausing when she was about fifteen feet away. Andy stared sullenly at his shoes.

'Look up at me,' she said.

'That would be a whole lot of effort.'

'Look up,' she said. There was a sharp edge on her voice. 'Whether you're a pardoner or not isn't the issue. We know you're a pardoner. I know you're a pardoner.' And she called him by a name he hadn't used in a very long time. 'You're Mickey Megabyte, aren't you?'

Now he looked at her.

Stared. Had trouble believing he was seeing what he saw. Felt a rush of memories come flooding up out of long ago.

The fluffy red hair was styled differently, now, clinging more tightly to her head. The five years had added a little flesh to her body here and there and some lines in her face. But she hadn't really changed all that much.

What was her name? Vanessa? Clarissa? Melissa?

Tessa. That was it. *Tessa.*

'Tessa?' he said hoarsely. 'Is that who you are?'

'Yes,' she said. 'That's who I am.'

Andy felt his jaw sagging stupidly. This promised to be even worse than what the hacker had done to him. But there was no way to run from it.

'You worked for LACON even then, yes. I remember.'

'That pardon you sold me wasn't any good, Mickey. You knew that, didn't you? I had someone waiting for me in San Diego, someone who was important to me, but when I tried to get through the wall they stopped me just like that, and dragged me away screaming. I could have killed you. I would have gone to San Diego and then Bill and I would have tried to make it to Hawaii in his boat. Instead he went without me. I never saw him again. And it cost me three years' worth of promotions. I was lucky that that was all.'

'I didn't know about the guy in San Diego,' Andy said.

'Why should you? It wasn't your business. You took my money, you were supposed to get me my pardon. That was the deal.'

Her eyes were gray with golden sparkles in them. It wasn't easy for him to look into them.

'You still feel like killing me?' Andy asked. 'Are you planning to have me executed?'

'No and no, Mickey. That isn't your name either, is it?'

'Not really.'

'I can't tell you how astounded I was, when they brought you in here. A pardoner, they said. John Doe, new in town and working the Pershing Square area. Pardoners, that's my department. They bring all of them to me. That's what they reassigned me to, after my hearing: dealing with pardoners. Isn't that cute, Mickey? Poetic justice. When they first assigned me to this job I used to wonder if they'd ever bring *you* in, but after a while I figured, no, not a chance, he's probably a million miles away, he'll never come back this way again. And then they pulled in this John Doe, and I went past you in the hall and saw your face.'

There was no hiding from the vindictive gleam in those gray eyes.

This called for desperate measures.

'Listen to me, Tessa,' Andy said, letting a little of that useful hoarseness come back into his voice. 'Do you think you could manage to believe that I've felt guilty for what I did to you ever since? You don't have to believe it. But it's God's own truth.'

'Right. My heart goes out to you. I'm sure it's been years of unending agony for you.'

'I mean it. Please. I've stiffed a lot of people, yes, and sometimes I've regretted it and sometimes I haven't, but you were one that I regretted, Tessa. You're the one I've regretted most. This is the absolute truth.'

She considered that. He couldn't tell whether she believed him even for a fraction of a second, but he could see that she was considering it.

'Why did you do it?' she asked, after a bit.

'I stiff people because I don't want to seem too perfect,' he told her. 'You have to stiff the customers once in a while or else you start looking too good, which can be dangerous. You deliver a pardon every single time, word gets around, people start talking, you start to become legendary. And then you're known everywhere and sooner or later the Entities get hold of you, and that's that. So I always make sure to write a lot of stiffs. One out of every five, approximately. I tell people I'll do my best, but there aren't any guarantees, and sometimes it doesn't work.'

'You deliberately cheated me.'

'Yes.'

'I thought that it must have been deliberate. You seemed so cool, so professional. So perfect, except for that dumb try at making a pass at me, and when you did that I just thought, oh, well, men, what can you expect? I was sure the pardon would be valid. I couldn't see how it would miss. And then I got to the wall and they grabbed me. And then I thought, that bastard purposely sold me out. He was too good just to have flubbed it up by accident.' Her tone was calm but the anger was all too evident in her eyes. 'Couldn't you have stiffed the next one, Mickey? Why did it have to be me?'

He looked at her for a long time, calculating things.

Then he took a deep breath and said, putting all he had into it, 'Because I had fallen for you in a big way.'

'Bullshit, Mickey. Bullshit. You didn't even know me. I was just some stranger who walked in off the street to hire you.'

'That's just it. It happened just like that.' He felt an inspired improvisation coming on, and went with it. 'There I was full of all kinds of crazy instant lunatic fantasies about you, all of a sudden ready to turn my nice orderly life upside down for you, write exit passes for both of us, take us on a trip around the world, the whole works. But all you could see was somebody you had hired to do a job. I didn't know about the guy from San Diego. All I knew was that I saw you and you were gorgeous and I wanted you. I fell in love with you right then and there.'

'Yeah. Fell in love. That's very touching.'

So far, not so good. But you can do this, he thought. Just let it come rolling out and see where it goes.

He said, 'You don't think that's love, Tessa? Well, call it something else, then, whatever you want. It was something that I had never let myself feel before. It isn't smart to get too involved, I always thought, it ties you down, the risks are too big. And then I saw you and I talked to you a little and right away I thought something could be happening between us and things started to change inside me, and I thought, Yeah, yeah, go with it this time, let it happen, this may make everything different. And you stood there not seeing it, not even beginning to notice, just jabbering on endlessly about how important the pardon was for you. Cold as ice, you were. That hurt me. It hurt me terribly, Tessa. So I stiffed you. And afterwards I thought, Jesus, I ruined that wonderful girl's life and it was just because I got myself into a snit, and that was a fucking petty thing to have done. I've been sorry ever since. You don't have to believe that. I didn't know about San Diego. That makes it even worse for me.'

She had not said anything all this time. Her implacable stony stillness began to get to him. To puncture it Andy said, 'Tell me one thing, at least. That guy who wrecked me in Pershing Square: who was he?'

'He wasn't anybody,' she said.

'What is that supposed to mean?'

'He isn't a who. He's a *what*. An *it*. An android, a mobile anti-pardoner unit, plugged right into the big Entity mainframe in Santa Monica. Something new that we have going around town looking for people like you.'

'Oh,' Andy said, stunned, as if she had kicked him. 'Oh.'

'The report is that you gave it one hell of a workout.'

'It gave me one too. Turned my brain half to mush.'

'There was no way you could have beaten it. You were trying to drink the sea through a straw. For a while it looked like you were really going to do it, too. You're one goddamned ace of a hacker, you know that? Yes, of course you do. Of course.'

'Why do you work for them?' Andy asked.

She shrugged. 'Everybody works for them, one way or another. Except people like you, I guess. Why shouldn't we? It's their world, isn't it?'

'It didn't used to be.'

'A lot of things didn't used to be. What does that matter now? And it's not such a bad job. At least I'm not out there on the wall. Or being sent off for TTD.'

'No,' he said. 'It's probably not so bad. If you don't mind working in a room with such a high ceiling. Is that what's going to happen to me? Sent off for TTD?'

'Don't be stupid. You're too valuable.'

'To whom?'

'The network always needs upgrading. You know it better than anyone alive, even from the outside. You'll work for us.'

'You think I'm going to turn borgmann?' Andy said, astonished.

'It beats TTD.'

She couldn't possibly be serious, he thought. This was some game she was playing with him. They would be fools to trust him in any kind of responsible position. And even bigger fools to give him any kind of access to their net.

'Well?' she said, when he remained silent. 'Is it a deal, Mickey?'

He was silent a little while longer. She was serious, he realized. Handing him the keys to the kingdom. Well, well, well. They must have their reasons, he supposed. *He'd* be the fool, if he said no.

He said, 'I'll do it, yes. On one condition.'

She whistled. 'You really have balls, don't you?'

'Let me have a rematch with that android of yours. I need to check something out. And afterward we can discuss what kind of work I'd be best suited for here. Okay?'

'You aren't in any position to lay down conditions, you know.'

'Sure I am. What I do with computers is a unique art. You can't make me do it against my will. You can't make me do anything against my will.'

She thought about that. 'What good is a rematch?'

'Nobody ever beat me before. I want a second try.'

'You know it'll be worse for you than before.'

'Let me find that out.'

'But what's the point?'

'Get me your android and I'll show you the point,' Andy said.

It surprised him tremendously that she would go along with it. But she did. Maybe it was curiosity, maybe it was something else, but she patched herself into the computer net and got off some orders, and pretty soon they brought in the android he had encountered in the park, or maybe another one that had the same bland face, the same general nondescript gray appearance. It looked him over pleasantly, without the slightest sign of interest.

Someone came in and took the security lock off Andy's wrists and fastened his ankles together with it, and left again. Tessa gave the android its instructions and it held out its wrist to him and they made contact. And Andy jumped right in.

He was raw and wobbly and pretty damned battered, still, but he knew what he needed to do and he knew he had to do it fast. The thing was to ignore the android completely – it was just a *terminal*, it was just a *unit* – and go for what lay behind it. He would offer no implant-to-implant access this time. No little one-on-one courtesies at all. Quickly he bypassed the android's own

identity program, which was clever but shallow. Moving intuitively and instantaneously, because he knew that he was finished
if he stopped to spell things out for himself, he leaped right over
it while the android was still setting up its combinations, piercing
its Borgmann interface and diving underneath it before the android could do anything to stop him. That took him instantly from
the unit level to the mainframe level, which was a machine of
unthinkably enormous capacity, and as he arrived he gave the
monster a hearty handshake.

There was a real thrill in that.

For the first time Andy understood, truly understood, what
old Borgmann had achieved by building the interface that linked
human biochips to Entity mainframes. All that power, all those
zillions of megabytes squatting there, and he was plugged right
into it. He felt like a mouse hitchhiking on the back of an elephant,
but that was all right. He might be only a mouse but that mouse
was getting a tremendous ride. Quickly he found the android's
data-chain and tied a bow-knot in it to keep it from coming after
him. Then, hanging on tight, he let himself go soaring along on
the hurricane winds of that colossal machine for the sheer fun
of the ride.

And as he soared he ripped out chunks of its memory by the
double handful and tossed them to the breeze.

Why not? What did he have to lose?

The mainframe didn't even notice for a good tenth of a second.
That was how big it was. There was Andy, tearing great blocks
of data out of its gut, joyously ripping and rending. And it didn't
even know it, because even the most magnificent computer ever
assembled is nevertheless stuck with the necessity of operating
at the speed of light, and when the best you can do is 186,000
miles a second it can take quite a while for the alarm to travel
the full distance down all your neural channels. That thing was
huge. Andy realized that it was wrong to think of himself as a
mouse riding on an elephant. Amoeba piggybacking on bronto-
saurus, was more like it.

But of course the guardian circuitry did cut in eventually.
Alarms went off, internal gates came clanging down, all sensitive
areas were sealed away, and Andy was shrugged off with the

greatest of ease. There was no sense staying around waiting to get trapped in there, so he pulled himself free.

The android, he saw, had crumpled to the carpet. It was nothing but an empty husk now.

Lights were flashing on the office wall.

Tessa looked at him, appalled. 'What did you *do*?'

'I beat your android,' he said. 'It wasn't all that hard, once I knew the scoop.'

'I heard an alarm. The emergency lights went on. You damaged the main computer!'

'Not really. Not in any significant way. That would have been very hard, staying in there long enough to do anything important. I just gave it a little tickle. It was surprised, seeing me get access in there, that's all.'

'No. I think you really damaged it.'

'Come on, Tessa. Now why would I want to do that?'

She didn't look amused. 'The question ought to be why you haven't done it already. Why you haven't gone in there somehow and crashed the hell out of their programs.'

'You actually think I could do something like that?'

She studied him. 'I think maybe you could, yes.'

'Well, maybe so. Or maybe not. I doubt it, myself. But I'm not a crusader, you know, Tessa. I like my life the way it is. I move around, I do as I please. It's a quiet life. I don't lead uprisings. I don't like to be out there on the firing line. When I need to gimmick things, I gimmick them just enough, and no more. And the Entities don't even know I exist. If I were to stick my finger in their eye, they'd cut my finger off. So I haven't done it.'

'But now you might,' she said.

He began to get uncomfortable. 'I don't follow you.'

'You don't like risk. You don't like being conspicuous. You keep yourself out of sight and all that, and don't start trouble just for the sake of making trouble. Fine. But if we take your freedom away, if we tie you down here in L.A. and put you to work, you'd strike back one way or another, wouldn't you? Sure you would. You'd go right in there, and you'd figure out a way to cover your tracks so the machine didn't know you were there. And you'd gimmick things but good. You'd do a ton of damage.'

She was silent for a time. 'Yes,' she said. 'You really would. You'd do such a job on their computer that they might have to scrap it and start all over again. I see it now, that you have the capability and that you could be put in a position where you'd be willing to use it. And so you'd screw everything up for all of us, wouldn't you?'

'What?'

'If we let you anywhere near the Entity net, you'd make such a mess of it that they'd feel obliged to do some sort of punitive strike to get back at us, and everybody in LACON would get fired, at the very least. Sent out for TTD, more likely.'

She was overestimating him, Andy saw. The machine was too well defended for anyone, even him, to damage it that way. If he got back inside he could make a little mess here and there, sure, a mouse-mess, but he wouldn't be able to hide from the guardian circuitry long enough to achieve anything important.

Let her think so, though. Being overestimated is a hell of a lot better than being underestimated.

'I'm not going to give you the chance,' she said. 'Because I'm not crazy. I understand you now, Mickey. It isn't safe to fool around with you. Whenever anybody does, you take your little revenge, and you don't give a damn what you bring down on anyone else's head. We'd all suffer, but you wouldn't care. No. Uh-uh, Mickey. My life isn't so terrible that I need you to turn it upside down for me. You've already done it to me once. I don't need it again.'

She was looking at him steadily. All the anger seemed to be gone from her and there was only contempt left.

But he was still a prisoner in this place with his ankles fastened together, and she still had total jurisdiction over him. He said nothing and waited to see what would happen next. She studied him for a moment without speaking.

Then she said something completely unexpected. 'Tell me, can you go in there again and gimmick things so that there's no record of your arrest today?'

Andy couldn't hide his surprise. 'Are you really serious about that?'

'I wouldn't have said it if I wasn't. Can you?'

'Yeah. Yeah, I suppose I could.'

'Do it, then. I'll give you exactly sixty seconds to do whatever it is you have to do, and God help you if you do anything else while you're in there, anything harmful. This is your dossier, here. Get rid of it.' She handed him a printout. 'And once you've wiped out your record, get yourself going, fast. Out of here, away from Los Angeles. And don't come back.'

'You're actually going to let me go?'

'I actually and sincerely am.' She made an impatient gesture, a shoo-fly gesture.

He wasn't able to believe it. Was there some catch? He couldn't see one. She genuinely appeared to be releasing him, just to get him out of her sight, evidently, before he could cause any trouble here that ultimately would come down on her own head.

He was so astounded that he felt he had to make some corresponding gesture, some kind of repayment, and suddenly a torrent of inane words came gushing from him. 'Look, Tessa, I just want to say – all that stuff about how guilty I've felt, how much I've regretted the thing I did to you back then – it was true. Every word of it.' It sounded foolish even to him.

'I'm sure that it all was,' she said drily. The gray eyes rested mercilessly on him for a long moment, shriveling him down to an ash. – 'Okay, Mickey. Spare me any further crap. Do your gimmicking and edit yourself out of the arrest records and then I want you to start moving. Out of the building. Out of the city. Okay? Do it now, and do it real quick.'

Andy hunted around for something else to say. Anything. Couldn't find a thing.

Quit while you're ahead, he thought.

She gave him her wrist and he did the interface with her.

As his implant access touched hers she shuddered a little. It wasn't much of a shudder, but he noticed it. She hadn't forgiven him for anything. She just wanted him gone.

He went in and found the John Doe arrest entry right away and got rid of it, and then, since he still had about twenty seconds left, he picked her I.D. number off his dossier and searched out her civil service file and promoted her up two grades and doubled her pay. His own outburst of sentimentality flabbergasted him.

But it was a nice gesture, Andy thought. And he never could tell when their paths might cross again someday.

He cleaned up his traces and exited the program.

'All right,' he said. 'It's done.'

'Fine,' she said, and rang for her cop squad. 'This is the wrong man,' she told them. 'Clean him up and send him on his way.'

One of the LACONs muttered an apology, more or less, for the case of mistaken identity, and they showed him out of the building and turned him loose on Figueroa Street. It was early afternoon. There were clouds overhead, and the air was cool with the kind of easy coolness that was typical of a Los Angeles winter day.

Andy went to a street access and summoned the Toshiba from wherever it had parked itself.

It came driving up, five or ten minutes later, and he told it to take him north, up the freeway, out of the city. He wasn't sure where he would go. San Francisco, maybe. It rained a lot in San Francisco in the winter, Andy knew, and from all he had heard it was colder than he liked a place to be. But still, it was a pretty town, and a port city besides, so he could probably arrange to get himself shipped out there to Hawaii or Australia or someplace like that, where it was warm, where he could leave all the tattered fragments of his old life behind him forever.

He reached the wall at the Sylmar gate, some fifty miles or so up the road. The gate asked him his name. 'Richard Roe,' he said. 'Beta Pi Upsilon l04324x. Destination San Francisco.'

Implant reading, now. He provided access. No problem. All cool.

The gate opened and the Toshiba went through, easy as Beta Pi.

The car went zooming northward. It would be about a five-hour drive, maybe six, Andy guessed, to Frisco. The freeway here seemed to be in unusually good shape, all things considered.

But then, when he was less than half an hour beyond the Sylmar gate, an idea came to him, an idea so strange and unexpected, so surprising and bewildering, that Andy couldn't quite make himself believe that he had actually thought of it. It was a crazy idea, absolutely crazy. He brushed it aside for the craziness that it was; but it had its hooks in him and would not release him. He struggled with it this way and that for about five minutes. And then he surrendered to it.

'Change of plan,' he told the Toshiba. 'Let's go to Santa Barbara.'

'Someone at the gate,' Frank said, as the honking sounded. 'I'll get it.'

It was a mild January day, getting toward evening, everything very green, the trees glistening from a recent drizzle. The weather had been very rainy lately; and more rain would be here before dawn, Frank figured, judging by the fishbelly clouds in the sky to the north. He grabbed the shotgun and went loping up the hill. He was a slender athletic young man, now, just on the cusp between adolescence and manhood, and he ran easily, gracefully, untiringly, in long loose strides.

The car sitting out there was an unfamiliar model, fairly new as cars went these days, very fancy. Looking through the bars of the gate, Frank was unable to make out the driver's face. With a wave of the shotgun he signalled to the man to get out of the car and show himself. The driver stayed where he was.

Suit yourself, Frank thought, and started to turn away.

'Hey, fellow – wait!' The car window was open, suddenly, and the man's head was sticking out. A strong face, just a little jowly, dark eyes, heavy frowning eyebrows, tough, scowling expression. The face looked familiar, somehow. But for a moment Frank wasn't quite able to place it. Then he gasped in astonishment as the click of recognition occurred.

'*Andy?*'

A nod and a grin from the man in the car. 'Me, yes. Who are you?'

'Frank.'

'Frank.' A moment's pause for contemplation. 'Anson's Frank? But you were just a little kid!'

'I'm nineteen,' Frank said, not troubling to keep the annoyance out of his voice. 'You've been gone better than five years, you know. Little kids grow up, sooner or later.' He pressed the button that opened the gate, and the bars slid back. But the car stayed where it was. That was puzzling. Frank said, frowning, 'Look, Andy, are you coming in or aren't you?'

'I don't know. That is, I'm not really sure.'

'Not *sure*? What do you mean, not sure?'

'I mean that I'm not sure, is what I mean.' Andy scrunched his eyes closed for a moment and shook his head, like a dog shaking off raindrops. ' – Shut up and let me think, will you, kid?'

Andy stayed put inside the car. What the hell was he waiting for? A little drizzle began to come down again. Frank began to fidget. Then he heard Andy say something in a low voice, obviously not intended for him. Speaking to the car, apparently. A model this recent would have a voice-actuated drive. 'Come on, will you?' Frank said, getting really irritated now, and beckoned once more with the shotgun. But then, grasping at last the fact that Andy had changed his mind about being here and was about to take off, he strode quickly out through the open gate and pushed the gun through the car window, right up against the side of Andy's jaw, just as the car began slowly to move in reverse along the muddy road. He kept pace easily with the vehicle, jogging alongside, holding the shotgun trained on Andy's forehead.

Andy gave the muzzle of the gun a pop-eyed disbelieving sidewise stare.

'You aren't leaving here,' Frank told him. 'Just forget about that idea. You've got about two seconds to put on the brakes.'

He heard Andy tell the car to stop. It came abruptly to a halt. 'What the fuck,' Andy said, glaring out at him.

Frank did not pull the shotgun away from the window. 'Okay, now get out of the car.'

'Listen, Frank, I've decided that I don't feel like visiting the ranch after all.'

'Tough. You should have decided that before you drove up the hill. Out.'

'It was a dumb idea, really. I never should have come back. Nobody here wants to see me again and there's nobody here I want to see. So would you very kindly get that goddamn cannon out of my face, please, if you don't mind, and let me move along?'

'Out,' Frank said once more. 'Now. Or I'll blow the hell out of your car's computer and you won't go anywhere at all.'

Andy gave him a surly look. 'Come *on.*'

'You come on.' Motioning with the gun.

'All right, kid. All *right*! I'm getting out. Cool down a little, okay? We can both ride down to the house together. It'll be a lot quicker. And I wish to hell you'd stop pointing that gun at me.'

'We'll walk,' Frank said. 'It's not that far, really. Let's go. Now. You're capable of walking, aren't you? Move it, Andy.'

Grumbling, Andy pushed the car door open and stepped out.

This was very hard to believe, Frank thought, that Andy was actually here. For the past couple of weeks Steve and Paul and all the other computer people at the ranch had been doing all sorts of on-line gymnastics, trying to trace this man's trail in Los Angeles, and here he was, turning up here all on his own. Operating under some confusion, apparently, about whether he should have come; but he was here. That was what mattered.

'The gun,' Andy said. Frank was still holding it at the ready. 'It really isn't necessary, you know. I'd like you to realize that it makes me very uncomfortable.'

'I suppose it does. But there's just the two of us up here and I don't know how dangerous you are, Andy.'

'Dangerous? Dangerous?'

'Walk on ahead, please. I'll be right behind you.'

'This is very shitty, Frank. I'm your own cousin.'

'Second cousin, I think. Come on. Keep it moving.'

'You taking me to your father?'

'No,' Frank said. 'Yours.'

'Where is he?' Steve asked.

'In the library,' said two of Anson's boys, speaking at the same time, as Anson's boys tended to do. Martin said, 'My brother Frank's keeping watch over him there.' 'He's got the shotgun on him,' added James, the other one. They both looked very pleased.

Steve hurried down the hall. In the library, a dark low-roofed room with floor-to-ceiling shelves crammed with hundreds and hundreds of rare and learned books on various Oriental cultures

that had belonged to the Colonel and had not been looked at by
anyone in fifteen or twenty years, a most unscholarly tableau
was on display. Frank was leaning casually against a bookcase
to the left of the door, with the shotgun that everyone carried
when going up to the gate resting lightly across his left forearm.
It was pointing in the general direction of a tense, scowling,
heavy-set man in loose-fitting denim trousers and a plaid flannel
shirt on the other side of the room. An angry-looking stranger,
whom Steve recognized, after a moment, as his son Andy.

'We probably don't need to hold him at gunpoint, Frank. Do
we, Andy?'

'*He* seems to think so,' Andy said balefully.

'Well, I don't. Is that all right with you, Frank?'

'Whatever you say, sir. Do you want me to leave the
room?'

'Yes. I think I do. Don't go very far, though.'

As Frank went out, Steve looked toward Andy and said, 'Am
I safe with you?'

'Don't talk crap, dad.'

'I can't be sure. You're a strange one, you are. Always were,
always will be.' Andy had put on more than a little weight, Steve
noticed. And his hair was beginning to recede. The Gannett genes
rising up in him. How old was he, anyway? Steve had to count
it up. Twenty-four, he decided. Yes. Twenty-four. He looked
considerably older than that, but then Steve reminded himself
that Andy had always had looked older than his years, even
when he was only a little boy. 'A strange one, yes, indeed, that's
you. Anson said he thought you were a mutant.'

'He did? Look, dad. Five fingers on each hand. Only one head.
Only two eyes, on different sides of my nose, the way they're
supposed to be.'

Steve was only faintly amused. 'Nevertheless,' he said, 'a
mutant. A mutant personality, is what Anson meant. Someone
who's not at all like any of us. – Here, look at it this way: I'm a
nerdy sort of guy, Andy. Fat and slow and cautious. Always
have been, always will be. I don't mind being like that. But I'm
also a decent and responsible and hard-working citizen. So tell
me this: How did I raise a criminal like you?'

'A criminal? Is that what I am?'

'Too harsh a word, is it? I don't think so. Not from the things I've heard. Why did you come back here, Andy?'

'I'm not sure. A touch of homesickness, maybe? I can't say. I was on my way to Frisco and suddenly something came over me and I thought, Well, what the hell, I'm driving up that way anyway, I think I'll go to the dear old ranch, I'll see the folks again, good old mom and dad, good old tight-assed Anson, good old red-hot La-La.'

'La-La, yes. She prefers to be called Lorraine now. That's her real name, you may remember. She'll be glad to see you. She can introduce you to your son.'

'My son.' Not a flicker of animation appeared on his chilly face.

Steve smiled. 'Your son, yes. He's five years old. Born not too long after you skipped out of here.'

'And what's his name, dad? Anson?'

'Well, actually, you'll be surprised to learn that it is. Anson Carmichael Gannett, Junior. Wasn't that sweet of Lorraine, naming him after you, all things considered?'

It was Andy's turn not to seem amused. He gave Steve a long, steady, sullen look. In an absolutely flat, cold voice he said, 'Well, well, well. Anson C. Gannett, Junior. That's very nice. I'm terribly, terribly flattered.'

Steve chose to take no notice of Andy's mocking tone. Smiling still, he said, 'I'm glad to hear it. He's a really lovely child. We call him "Anse". – And just how long are you planning to stay with us, son, now that you're here?'

'As least as long as Frank is sitting out there in the hall with his shotgun, I guess.'

'I'm sorry about the gun. Frank overreacted a little, I think. But he didn't know what to expect from you. We know that you've been living on the edge of law ever since you left here. Working as a pardoner, right?'

Stiffly Andy said, 'The laws that pardoners break are Entity laws. The things that pardoners do save people from Entity oppression. I could make out a case for looking upon pardoner activity as being one aspect of the Resistance. A kind of free-lance

Resistance effort. Which would make me just as decent and law
abiding a citizen as you claim to be.'

'I understand what you're saying, Andy. Even so, the fact
remains that pardoners live a kind of shady underground exist
ence and not all of them are completely honest. I like to think
that you were more honest than most, though.'

'As a matter of fact, I was.' There was a crackle in Andy's voice
and a glint in his eye that led Steve to think that he might actually
be telling the truth, for a change. 'I wrote a few stiffs, yes – you
know what those are? – but only because the pardoner guild told
me I had to. Guild rules. Most of the time I played it straight
and did the job right. A matter of professional pride as a hacker
I got to know the Entity net inside and out, too.'

'That's good to know. We rather hoped you had. That's why
we've been looking all over for you, all these years.'

'Have you, now? What for?'

'Because we're still running the Resistance up here, and you
have unique skills that could be of service to us in a major enter
prise that we've been working on for a long time.'

'And what kind of enterprise might that be? Let's get down to
it, all right. Just what do you want from me, dad?'

'To begin with, your cooperation on a little hacking project of
critical importance, one that happens to be too tough even for
me, but which I think you can handle.'

'And if I don't cooperate?'

'You will,' Steve said.

Andy was astonished. The Borgmann archive! Well, well, well.

He remembered having gone looking for it once or twice or
thrice – when he was fourteen, fifteen, somewhere back there
Everyone did. It was like looking for El Dorado, King Solomon's
mines, the pot of gold at the end of the rainbow. The legendary
Borgmann data cache, the key to all the Entity mysteries.

But the quest had brought no payoff for him, and he had lost
interest quickly enough, once it started petering out into useless
trails. You went sniffing up this promising pathway and that
one, and for a time you were sure that you actually had found
the way to reach the goodies that the sly and malevolent Borg

mann had stashed away for his own private amusement in some unspecified zone of memory in somebody's computer somewhere on Earth. And then just as you were pounding down the road to success and had worked up a really good sweat you discovered that you had been turned around without noticing it and were disappearing up your own anal orifice, so to speak, and the ghostly cackle of Borgmann's laughter was resounding in your ears. Andy had decided, after a few such experiences, that there were better things in life for him to be doing.

He told all that to Steve and Anson, and to Frank, who had accompanied them on the way over to the communications center. Despite his tender years, Frank seemed to have become very important here during Andy's absence.

'We want you to give it another try,' said Anson.

'What makes you think I'm going to get anywhere now?'

'Because,' said Steve, 'I've got a data path here that I don't think anybody's ever traveled up before, not very far, anyway, and I'm convinced it leads right to Borgmann. I've known about it for years. I fool with it, every once in a while. But there's a lock across it that I can't get through. Perhaps you can.'

'You never told me anything about it. Why didn't you bring me in on it then?'

'Because you weren't here. You chose to head out for Los Angeles the very night I stumbled on it, my friend. So how was I going to tell you?'

'Right,' Andy said. 'Right. And if I do get in there now, what is it that I'm supposed to find for you, pray tell?'

'The location of Entity Prime,' said Anson.

Andy turned and stared at him. 'You still hung up on that bullshit, are you? Wasn't getting Tony killed enough for you?'

He saw Anson flinch, as though Andy had gone at him with his fist. And for a moment Andy almost regretted having said what he had said. It was a dirty shot, he knew. Anson was too vulnerable in that area. Even more so than he had been before, possibly. Something had changed in Anson during the years Andy had been gone, he realized, and not for the better. As though some key part had broken inside him. Or as though he had aged thirty years in five. All those deaths hitting Anson one after another: his wife, his father, then his brother. The pain of all that must still be with him.

Still, Andy had never liked Anson much. A stuffed shirt; a fanatic; a pain in the ass. A *Carmichael*. If he was still hurting for people who had died five or ten years ago, too bad. To hell with him and his tender feelings, Andy thought.

Anson said, obviously keeping himself under tight check, 'We still believe that there is such a being as Entity Prime, Andy, and that if we can find him and kill him we'll do tremendous damage to the whole Entity control structure.' He clamped his lips tightly together for a moment, a thin straight line. 'We sent Tony, but Tony wasn't good enough, somehow. Somehow they caught wise to what he was going to do, but they let him plant the bomb anyway, because we had the wrong place. And then they grabbed him. The next time, we need to have the right place. Which we hope you can find for us.'

'And who's going to be the next Tony, if I do?'

'Let me worry about that. Your job is to go into the Borgmann archive and tell us where Prime is and how we can get access to him.'

'What makes you so sure I'll find any such material?'

Anson shot an exasperated look at Steve. But otherwise he continued to hold himself under steely control.

'I'm not in any way sure of that. But it's a reasonable assumption that Borgmann, considering all that he achieved and the degree of authority that he was able to attain under the Entities in the earliest days of the Conquest, had found some way of making direct contact with the Entity leadership. Which we define as the creature we call Entity Prime. It's reasonable to believe, therefore, that Borgmann's protocols for approaching Prime are archived somewhere in his files. I don't know that they are. Nobody does. But if we don't go in there and *look*, God damn it –'

Anson's forehead and cheeks, seamed and corrugated by lines of stress that Andy did not remember, now had begun to turn very red. His left arm was shaking, apparently uncontrollably. Frank, looking worried, moved closer to Anson's side. Steve gave

Andy the most ferocious look of rage that Andy had ever seen to cross his father's bland, plump face.

'All right,' Andy said. 'All *right*, Anson. Show me the stuff and I'll see what I can do.'

It was a little before midnight. They sat side by side, Steve and Andy, father and son, in the communications center with Anson and Frank standing behind them. Steve had one screen, Andy had another. As Andy watched, abstract patterns began to stream across his father's screen, the fluid lines of data trails that had been converted into visual equivalents.

'Give me your wrist,' Steve said.

Andy looked at him uneasily. It was a long, long time since the two of them had done any implant stuff with each other. Andy had never had any trouble with making biocomputer connections with anyone before, but suddenly he felt himself hesitating at opening his biochip to Steve, as though even a mere interflow of data was too terrifying an intimacy.

'Your wrist,' Steve said again.

Andy stretched forth his arm. They made contact.

'This is what I think might be the Borgmann access line,' Steve said. 'This, this here.' Data began to cross over from father to son. Steve pointed to nodes in the picture on Andy's screen, whorls of green and purple against a salmon-toned background. Andy cut his bioprocessor into the system and began to manipulate the data that had come to him by way of his father's implant. What had seemed abstract, even formless, a moment ago now began to have meaning. He followed along, nodding, humming, murmuring to himself.

'And here,' Steve said, 'is where I ran into the blockage.'

'Right. I see. Okay, dad. Everybody all quiet now, please.'

He leaned into the screen. He saw nothing else but that glowing rectangular surface. He was alone in the room, alone in the world, alone in the universe. Anson, Frank, Steve, were gone from his perceptions.

Some mainframe in Europe was welcoming him on line, now. Andy clicked himself into it.

Where was he? France? Germany? Those were only names.

All foreign places were mere names to him. He had never been anywhere in the world beyond the land of his birth – it was the only country he knew.

Prague, I want. Which is in Czech-land. Czechia. Whatever the hell they call the place. Click, click, click. Give me Prague, Prague, Prague. *Prague.* Borgmann's home town. Is that it? Yes. That's it. The city of Prague, in Czecho-whatever.

The patterns on the screen looked very familiar. He had been down this trail once before, he realized. Long ago, when he was a boy: this narrowing tunnel, this set of branching forks. Yes. Yes. He had entered it and hadn't even known where he was, how close he stood to the pot of gold.

But of course he had lost his way, then. Would he lose it now?

He was starting to get verbals. Words in some foreign language floated up to him. But which language? He had no idea. There must have been some reason why his father had thought this path was the way into Borgmann's files, though. Well, Borgmann had been a Czech, hadn't he? So maybe this language was Czechian, or whatever it was that they spoke in the Czech country. Andy called up a translator file and asked it to do Czech, and got an error message back. He told the translator to run a linguistic scan for him. Mystery language, here. What is it?

Deutsch.

Deutsch? What the fuck was Deutsch? The language of Czechia? That didn't sound right. Whatever Deutsch was, though, Andy needed it translated. He gave the translator a nudge and told it to do Deutsch. *Jawohl.* It did Deutsch for him.

Dirty Deutsch, at that. A spew of filthy words such as startled even Andy went rocketing across the screen. Whoever had written that file was foaming at the mouth at him across the decades, really running berserk, welcoming him to this sealed archive with an unparalleled stream of derisive muck.

Yes. Yes. Yes. This had to be the Borgmann trail, all right!

He went a little deeper, down that tunnel of forking paths.

'And now,' Andy said, talking entirely to himself, because there was no one left in the universe except him, 'I should hit the lock that Steve ran into, right – around – *here*.'

Yes.

It was a real lulu, that lock. On the surface it was very innocent. It looked like a friendly invitation to go forward. Which Andy proceeded to do, knowing full well what would happen, and carefully marking his position before it did. Onward, onward, onward. Then one step too many, and he found himself crashed. There was nothing he could have done to save himself. The trapdoor had opened in a billionth of a nanosecond and that was that, *whoosh, gone!* Goodbye, chump.

Right. If this lock had defeated a hacker like Steve, again and again over the past five years, it had to be something special. And it was.

Andy got himself back to his marker and started again. Down the tunnel, yes, take this fork, take that one. Yes. There was the lock coming into view a second time, so beguilingly telling him that he was going the right away, urging him to continue moving ahead. Instead of moving ahead, though, Andy simply *looked* ahead, sending a virtual scout forward and watching through the scout's eyes until he could see the pincers of the lock coyly waiting for him at the edges of the data trail a short distance onward. He let them grab the scout and backed up once again to his point of entry.

Slowly, slowly. This thing could be beaten.

His many trips through the Entity mainframes in the course of his pardoning work had taught him how to deal with stuff of this kind. You don't like one route, just carve yourself another. There's plenty of megabytage in here to work with. Call in assistance if you need it; link yourself up with other areas of the operation. Tunnel *around* the block. Borgmann had been one clever cookie, that was clear, but a whole lot of interfacing had gone on since Borgmann's day, and Andy had the benefit of everything that had been learned about the Entity computers in the past quarter of a century.

He came at the Borgmann data sideways. He routed himself through computers in Istanbul, in Johannesburg, in Jakarta; and also he went through Moscow, through Bombay, through London, simultaneously tiptoeing up on the Czecho data cache from any number of different directions. He built a double trail for himself, a triple trail, letting himself seem to be in all sorts of places at once, so that nobody could possibly could track him to any one point in his journey and come along in back of him and short him out. And finally he shot into the Prague mainframe through the back door and went whizzing toward the Borgmann cache hind-end first.

He could see the lock, shining bright as daylight, up there in the tunnel waiting for new patsies to show up. But he was *behind* it.

'Hello, there,' he said, as the secret files of Karl-Heinrich Borgmann came swimming up into his grasp like so many friendly little fish asking to be tickled.

It was amazing, even to Andy, how disgusting some of Borgmann's stuff was.

Layer after layer of porno, stacked a mile high. Videos of naked European-looking women with hairy armpits and spread crotches, staring into the camera lens in sullen resignation as they went through curious and, to Andy, highly non-enthralling movements of a blatantly sexual nature.

Andy didn't have any particular problem with the sight of naked women. But the sullen looks, the barely concealed anger of these women, the absolutely unavoidable sense that the camera was *raping* them – all that was very distasteful. Andy could imagine, easily enough, what must have gone on. Borgmann had been the boss puppet-master, hadn't he, the voice through which the Entities made known their commands to the conquered planet? The Emperor of Earth, pretty much, the highest authority in the world below Entity level. He had been that for a while, anyway, until that woman had walked into his private office – she had been someone he must have trusted, it would seem – and put the knife into his guts. With the powers he held he could have made anybody do anything he wanted, or else they would face the worst of punishments. And what Borgmann had wanted, evidently, was nothing more profound than for women to take off their clothes in front of him and follow his loathsome instructions while he made videos of them and filed them in his permanent archive.

There was other stuff here, too, that indicated that Borgmann had done even creepier things than making unwilling women gyrate on command while he sat there drooling and took movies of them. Borgmann had been a secret voyeur, too, a peeping Tom, spying on the women of Prague from afar.

Moving deeper, Andy found whole cabinets of video documents that could only have been made by snaking spy-eyes into people's houses. These women were alone, unsuspecting, going about their business, changing their clothes, brushing their teeth, taking baths, sitting on the john. Or making love, even, with boyfriends or husbands. And all the while there was sweet lovely Karl-Heinrich gobbling it all up by remote wire, taping it and stashing it away where it would eventually be found, twenty or thirty years later, by none other than Anson Carmichael ('Andy') Gannett, Senior.

They went on and on and on, these porno films. Borgmann must have had half the city of Prague wired up with his spy-eyes. No doubt he had put the cost of it all into the municipal budget as necessary security monitoring. But the only thing he had monitored, it seemed, was female flesh. You didn't have to be any kind of puritan to find the Borgmann files repellent. Moving swiftly from cabinet to cabinet, Andy felt his eyes glazing over, his head beginning to throb. How many breasts could you stare at before they came to lose all erotic value? How many crotches? How many waggling fannies?

Sick, he thought. Sick, sick, sick, sick, sick.

But there was no way to get to the Entity material he was looking for, it appeared, except by wading through these mountains of muck. Perhaps Borgmann himself had had an automatic jump-command that took him past them, but Andy didn't see any quick and convenient way of looking for it and was unwilling to try anything that might deflect him from the main path. So he went on slogging inward the old-fashioned way, file by file by file, through mountains of flesh, tons of tits and ass, hoping that there would indeed be something in this much-sought-after archive of Borgmann's beside this unthinkable record of the invasion of the privacy of hundreds and hundreds of girls and women of a bygone era.

He got past the porno levels, an endless time later.

He thought for a while that he never would. But then, abruptly, he found himself among files that had an entirely new inventorying system, an archive buried *within* the archive, and knew, after a few minutes of poking around, that he had hit the jackpot.

It was awesome, how thoroughly Borgmann had infiltrated himself into the Entities' mysterious data systems, starting absolutely from scratch. How much he had perceived, and achieved, and squirreled away under lock and key right there in one of the main machines of the Entities' own computational network, there to rest undisturbed until Andy Gannett came chopping his way in to find it. He had been a creep, old Borgmann had been, but he also must have been a supreme master of data-handling to have penetrated this deeply into an alien code system and learned how to deal with it. In the midst of his distaste for the man Andy could not help feeling a certain degree of reverence for the great master he had been.

There was plenty here that would be useful to the Resistance. The record of all of Borgmann's one-on-one dealings with the occupying administration of Central Europe. His interfacing lines, the ones that had enabled him to communicate with the high Entity offices. His lists of useful channels to use when relaying data to them. His classified set of Entity decrees and promulgations. Best of all, here was his digital dictionary, Borgmann language lined up against Entity language, the whole set of code equivalencies – the key to full translation, perhaps, of the secret Entity communications system.

Andy didn't stop to make any sort of detailed investigation of this material. His job now was just to collect it and make it accessible for later study. Working quickly, he lassoed great gobs of it, anything that seemed even halfway relevant, copied it file by file and kicked it on through his parallel data chains, Moscow to Bombay to Istanbul, Jakarta to Johannesburg to London, letting the chains snarl and overlap and become corrupted beyond anybody's comprehension, human or Entity, while at the same time coding them to reconstruct themselves in some mysterious midpoint zone where he could find them and bring them up again right here at the ranch. Which he did. One by one, everything useful that he could find, neatly carried around Borgmann's nasty little lock into an open file so that it would not be necessary for anyone ever again to go through all that Andy had gone through this night.

He looked up at last from his screen.

His father, red-eyed and bleary-faced, still sat beside him, watching him in undisguised astonishment. Frank leaned yawning against the wall. Anson had fallen asleep on the couch near the door. Andy heard the patter of rainfall outside. There was a gray light in the sky.

'What time is it?' he asked.

'Half past six in the morning. You haven't stopped going for a moment, Andy.'

'No. I guess I haven't, have I?' He rose, stretched, yawned, pressed his knuckles against his eyeballs. He felt creaky, tired, hungry, empty. 'I think I'd like to pee, now, okay? And then maybe somebody could bring me a cup of coffee.'

'Right.' Steve gestured to Frank, who got up immediately and left. As Andy, still yawning, started to amble toward the washroom, Steve said, making no attempt at concealing his eagerness to know, 'Well, boy, any luck? What did you find in there?'

'Everything,' Andy said.

So it had worked out after all, their long shot. The unfindable Andy had returned to the ranch and entered the unenterable archive for them, and now they had confirmation of the unconfirmable Prime hypothesis. Looking in wonder and jubilation through the synopsis that Steve had prepared for him from Andy's early analysis of his preliminary tour of the Borgmann file, Anson felt the burdens dropping away from him, that leaden weight of grief and regret and self-denunciation. All of that had turned him into an old man for the past five years, but now he was miraculously rejuvenated, full of energy and dreams, ready once more to rush forth and rescue the world from its conquerors. Or so it seemed to him just now. He hoped the feeling would last.

He paged through the glossy, neatly printed sheets for three or four minutes, while the others watched without speaking.

Then he looked up and said, 'How soon can we get moving on this, do you think? Do we have enough information to move against Prime yet?'

With him in the chart room were Steve Gannett, and Steve's wife Lisa, and Paul's oldest son Mark and Mark's sister Julie, and Charlie Carmichael with his wife Cassandra. The inner circle, pretty much, of the family now, everyone but Cindy, the ancient and ageless, the matriarch of the clan, who was somewhere else just then. But it was Steve to whom Anson looked for most of his answers now.

And the answer that Steve gave him was not the one he wanted to hear.

'Actually,' Steve said, 'we've still got quite a bit of work ahead of us first, Anson.'

'Oh?'

'The honcho Entity that Borgmann was dealing with – and we can assume, I think, that that really was the one we call Prime – was based in Prague, in a big castle that they have there up on a hill. As you already know, I think, we believe that the Prague headquarters was de-emphasized quite some time ago, and that Prime was moved to Los Angeles. But we need to confirm that, which I intend to have Andy do for us as soon as he's worked out the access path. Once we've pinned down the location of Prime, we can start thinking of ways to take him out.'

'What if Andy should decide to vanish again?' Anson asked. 'Will you be able to come up with the necessary data yourself, Steve?'

'He won't vanish.'

'And if you're wrong?'

'I think he genuinely wants to be part of this, Anson. He knows how essential he is to the project. He won't let us down.'

'All the same, I'd like to keep your son under twenty-four-hour-a-day guard. To insure that he sticks around until he's finished massaging the Borgmann data. Is that very offensive to you, Steve?'

'It's certainly going to be offensive to Andy.'

'Andy has let us down before. I don't want to take any further risks of losing him. I suppose I might as well tell you: I've asked

Frank and a couple of my other boys to take turns guarding him while he's here at the ranch.'

'Well,' Steve said, letting some displeasure show. 'Whatever you want, Anson. Especially since you seem already to have done it. My opinion about the need for treating him like a prisoner is on record.'

'Lisa?' Anson said. 'He's your son. How do you feel about this?'

'I think you should watch him like a hawk until you get what you need from him.'

'There you are,' said Anson triumphantly. 'Watch him like a hawk! Which Frank will do. Which he is doing right at this very moment, as a matter of fact. Martin and James are going to take turns with him, eight hours per day each. That much is settled, all right? – Steve, how soon are you likely to have anything hard concerning Prime's location?'

'I'll have it when I have it, okay? We're making it our highest priority.'

'Easy. Easy. I just wanted an estimate.'

'Well,' Steve said, seeming almost to be pouting, 'I can't give you one. And I don't think putting Andy under round-the-clock guard is going to improve his motivation for helping us, either. But let that pass. Maybe he'll be willing to cooperate anyway. I certainly want to think so. Once we *do* get you your information, incidentally, what method do you have in mind for taking Prime out?'

'We'll do it the way we did before. Only better, this time, I hope. – Hello, Cindy,' Anson said, as she came into the room. She moved serenely across it with the stately grace of the frail old woman that she was, eyes bright as ever, head held alertly forward, and took a seat next to Mark. 'We're talking about the assault on Prime,' Anson told her. 'I've just explained to Steve that I intend to carry it out pretty much the same way as the first time, sending someone in to plant a bomb right against the side of Prime's house. Or even inside it, if we can. This time Andy should be able to provide us with the precise location of Prime, and also the right computer passwords to get our man through Entity security.'

Mark said, 'Do you have anyone in mind for the job yet, Anson?'

'Yes. Yes, I do. My son Frank.'

That was something Anson hadn't shared with anyone, not even Frank, until this moment. The uproar was instant and vehement. They all were talking at once right away, yelling, gesticulating. In the midst of the sudden chaos Anson saw Cindy, sitting bolt upright, as rigid and gaunt and grim-faced as the mummy of some ancient Pharaoh, staring at him with a look of such wholehearted truculent violence in her intense and glittering eyes that it struck him with an almost tangible force.

'*No*,' she said, a deep icy contralto that sliced through the din like a scimitar. 'Not Frank. Don't even think of sending Frank, Anson.'

The room fell silent, and stayed that way until Anson could find his voice.

'You see some problem with that, Cindy?' he asked, finally.

'Five years ago you sent your only brother down there to die. Now you want to send your son? Don't tell me that you have three more in reserve, either. No, Anson, no, we aren't going to let you risk Frank's life on this thing.'

Anson pressed his lips into a thin, tight line.

'Frank won't be at risk. We know what mistakes we made the last time. We aren't going to repeat them.'

'Can you be sure of that?'

'We're going to take every precaution. Don't you think I'll do everything in my power to see to it that Frank gets safely through the mission? But this is a war, Cindy. Risk is inevitable. So is sacrifice.'

But she was inexorable. 'Tony was your sacrifice. You aren't required to make a second one. What kind of crazy demonstration of macho toughness is this, anyway? Do you think we don't know what you've already given, and how much it cost you? Frank's the hope of the future, Anson. He's the next generation of leadership here. You know that: everyone does. He mustn't be wasted. Even if there's only one chance in ten that he wouldn't come back, that's too much of a chance. – Besides, there's someone else at the ranch who's far better fitted for the job than Frank is.'

'Who's that?' Anson demanded harshly. 'You? Me? Or do you mean Andy, maybe?'

'Talk to Khalid,' Cindy said. 'He's got someone who can do this job just fine.'

Anson was mystified. 'Who? Tell me. Who?'

'Talk to Khalid,' she said.

'I would want certain safeguards for him,' Khalid said. 'He is my eldest son. His life is sacred to me.'

He stood before them straight as a soldier on patrol, as cool and self-possessed as though he and not Anson were in charge of this meeting. Only in the moment of entering the chart room had Khalid betrayed a touch of uneasiness, seeing so many family members gathered there, like a court in session with Anson as the high judge; but that had very quickly passed and his normal aura of preternatural calm had reasserted itself.

Khalid was an unfamiliar figure here. He was never present at any of the chart room meetings; he had amply let it be known years ago that the Resistance was no concern of his. Indeed he very rarely had been in the main house at all in recent years. Khalid spent most of his time in and about his little cabin on the far side of the vegetable patch, with the equally reclusive Jill and their multitude of strange, lovely-looking children. There he carved his little statuettes and the occasional larger work, and raised crops for his family, and sat in the wonderful California sunlight reading and re-reading the Word of God. Sometimes he went roving along the back reaches of the mountain, hunting the wild animals that had come to flourish there in these days of diminished human population, the deer and boars and such. His son Rasheed occasionally went with him; more usually he went alone. He lived a private, inward life, needing very little beyond the company of his wife and children, and often content to hold himself apart even from them.

Anson said, 'What safeguards do you mean, specifically?'

'I mean I will not let you send him to his death. He must not perish the way Tony perished.'

'*Specifically*, I said.'

'Very well. He will not go on this mission unless you prepare the way fully for him. What I mean by that is that you must be altogether sure that you are sending him to the right place, and that when he gets there, the doors of it must be open to him. He must know the passwords that will admit him. I understand about these passwords. He must be able to walk into the place of Prime in complete safety.'

'We have Andy working on extracting the location of Prime and the password protocols right this minute. We won't be sending Rasheed until we have them, I assure you.'

'Assurance is not enough. This is a sacred promise?'

'A sacred promise, yes,' Anson said.

'There is more,' said Khalid. 'You will see to it that he comes safely back. There will be cars waiting, several cars, and care will be taken that confusion is created so that the police do not know which car he is in, and so he can be returned to the ranch.'

'Agreed.'

'You agree very quickly, Anson. But I must be convinced that you are sincere, or otherwise I will see to it that he does not go. I know how to make a tool, but I know how to blunt its edge, too.'

'I lost my brother to this project,' Anson said. 'I haven't forgotten what that felt like. I don't intend to lose your son.'

'Very good. See to that, Anson.'

Anson made no immediate reply. He wished there were some way that he could transmit telepathically to Khalid his absolute conviction that this time the thing would be done right, that Andy would find in Borgmann's archive every scrap of information that they would need in order to send Rasheed to the true location of Prime and to open all the hidden doors for him, so that Rasheed could carry out the assassination and make good his escape. But there was no way for Anson to do that. He could only ask for Khalid's help, and hope for the best.

Khalid was watching him calmly.

That cool gaze of Khalid was unnerving. He was so *alien*, was Khalid. That was how he had seemed to the sixteen-year-old Anson on that day, decades ago, when he had turned up here out of the blue, traveling with Cindy; and after all this time, he was alien still. Even though he had lived among them for so many years, had married into their family, had shared in the splendor and isolation of their mountaintop existence as though he were a born Carmichael himself. He still remained, Anson thought, something mysterious, something *other*. It wasn't so much that he was of foreign birth, or that he had that strange, almost unearthly physical beauty, or that he worshipped a god named Allah and lived by the book of Mohammed, who had been a desert prince in some unimaginably alien land thousands of years ago. That was part of it, but only part. Those things couldn't account for Khalid's formidable inner discipline, that granite-hard calm of his, the lofty detachment of his spirit. No, no, the explanation of his mystery must lie somewhere in Khalid's childhood, in the very shaping of him, born as he had been in the earliest and harshest years of the Conquest and raised in a town infested by Entities, under hardships and tensions whose nature Anson could scarcely begin to guess at. It was those hardships and tensions that must have led to his becoming what he was. But Khalid never would speak of his early years.

'There's one thing I'd like to know,' Anson said. 'If you have so little desire to place Rasheed at risk, why did you give him the same assassin training you gave Tony? I remember very clearly the time you told me that you didn't give a damn about killing Prime, that the whole project was simply no concern of yours. So surely it wasn't your intention to set up Rasheed as someone to be put into play if Tony failed.'

'No. That was not my intention at all. I was training Tony to be your assassin. I was training Rasheed to be Rasheed. The training happened to be the same; the goals were different. Tony became a perfect machine. Rasheed became perfect too, but he is much more than a machine. He is a work of art.'

'Which you now are willing to place at our service for a very dangerous mission, knowing that we're going to do everything we can to protect him, but there's going to be some element of risk nevertheless. Why? We would never have known what Rasheed was, if you hadn't happened to say to Cindy that you felt he could handle the job. What made you tell her that?'

'Because I have found a life here among you,' said Khalid unhesitatingly. 'I was no one, a man without a home, a family, an existence, even. All that had been stripped from me when I was a child. I was merely a prisoner; but Cindy found me, and brought me here, and everything changed for me after that. I owe you something back. I give you Rasheed; but I want you to use him wisely or else not at all. Those are the terms, Anson. You will protect him, or you will not have him.'

'He'll be protected,' Anson said. 'We aren't going to repeat the Tony event. I swear it, Khalid.'

'Are you getting anywhere?' Frank asked, as Andy looked wearily up from the screen.

'Depends how you define "anywhere". I'm discovering new things all the time. Some of them are actually useful. – Would you mind getting me another beer, Frank? And have one for yourself.'

'Right.' Frank moved hesitantly toward the door.

'Don't worry,' Andy said. 'I'm not going to jump through that window and run away the moment you leave the room.'

'I know that. But I'm supposed to be guarding you, you know.'

'You think I'm going to try to escape? When I'm this close to breaking through into the most secret Entity code?'

'I'm supposed to be guarding you,' Frank said again, patiently. 'Not thinking about what you might or might not do. My father would roast me alive if I let you get away.'

'I would work much better if I weren't so thirsty, Frank. Get me a beer. I'm not going anywhere. Trust me.' Andy smiled slyly. 'Don't you think I'm a trustworthy person, Frank?'

'If you *do* go anywhere, and I don't get roasted alive because you do, I'll personally hunt you down and roast you myself,' Frank said. 'I swear that by the Colonel's bones, Andy.'

He went down the hall. When he returned, about a minute and a half later, Andy was bent over the computer screen again.

'Well, I escaped,' Andy said. 'Then I thought of a new approach I wanted to try, and I decided to come back. Give me the god-damned beer.'

'Andy –' Frank said, handing the bottle over.

'Yes?'

'Look, there's something I've been intending to tell you. I want to apologize for all that shotgun stuff, the day you arrived. It wasn't very pretty. But I knew what my father and Steve would say if they found out you had been here and I had let you go away again. I couldn't take the chance that you would.'

'Forget it, Frank. Don't you think I understand why you pushed that gun in my face? I'm not holding any grudge.'

'I'd like to believe that.'

'You might just as well, then.'

'Just why did you come back here?' Frank asked him.

'That's a good question. I don't know if I have a good answer. Part of it was just a wild impulse, I guess. But also – well – look, Frank, I'll kill you if you say anything about this to anybody else. But there was something else going on in my mind too. I did some shitty things while I was wandering around the country. And when I headed north out of Los Angeles I found myself thinking that maybe I just ought to stop off here and make myself of some use to my family, if I could, instead of acting like a selfish asshole all of the time. Something like that.'

'You almost turned right around and left again, though. Before you were even inside the gate.'

Andy grinned. 'It isn't easy for me not to act like a selfish asshole. Don't you know that about me, Frank?'

Eleven at night. No moon, no clouds, plenty of stars. Frank was off duty now; Martin had taken over the job of guarding Andy. He stood outside the communications center, looking up into the darkness, thinking about too many things at once.

His father. This mission, and whether it would achieve anything. Andy, about whom so many terrible things had been said, suddenly becoming so repentant, sweating away in there to find the secret that would let them overthrow the Entities. And how wonderful everything would be if by some miracle they *did* overthrow the Entities and regain their freedom.

He closed his eyes for a moment; and when he opened them again, the blazing stars arrayed in that great arch above him seemed to engulf him, to draw him up into their midst.

Cindy knew all their names. She had taught them to him long ago, and he still remembered a great many of them. That was

Orion up there, an easy one to find because of the three stars of his belt. Mintak, Alnillam, Alnitak, they were. Strange names. Who had first called them that, and why? The one in the right shoulder, that was Betelgeuse. And there, there in the warrior-god's left knee, that was Rigel.

Frank wondered which star the Entities had come from. We'll probably never know, he thought. Were there different kinds of Entities living on the different stars? Might there be a world of Entities greater than *our* Entities somewhere, beings that would conquer ours some day, and devour their civilization, and set free their slaves? Oh, how he hoped that would happen! He loathed the Entities for what they had done to the world. He despised them. He envied Rasheed for being the one who had been chosen to kill Entity Prime, a task he had desperately wanted for himself.

Stars are suns, he told himself. And suns have planets, and planets have people.

He wondered what kept the stars from falling out of the sky. Some of them did, he knew. He had seen it happen. Often on August nights they would go streaking across the sky, plummeting toward doom somewhere far away. But why did some fall, and not others? There was so much that he didn't know. He would have to ask Andy some of these questions, one of these days.

Maybe the Entities' star was one of those that had fallen. Was that why they went around to other stars and stole the worlds of those who lived there? Yes, Frank thought, that must be it. The Entities' star *has* fallen. And so have the Entities, in a way: they have fallen on us. Looking up into the dark glittering beauty of the night sky, Frank felt a second fierce surge of hatred for the conquerors of Earth who had come out of that sky to steal Earth from its rightful owners.

One day we'll rise up and kill them all.

It felt very good to think that, even though he had trouble making himself believe it ever would happen.

He glanced toward the communications center, and wondered how Andy was coming along in there. Then Frank looked up at the stars one last time; and then he went off to get some sleep.

* * *

Andy worked through the night, which was the way he preferred to do things, and put the last pieces of the puzzle together at the very moment when the sun was coming up. It was the time of the changing of his guard, too, James's shift ending and Martin's beginning.

Or perhaps it was the other way around, Martin going off duty and James arriving. Andy had never been very good at telling them apart. Frank stood out from the others to some degree – there was an extra spark of intelligence or intuition somewhere in him, Andy thought – but the rest of Anson's kids all seemed interchangeable, like a bunch of androids. It was mostly that they all looked alike, poured from the same mold: that awesome Carmichael mold that never seemed to relinquish its grip on the family protoplasm. Glossy blond hair, chilly blue eyes, smooth even features, long legs, flat bellies – the entire crowd of them here at the ranch had been like that, boys and girls alike, decade after decade. Martin and James and Frank and Maggie and Cheryl in this generation; La-La, Jane, Ansonia, that whole bunch, too, just the same; Anson and Tony before them, and Heather and Leslyn, Cassandra and Julie and Mark, Jill and Charlie and Mike; and, even further back, the Colonel's three children, Ron and Anse and Rosalie. And the near-mythical Colonel himself. Generation after generation, going back to the primordial Carmichael at the beginning of time. Outsiders might come in, Peggy, Eloise, Carole, Raven, but the genes of most of them were gobbled up, never to be seen again. Only the Gannett input, the genes for brown eyes and too much weight and brown hair that went thin early, had somehow persevered. And, of course, so had Khalid's, in spades; Khalid's huge brood only too plainly bore the mark of Khalid. But Khalid was truly an outsider, so thoroughly non-Carmichael that his genetic heritage had succeeded in dominating even that of the indomitable Colonel.

Andy knew that he was being unfair: they must really be very different inside, Martin and James and Maggie and all the rest of the tribe, actual separate persons with individual identities. No doubt they would be indignant at being clumped together like this. So let them be indignant, and to hell with them. Andy had always felt overwhelmed by them all, outnumbered, out-

blonded. As his father also had been, Andy was sure. And probably his grandfather, also, Doug, whom he only faintly
remembered.

'Tell your father I've finished the job and I've got the stuff he
wants,' Andy said to Martin, or perhaps it was James, as the
young man went off duty. 'The whole business, every parameter
lined up just right. No question of it. If he'll come over here, I'll
lay it all out for him.'

'Yes,' said James, or perhaps it was Martin, with absolutely no
inflection in his voice. He showed hardly any more comprehension of what Andy had just told him than if Andy had said to
him that he had discovered a method for transforming latitude
into longitude. And off he went to bear the news to Anson.

'Good morning, Andy,' the newly arrived brother said, settling
in for his shift.

'Morning, Martin.'

'I'm James.'

'Ah. Yes. James.' Andy acknowledged the correction with a
nod and turned his attention back to the screen.

The yellow lines cutting across the pink field, the splashes of
blue, the burning scarlet circle. It was all there, yes. He felt no
particular sensation of triumph: a little of the opposite emotion,
perhaps. After days and days of rummaging through the foul
sewer that was the Borgmann archive, and then a gradual direct
thrust through the area of essential Entity-relationship files, and
now this sustained ten-hour burst of drilling down into the core
of the matter, he had laid bare everything that Anson had asked
him to find. Anson now could go out and strike the blow that
would win his war against the Entities, and hoorah for Anson.
What Andy was thinking in the moment of glorious attainment,
mainly, was that now they would let him have his life back.

'I hear you've got some great news for us,' said a voice from
the door.

Frank stood there, beaming like the newly risen sun.

'I was expecting your father,' Andy said.

'He's still asleep. He's been feeling poorly lately, you know.
Let's see what you've got.'

Andy decided not to stand on ceremony. If they didn't feel

like sending Anson over, well, he would explain things to Frank, and so be it. During the search Frank had appeared to understand more of what he was doing than Anson, anyway.

'Here,' Andy said, 'this is where they keep Prime.' He indicated the scarlet circle. 'Downtown Los Angeles, in the strip between the Santa Ana Freeway and the dry bed of the old Los Angeles River. That's just a couple of miles south and east of the place where my father thought he was being kept at the time of the Tony episode. I tracked down an ancient city gazetteer that says the neighborhood is a warehouse district, but of course that was back in the twentieth century, and things may have changed a lot. The Entities' own digital code for Prime translates out to Oneness, so our name for him was pretty damned close.'

Frank's grin grew broader. 'That's terrific. What kind of security arrangements do they have for him?'

'A ring of three gates. They work just like the gates in the city walls, with biochip-driven gatekeepers.' Andy sent two clicks along the line that connected him to the computer and a batch of code jumped out into a window on the auxiliary screen. 'These are access protocols, which I've derived from stuff that Borgmann had collected and stashed away in Prague. They were operative when Prime was being kept in the castle there, and I think they'll still be good. From what I can tell, they don't seem to have changed any of the numbers after the move to L.A. The protocols will take your man through the gates one by one, pretty much as far as he wants to go, and his mission ought to seem perfectly legitimate to the security screens.'

'What about the centrality of Prime to the Entity neural framework?' Frank asked. 'Do you see any sign of a communal linkage?'

Those were fancy words. Andy gave him a quick look tinged with new respect. 'I can only offer you an informed guess about that,' Andy said.

'Okay.'

'In Borgmann's time, all the lines of communication, everywhere around the world, ran to Prime's nest in Prague. I'm talking about computer access. There's a similar heavy convergence on the Los Angeles nest today. Which is a good argument for the centrality of Prime to their computer system, but it doesn't prove anything about the supposed *telepathic* linkage between Prime and the other Entities that Anson believes exists, and which I gather is critical to the whole assassination plan. On the other hand, if there's no such telepathic linkage I think there would have to be a great many more strands of on-line communication than I've been able to find. And that leads me to think that a portion, perhaps the greater portion, of the communication between Prime and the lesser Entities must be carried out by some form of telepathy. Which, of course, we aren't capable of detecting.'

'This is all a guess, you say.'

'All a guess, yes.'

'Show me Prime's nest again.'

Andy brought the scarlet circle onto the screen once more, standing out brightly against the gray backdrop of a Los Angeles street map.

'We'll blow him halfway to the moon,' said Frank.

Rasheed had no implant, and Khalid didn't want him to have one installed. Implants, Khalid said firmly, were devices of Satan. Since Andy saw no way to carry out the Prime mission other than by moving Rasheed through the Entity security lines by remote-control on-line impulse, this created a certain problem, which required weeks of negotiation to resolve. In the end Khalid backed off, after Anson convinced him that the only way to bring Rasheed back alive from the venture was to guide him via an implant. Without an implant it became a suicide mission or no mission at all, and, faced with that choice, Khalid opted to let the Devil's gadget be inserted into his eldest son's forearm, with the proviso that the dread thing be taken out again once the mission had been carried out. But by the time all that was agreed on, it was June.

Now the implant had to be put in, which was done by the man from San Francisco who had built the one for Tony. Rasheed's was of similar but improved design, with all the tracer features that its predecessor had had, but a wider and more versatile range of audio signals by which the remote operator –

Andy, that would be – could guide Rasheed through his tasks by wireless modem, or, if need be, by direct vocal instruction. Another three months went by while the implant was constructed and installed and Rasheed went through the necessary period of healing and training.

Andy was impressed by the swiftness with which Rasheed learned how to interpret and act on the signals he received from his implant. Rasheed, who was twenty years old, slender and fragile-looking and taller even than his long-shanked father, had the shy, alert look of some delicate forest creature that was always ready to break into flight at the crackling of a twig. To Andy he was an enigma of the most profound sort, elusive and remote, indeed virtually unreachable. Rasheed could easily have been something that had descended from space with the Entities. He hardly ever spoke, except in answer to a direct question and not always even then; and when he did respond it was inevitably with a parsimonious syllable or two uttered just at the threshold of audibility, rarely anything more. The extraordinary grace and beauty of his appearance, verging on the angelic, contributed to the extraterrestrial aura that forever cloaked him: the great dark liquid eyes, the finely chiseled features, the luminous glinting of his skin, the swirling halo of glowing hair. He listened gravely to everything that Andy had to tell him, filing it all away in some retentive recess of his inscrutable soul and giving it back perfectly whenever Andy quizzed him on it. That was very impressive. Rasheed had the efficiency of a computer; and Andy understood computers very well. Yet Rasheed was more than just a mechanism, Andy sensed. There seemed to be a person inside there, an actual human being, shy, sensitive, perceptive, highly intelligent. One thing Andy understood above all else about computers was that they were not intelligent in the least.

At the end of November Andy pronounced him ready to go.

'In the beginning, you know, I thought that this was an absolutely crazy plan,' he said to Frank. Andy and Frank had become friends, of a sort, lately. Andy was no longer under round-the-clock guard; but Frank was with him much of the time, simply to keep him company. They had both become accustomed to that. 'I didn't see, from the moment when Anson and my father first explained it to me, how it could possibly have any chance of succeeding. Send your assassin into a den of telepathic aliens and expect that he'd go unnoticed? Lunacy, is what I thought. Rasheed's mind will be broadcasting his lethal intentions at every step of the way, and the Entities will pick up on them before he ever gets within five miles of Prime. And as soon as they decide that this is something serious, not just some deranged joke, they'll give him a Push – hell, man, they'll fucking give him a *Shove* – and it'll be goodbye, Rasheed.'

But that, Andy went on, had been before his first meeting with Rasheed. He knew better now. His months with Rasheed had brought him to an awareness of Rasheed's special skill, the great thing that Rasheed had learned from his equally mysterious father: the art of Not Being There. Rasheed was capable of disappearing totally behind the wall of his forehead. His training had taught him how to reduce his mind to an absolute blank. The Entities would find nothing to read if they turned their telepathy on Rasheed. It was Andy himself, far away, who would be the true assassin. *Do this, do that, turn right, turn left.* All of which Rasheed would do, without thinking about it. And even the Entities would have no means of picking up Andy's remote-control computer commands with their telepathy.

Anson, who had kept out of the picture all summer long, now emerged from his seclusion to issue the final directives. 'Four cars,' Anson said crisply, when all the relevant personnel had gathered in the chart room, 'will be dispatched to Los Angeles at intervals of ten to fifteen minutes. The drivers are to be Frank, Mark, Charlie, and Cheryl. Rasheed will ride with Cheryl at the outset, but somewhere around Camarillo she will drop him off to be picked up by Mark, and Mark will hand him off to Frank in Northridge –'

He shot a glance toward Andy, who was sitting slouched at his keyboard, languidly bringing all this stuff up in three dimensions on the big chart-room screen as Anson laid it out.

'Are you getting all this, Andy?' he asked, using the hard, crisp tone that everyone at the ranch thought of as the Colonel-voice, though the Colonel himself might have been surprised to know that.

'I'm right with you, commander,' Andy said. 'Just keep on rapping it forth.'

Anson glowered a little. He looked haggard and there were dark rings under his eyes. In his left hand he held a zigzaggy walking-stick that he had carved some time back from the glossy red wood of a manzanita branch, and he was tapping it steadily against his left boot, as though to keep his toes awake.

'Well, then. To continue. Over in Glendale Frank gives him to Charlie, and Charlie takes him on eastward and then down through Pasadena and gives him back to Cheryl near the Monterey Park Golf Course. Cheryl is the one who'll take him on through the wall, by way of the Alhambra gate, as we'll discuss in a moment. Now, as for the explosive device itself,' Anson said, 'which has been produced at the Resistance factory that's located in Vista, in northern San Diego County, it will be brought up to Los Angeles in a nursery truck loaded with poinsettia plants for sale as Christmas decorations –'

So, then. The big day. Second week in December, bright and clear and warm in Southern California, a little high cloudiness, no rain in the offing. Andy in the communications center, wearing a headset with one earpiece and a throat-pad microphone, with a phalanx of computers all around him. He was ready to go to work. He was going become a great hero of the Resistance today, if he wasn't one already. Today he was going to kill Entity Prime by proxy, reaching out across some hundred fifty miles to do the job as puppet-master for Rasheed.

Andy would, in fact, be controlling everyone involved in the mission, guiding them into position, moving them about from place to place as things unfolded. His hour of glory; his greatest hack ever.

Steve was sitting beside him, ready to take over if he should grow weary. Andy didn't expect to grow weary. Nor did he think that Steve, or anyone else except himself, would be capable of managing an operation that involved maintaining constant simultaneous contact with four vehicles plus an ambulatory assassin, and auxiliary spotter input besides. But let him stay, if he liked. Let him get a good look at what kind of hacker he had brought into the world. Eloise was there, too, and Mike, and some of the others, a constantly shifting crew. La-La for a while, with little Andy Junior in tow to stare at his still unfamiliar daddy. Leslyn. Peggy. Jane. People came and went. Nothing much was happening yet, anyway. Anson, though he was nominally in command of the mission, was in and out every half hour or so, very fidgety, unable to remain in one place for very long. Cindy stopped in for a while to watch things too, but likewise didn't stay.

The first of the four cars, Charlie's, had set out at eight that morning, with the others leaving soon after. Two had gone by the coast road and two the inland route, all of them zigging and zagging like Anson's walking-stick to get themselves around the various blockages and pitfalls that the Entities, over the years, had whimsically established on the highways linking Santa Barbara with Los Angeles. Andy had each driver pegged on the screen. The scarlet line was Frank; the blue one, Mark; the deep purple, Cheryl; the bright green, Charlie. Whichever car was currently carrying Rasheed got a halo in crimson around it. Right now Rasheed was traveling with Frank, in the San Fernando Valley, heading around the northern side of the Los Angeles city wall toward his rendezvous with Charlie far to the east in Glendale.

There was no indication of unusual activity on the part of the Entities or the LACON police. Why should there be? At any given moment there might be half a million cars in motion in and around the Los Angeles area. What reason was there to think that some villainous conspiracy had been launched, aimed at taking the life of the supreme Entity himself? But Andy had spotters located all around the periphery of the L.A. wall, Resistance people from the subsidiary organizations down there, just in case. They would let him know what was going on, if anything did.

'We are approaching the next Rasheed rendezvous now,' Andy announced grandly. 'Frank and Charlie, West Colorado Street at the corner of Pacific.'

Did those street names mean anything to any of them? Probably not, except maybe to Cindy, if at her age she could still remember anything about her life in Los Angeles. Or Peggy, perhaps, though the years had made her mind pretty foggy too. But Andy had actually been in Glendale within the past five years. Had known a reasonably amusing woman there, for a time, in his pardoner days. Had in fact set foot once or twice on Colorado Street. Whereas these others had lived their lives out hidden away safely here at the ranch, largely ignorant of the world beyond.

Anson was getting edgy again. He went out for another walk.

'Coming up on Rasheed transfer,' Andy said, as the crimson halo left Frank's car and shifted to Charlie's. Andy, who was in touch with everyone by audio as well as on-line, sent a couple of quick impulses down to Frank to tell him to get over to the Glendale gate and wait there for further instructions, now that he had dropped off his passenger. Mark, his morning's work also behind him, was already parked outside the Burbank gate. Cheryl was still in motion, well east of Charlie's position, making her southward journey around the city through Arcadia and Temple City and looping upward toward her rendezvous with Charlie in Monterey Park. They were nearly four hours into the mission.

That was interesting, Andy thought, that Anson would have given the key assignment to Cheryl. Andy could remember some cheery romps with her when he was in his mid-teens and she a year or two older; but mostly what he remembered was that she had kept her eyes open even when she was coming. Those big blue Carmichael eyes, with nothing much behind them. It had never seemed to Andy that there was anything to her, except, of course, a trim and pleasantly rounded body that she had used skilfully but without much imagination on their sporadic encounters in bed. And now here she was getting the job of taking Rasheed right into Los Angeles, delivering him to the very perimeter of the Objective Zone, and getting him out of there again after the assassination. You never could tell about people. Maybe she was smarter than he had supposed. She was the daughter of Mike and Cassandra, he reminded himself, and Mike was a capable guy in his way, and Cassandra was the closest thing to a doctor they had here.

'Approaching acquisition of explosive device,' Andy said loud and clear, since no one in the room except, perhaps, Steve, would be capable of making sense out of the scrambled macaroni on the screen without Andy's verbal guidance. His audience just now, a quick glance over his shoulder told him, consisted of his sister Sabrina and her husband Tad, Mike and his sister-in-law Julie, and Anson's sister Heather. Cindy had returned, also, but she already seemed to be on her way out the door again, walking in that painfully slow but fiercely determined way of hers.

A dotted yellow line marked the progress of the nursery truck that was bearing the bomb up from the factory in Vista. Nestling among the poinsettias, it was, tucked away amid all that gaudy red holiday foliage. He liked that idea. A sweet little premature Christmas present for Prime.

The nursery truck was in Norwalk, now, chugging up the Santa Ana Freeway toward Santa Fe Springs. Andy got in touch with the driver by audio and told him to get a move on. 'Your client is heading toward the depot,' Andy said. 'We don't want to keep him waiting.'

Charlie, with Rasheed aboard, had reached Pasadena, and was moving south on San Gabriel Boulevard toward Monterey Park. It was in Monterey Park that the transfer of the explosive device to Rasheed was supposed to take place, just before Charlie handed him over to Cheryl.

Dotted yellow line, moving faster now.

Green line with crimson halo, traveling toward rendezvous.

Deep-purple line heading in the same direction from the opposite side.

Dotted yellow converging with green. The signal coming from Charlie: successful acquisition.

'Rasheed's got the bomb, now,' Andy announced. 'Going on to rendezvous with Cheryl.'

This is easy, he thought. Fun, even.

We should do one of these every day.

Half an hour later. Deep-purple line bearing crimson halo now approaches great black slash that represents the Los Angeles wall on Andy's master screen. Shimmering vermilion chevrons indicate the Alhambra gate. On audio Andy asks Cheryl for confirmation of position and gets it. All is well. Cheryl is about to enter the city, with Rasheed sitting quietly beside her and the bomb reposing in his backpack.

Andy listens in. Gatekeeper stuff going on. Routine demand for identification.

Cheryl must be making her reply, now, sticking out her implant to be scanned by the gatekeeper. A pass number has been provided for her use. It is, in fact, the pass number of one of the LACON men who had so unkindly trussed Andy in that straitjacket on that bad day on Figueroa Street. Will it work? Yes, it works. The Alhambra barrier opens. Cheryl passes unchallenged through the wall.

Beaming in satisfaction, Andy glances up and around at the current group of onlookers in the communication center: Steve, Cindy, Cassandra, La-La and the wide-eyed little boy. Why aren't the rest of them here, all of them, now that the big moment is practically at hand? Aren't they interested? Especially Anson. Where the fuck is Anson? Off playing golf? Is the suspense too much for him?

To hell with Anson.

'Rasheed is now within the wall,' Andy says, resonantly, majestically.

The crimson circle has separated from the deep-purple line and is moving at a nice steady clip through the shabby streets of the Los Angeles warehouse district. Andy brings up the resolution on his street-map underlay, and sees that Cheryl is parked just east of Santa Fe Avenue near the old and rusting railway tracks, and that the street along which long-legged Rasheed is currently briskly striding is Second Street, heading toward Alameda.

Andy lets five minutes more elapse. According to the screen, Rasheed now is practically on the threshold of Prime's snug little hideout. Time for one final bit of voice-to-voice confirmation.

'Rasheed?' Andy says, via the audio channel.

'I am here, Andy.'

'Where is that?'

'Perimeter of Objective Zone.'

Rasheed's voice, tiny in Andy's headphone, does not waver in the slightest. To Andy he sounds marvelously cool, calm, completely serene. Pulse rate normal, absolutely unhurried, no doubt. All quiet within Rasheed, quiet as the grave. That boy is a wonder, Andy thinks. He is a superhuman. Walking right up to that building with a bomb on his back and he's not even perspiring.

'This is our last audio contact, Rasheed. Everything digital from here on. Acknowledge digitally.'

A trio of pulses light up Andy's screen. Rasheed's implant is operating properly, therefore. So is Rasheed.

Steve reaches over, just then, and lets his hand rest lightly on Andy's forearm, only for a moment. Offering reassurance? Making a show of confidence in Andy's capabilities? In Rasheed's? All three, maybe. Andy gives his father a quick smile and goes back to his screens. The hand is withdrawn.

Crimson circle advancing unmolested. Rasheed must be almost at the first checkpoint. He will be moving with a sleepwalker's ghostly tranquility, untroubled in any way by thoughts of the thing he has come here to do, because that is what his training has equipped him to do. Andy sees to it that his own breathing is slow and regular, his heartbeat normal. He will never have the same kind of supernatural bodily control that Rasheed has achieved, but he wants to keep himself as calm as he can, anyway. This is not the moment to get overexcited.

Checkpoint.

Rasheed has halted. Implant access is being provided. The password-protocol code that Andy has dredged up out of Borgmann's antiquated files, and refreshed by a probe only yesterday through the interface into the heart of the Entity security spookware, will be tested now.

A long moment slides by. Then crimson circle begins moving forward again. Password accepted!

'In like Flynn,' Andy says, speaking to no one in particular. He wonders what the phrase means. But he likes the sound of it. 'In like Flynn.'

Checkpoint Number Two.

Where the hell is Rasheed now, actually? Andy can't even imagine what sort of lair they might keep Prime in. A pity that there's no video on this link-up. Well, Rasheed can tell us all about it afterward. If he survives.

Is he moving between rows of lofty gleaming marble walls? Or, Andy wonders, circling past some fearsome ring of fire behind which the overlord of overlords reclines in splendor? Are there subordinate Entities sitting around casually in there, sipping soft drinks, playing pinochle, amiably waving their tentacles at Rasheed as the unflappable human intruder, rock-solid in his serenity of soul, equipped with all the right passwords and broadcasting not one telepathic smidgeon of his sinister purpose, goes deeper and deeper into the inner sanctum? And, Andy supposes, there are some humans in there too, Entity slaves, humble servants of the great monarch. Borgmann's files had indicated that that was the case. They would pay no attention to Rasheed, naturally, because he would not be in here unless it was all right for him to be in here, and therefore it was all right for him to be here. The slave mentality, yes.

The Checkpoint Number Two password is requested. Rasheed obliges, giving implant access.

Streams of digits provided by Andy flash from Rasheed to whatever kind of thing is guarding the door at this checkpoint.

Password accepted.

Once again, crimson circle goes forward.

Sixty seconds elapse. No further news from Rasheed. But he's still moving. Eighty seconds. One hundred. Andy stares and waits. Blue shadows surround his master screen. The faint hum of the equipment starts to turn into a tune, something out of grand opera, Mozart, Wagner, Verdi.

No news from Rasheed. No news. No news. De-dum, de-dum, de-dum, de-*dah*.

Andy wonders how long it actually takes for Rasheed's coded messages to travel up to him across the 150 miles that separate him from Los Angeles. Speed of light: fast, but not instantaneous. He divides 186,000 miles per second by 150 miles, which is easy enough to do, somewhere about 1200, but when he tries to convert that result into the appropriate fraction of a second that is the actual lag his mental arithmetic fails him. He must be doing this all wrong, he decides. Maybe he should have divided 150 by 186,000. Usually he's better at stuff like this. Difficult to concentrate. *Where the hell is Rasheed?* Has someone caught on to the fact that this big-eyed and elongated young human has no business being where he is?

Impulse from Rasheed arrives. Thank God.

Checkpoint Number Three.

Okay. This is a major decision point, and only Rasheed can make the decision. Perhaps he's far enough inside the Objective Zone now so that he can plant the bomb right where he is. Or perhaps he needs to go through one more checkpoint. Andy can't tell Rasheed what to do; Andy has no way of seeing what's actually there, no idea of the distances involved, and Rasheed can't describe anything except by audio, which now is too dangerous to use. Rasheed will have to use his own judgment about whether to continue on through Checkpoint Three. But these password protocols come without guarantees. Two have worked, but will the third? If Rasheed tries it and it bounces, they will grab him with their nasty elastic tongues and stuff him into a gunnysack and haul him away for interrogation, and God help us all.

Andy has one fallback, if that happens. He can detonate the bomb while it's still in Rasheed's backpack, which would not be very nice for Rasheed, but which might just get Prime as well, even as Rasheed is being spirited off for questioning. Rasheed is aware of this option. Rasheed is supposed to send the appropriate signal to Andy if it should become necessary to make use of it.

But that is very much a last resort.

Andy waits. Breathes. Counts heartbeats. Tries to divide 150 by 186,000 in his head.

Rasheed is offering the password for Checkpoint Number Three. He has decided, evidently, that he is not yet sufficiently close to Prime's personal place to plant the bomb.

Andy realizes that he has stopped breathing. No heartbeat to speak of, either. He is suspended between one second and the next. Through Andy's mind race, over and over, the combinations that will trigger the fallback detonation. A mere quick twitch of his fingers will set them up. All Rasheed needs to do is send him the one despairing signal that means he has been caught, and –

Crimson circle starting to go forward again.

Rasheed has passed through Checkpoint Number Three.

Andy resumes regular breathing patterns. Time begins moving along once more.

But Rasheed isn't telling him anything as the moments go by. The only information Andy has is that crimson circle gliding across his screen – the symbol for Rasheed, coming to him by telemetry. Tick. Tick. Ninety seconds. Nothing happening.

Now what? An unsuspected fourth checkpoint? Some formidably efficient security device that has instantaneously and fatally taken Rasheed out of the picture, before he could even sound a distress signal? Or – surprise! – Rasheed has discovered that Prime has gone on vacation in Puerta Vallarta?

Signal coming through now from Rasheed.

Andy, his senses phenomenally over-sharpened by all this, experiences an interval of about six years between each incoming digit.

Is Rasheed telling him that he has been caught? That he has lost his way? That this is the wrong building altogether?

No.

Rasheed is saying that he has reached the Objective.

That he has taken the bomb from his backpack and is sticking it to the wall of wherever-he-is, neatly affixing it in some nice snug insignificant place. That he has done his job and is coming out.

The whole thing unwinds in reverse, now. Rasheed is heading back toward Checkpoint Three. Yes. There he goes, right through it. All is well.

Checkpoint Two. Crimson circle moving nicely.

Checkpoint One. Will they collar him here? 'We're very sorry, young man, we simply can't permit you to plant bombs within this area.' *Zap!*

No zap. He's made it. He's outside Checkpoint One. Outside the sanctuary entirely. Leaving the Objective Zone quickly, not running, of course, oh, no, not cool calm Rasheed, just moving along through the streets with his usual long-legged **stride.**

Andy is dealing with four people at once, now, shooting a

welter of coded messages to them. At Andy's command Cheryl
has left her parking spot and is coming forward to collect Rasheed
as he moves eastward toward her. She will try to get out the
Alhambra gate, the same one through which she entered. Charlie
is parked outside that gate and will take Rasheed from her,
assuming she can get through. Frank, at the Glendale gate, and
Mark, at Burbank, are the fallback drivers if for some reason the
Alhambra gate has been closed to vehicular traffic; if that is the
case one or the other of them will enter the city, if they can, and
rendezvous with Cheryl at a point to be determined by Andy, if
it can be managed, and take Rasheed from her and spirit him
back out through some gate or other, whichever one they can.
If. If. If. If.

Andy wants to ask all sorts of questions, now, but he doesn't
dare use the audio line. Too easy to intercept that; this all has
to be done by coded impulse, cryptic blips coursing along the
electronic highway between the ranch and the city. Sparks seem
to fly on the screen as the colors dance. Andy leans forward until
his nose is practically touching the screen. His fingers caress its
cool plastic surface as though he has abruptly decided to conduct
the rest of this operation in Braille.

Crimson circle is now a halo around the midsection of the
deep-purple line. Cheryl has picked up Rasheed. Heading for
Alhambra gate.

The moment has arrived when the greatest of this series of
gambles must be played out. Detonation has to wait until
Rasheed is safely through the gate. They will surely close all the
gates the moment the bomb blows. Rasheed needs to be outside
the wall first: there's no choice about that. But what if Andy waits
too long to give the detonation signal, and Prime's attendants
notice the bomb? It is inconspicuous but definitely not invisible.
If the Alhambra gate is shut down and he has to futz around with
arranging a second rendezvous, bringing Rasheed out through
Burbank or Glendale, and meanwhile they find the bomb and
are able to defuse it –

If. If. If. If.

But Alhambra is open. Crimson halo passes to green line.
Rasheed is safely outside the wall, and he is in Charlie's car

now. Using five hands and at least ninety fingers, Andy sends simultaneous signals to all parties concerned.

Frank – Mark – head homeward right away.

Charlie – get your ass up toward the 210 Freeway and cruise toward Sylmar, where you will rendezvous with Cheryl and give Rasheed back to her.

And you, Cheryl – shadow Charlie on the freeway, just in case he runs into a roadblock, in which case you can grab Rasheed and dart off in the other direction with him.

Plus one message more.

Hey – Prime! Here's something for you!

Andy grins and keys in the detonator code.

There was no way for him to feel the explosion from 150 miles away, no, sirree. Except in his imagination. In Andy's imagination, the whole world shook with the force of a Richter Ten, the sky turned black with red streaks, the stars began to run backward in their courses. But of course it was impossible really to know, at least not right away, what had actually happened in Los Angeles. The bomb was a potent one but it hadn't been Anson's plan to blow up the whole city with it. Most likely it hadn't been noticed even in places as close to the site as Hollywood.

But then a voice in Andy's headphone said, 'I'm just off Sunset Boulevard, not far from Dodger Stadium. Two Entities just went by in a wagon, and they were, like, screaming. Shrieking. You know, like they were in the most extreme pain. The explosion must have, like, driven them out of their minds. The death of Prime.'

'Who is this, please?' Andy said.

'Sorry. This is Hawk.'

One of the spotters, that was. Andy said, 'You can see the Figueroa Street headquarters from where you are, can't you? What's happening there?'

'Lights blinking on and off all over the upper stories. It seems pretty frantic. That's all I can see, the upper stories. I hear sirens, too.'

'You felt the explosion?'

'Oh, yeah. Yeah. Most definitely. And, like –'

But another of the Los Angeles spotters had begun to signal for his attention. Andy cut over to him. This one was Redwood, calling in from Wilshire and Alvarado, the eastern side of Mac-Arthur Park. 'There's an Entity keeled over at the edge of the lake,' Redwood said. 'It just fell right down the minute the bomb went off.'

'Is it alive?'

'It's alive, all right. I can see it writhing. It's laying there hollering blue murder. You have to cover your ears, practically.'

'Thank you,' Andy said. He felt a wild surge of joy go running through him like an electrical jolt. *Writhing. Hollering blue murder.* Music to his ears. Grinning, he switched to another line, and it was Clipper, calling in from far-off Santa Monica with news of great confusion there, and Rowboat waiting right behind him with a similar report from Pasadena. Someone had seen an Entity that seemed to be lying unconscious in the street, and someone else had seen four greatly agitated aliens of the Spook variety running around in mindless circles.

Andy felt a nudge from Steve, beside him. 'Hey, tell us what's going on.'

He realized that for the past couple of minutes he had been in Los Angeles in his mind. Los Angeles, with its writhing, shrieking Entities, was more vivid to him than the ranch. It was a serious effort for him to bring the scene in the communications center back into focus. Faces peered into his. Anson stood beside him now, and Mike, Cassandra, half a dozen others. Even Jill had turned up, though not Khalid. Staring eyes. Tense faces. They had figured out something of what had taken place by listening to his audio exchanges with the spotters within the city, but they only had part of the story, and now they wanted the rest of it, and they were all yelling questions at him at the same time.

Andy began yelling answers back at them. Telling them that Rasheed had done it, that the bomb had gone off, that Prime was dead, that the Entities were crazy with shock, that they were falling down in the streets and moaning – no, *shrieking* – shrieking like lunatics, all of them going berserk down there and probably all around the world too, a single great shriek coming out of

every Entity at once, everywhere, a terrible sound that rose and
fell like a siren, *yow wow wow wow yow* –

'What? What? What? What are you trying to say, Andy?'

A ring of baffled faces confronted him. He suspected that he
wasn't getting the information to them quite in the right order,
that carts were being put before horses, that he might in truth
be babbling a little. He didn't care. He had been in six places at
once all morning, six at the very least, and now he just wanted
to go off somewhere quiet and lie down for a while.

He wished he could hear that shriek, though. The stars themselves must be shrieking. The galaxies.

'We did it,' he blurted. 'We won! Prime's dead and the Entities
are going nuts!'

That got through to them, all right.

Steve began to drum jubilantly on the table. Mike was dancing
with Cassandra. Cindy was dancing with herself.

But Anson wasn't dancing. He was standing all by himself in
the middle of the room, looking a little dazed. 'I just can't believe
that it worked,' he said wonderingly, slowly shaking his head.
'It's almost too good to be true.'

In one ear Andy heard his father telling Anson not to be such
a goddamned pessimist for once, and in the other ear, the one
that had the earpiece over it, he heard the spotter called Redwood,
the one out by MacArthur Park, clamoring for his attention, begging for it. Telling him something very peculiar now was going
on, that the Entity who had fallen down at the edge of the lake
now was upright again and starting to move around pretty vigor-
ously; and then Hawk was trying to cut in with some bulletin
from his district, unsettling news from that quarter also, a few
Entities apparently beginning to get themselves back together
after that little fit that they had had. Two or three of the other
spotters were trying to get through to Andy too, lighting up his
whole switchboard. 'LACON,' someone was saying. 'LACON
guys all over the place!'

Something fishy very definitely was occurring. Andy shook
his hands furiously in the air. 'Quiet, everyone! *Quiet!* Let me
hear!'

The room was suddenly silent.

Andy listened to Hawk, listened to Clipper, listened to Rowboat and the rest of the spotters down there in Los Angeles. He cut from line to line, saying very little, just listening. Listening hard. No one around him said anything.

Then he looked up, at Anson, at Steve, at Cindy, Jill, La-La, going one by one around the room. All those inquiring eyes, pleading for information, staring at him, reading his face. Pins could drop and the sound would be like thunder. They all could tell from his expression, Andy knew, that the news was ungood. That some unexpected extra factor had entered the equation, something they had not in the least reckoned on, and the situation was not quite as satisfactory as had been thought. Might, in fact, be suddenly starting to look pretty disastrous.

'Well?' Steve asked.

Andy slowly shook his head. 'Oh, shit,' was all he could bring himself to say. 'Shit! Shit! Shit! Shit!'

Frank had left the freeway in favor of a surface-streets route that would take him around the place where the northernmost bulge of the city wall bisected Topanga Canyon Boulevard. Now, as he was moving quickly through the town of Reseda in the San Fernando Valley, he glanced at his rear-view mirror and saw a great pillar of black smoke rising into the sky behind him.

That puzzled him at first. Then he realized what it probably was, and the excitement that he had felt ever since Andy had sent word of the successful detonation, the wild euphoria that had been powering him for the last forty minutes, evaporated faster than snow in July.

'Andy?' he said, on the audio channel to the ranch. 'Andy, listen, there's a big fire, or something, going on somewhere around Beverly Hills or Bel Air. I can see the smoke coming right up over the top of the hills, a huge plume rising, out there on the far side of Mulholland Drive.'

There was no immediate reply from the ranch.

'Andy? Andy, are you receiving me? This is Frank, at Reseda Boulevard and Sherman Way.'

He got back only crackling noises. The continued silence was unsettling. The column of smoke behind him was still rising. It looked to be half a mile high. Frank thought he heard the sound of distant explosions, now.

'Andy?'

Another minute or so, still no Andy.

Then: 'Sorry. That you, Frank?' At last. 'I've been busy. Where did you say you are?'

'Heading northward across the Valley along Reseda Boulevard. There's a tremendous fire happening behind me.'

'I know. There are a lot of fires. The Entities are hitting back, doing reprisals for killing Prime.'

'*Reprisals?*' The word went ricocheting around in Frank's head, pummeling his brain.

'Damn right. LACON planes are bombing the shit out of everything all over town.'

'But the mission was successful,' Frank said uncomprehendingly. 'Prime is dead.'

'Yes. Apparently he is.'

'And half an hour ago you told me the Entities all over the world were going completely around the bend from the shock of his death. That they were crazed and staggering, berserk with pain, falling down all over the place. They were finished, you said.'

'I did say that, yes.'

'So who ordered the reprisals?' Frank asked, pushing his words out slowly and thickly, as though trying to speak through wads of cotton.

'The Entities did.' Andy sounded tired, terribly tired. 'They seem to have picked themselves up somehow and put themselves back together again. And they've sent out a whole armada of LACON people and other assorted quislings to make air raids, pretty much at random, from the looks of it, by way of showing how annoyed they are with us.'

Frank leaned forward over the steering wheel, breathing slowly in and out. It was hard, very hard, assimilating all this. 'Then it was just a waste of time, everything we just did? Knocking out Prime didn't really achieve anything?'

'For about ten minutes, it did. But what it looks like is that they have backup Primes. Which is something that Borgmann's files didn't tell me.'

'No! Oh, Jesus, Andy! Jesus!'

'Once I got the picture of what was going on in Los Angeles,' Andy said, 'I went back in and hunted around and discovered that there's evidently another Prime in London, and one in Istanbul, and the original one still in Prague. And more, maybe. They're all interchangeable and linked in series. If one dies, the next one is activated right away.'

'Jesus,' Frank said again. And then, anguishedly: 'What about Rasheed? And the others.'

'All okay. Rasheed's currently riding with Charlie, traveling westward on the Foothill Freeway, somewhere near La Canada. Cheryl's coming right up behind him. Mark's on the Golden State Freeway in the vicinity of Mission Hills, heading north.'

'Well, thank God for that much. But I thought we had them beaten,' Frank said.

'Me too, for about five minutes.'

'Finished them all off at once, with one big bang.'

'That would have been nice, wouldn't it? Well, we gave them a pretty good hit, anyway. But now they're banging us back. And then, I guess, everything will go on pretty much as before.' The sound that came over the line from Andy was one that Frank interpreted as laughter, more or less. 'Makes you feel like shit, doesn't it, cuz?'

'I thought we had them,' Frank said. 'I really did.'

A sensation that was entirely new to him, a feeling of utter and overwhelming hopelessness, swept through him like a cold bitter wind. They had been so completely absorbed in the project for so long, convinced that it would bring them to their goal. They had given it their best shot: all that ingenuity, all that sweat, all that bravery. Rasheed walking right into the lion's den and sticking the bomb to the wall. And for what? For what? There had been one little fact they didn't know; and because of it they hadn't accomplished a damn thing.

It was maddening. Frank wanted to yell and kick and break things. But that wouldn't make anything any better. He drew a deep breath, another, another. It didn't help. He might just as well have been breathing ashes.

'God *damn* it, Andy. You worked so hard.'

'We all did. The only trouble was that the theory behind what we were doing didn't happen to be valid. – Look, kiddo, just get yourself back to the ranch, and we'll try to figure out something else, okay? I've got other calls to make. See you in about an hour, Frank. Over and out.'

Over, yes. Out.

Try not to think about it, Frank told himself. It hurts too much to think. Pretend you're Rasheed. Empty your mind of everything except the job of getting home.

That worked, for a while. Then it didn't.

And then, about an hour later, he had something new to think about. He was far up the coast, just past Carpinteria, practically on the outskirts of Santa Barbara, when he saw strange streaks of light in the sky ahead of him, something that might have been a golden comet that exploded into a shower of green and purple sparkles. Fireworks? He heard muffled booming sounds. A moment later the dark slim shapes of three swiftly moving planes passed overhead, high up, heading south, back toward Los Angeles.

A bombing mission? All the way up here?

He told the audio to kick in.

'Andy? Andy?'

The crackle of static. Otherwise, silence.

'Andy?'

He kept trying. No reply from the ranch.

He was past Summerland now, past Montecito, moving on into downtown Santa Barbara. The familiar hills of home rose up back of the city. Another couple of miles up the freeway and he would be able to see the ranch itself, nestling high on its mountain among the folded canyons that sheltered it.

And now Frank saw it. Or the place where he knew it to be. Smoke was rising from it, not a gigantic black pillar like the one he had seen when leaving Los Angeles, but only a small spiralling trail, wisping out at its upper end and losing itself in the darkening late-afternoon sky.

Stunned, he traversed the city and made his way up the mountain road, keeping his eyes on the smoke and trying to make himself believe that it was coming from some other hilltop. The road twisted about so much as it ascended that perspectives were tricky, and for a time Frank actually did believe that the fire was on another hill entirely, but then he was on the final stretch, where the road hooked around and leveled out on the approach to the ranch gate, and there could be no doubt of it. The ranch had been bombed. All these years it had been sacrosanct, as though exempt by some special sanction from the direct touch of the conquerors. But that exemption had ended now.

He gave the signal that would open the gate, and the bars went sliding back.

As he drove in, down the little road, Frank could see that the main house was on fire. Flames were dancing across its rear facade. The whole front of the building looked to be gone, and the tiled roof over the middle section had fallen in. There was a shallow crater behind the house, where the path to the communications center had been. The communications center itself was still standing, but it had taken some damage, and appeared to have been knocked off its foundation. Most of the other structures, the minor outbuildings, looked more or less intact. Little fires were burning here and there in the trees behind them.

Through the haze and smoke Frank saw a small figure wandering about outside, moving as though in a daze. Cindy. Ancient, tottering little Cindy. Her face was smudged and blackened. He got out of the car and ran toward her, and embraced her. It was like clutching a bundle of sticks.

'Frank,' she said. 'Oh, look at everything, Frank! Look at it!'

'I saw the planes leaving. Three of them, I saw.'

'Three, yes. They came right overhead. They fired missiles, but a lot of them missed. Some didn't. The one direct hit, that was a good one.'

'I see. The main house. Is anyone else alive?'

'Some,' she said. 'Some. It's bad, Frank.'

He nodded. He caught sight of Andy, now, standing in the skewed doorway of the communications center. He looked about ready to drop from exhaustion. Somehow, though, he managed a grin, the smirking one-side-of-mouth Andy-grin that always looked so sneaky and false to Frank. But that grin was a welcome sight now.

Frank went trotting over to him.

'You okay?'

The grin became a weary smile. 'Fine, yes. Real fine. A little concussion, is all. Not too serious. Slight dislocation of the brain, nothing more. But the whole communications system got wrecked. If you were wondering why I've been off the air, now you know.' Andy pointed to the crater on the path. 'They didn't miss by much. And the main house –'

'I can see.'

'We were leading a charmed life up here for a hell of a long time, boy. But I guess we tried one little trick too many. It all happened very fast, the raid. Whoosh, whoosh, whoosh, blam, blam, blam, and they were here and gone. Of course, they might come back and finish the job half an hour from now.'

'You think?'

'Who knows? Anything's possible.'

'Where are the others?' Frank asked, glancing around. 'What about my father?'

Andy hesitated just a moment too long. 'I'm sorry to have to tell you this, Frank. Anson was in the main house when the bomb hit it. – I'm very sorry, Frank. Very sorry.'

A dull thudding sensation was all that Frank felt. The real shock, he suspected, was going to hit later.

'My father was in there with him,' Andy added. 'My mother, too.'

'Oh, Andy. Andy.'

'And also your father's sister.' Andy stumbled over the name. ' – Les – Leh – Lesl –' He was right at the edge of collapse, Frank realized.

'Leslyn,' Frank supplied. 'You ought to go inside and get off your feet, Andy.'

'Yes. I really should, shouldn't I?' But he stayed where he was, bracing himself against the frame of the door. His voice came to Frank as though from very far away: 'Mike is okay. Cassandra, too. And La-La. Lorraine, I mean. Peggy was pretty badly hurt. She may not pull through. I'm not sure what happened to Julie. The whole ranch-hand compound got smashed. But Khalid's place wasn't even touched. It's the infirmary for the survivors, right now. Mike and Khalid went into the main house and brought out anybody who was still alive, just before the roof fell in. Cassandra's looking after them.'

Frank made a vague sound of acknowledgment. Turning away from Andy for a moment, he stared across the way, toward the burning building. Through his numbed mind went the thought of the Colonel's books, of the maps and charts in the chart room, of all that history of the vanished free human world going up in flames. He wondered why he should think about anything as irrelevant as that just now.

'My brothers and sisters?' he asked.

'Most of them okay, just shaken up. But one of your brothers died. I don't know if it was Martin or James.' Andy gave him a sheepish look. 'Sorry about that, Frank: I never could keep them straight in my head.' In a mechanical way he went on, now that Frank had started him going again: 'My sister Sabrina, she's okay. Not Irene. As for Jane – Ansonia –'

'All right,' Frank said. 'I don't need to hear the whole list now. You ought to get yourself over to Khalid's house and lie down, Andy. You hear me? Go over there and lie down.'

'Yeah,' Andy said. 'That sounds like a good idea.' He went lurching away.

Frank glanced up and off toward the left, where the road that came from town could be seen, snaking along the flank of the mountain. The other cars would be arriving soon – Cheryl, Mark, Charlie. Some splendid homecoming this would be for them, too, after the excitement of the grand and glorious expedition to Los Angeles. Perhaps they already knew of the mission's failure. But then, to learn of the raid on the house, to see the damage, to hear of the deaths –

Rasheed was the only one who would ride with the blow, Frank suspected, out of the entire group that had gone to Los Angeles. The strangely superhuman Rasheed, who had been designed and constructed by his father, the equally strange Khalid, to handle any kind of jolt without batting an eye. That eerie detachment of his, the other-worldly calm that had allowed him to venture right into the den of Entity Prime and fasten a bomb to the wall: that would carry him through the shock of returning to the gutted ranch without any difficulty at all. Of course, Rasheed's mother and father and brothers and sisters hadn't been touched. And he might not have given a damn about the success or failure of the mission in the first place. Did Rasheed give a damn about anything? Probably not.

And very likely that was the attitude they would all need to cultivate now: detachment, indifference, resignation. There was no hope left, was there? No remaining fantasies to cling to now.

He walked slowly back toward the parking area.

Cindy was still standing by his car, running her hands over its sleek flanks in a weird caressing way. It occurred to Frank that the frail old woman's mind must be gone, that she had been driven insane by the noise and fury of the bombing raid; but she turned toward him as he approached, and he saw the unmistakable clear, cool look of sanity in her eyes.

'He told you who the dead ones are?' she asked him.

'Most of them, I guess. Steve, Lisa, Leslyn, and others, too. One of my brothers. And my father, too.'

'Poor Anson, yes. Let me tell you something, though. It was just as well, I think, that he died when he did.'

The casual brutality of the remark startled him. But Frank had seen on other occasions how merciless the very old could be.

'Just as well? Why do you say that?'

Cindy waved one claw-like hand at the scene of destruction. 'He couldn't have lived with himself after seeing *this*, Frank. His grandfather's ranch in ruins. Half the family dead. And the Entities still running the world, despite everything. He was a very proud man, your father. All the Carmichaels are.' The hand swiveled around and came to rest across Frank's forearm, grasping it tightly. Her eyes glittered up into his like those of a witch. 'It was bad enough for him when Tony was killed. But Anson would have died a thousand deaths a day if he had survived *this*. Knowing that his second great plan for ridding the world of the Entities had been an even bigger failure than the first – that it had ended by bringing all this wreckage upon us. He's a lot better off not being here now. A lot better off.'

*   *   *

Better off? Could that be true? Frank needed to think about that.

He disengaged his arm and took a few steps away from her, toward the jumble of blackened granite and flagstone that was the smoldering house, and dug the toe of his boot into the heaps of charred wood scattered along the path.

The bitter smell of burning things stung his nostrils. Cindy's harsh words sounded and resounded in his ears, a doleful clamor that would not cease.

Anson would have died a thousand deaths a day – a thousand deaths – a thousand deaths –

His great plan a failure –

A failure –

A failure –

Failure – failure – failure – failure –

After a few moments it seemed to Frank that he could almost agree with her about Anson. He could never have withstood the immensity of the fiasco, the totality of it. It would have wrecked him. Not that that made his death any easier to accept, though. Or any of the rest of this. It was hard to take, all of it. It stripped all meaning from everything Frank had ever believed in. They had made their big move, and it had failed, and that was that. The game was over and they had lost. Wasn't that the truth? And now what? Frank wondered.

Now, he supposed, nothing at all. No more great plans. No grand new schemes for throwing off the Entity yoke with a single dramatic thrust. They were finished with such projects now.

A strange dark thought, that was. For generations now his whole family had channeled its energies into the dream of undoing the Conquest. His whole life had been directed toward that goal, ever since he was old enough to understand that the Earth once had been free and then had been enslaved by beings from the stars: that he was a Carmichael, and the defining trait of Carmichaels was that they yearned to rid the world of its alien masters. Now he had to turn his back on all that. That was sad. But, he asked himself, standing there at the edge of the rubble that had been the ranch, what other attitude was possible, now that this had happened? What point was there in continuing to pretend that a way might yet be be found to drive the Entities away?

His great plan –

A failure – a failure – a failure –

A thousand deaths a day. A thousand deaths a day. Anson would have died a thousand deaths a day.

'Penny for your thoughts,' Cindy said.

He managed a feeble smile. 'You really want to know?'

She didn't even bother to answer. She simply repeated the question with her unrelenting eyes. He knew better than to refuse again. 'That it's all over with, now that the mission's failed,' he said. 'That I guess we're done with dreaming up grand projects for the liberation, now. That we'll just have to resign ourselves to the fact that the Entities are going to own the world forever.'

'Oh, no,' she said, astounding him for the second time in the past two minutes. 'No. Wrong, Frank. Don't you dare think any such thing.'

'Why shouldn't I, then?'

'Your father's not even in his grave yet, but he'd be turning in it already if he was. And Ron, and Anse, and the Colonel, in theirs. Listen to you! "*We just have to resign ourselves*".'

The sharpness of her mockery, the vehemence of it, caught Frank off guard. Color came to his cheeks. He struggled to make sense of this. 'I don't mean to sound like a quitter, Cindy. But what *can* we do? You just said yourself that my father's plan had failed. Doesn't that end it for us? Is it realistic to go on thinking we can defeat them, somehow? Was it ever?'

'Pay attention to me,' she said. She impaled him with a stark, unanswerable glare from which there could be no flinching. 'You're right that we've just proved that we can't defeat them. But completely wrong to say that because we can't beat them we should give up all hope of being free.'

'I don't underst –'

She went right on. 'Frank, I know better than anyone alive how far beyond us the Entities are in every way. I'm eighty-five years old. I was right on the scene, the day the Entities came. I spent weeks aboard one of their starships. I stood right before them, no farther from them than you are from me, and I felt the power of their minds. They're like gods, Frank. I knew that from the moment they came. We can hurt them – we just demonstrated that – but we can't seriously damage them and we certainly can't overthrow them.'

'Right. And therefore it seems to me that it's useless to put any energy into the false hope of –'

'Pay attention to me, is what I said. I was with the Colonel just before he died. You never knew him, did you? – No, I didn't think so. He was a great man, Frank, and a very wise one. He understood the power of the Entities. He liked to compare them to gods, too. That was the very term he used, and he was right. But then he said that we had to keep on dreaming of a day when they'd no longer be here, nevertheless. Keeping the *idea* of resistance alive despite everything, is what he said. Remembering what it was like to have lived in a free world.'

'How can we remember something we never knew? The Colonel remembered it, yes. You remember. But the Entities have been here almost fifty years. They were already here before my father was born. There are two whole generations of people in the world who never –'

Again the glare. His voice died away.

'Sure,' Cindy said scornfully. 'I understand that. Out there are millions of people, billions, who don't know what it ever was like to live in a world where it was possible to make free choices. They don't mind having the Entities here. Maybe they're even happy about it, most of them. Life is easier for them, maybe, than it would have been fifty years ago. They don't have to think. They don't have to shape themselves into anything. They just do what the Entity computers and the quisling bosses tell them to do. But this is Carmichael territory, up here, what's left of it. We think differently. And what we think is, the Entities have turned us into nothing, but we can be something again, some day. Somehow. Provided we don't allow ourselves to forget what we once were. A time will come, I don't know how or when, when we can get out from under the Entities and fix things so that we can live as free people again. And we have to keep that idea alive until it does. Do you follow me, Frank?'

She was frail and unsteady and trembling. But her voice, deep and harsh and full, was as strong as an iron rod.

Frank searched for a reply, but none that had any logic to it would come. Of *course* he wanted to maintain the traditions of his ancestors. Of *course* he felt the weight of all the Carmichaels he had never known, and those that he had, pressing on his soul, goading him to lead some wonderful crusade against the enemies of mankind. But he had just returned from such a crusade, and the ruins of his home lay smoldering all around him. What was important now was burying the dead and rebuilding the ranch, not thinking about the next futile crusade.

So there was nothing he could say. He would not deny his heritage; but it seemed foolish to utter some noble vow binding him to make one more attempt at attaining the impossible.

Abruptly Cindy's expression softened. 'All right,' she said. 'Just think about what I've been saying. Think about it.'

A horn sounded in the distance, three honks. Cheryl returning, or Mark, or Charlie.

'You'd better go up there and meet them,' Cindy said. 'You're in charge, now, boy. Let them know what's taken place here. Go on, will you? Hurry along. See who it is.' And as he started up the path to the gate he heard her voice trailing after him, a softer tone now: 'Break it to them gently, Frank. If you can.'

IX

Fifty-Five Years
from Now

It was the third spring after the bombing of the ranch before the scars of the raid really began to fade. The dead had been laid to rest and mourned, and things went on. New plantings now covered the bomb craters, and generous winter rains had nurtured the young shrubs and freshly seeded grass into healthy growth.

The damaged buildings had been either repaired or demolished, and some new ones constructed. Removing the debris of the burned-out main house had been the biggest task, a two-year job; the place had been built to last through the ages, and dismantling it using simple hand tools was a monumental task for one small band of people. But finally that was done, too. They had managed to salvage the rear wing of the house, at least, the five rooms that were still intact, and had recycled sections of wall and flooring from the rest to construct a few rooms more. The communications center was back on its foundation also, and Andy had even succeeded in reopening on-line contact with people elsewhere in California and other parts of the country.

It was a quiet existence. The crops thrived. The flocks flourished. Children grew toward maturity; couples came together; new children were born. Frank himself, almost twenty-two years old, was a father now. He had married Mark's daughter Helena, and they had two so far, both named for his parents: Raven was the girl's name, and Anson the boy's – the newest Anson Carmichael in the long sequence. Some things would never change.

The Colonel's library was gone forever, but at Frank's suggestion Andy succeeded in downloading books from libraries as far away as Washington and New York, and Frank spent much of his time reading, now. History was his great passion. He had not known much about the world that had existed before the Entities, but he spent endless hours now discovering it, Roman history, Greek, British, French, the whole human saga swimming about in his bedazzled mind, a horde of great names all mixed together, builders and destroyers both, Alexander the Great, William the Conqueror, Julius Caesar, Napoleon, Augustus, Hitler, Stalin, Winston Churchill, Genghis Khan. He knew that California had once been a part of the country that had been known as the United States of America, and he pored over that country's history, too, swallowing it whole, learning how it had been put together out of little states and then had nearly come apart and had been united again, supposedly for all time, and had grown to be the most powerful nation in the world. He heard for the first time the names of its famous presidents, Washington, Jefferson, Lincoln, Roosevelt, and the two great generals Grant and Eisenhower, who had become presidents also.

The names and details quickly lost themselves in a chaotic welter. But the patterns remained discernible enough, how all through history countries and empires had been formed, had grown to greatness, had overreached themselves and crumbled and been replaced by new ones, while in each of those countries and empires people constantly struggled toward creating a civilization built on justice, on fairness, on open opportunity in life for all. The world had, perhaps, finally been on the verge of attaining those things just when the Entities arrived. Or so it seemed to him, anyway, half a conquered century later, knowing nothing but what he could find in the books that Andy plundered for him from the on-line archives of the conquered world.

No one spoke of the Resistance now, or of assassinating Entities, or of anything much but the need to get the crops planted on time and to bring in a good harvest and to look after the livestock. Frank had not lost his hatred for the Entities who had stolen the world and killed his father. It was practically in his genes, that hatred. Nor had he forgotten the things Cindy had said to him the day he had returned from Los Angeles to find the ranch in ruins. That conversation – the last one he had ever had with Cindy, for she had died a few days later, peacefully, surrounded by people who loved her – was forever in the back of his mind, and now and again he took out the ideas she had expounded and looked at them for a while, and then put them away again. He could see the strength of them. He understood the worth of them. He would pass them dutifully along to his children. But he saw no practical way to give them any life.

On an April day in the third year after the bombing, with the rainy season finished for the year and the air warm and fragrant, Frank set out across the ravine to Khalid's compound, where Khalid and Jill and their many children lived apart from the others in an ever-expanding settlement.

Frank went there often to visit with Khalid and sometimes with his gentle, elusive son Rasheed. He found it curiously comforting to spend time with them, savoring the peacefulness that was at the core of their souls, watching Khalid carve his lovely sculptures, abstract forms now rather than the portraits of earlier years.

He liked also to talk with Khalid about God. *Allah*, is what Khalid called Him, but Khalid said that it made little difference what name one used for God, so long as one accepted the truth of His wisdom and perfection and omnipotence. No one had ever said much to Frank about God while he was growing up, nor could he find much evidence for His existence as he contemplated the bloody saga that was human history. But Khalid believed unquestioningly in Him. 'It is a matter of faith,' Khalid said softly. 'Without Him, there is no meaning in the world. How could the world exist, if He had not fashioned it? He is the Lord of the Universe. And He is our protector: the Compassionate, the Merciful. To Him alone do we turn for help.'

'If God is our compassionate and merciful protector,' said Frank, 'why did He send the Entities to us? And, for that matter, why did He create sickness and death and war and all other evil things?'

Khalid smiled. 'I asked these same questions when I was a small boy. You must understand that God's ways are not for us to question. He is beyond our comprehension. But those who are rightly guided by God, they shall surely triumph. As is revealed on the very first page of this book.' And he held out to Frank his old, worn copy of the Koran, the one that he had carried around from place to place all his life.

The problem of the existence of God continued to mystify Frank. Again and again he went to Khalid for instruction; and again and again he came away unconvinced, and yet still fascinated. He wanted the world to have pattern and meaning; and he could see that for Khalid it did; and yet he could not help wishing that God had given the world some tangible evidence of His presence, revealing Himself not just to specially chosen prophets who had lived long ago in far-off lands, but in modern times, day in and day out, everywhere and to everyone. God remained invisible, though. 'God's ways are not for us to question,' Khalid would say. 'He is beyond our comprehension.' The ways of the Entities were also, apparently, not for us to question; they were as mysterious in their aloofness as was God, and just as incomprehensible. But the Entities had been visible from the first. Why would God not show Himself to His people even for a moment?

When he went to visit with Khalid, Frank usually would stop also at the nearby cemetery to pass a quick moment at the graves of his father and mother, and at Cindy's grave; and sometimes at those of others who had died in the bombing attack, Steve and Peggy and Leslyn and James and the rest, and even the graves of people of the olden days whom he had never known, the Colonel and the Colonel's son Anse and Andy's grandfather Doug. It gave him a sense of the long past, of the continuity of human life across time, to walk among the resting-places of all these people and contemplate the lives they had led and the things they had sought to achieve.

But this day he never quite got as far as the graveyard, because he was only a few paces along the path when he heard Andy calling to him in an oddly hoarse voice from the porch of the communications center. 'Frank! Frank! Get in here, on the double!'

'What is it?' Frank asked. He took in at a glance Andy's flushed face, his staring eyes. Andy looked badly shaken: stunned, almost dazed. 'Something wrong?'

Andy shook his head. His lips were moving, but nothing coherent seemed to be coming out. Frank ran to him. *The Entities*, Andy seemed to be saying. *The Entities. The Entities.* He sounded so strange: thick-tongued, almost inaudible. Drunk, maybe?

'What about them?' Frank asked. 'Is a party of Entities heading toward the ranch right now? Is that what you're telling me?'

'No. No. Nothing like that.' And then, with an effort: 'They're *leaving*, Frank!'

'Leaving?' Frank blinked. The unexpected word hit him with enormous force. *What are you talking about, Andy?* 'Leaving where?'

'Leaving the Earth. Packing up, clearing out!' Andy's eyes looked wild. 'Some are gone already. The rest will be going soon.'

Strange, incomprehensible words. They fell upon Frank like an avalanche. But they had no meaning at first, any more than an avalanche would, only impact. They were mere noises without relevance to anything Frank could understand.

The Entities are leaving the Earth. Leaving, packing, clearing out.

What? What? What? Gradually Frank decoded what Andy had said, extracting actual concepts from it, but even so he had trouble getting his mind fully around it. *Leaving? The Entities?* Andy was speaking craziness. He must be in some delusional state. All the same, Frank felt a dizzying wave of astonishment and bewilderment engulf him. Almost without thinking he looked up, staring into the sky, as though he might find it full of Entity starships this very minute, dwindling and vanishing against the blueness. But all he saw was the great arching dome of the heavens and a few fluffy clouds off to the east.

Then Andy seized his wrist, tugging at him, drawing him into the communications center. Pointing at the screen of the nearest computer, he said, 'I'm pulling it in from everywhere – New York, London, Europe, a bunch of places. Including Los Angeles. It's been happening all morning. They're packing up, getting aboard their ships, moving on out. In some areas they're completely gone already. You can walk right into their compounds, nothing to stop you. Nobody's there.'

'Let me see.'

Frank peered at the screen. Words sprawled across it. Andy touched a button; the words moved along, other words took their place. The words, like Andy's spoken ones of a few moments before, were reluctant to yield any meaning to him. Frank conjured significance out of them slowly, with a great effort. *Leaving . . . leaving . . . leaving.* It was so unexpected, and so strange. So damned confusing.

'Look here,' Andy said. He did something to his computer. The words disappeared and a picture blossomed on the screen. 'This is London,' he said.

An Entity starship standing in a field, a park, some broad flat expanse of greenery. Half a dozen colossal Entities solemnly parading toward it in single file, stepping aboard a platform, riding up toward the hatch that opened for them in the starship's side. The hatch closing. The ship rising on a column of flame.

'You see?' Andy cried. 'The same thing, all over the world. They're tired of being here. They're bored with Earth. They're going home, Frank!'

So it seemed. Frank began to laugh.

'Yes. Pretty fucking funny, isn't it?' Andy said.

'Very funny, yes. A riot.' The laughter was coming from Frank in unstoppable gales. He fought to pull himself together. 'We sit up on this mountainside for fifty years trying to figure out ways of making them go away, and nothing works, and finally we decide that we're simply never going to succeed. We give the whole thing up. And then a couple of years later they go away anyhow, just like that. Why? Why?' He wasn't laughing any more. 'For God's sake, Andy, why? What sense does any of it make?'

'Sense? You should know better than to expect anything that the Entities do to make sense to us. The Entities do what the Entities do, and we're not meant to know why. And never will know, I guess. – Hey, you know something, Frank, you look like you're almost about to cry!'

'I do?'

'You ought to see your face right now.'

'I don't think I want to.' Frank turned away from Andy's computers and wandered around the room, bewildered, confounded.

The possibility that all this might actually be happening was starting to sink in. And, as it did, he felt a sensation as of the ground liquefying beneath him, of the whole mountain atop which he stood turning plastic and insubstantial and beginning slowly to flow down itself toward the sea.

The Entities are leaving? Leaving? Leaving?

Then he should be dancing with glee. But no, no; he was lost in perplexity instead. His eyes stung with anger. And suddenly he understood why.

It maddened him that they might be gone from the world before he had found a way of driving them out. He realized in amazement that the sudden departure of the Entities, if indeed they had departed, would create a yawning vacancy in his soul. His hatred for their presence on Earth was a huge part of him; and if they were gone, without his ever having had a chance to express that hatred properly, it would leave a mighty absence where that presence had been.

Andy came up behind him.

'Frank? What's going on, Frank?'

'It's hard to explain. I feel so goddamned peculiar all of a sudden. It's like – well, we had this big high holy purpose here, you know. Which was to get rid of the Entities. But we couldn't bring it off, and then it happened anyway, without our even lifting a finger, and here we all are. Here. We. Are.'

'So? I don't get what you're saying.'

Frank groped for the right words. 'What I'm saying is that I feel – I don't know, some kind of letdown, I guess. A kind of hollowness. It's like you push and push against a door all your life, and the door won't budge, and then you stop pushing and walk away, and then – Surprise! Surprise! – the door opens by itself. It bewilders you, you know what I mean? It unsettles you.'

'I suppose it would, yes. I can see that.'

But Frank saw that Andy didn't see it at all. And then his thoughts raced off in the other direction entirely. None of this could actually be occurring. It was idiotic to believe that any such thing as a voluntary Entity withdrawal was going on.

He nodded toward the screen. 'Look, what if what we see here isn't real?'

Andy gave him a vexed look. 'Of course it's real. How can it not be real?'

'You of all people shouldn't need to ask that. It could be some kind of hacker hoax, couldn't it? You know more about these things than I do. Couldn't it be that somebody has worked up all these pictures, these bulletins, and sent them out over the Net, and that there isn't a shred of truth to any of them? That would be possible, wouldn't it?'

'Possible, yes. But I don't think that's what's happening.' Andy smiled. 'If you want, though, we could check it out at first hand, you know.'

'I don't understand. How?'

'Get in a car. Drive down to Los Angeles right now.'

They made the journey in just two and a half hours, which was an hour less than usual. The roads were deserted. The LACON checkpoints were unmanned.

The route Frank had chosen brought them into the city via the Pacific Coast Highway, which took them along the western rim of the wall and delivered them to the Santa Monica gate. As he made his inland turn toward the wall he saw that the gate was wide open, and that there were no LACON functionaries anywhere in sight. He drove on through, into downtown Santa Monica.

'You see?' Andy asked. 'You believe, now?'

Frank answered with a curt nod. He believed, yes. The unthinkable, altogether inexplicable thing seemed really to be true. But he was finding all of this harder to digest than he could ever have expected. It was as though some great inner wall cut him off from the joy he should be feeling over the bewildering departure of the Entities. What he felt instead of happiness was something closer to despair, a profound inner confusion. That was the last thing he would have expected to feel on a day like this.

It's that sudden sense of *absence*, he thought. He saw that clearly now. The central purpose of his life had been stripped from him in the course of a single day, had been yanked away lightheartedly, almost flippantly, by the ever-mystifying beings from the stars, and it might not be easy for him to find a way to cope with that.

*   *   *

Frank parked the car a few blocks inside the wall, just at the edge of the old Third Street Promenade. There had been a huge shopping mall there once, but the shops had been abandoned long ago and boarded up. Santa Monica was a silent city. Here and there, little scatterings of people could be seen moving slowly about in a dazed, blank-faced way, as though they had been drugged, or were walking in their sleep, lost in trances. No one was looking at anyone else. No one was saying anything. They were like ghosts.

'I thought a wild celebration would be going on,' Frank said puzzledly. 'People dancing in the streets.'

Andy shook his head. 'No. Wrong, Frank. You don't understand what they're like, these people. You haven't lived among them the way I did.'

'What do you mean?'

'Look over there.'

On the street facing the abandoned mall was an old gray-walled high-rise building that bore the LACON insignia over its entrance. A small crowd had gathered in front of it: another group of silent, stunned people, standing side by side in five or six ragged lines, gazing upward at the building. A solitary LACON man stared back at them from a high window. He was pale, dead-eyed, frozen-faced.

Andy gestured toward the building. 'There's your celebration,' he said.

'I don't get it. What's he looking at them like that for? Is he afraid that they're going to come upstairs and lynch him?'

'Maybe they will, later on. It wouldn't take much to trigger it. But right now they just want him to give them the Entities back. And the look on his face is his way of saying that he can't.'

'They want to have them *back*?'

'They miss them, Frank. They *love* them. Don't you get it?'

Frank swung around to face him. He felt his face growing hot. 'Please don't joke around with me, Andy. Not now.'

'I'm not joking. Put your mind to it, man. The Entities have been here since before either of us was born. *Long* before. They gave one little nudge and civilization simply fell apart, governments, armies, everything. And after they killed off something like half the population of the world to show that they meant business, they put a new system together in which they made all the rules and everybody did whatever they told them to do. No more private ownership of anything, no more individual initiative, just keep your head down and work at whatever job the Entities may give you and live wherever the Entities want you to live and it'll all be nice and sweet, no war, no poverty, nobody going hungry or sleeping in the streets.'

'I know all this,' Frank said, irked a little by Andy's tone.

'But do you understand that in time most people came to prefer the new system to the old one? They *adored* it, Frank. Only a few isolated crackpots like the ones at a certain ranch in the hills above Santa Barbara thought there might be anything wrong with it. For some reason the Entities chose to leave those crackpots alone, but just about everybody else who didn't love the system wound up in prison somewhere, or getting dead very fast. And now, poof, the Entities are gone and there's no system any more. All these people feel *abandoned*. They don't know how to deal with things on their own, and there's no one to tell them. Do you see, Frank? Do you see?'

He nodded, his face reddening.

Yes, Andy. Yes. He saw. Of course he saw. And felt very foolish for having needed to have it all spelled out for him. He supposed he was just being slow-witted today, amidst the general startlement of this day's bewildering events.

'You know,' Frank said, 'Cindy made pretty much the same point to me, the day the ranch was bombed. How there were all these millions of people in the world who found life much easier just doing what the Entities told them to do.' He chuckled. 'It was like, the gods were here and then just like that they went home, and now nobody can figure out what it all means. As Khalid likes to say, the ways of Allah are beyond our comprehension.'

Now it was Andy's turn to look baffled. 'Gods? What the fuck are you talking about, Frank?'

'That was something else Cindy said to me, once. That the Entities were like gods who had come down among us from heaven. The Colonel believed that too, she said. We never understood a damned thing about them. They were too far beyond us. Nobody ever figured out why they came here or what they wanted from us. They simply came, that's all. Saw. Conquered. Rearranged the whole goddamned world to suit themselves. And when they had accomplished whatever it was that they had wanted to accomplish, they went away, without even telling us why they were going. So the gods were here, and then they went home, and now we're left in the dark without them. That's it, isn't it, Andy? What do you do, when the gods go home?'

Andy was looking at him strangely. 'And was that what they were for you, too, Frank? Gods?'

'For me? No. Devils, is what they were, for me. Devils. I hated them.' He walked away from Andy and began to move forward through the lines of numbed, dazed-looking people standing in front of the LACON building. No one paid any attention to him.

He passed among them, peering into their faces, their empty eyes. They were like sleepwalkers. It was frightening to look at them. But he understood their fear. He felt some of it himself. That confusion, that despair, that had come over him when he first heard that the Entities were leaving: it stemmed from the same uncertainty as theirs. What, Frank wondered, was going to happen in the world now that the Entity episode was over?

Episode. That was what it had been, he knew. The invasion, the conquest, the years of alien rule – just a single episode, if a very strange one, in humanity's long history. Fifty-some years, out of thousands. The *alien* years, is what they would be called. And, thinking about it that way, giving it that name, *episode*, Frank felt himself at last beginning to come out of the fog of bewilderment that had engulfed him these few hours past since Andy first had told him of the Entities' withdrawal.

The alien years had changed things very greatly, yes. Such episodes always did. But this wasn't the first time that some great calamity had transformed the world. It had happened again and again. The Assyrians would come, or the Mongol hordes, or the Nazis, or the Black Death, or alien beings from the stars – whatever – and afterward nothing would be the same again.

But still, Frank thought, come what may, the basic things always continued: breakfast, lunch, love, sex, sunshine, rain, fear, hope, ambition, dreams, gratification, disappointment, victory, defeat, youth, age, birth, death. The Entities had arrived and they had wiped the world clean of everything fixed and stable, God only knew why; and then they went away, he thought, God knows why; and we are still here, and now we must start over, just as inevitably as spring starts everything over once winter is done with us. *Now we must start over.* God knows why, yes, and we don't. He would have to talk to Khalid about that when he returned to the ranch.

'Frank?'

Andy had come up behind him. Frank glanced at him over his shoulder, but said nothing.

'Are you all right, Frank?'

'Of course I'm all right.'

'Walking away from me like that. Wandering around among these people. Something's bothering you in a big way. You miss the Entities as much as they do, is that it?'

'I said I hated them. I said they were devils. But yes, yes, I do miss them, in a way. Because now I know that I won't ever get a chance to kill any of them.' Turning, Frank faced Andy squarely. 'You know,' he said, 'when you told me they were gone, it made me furious. After my father died, I had wanted so bad to be the one who drove them away. Even though I knew we probably weren't capable of doing it. But now, coming right out of the blue, I lose even the possibility of my doing it.'

'Like father, like son, eh?'

'What's wrong with that?' Frank asked.

'Right. Anson was so goddamned eager to go down in history as the man who got us out from under the Entities. And it broke him in half, wanting that. Broke him right in half. Is that what you want to happen to you?'

'I'm not as brittle as my father was,' said Frank. ' – You know, Andy, the only people who ever actually killed any Entities were Khalid and Rasheed, and they hadn't given a damn about it at all. Which was why they were able to succeed at it. And I *did* give a damn, but I'm not ever going to get a chance to do anything about it, and for a while today it really set me back, realizing that. So I guess it's pretty much the same for me as for them,' he said, waving an arm at the ghostly, shuffling people all around them. 'They're upset because they've lost their beloved Entities. I'm upset because I don't have the Entities to hate any more.'

'You want to do something to work the hate out of your system, then? Go into that building and drag that LACON quisling out of it, and get these people here to string him up to a lamppost. He collaborated with the enemy. Collaborators will have to be punished, won't they?'

'I don't think killing quislings is the answer, Andy.'

'What is, then?'

'Tearing down the walls, for a starter. How big a job will it be, do you think, tearing down the walls?'

Andy was staring at him as if he had lost his mind. 'Plenty big. Plenty.'

'Well, we'll do it anyway. We built them, we can tear them down.' Frank took a deep breath. That other wall, the one within him, that wall of numb despair and bafflement, was beginning to break up and fall away. It was all going from him, his uncertainty, his confusion in the face of the Entities' departure.

He looked up into the bright, clear sky: *through* the sky, to the hidden stars, to the unknown star that was the home of the Entities. He would have incinerated that star with his gaze, if he could, so hungry was he for revenge against them.

But what revenge was possible against gods who had come here and changed the world beyond recognition, and then had fled like thieves in the night?

Why, to restore the world to what it had been; and then to make it even finer than that. That was what he would do. That would be his revenge.

He thought he understood, now, what had happened to the world.

By sending us the Entities, the universe has sent us a message. The problem is that we don't know what it is. The job that faces us in the next hundred years, or five hundred, or however long it takes, is to find the meaning in the message that came to us from the stars.

And meanwhile –

Meanwhile, through some miracle, we are free again, and now, he thought, someone has to step forward and say, *This is what freedom is like, this is how free people behave.* And a new world would come forth out of the rubble of the one that the Entities had abandoned.

'We'll take the walls down everywhere,' Frank said. 'I want to travel around and watch it happening. New York, Chicago, Washington, all those places they have back east that I've heard of. Even London. Paris. Rome. Why not? We'll do it.'

Andy was still staring at him.

'You think I'm crazy?' Frank asked. 'Look, we can't just sit around on our asses. There's going to be chaos now. Anarchy. I've read about what happens when a central power suddenly evaporates, and it isn't good. We have to do something, Andy. *Something.* I don't know what, but tearing down the walls is a good place to start. Tear down first, then rebuild. Is that so crazy, Andy? Is it?'

He didn't stay for an answer. He began once more to walk away, moving quickly this time.

'Hey!' Andy called. 'Hey, where are you going?'

'Back to the car. I want to take a close look at the wall and see how it's put together. So I can figure out the best way of blasting it apart.'

Andy stayed where he was, looking toward Frank's rapidly retreating back.

It crossed his mind that he had badly underestimated Frank all along. Thinking of him as a mere lightweight, just another of that swarm of interchangeable blond kids all over the ranch. No, Andy thought. Wrong. Frank is different. Frank will be the one to build something – who the hell could say what it would be? – out of this nothingness that the Entities have left us. Not even Frank knew, just now, what Frank was going to do. But Frank would give the world a second chance. Or kill us all, trying.

He grinned. Slowly shook his head.

'Carmichaels,' he muttered.

Frank was at the car now. Andy realized that if he waited

any longer, Frank was going to get in and drive away without him.

'Hey! Hey, Frank, wait for me!' he yelled. And began to run toward the car.